"Make the World Safe for Democracy!"

"Remember Pearl Harbor!"

"Hell, No, We Won't Go!"

Three wars . . . three eras . . . three men . . . Bert, Will and Wat Tyler . . . the battles they fought, the women they loved, the passions that swayed them, the decisions they made.

Here, by one of the major writers of our time, is a spellbinding novel that spans fifty years of war and peace—and traces the individual destinies of three vivid human beings who each went his own way, and paid his own price.

SONS

Other SIGNET Titles You Will Enjoy

SONS

by Evan Hunter

A SIGNET BOOK from
NEW AMERICAN LIBRARY
TIMES MIRROR

Library of Congress Catalog Card Number: 78-79415

Grateful acknowledgment is made to the following for their copyrighted material: *HARCOURT, BRACE & WORLD, INC.* "Buffalo Bill," by E. E. Cummings. Copyright 1923, 1951 by E. E. Cummings. Reprinted from his volume *Poems 1923–1954; EDWIN H. MORRIS & COMPANY, INC.* Lines from "I've Heard That Song Before," by Sammy Cahn and Jule Styne. © 1942 Morley Music Co.; *WARNER BROS.—SEVEN ARTS MUSIC* Lines from "Till We Meet Again," by Raymond B. Egan & Richard A. Whiting. © 1918 by Remick Music Corp.; Lines from "Avalon," by Al Jolson & Vincent Rose. © 1920 by Remick Music Corp. All reprinted by permission of the publishers.

This is an authorized reprint of a hardcover edition published by Doubleday & Company, Inc.

THIRD PRINTING

SIGNET, SIGNET CLASSICS, MENTOR AND PLUME BOOKS
are published by *The New American Library, Inc.,*
1301 Avenue of the Americas, New York, New York 10019

FIRST PRINTING, JUNE, 1970

This is for my sons

TED • MARK • RICHARD

Buffalo Bill's
defunct
            who used to
            ride a watersmooth-silver
                                    stallion
and break onetwothreefourfive pigeonsjustlikethat
                                                Jesus

he was a handsome man
                        and what i want to know is
how do you like your blueeyed boy
Mister Death

                                    e. e. cummings

I

November ♣ ♣ ♣

I felt like a spectator and a participant both.

From somewhere outside of myself, as if I were watching myself perform in the Friday night game films, I could see my own slow-motion image leaning into the huddle, sunshine splintering jaggedly from my helmet. Inside the shadowed huddle, dark and secret, the players' faces took on a surrealistic look, foreshortened, faintly reflecting the green of the field, cheekbones smeared with grease, eyes narrowed in nothing less than murderous intent. Watching this from outside myself, seeing the homicidal glitter in the eyes of the team and in my own eyes too, I was almost tempted to laugh. But here, actually here in the huddle, the serious faces turned expectantly toward mine, the click of plastic as helmets touched and shoulders touched, there was nothing to laugh at, there was just a game to be won, although only against the junior varsity.

I whispered a Roger-Hook-Go, and we clapped out of the huddle, and rushed toward the line of scrimmage as the camera eye above me and outside of me somewhere panned the rows of naked sycamores flanking the field against a painfully blue sky. We lined up with the strong side on the left, Roger-Hook-Go calling for a fake pass to that side, with the right end cutting wide and fast on the outside instead, hooking around behind the cornerback's block, and then running straight downfield to receive my long, accurate, touchdown pass, amen.

I crouched behind the center, seeing my own fanned expectant hands in huge closeup, as through the camera eye again, "One, two, three," the ball was snapped. The j.v. were expecting a pass, the formation had told them that. I made no attempt to deceive them now, no attempt to fake a running play (seventeen-year-old Wat Tyler fades back in black-and-white slow motion, searching for a receiver, never once looking at his true receiver, a quarterback's eyes are his own worst enemy), I turned to the left, faked a pass in that direction, with the weight on my rear foot, and then swung my left leg around, swiveling to locate the end just as he broke out of the hook and went sprinting downfield. The ball was level with my eyes now, fingers widespread over the laces, my right arm cocked and poised (Timing is essential to a passer, a voice says over the black-and-white film, he must lead his receiver and get the ball to him while he is still in the open). Turn, I thought, goddamn you, Frank, *turn*, and suddenly I was hit by two men, the right guard who had broken through, and a linebacker who had got in around the tackle. I tucked the ball in against my chest and allowed myself to go limp.

(In black-and-white, disrupted grass rises in soundless clods exploding on the air, rolling and tumbling slowly, Wat Tyler feels the weight of the linebacker shoving against his chest, the strong grip of the guard around his knees, relaxing, in black-and-white, he rolls with their force and hits the ground in cushioned unreality.)

The others had broken through the line now, I could feel the weight of additional bodies as they piled on, Yeah, get the quarterback, men, break his ass even though he's our own school's varsity quarterback, stomp him into the earth. I lay soft and still under the mound, the ball securely tight against my chest. My leg hurt, but I knew nothing had been broken, and the fear I always experienced before each tackle left with a rush as sweet and as clean as the November wind. I got to my feet, grinned, tossed the ball away, and ran quickly back to the huddle.

Something was wrong.

This was only a scrimmage between the varsity and the

j.v., Friday afternoon's warmup for the game against Greer tomorrow, having started at one p.m., and now only in its first quarter. But as I turned in mid-stride to glance at the high school's white main building, sleekly rectangular on a knoll against the piercing sky, I saw far too many teachers and students coming down the steps and heading for the bleachers, why would a mere scrimmage be attracting such a crowd? Something was wrong, and yet the coaches paced nervously before the bench as usual, Mr. Cowley wore his long red muffler with usual affectation, the team was waiting as usual, but something was wrong.

(Wat Tyler leans into the huddle. Again, there is the click of plastic as white helmets join in muted strategy. "Same play," he says, "Roger-Hook-Go, on two," and ends with the word "Pass"—it is always advisable to end the call with the type of play, so that linemen missing the pattern will at least know whether the team is running or passing.)

We clapped out of the huddle (but something was wrong) and ran toward the line of scrimmage. From the corner of my eye, I could see Mr. Cowley talking to Miss Huber, who had come out of the school without a coat. The coach was not watching the play, he was instead nodding in serious attention, and now more students and teachers were coming out of Main, was it a fire drill? I spread my hands fanlike behind the center's ass, "One, two," I said, and the ball was snapped, and again I turned and ran directly back for five yards, wheeled, faked my eyes to the false receiver on the left, stepped to the right to avoid the opposing guard who had again come crashing through the line, ball back, the right end had hooked and was clear, I had about two seconds to get off the pass. The line was buckling, I was forced to go back deeper, and saw that my receiver was being double-teamed, the little j.v. bastards had second-guessed the repeat play. I looked far downfield for my alternate, found him covered man-for-man, and abruptly cut left to try a run through the strong side.

I was ganged before I covered three yards. They hit me from every possible direction this time, fear spit into my head, I thought they'd break every bone in my body. Pumping my legs wildly, I tried to break away, hands clutching at my jersey, "Oh God!" I heard someone say, and then I was falling. (The ground seems very far away this time, the sky wheels overhead, Hold the ball, he tells himself in litany against the fear, Hold the ball, and clutches it to him like a woman. A helmet smashes into his face guard, his neck snaps back, he thinks for a moment he has broken something in his spine, and then the ground hits him, and he is splayed flat against the unyielding earth by five hundred pounds of muscle and bone.)

The pile-on began.

I clung to the ball against my chest, I could smell the tumbled earth and grass, that's right you little shits, I thought, kill your star quarterback, and smiled, and lay still and helpless, and thought suddenly of something Mr. Jarrel had said in American History I, about Giles Corey being pressed to death in Salem, Massachusetts, because he would not admit he was a witch, rock after rock being piled upon his chest, and all he ever said was, "More weight," and had died for his refusal to betray his own conscience. I lay still and waited, my eyes squeezed shut. They were climbing off me now. I opened my eyes, saw an untangling scramble of cleats and muscles, fallen socks and grass-stained knee pads. Free, I got to my feet and grinned. I had read somewhere that Jim Brown always grinned when he got up after a tackle, grinned and walked slowly back to the huddle, no matter how hard he'd been hit.

An odd buzz hovered over the field. I thought I was hearing things at first, thought they had done something to my brain. I tossed the ball away and began sprinting back for the huddle.

There was no huddle.

Mr. Cowley was on the field, and he was whispering to the referee, and the guys were all talking at once, not standing with that patient hands-on-hips posture of football players waiting for a decision, but gesturing wildly instead. I could hear them saying, "The head, the head," and I listened in bewilderment and fear because I was sure now that something terrible had happened to *me*, that they were all talking about *my* head, that maybe there was my neck was twisted at a funny angle, maybe there was a line of blood trickling from under my white helmet. The playing field was crowded with people now, what were they all doing on the field? The buzz was incredible, the referee finally blew his whistle to stop it, and a hush fell over the

12

field, broken only by the keening of the November wind and the empty rattle of the sycamores lining the field.

Mr. Cowley cleared his throat. He seemed embarrassed.

"We're calling the game," he said.

"I cannot reconcile the events of this past week," my grandfather said, tall and white-haired at sixty-three, sitting at the head of the table, the family patriarch, though I could sense my father's displeasure with the old man for taking his usual seat. "To believe that in this day and age, in a country as sophisticated as America . . ."

"Is there any cranberry sauce?" one of the twins asked. She was my cousin, eight years old, the prettier of the two girls, though frankly neither of them was worth a glance, even in the third grade. She smiled at my grandfather because she knew she had interrupted him, and he reached over to touch her straight brown hair for just an instant before Aunt Linda said, "Your grandfather's speaking, Mary. You can just wait for the cranberry sauce."

"I'll get it," my mother said, and rose from the table.

"She can *wait,* Lolly."

My mother's name was Dolores, and the "Lolly" was a hangover from the days of her youth. I saw a small twinge of displeasure in her eyes as my aunt used the name now, but she recovered immediately and said, "I want to see how *she's* doing, anyway," referring to the new maid, a priceless gem from Georgia. She put down her napkin, and then left the dining room and went into the kitchen. The other twin, Marcia, yelled, "I want some, too, Aunt Lolly!" and my mother shouted, "Yes, Marcy!" from the kitchen, and Uncle Stanley said, "I want some, too, *please,* Aunt Lolly."

"Please!" Marcy shouted to the closed kitchen door.

"The whole thing was a spectacle," my father said. He said it very softly, I knew that voice, as if he hadn't been patiently waiting through the twins' nonsense for this moment when he could openly challenge Grandpa sitting in his place at the head of the table. Grandpa's brows went up just a trifle. There was a glint of humor in his blue eyes. The two men squared off across two yards of white tablecloth. "That whole damn funeral was a theatrical production," my father said.

"Well," Grandpa seemed to agree, "there *is* something

13

very theatrical about an assassination, wouldn't you say?"

"Not to mention *another* murder following it," I offered.

"I'm not talking about *that* aspect of it," my father said.

"Are there any more yams?" Uncle Stanley asked.

"I'm talking about the funeral—the horses, the drums, all that overproduced crap."

Aunt Linda shot my father a warning look: the children.

My father turned with a faint glance of annoyance, and then passed the candied yams to Uncle Stanley. Stanley was a heavy-set man with a bland open face, thinning blond hair, gold-rimmed spectacles, a Phi Beta Kappa key hanging on a gold chain across the front of his vest. He was wearing a brown suit (he *always* wore brown), a white shirt, and a brown tie upon which there were now several specks of gravy he hadn't yet noticed. He accepted the proffered yams in the silver dish that had once been my grandmother's, said, "Thank you, Will," and promptly served himself the last two potatoes in the dish.

"Someone else may want some," Aunt Linda said.

"I hate yams," Mary said.

"*I* hate yams, too," Marcy said.

"I'll grant you," my grandfather said, "that the Kennedy women have a certain flair about them, and that perhaps . . ."

"Even *that* annoys me."

"What does?"

"*That*," my father said. " 'The *Kennedy* Women!' " He shook his head. "That's for O'Hara novels, not real life."

"The assassination was real life," I said.

"I beg your pardon," my grandfather said, turning to me with a small pleased smile, "but that's where I disagree. That's exactly my point, Walter, it's exactly what I was trying to say."

"Lolly, we need some more butter, please," Uncle Stanley shouted to the kitchen.

"Coming!"

"I was trying to say that there is an air of total unreality to the events of this past week. The assassination

14

itself, the television murder, the funeral, *all* of it. Unreal. Incredible."

"The only unreality was the funeral," my father insisted. "A play in three acts, produced and directed by Jacqueline Kennedy. The rest is only America."

"What do you mean?" I asked him.

"I mean that this concept of America as a *sophisticated* nation is all a lot of crap. We're barely out of . . ."

"Oh, really, Will, *I* think . . ."

". . . our infancy."

". . . America's a pretty sophisticated country," Uncle Stanley concluded, and stuffed a whole candied yam into his mouth. Aunt Linda shot my father another warning glance. She really looked a lot like him, I suppose, especially now when her blue eyes were flashing the same anger as his. They'd both inherited Grandpa's high cheekbones and prominent nose, as well as the somewhat thin-lipped Bertram Tyler mouth—which I had also inherited—and which I felt looked more attractive on a man than on Aunt Linda, who always wore the look of a maiden lady about to peer under the bed, straight blond hair pulled into an old-fashioned bun at the back of her head, good breasts hidden in a high-necked blouse. "This is 1963, Linda," my father said emphatically, half in response to Uncle Stanley, and half in reprimand to his sister for her prissy-assed ways.

"Yes, and we're almost . . ."

"We're less than two hundred . . ."

". . . on the moon," Uncle Stanley said.

"Are we *ever* getting that cranberry sauce?" Mary asked.

"Hush, Mary!"

My mother came from the kitchen. The new maid trailed behind her with a bewildered look, carrying hot bread and two butter dishes, as well as the celery and olives she'd forgotten to put on the table at the start of the meal. My mother put down the cranberry sauce, and then tucked a stray wisp of brown hair behind her ear, and smiled at me suddenly and radiantly when she realized I was watching her.

"Why, it's one of the Tyler Women!" I said, and opened my eyes wide in fake astonishment.

"Yes, of course," my mother said simply, smiling, and suddenly her eyes met with my father's, her eyes clashed

15

with the eyes of Will Tyler across those yards of white linen, and held, and I was reminded of the cold hard intelligent waiting eyes of a football team in a huddle, waiting for the play to be called, and my father mimicked in precise derision, "Yes, of course," and it was as if the play had been called, and their eyes broke contact, I almost expected to hear the clap of hands as the huddle opened. I felt what I had felt last Friday, that something was terribly wrong. I almost expected to learn momentarily that yet another person had been killed. I guess I experienced in that instant an uncertainty I had never before known in my life, the rising fear that everything I'd learned to count on before then, a sane and ordered existence, an America comforting and secure, was rapidly crumbling all around me. And then I realized that the sharp crack of eyes across that Connecticut dining room table had been every bit as fatal as the rifle shots that shattered the Dallas stillness, and I knew further that my mother had been the victim.

"The only thing we've got to be thankful for this year," my father said, "is that we're still alive."

December ✿ ✿

It was almost midnight, it was almost 1943.

Michael had decorated the room with war posters, and I squinted at the one on the farthest wall, trying to read it like an eye chart, struggling under the slight handicap of having consumed twelve beers since the start of the party. The poster showed a workingman behind a riveting gun, and a soldier behind a machine gun, and the big lettering on the bottom of the poster read BOTH BARRELS, but I couldn't make out the smaller type to the left of the workingman's head. I rose unsteadily, navigated my way across the room and past the wilting Christmas tree, and peered at the full message: GIVE 'EM BOTH BARRELS. Very good, I thought, and remembered the barrel of beer in the kitchen, and thought it was time to have another little brew.

16

I was very depressed.

First of all, whereas Michael Mallory was a close friend of mine, I did not wish to be in his house this New Year's Eve. I had been in his house last New Year's Eve, and that had been depressing as hell because the Japanese had practically just finished bombing Pearl Harbor, and nobody was exactly in the mood for revelry and gay abandon. But *this* year's party was turning out to be just as depressing as last year's, so naturally I blamed my father. If he had given me permission to join the Air Force, I wouldn't have been here in Chicago at all, but instead would be up there someplace in the wild blue yonder, being all of seventeen years old and five feet eleven inches bone-dry, which was old enough and tall too for a fighter pilot, so why wouldn't he sign?

It was all quite depressing.

It was also quite depressing, believe me, that I had been flirting with a redheaded girl all night long, and she was now necking on the sofa with Matty Walsh. Walsh kept trying to sneak his sneaky little hand up under her skirt, but the girl had the good sense to pull it away each time, which certainly didn't excuse my father. I remembered abruptly that tomorrow was his birthday, that at exactly 12:01 on the first day of January in the year 1900, my dear daddy, Bertram Tyler, had been brought into the world and the century, doubtless screaming his head off. I had already planned to call him after midnight. I would call at exactly 12:01 and listen to the phone ringing in the old house on East Scott Street, and when my father came onto the line, I would say, "This is Western Union, we have a message for Mr. Bertram Tyler, is he there please?" knowing full well he was of course there. And then I would sing "Happy Birthday to You," and as a final I would say, "Pop, this is Will. Can I please join the Air Force?"

I wondered why Walsh didn't take the redhead into one of the bedrooms. It occurred to me in my foamy stupor that perhaps the redheaded girl did not *wish* Walsh to take her into one of the bedrooms, and thus emboldened I staggered across the room doing my imitation of John Wayne, found the record player, and with no little difficulty picked out ten or twelve very good records for dancing close to, all fox trots. I hesitated a moment before approaching Walsh and the girl, partially because they were at the moment kissing, and partially because I was trying to think of a good joke I could tell when I got over to the couch, but all I could think of was the one about the guy at the induction center with a hard-on, and I didn't think I should risk *that* one with the girl, not having said two words to her all night long. So I shrugged and went into the kitchen instead. Russo and another guy were standing near the keg of beer, talking to two girls from Evanston.

"Hello, hello," I said.

"What's going on out there?" Russo asked.

"Walsh is necking," I said, and heard the first of my records fall into place on the turntable, Jimmy Dorsey's "Star Eyes."

"Isn't everybody?" the other guy said.

"We're not," the girl closest to the keg said, nor was it any wonder since she was possibly ugly as sin or worse, and since she immediately giggled after her funny remark and nudged her friend, who giggled too, a nice ugly pair of gigglers. They were both blondes, both wearing their hair in shoulder-length pageboys, both wearing navy blue taffetas with gold buttons down the front, flaring from the waist over thick legs, their beauty was so fantastic they had to duplicate it.

"Well," I said, "I think I'll have another brew."

I opened the tap and poured myself a foaming glass of beer, and then chug-a-lugged it, aware of the no-doubt-admiring glances of the two ugly gigglers, and then looking toward the living room and wondering what was keeping the redhead. I figured maybe I would have to hit Walsh, but that was okay. He had no right trying to sneak his hand up under, sneaky little Jap. I wondered why my father wouldn't let me join the Air Force. I opened the tap again. One of the gigglers said, "May I have one, too?"

"Sure," I said, and handed her the glass I'd already filled.

"Why, thank you," she said, and giggled again.

"Are you sure you're old enough to drink?" Russo asked.

"I'm sixteen," she answered, which meant she was fifteen, and which meant she was just as old as my kid sister Linda who was definitely *not* old enough to drink.

"She's sixteen," Russo said.

18

"Mmm," I said.

"Yes, I'm sixteen," the girl said again.

"That's certainly old enough to drink," Russo said.

"That's certainly old enough for a lot of things," the other guy said.

I didn't say anything.

There was a momentary silence as "Star Eyes" cleared the record player, a click, and then the next record dropped, the tone arm moved into place, and Frank Sinatra began singing "Sunday, Monday or Always" with a choral background. I began thinking about musicians' union strikes and things like that, and started getting very depressed again, and just then the redhead walked into the kitchen. Her lipstick had all been kissed off, and she was very flushed from all that Walsh activity. Her hair was rolled up from either side of her head into twin pompadours, falling straight and free behind in a cascade around her shoulders, burnished copper against a black crepe dress, three rhinestone buttons over her bosom. She came directly to the beer keg and said, "Can I have a beer?"

"Sure," I said.

"Will's the bartender tonight," Russo said, and laughed, I didn't know at what.

"Looks that way," I said, and smiled, not at Russo but at the redhead.

"Is that your name?" she asked. "Will?"

"That's right." I handed her the brimming glass. "What's yours?"

"Marge."

"That's a good name for a redhead."

"Is it?"

"Sure. All beautiful redheads should be named Marge."

"Oh boy," she said, "what a line," and rolled her green eyes, and sipped at the beer.

I poured myself a fresh glass from the open tap. Russo and the other guy had moved toward the sink, the two gigglers following them. "What's your connection with Walsh?" I asked.

"Who's Walsh?" she said.

"The guy you were necking with on the couch."

"No connection," she said, and shrugged, and sipped some more beer.

"Did he bring you?"

"No."

"Who did?"

"I came alone. Michael invited me, so I came."

"How old are you?"

"How old do I look?" she asked.

"Fifteen."

"Oh, come on, I'll be eighteen in April."

"Marge what? Did you say Marge?"

"Yes."

"Marge what?"

"Marge Penner."

"Wanna buy a duck?"

"No relation."

"I'll bet you hear that a lot, though."

"No, this is only the ten thousandth time," she said.

"I get the same thing," I said. "My last name's Tyler. Everybody always wants to know if I'm related to the President."

"To Roosevelt? I don't get it."

"No, to Tyler. John Tyler. He was the tenth President. Of the United States."

"Oh," she said. "*Are* you?"

"No, no. You want to dance?"

"Sure."

"What about Walsh?"

"What about him?"

"Won't he mind?"

"Who cares what he minds?"

"Not me, that's for sure," I said, and we went into the other room. Walsh was still on the couch. I gave him my John Wayne look, and then took the girl into my arms.

"Where do you live?" I whispered in her ear.

"On Halsted."

"Halsted and where?"

"Halsted and Sixty-first."

"Near the university?"

"Yes."

"That's very nice there."

"Yes, it's beautiful. You dance awfully close, do you know that?"

"So do you."

"That's only because you're holding me so tight."

"Do you mind?"

20

"Well . . . no. But don't get the wrong idea."

"What's the wrong idea?"

"You know," she whispered.

"No, I don't."

"Well, you just figure it out."

"I'll try."

"Yes, do try," she said.

Walsh was still watching us. There was only one other couple in the room and they were standing near the record player. Walsh glanced at them as though seeking their sympathy, but they were chattering about the poster hanging over the phonograph, a huge cartoon showing Hitler saying, "It is goot to hear Americans are now pudding 10% of der pay into Bunds!" and Goebbels whispering to a glum Goering, "Hermann, you tell him it iss BONDS—not BUNDS!" Neither of them even noticed Walsh's imploring look, and he seemed to take their indifference as a personal affront.

"How old are *you?*" the girl asked me.

"I'll be eighteen in June. I may join the Air Force," I said. "I want to fly. I want to be a fighter pilot."

"Seems like everybody interesting is either already drafted or about to be," the girl said.

"Oh? You think I'm interesting?"

"You're okay," she said indifferently.

Walsh came up off the couch in that moment, apparently having made his big decision. He walked directly to where we were dancing, and politely tapped me on the shoulder. I looked at his hand, and I said, "Sorry, no cutting in."

"Who says so?" Walsh asked.

"Me."

"Look, Tyler . . ."

"Yes, Walsh?"

"What's the idea?"

"What's the *big* idea," I said. "You're supposed to say 'What's the *big* idea?' "

"All right, what's the *big* idea?" Walsh said.

"The idea is no cutting in," I said. "That's also the *big* idea."

"Look, Tyler . . ."

"Yes, Walsh?"

"You know, Tyler . . ."

"Yes, Walsh?"

21

Walsh stood looking into my face, pained. I figured he didn't know whether to press the issue or to retreat gracefully. He knew I could take him, but he also knew there were several close friends of his at the party, and yet he further knew I could take *them,* too. Besides, he knew I'd had a few beers, and he knew I could be terribly dangerous when I was John Wayne, but at the same time he wanted this girl, probably because he'd had such a promising beginning with her, his hand only having been removed from the hem of her skirt some sixty-four times in the length of a half-hour. So he stood in the center of the room, not wanting to walk away from a fight, and yet hoping he would not have to fight. Realizing all this, I refused to make things easier for him. Instead of dancing the girl away and allowing Walsh to save face, I kept circling in the same spot, waiting for him to make his move.

"Aw, go fuck yourself," he finally said cleverly, and went out into the kitchen.

"Nice fellow," I said, and smiled.

"Charming."

"You still want to dance?"

"What else is there to do?"

"I thought we'd explore the house a little."

"What's there to explore?"

"Well, the thing about exploration is you never know what you'll be exploring until you start."

"I've got a pretty good idea what we'll be exploring," the girl said.

"Well, don't be too sure."

"Maybe we ought to keep dancing."

"Sure, whatever you say."

"Anyway, it seems as if too many people are *already* out exploring."

"Oh, there're always new worlds," I said.

"What time is it?"

"Eleven-thirty."

"At midnight, you know . . ."

"Sure, we'll be back. What do you say?"

"Why not?"

I took her hand. I deliberately avoided going through the kitchen to the bedrooms at the back of the house, not wanting an encounter with Walsh, not now. Instead, I led her through the entryway and up a flight of steps to the second floor. A boy and a girl were necking in the hallway. They broke apart as we went by, and then began kissing again almost immediately. I had practically grown up with Michael Mallory, could in fact remember the time he had wet his pants in the first grade of the Norwood Park elementary school on West Pratt Avenue, and I knew of course that his bedroom was around the turn at the far end of the hall, out of sight, heh-heh, unbeknownst except to people like myself who had been in and out of this house for the better part of ten years. I tiptoed down the hall and hoped that Michael himself wasn't using the bedroom, because that would have been possibly the *most* depressing thing that could happen on this otherwise totally depressing night.

"Where are we going?" the girl whispered.

"Exploring," I whispered back.

I tried the doorknob, and gently eased the door open. Wherever Michael was, he was not in his own bedroom. I led the girl inside, and locked the door behind me. When I turned, she was walking toward the bed, and I watched the black dress tighten across her ass as she moved in the semi-darkness, something about her deliberate walk as suddenly provocative as the whisper of a streetwalker on West Madison. The outside porch light was on, and it threw enough illumination into the room so that I could make out a framed picture of Michael on the table near the bed. He was smiling, his cherubic face retouched free of acne, his curly hair sitting on his head like a pile of wood shavings. The girl sat on the edge of the bed and crossed her legs. My heart was suddenly pounding. I looked at my watch. It was twenty minutes to twelve. I didn't want to forget to call my father. "Western Union calling," I would say.

I thought at first that she, this Margaret, Marge, or Margie Penner, this cotton candy concoction with bright red hair, would allow me to do whatever I had wildly imagined in my midnight bed, holding myself stiff and throbbing while my sister Linda slept in the room next door, would give herself to me as freely as the old year was giving itself to the new. There was no reluctance in her bold unfolding, she allowed me to take her breast in my hand, the way Michael had taught me to do one rainy

23

afternoon in the basement of this selfsame house when we were both twelve years old and discussing all the things we'd never done to girls, permitted me to explore and exploit, offering her pink-white softness like a sacrificial maiden helpless in the grip of a greedy priest, allowing me the secret electric touch of all her silken underthings, and then opening to receive my hand. I was astonished by my own success, I had never before, she was wet and warm and suddenly entreating beneath me, suddenly transformed into something to tell the truth a little frightening. "Oh Jesus," she whispered, "put on a rubber," and I said, "I haven't got one," and she said, "Oh Jesus," again and the stench of fear rose from her as overpowering as that other dizzying musk. Her hand expertly found me and she urged me against her belly in quick sharp jerks, while I begged, "Let me fuck you, let me fuck you," and she answered now the cool determined mistress, "No, you'll get me pregnant," and I pleaded, "I'll pull out, I swear to God," and she said as Michael smiled in black and white beside the bed, "No, you won't, you won't, you won't, you won't," and I came against her leg, spurting dizzily onto her thigh and her garters and the ribbed tops of her stockings.

Downstairs, I could hear the others in the living room. Someone had turned off the Victrola and put on the radio. An announcer was broadcasting from The Loop, describing the crowds of people in the street. I took out my handkerchief. She was lying crosswise on the bed, one arm up and folded, the back of her hand against her closed eyes. Her legs were still spread. I handed her the handkerchief, and she murmured, "Thank you, Will."

She sat up then and clasped her bra, though I couldn't remember having unclasped it, and then she turned for me to zip up the back of the black dress, and said, "Will, I hope you don't think . . ." and I immediately said, "Of course not." Downstairs, the announcer was saying it was four minutes to midnight. Someone had given out noise-makers and the kids were already beginning to use them as the redhead and I came into the living room.

Just after midnight, I went into the kitchen and dialed my home number. My father answered on the first ring. I didn't even pretend I was Western Union with a message for Mr. Bertram Tyler.

24

"Pop?" I said.

"Yes."

"Happy New Year. And happy birthday."

"Thank you," my father said.

January ⚘

Mama always said, "Bertram, we've only got two seasons here in Wisconsin, winter and the Fourth of July," but I never minded the cold, and I didn't mind it now. I was working late and alone in the forest because I'd taken an hour off that morning to ride one of the wagons into Eau Fraiche. With two thousand men working in the bush during cutting season, seven supply wagons made the trip to town every Friday, coming back loaded with beans and butter and coffee and potatoes and molasses and eggs and beef. Flour was still a problem because there'd been an epidemic of black stem rust in 1916, followed by another poor wheat season last year, and what with trying to keep France and England supplied with grain, there was a severe shortage all over the country, not only in Eau Fraiche. The same applied to pork and sugar, which the Allies desperately needed. I couldn't remember having had a strip of bacon since I began working at the camp, and last year we were actually pouring corn syrup into our coffee to sweeten it.

I'd asked Hal, the head-chopper, if I could take a few hours off that morning because I had something to do in town. I didn't tell him what it was I had to do, but I think he knew what I was up to because he just grinned and clapped me on the shoulder and said, "Sure, Bert, you just take all the time you need." As it turned out, I hadn't needed much time at all. In fact, I was able to catch the first loaded wagon back to camp. Still, I'd lost an hour's work, and when you were cutting pulpwood, you got paid by how many cords of wood you cut, and not by how much time you spent in town. The standard cord was eight feet long, four feet high, and four feet wide. A scaler measured each pile of logs at the end of the day, figured out how many cords they added up to, and that way was able to tell how much pay you had coming. Anyway, I thought I might still be able to hit my quota if I could bring down the tree I'd been working on.

The tree was a huge spruce, probably there since the days of old Frenchy La Pierre, towering up against a sky brittle with dusk. I'd cleared a working space around the tree, clipping off the brush and saplings, holding the ax in one hand near the point of balance and cutting very close to the ground. I'd hung the ax myself because I never did trust factory-hung axes, and I'd also tapered the blade—a single-bit Michigan—on a wet grindstone, and then honed it razor-sharp, taking off the wire edges; a dull ax is much more dangerous than a sharp one, that was something you learned very quickly in the woods. I'd also cut off all the low-hanging branches to give me plenty of swinging room, and I'd checked the direction of fall, to make sure there weren't any widow-makers on any of the surrounding trees. I was ready to start my undercut now, and as I moved around to the side toward which the tree would fall, I looked up at the sky and saw a pair of geese silhouetted against the deepening red, and saw my own breath blowing white out of my mouth, and I grinned and picked up the saw and began making the horizontal cut, and thought again of what I'd done that morning.

Nancy wasn't going to like it, that was for sure. I couldn't wait to tell her about it, and yet I was really sort of scared to tell her. She was five feet four inches tall, thinner than a rake handle, but when she got mad, thunder could boom out of those green eyes of hers. I knew all the arguments she'd give me (even though it was too late now) because I'd given myself the very same arguments all this past week before finally deciding this morning to go over to Eau Fraiche and get the thing done. There were some things a man *had* to do, that was all, but I guessed Nancy wasn't going to understand that too well. All I knew was I was eighteen years old, and I was strong and healthy, and I wanted to do my part. It was as simple as that.

(When did you all of a sudden get so thick with Mr. Wilson? Nancy would ask. It was you who said Wisconsin should go all-out for Hughes, which we most surely did, and now you're thick as the devil and the old green snake, how do you explain that, Bert?)

26

Well, there *was* no explaining it, I guessed. It was just something you had to do, that was all.

I freed the saw and picked up my ax. There was perhaps half an hour of light left, oh, maybe just a bit longer, and with luck I could have my notch cut in half an hour, and then I could start on my backcut. I was beginning to doubt I would get any bucking done before dark, but if I could at least get her felled and limbed, why then I could get to work with the bow saw in the morning, and cut her into log lengths then. I began to chop. She was a big tree, so I decided to make two smaller notches, working them eventually into a single large one. I worked with an easy steady swing, my legs widespread, my right hand just above the bulge at the end of the ax handle, sliding my left hand up close to the head on the upstroke, and then toward my right hand again on the downstroke. I kept one corner of the blade always free of the wood, giving it a slight twist each time to free the chip and release the bit. I put each stroke exactly where I wanted it, the chips falling away yellow-white and thick into the snow. I took off my jacket after twenty minutes of hard chopping, working in my sweater now, swinging the ax in long steady arcs, joining the two notches and making a big notch that slanted down at a forty-five degree angle toward the saw cut.

The sky was streaked with purple, the trees looming high against it, the snow tinted a fainter lavender. From far away in one of the bunkhouses, I heard a lumberjack's laughter cracking across the snowbound silence. A dog began barking and then was still.

I began my backcut.

Maybe I could help Nancy to see it my way. There was talk around, I'd tell her, that they were going to lower the age to eighteen by June, so what difference would a few months make? Wasn't it better to get into the thing now, and help get it over with, so we could later go on with our normal lives? Wasn't that better, Nance?

Bert, she would say, they can kill you clear up to your navel, is that what you want them to do?

I was using the bow saw for my backcut, but I was beginning to think I'd made a mistake, she was much too big to fell this way. What I needed was a crosscut saw with two men on it. At least, that's the way it looked to me now, with darkness fast coming on and the bow saw sinking into the trunk far too close to its frame without getting anywhere near enough to my undercut. I needed only an inch or two of holding-wood to serve as my hinge when the tree fell, but here I was almost up tight against the frame of the saw now, and still three inches away from my undercut; nope, it wasn't going to work. I eased the saw free and wondered what I should do. Suppose I left her this way, and a strong wind came along and topped her over tomorrow morning when some poor fellow was out honing his ax and never suspecting somebody had left a tree hanging? I decided to try poling her over, and if that didn't work, I'd head back for the bunkhouse and get some help.

I hadn't even told my mother yet, that was going to be still another fracas. I could see us all sitting around the table Sunday after church, and Papa saying the blessing, while Harriet and Fanny and little brother John fidgeted and squirmed, and then Mama would come in from the kitchen carrying our usual Sunday meal—corned beef, boiled for almost two and a half hours, after which carrots, onions, turnips, cabbage, and potatoes were added to the pot to simmer in the meat juices for another half hour or so. Harriet would rise immediately to go into the kitchen for the freshly baked loaf of bread and Fanny would only reluctantly follow, coming back with the ironstone pitcher full of milk in one hand, and the butter urn in the other. We would eat silently and gratefully, the huge table (which Papa had made himself from an oak on our own land) clinking and clattering with the sound of silver and china, and me with a secret to tell. I'd probably wait until the girls and Mama had cleared the table and were bringing in the Queen's pudding, which she would dish out to us from her place opposite Papa, ladling the pale tart lemon sauce onto each moist coconut-shredded mound. I would tell her then. There was nothing she could do about it: I was eighteen, and Papa had given me written consent.

The pole was twelve feet long, with a metal spike on one end. I planned my getaway and then braced the pole against my hip and began shoving. The tree wouldn't budge. I didn't know whether or not I had time to rig a killig, but it looked as if I'd need one, and I figured I ought to try before going back to the bunkhouse. I cut myself a long hardwood pole, the light fading fast now, a wolf howling somewhere off against the approaching night, notched one end of it and made a wedge point on the other end. I reached up as high as I could then, and cut a notch into the tree trunk with my ax. I'd left my peavy over by the bow saw, and I went to get it now, and then fitted the pointed end of the pole into the notch I'd just cut in the tree, and then braced the wedged end of the pole against the thick wooden handle of the peavy, just above the hinge. I shoved the pick end of the tool deep into firm ground, through the crusting layer of snow. My killig was ready. I shoved forward on the handle, just testing, seeing if I'd get enough leverage to fell her this way. She began to groan a little, and I nodded silently, the sun was all but gone now, the air seemed suddenly very cold. I shouted "Timberrrrrrr," knowing I was the only soul in the woods, but remembering what Tiny, the camp's wood butcher had told me about it being better to feel a little foolish yelling to nobody than to look around later and find a man squashed flat under the tree you'd just knocked down. I shoved forward on the peavy handle.

There was, as always, that moment when she seemed to resist, seemed to cling to whatever slender fiber still connected her to life. And then she trembled, and I could hear her groan again, almost as if she were in pain, and suddenly she began to topple, the weight of her upper branches pulling her down toward the earth. I dropped the peavy and ran back toward the cord of pulpwood, and behind it, and I heard the huge spruce whispering through the icy air, and then she hit the ground and snowdust billowed up from her branches and there was a long heavy shudder and then a hundred echoing crackings, and then there was silence.

There was never much doing in Eau Fraiche on a Friday night, except for the first Friday of every month, when a dance was held at the Grange Hall on Buffalo Street. Anybody who owned a car, though, usually drove into Eau Claire, twelve miles to the west, or preferably made the trip down to La Crosse, which was about sixty miles away due south, on the Minnesota border. The trip to La Crosse, figuring on a top speed of about thirty miles an hour on a road like Route 12, took at least two hours, but it was worth it once you got there. La Crosse wasn't

Madison either, but it was a darn sight more interesting than Eau Fraiche.

The main street of Eau Fraiche was called Chenemeke Avenue, and the name was supposed to have derived from an old Chippewa legend about an invisible bird messenger of the Great Spirit. I never did get the story straight, even though Nancy told it time and again, something about lightning flashing from the bird's eyes, and retribution for deeds that were un-Christian—genuine Indian superstition sifted through her own Wisconsin background and temperament. In any event, Chenemeke (which we pronounced Chain-make; God knew how the Indians pronounced it) was a narrow street that cut a wandering path through the center of town. The railroad tracks were off to the east of Chenemeke, and beyond those and running parallel to them were the paper and pulp plants, the furniture factory, and the big rubber plant that covered two full city blocks and employed more than a thousand men at peak production. We had a state fish hatchery running along the base of the town's southern bluffs, and off to the west there was a really good park named Juneau Park, with picnic grounds and tennis courts, baseball and football fields, and good swimming and boating off the peninsula. According to the 1910 census, there were 7000 people living in the town of Eau Fraiche, but I guessed that by now, in 1918, the figure was closer to 9000. Some of these people lived on the southern and eastern outskirts, but most of them preferred living right in town where, on a good day, you could see both the Eau Claire and the Chippewa Rivers from the upstairs bedroom of your house. Our own house, white clapboard and slate, was down near the peninsula overlooking Lake Juneau, which was a spring-fed body of water actually closer to Eau Claire than it was to Eau Fraiche, but nonetheless within the city limits.

There were two hotels in town, the United being the best of them, and there were at least a dozen very bad restaurants. The only halfway decent restaurant, in fact, was French, and was called Coin de Lorraine, which meant Corner of Lorraine. It was run by a man named Claude Rabillon, who used to be a cook at one of the big lumber camps. That was in the good old days when timber was truly a crop, and when fortunes were being made in the wilderness. Today, most of the sawmills had already

30

packed up their machinery and moved to the West Coast, and we were cutting trees almost exclusively for the production of paper. Eau Fraiche used to be a livelier town when the industry was at its peak. In fact, the census for 1900 showed the town to be twice the size it later became in 1910, and most of those people were lumberjacks or people otherwise connected with timber—brawny two-fisted men who worked hard all day long, and then caught the wagons into town to drink half the night away. (You were *still* permitted to drink in Wisconsin, which continued to amaze many of us in Eau Fraiche, considering the fact that three-quarters of the states had gone dry, including nearby Iowa and everything west of the Mississippi—with the exception of California, where booze and bimbos were to be expected.)

The one movie theater in town was called The Chenemeke, and it was of course on Chenemeke Avenue. That week, it was playing Theda Bara in *Cleopatra,* which Nance and I had seen in La Crosse just before Christmas. There was another theater, called the Wisconsin, but it was strictly vaudeville. The Wisconsin was owned and managed by a Swede named Kurt Elfstrom, who was reputed to have earned four million dollars from his two theaters, the one here in Eau Fraiche and the other in Eau Claire. Personally, I couldn't see how he'd made that much money, because whereas he charged some pretty good admission prices—a quarter for a box seat, and fifteen cents for an orchestra seat—he still had to pay his performers, didn't he? And he booked some really good acts into the theater, too, considering the fact that this was just a dying little timber town in Wisconsin. I could remember my father taking me to see Charlie Chaplin, in person, in a thing called *A Night in a London Club,* even before Mr. Elfstrom renovated The Wisconsin and put in the red velvet seats. That must have been in 1912 or 1913, sometime around then, when I was still a little kid and before Chaplin got to be a famous movie star, of course. This week at The Wisconsin, Mr. Elfstrom was showing the Greater Morgan Dancers in a historical Roman ballet; Eddie Leonard & Co., who were blackface singers, dancers, and comedians; and Blossom Seeley with her "Jazz Melodical Delirium." Nancy and I were keeping steady company, so I would probably take her there tomorrow night. Tonight, of course, was the monthly

31

dance, and neither of us wanted to miss that. Besides, I had worked late at the camp (even though I'd never got close to starting my bucking), and it wouldn't have paid to drive the tin Lizzie all the way down to La Crosse, not with the roads still pretty bad after the last snowfall.

There were, I guessed, about thirty Fords parked behind the Grange Hall, as well as one of the only two Pierce-Arrow touring cars in town, this one being yellow, which meant it belonged to Daniel Talbot, whose father owned the furniture company on Carey Avenue. Just to be perverse (and also so I'd be able to find the car again when I came out, all the other Fords being as black as my father's), I parked directly alongside Mr. Talbot's snazzy automobile, and then led Nancy carefully over the hard, rutted, frozen mud of the back lot, around to the front of the hall. There was music coming from inside the gray frame building, two bands having been hired as usual for the occasion; Red Reynolds' local dance orchestra, and a colored jazz band from Chicago that called itself the "Original" something or other.

I still hadn't told Nancy what I'd done that morning.

She looked about as pretty as a skyful of stars, her hair coiled at the back of her neck beneath a simple black velvet hat, glistening pale and gold above the high crushed collar of her coat. Picking her way delicately over the sidewalk, she skirted the patches of ice, one ungloved hand raising the hem of her skirt as she navigated the slippery pavement, her muffed hand resting on my bent arm. When we got inside, I checked our coats and then went into the main hall with her. Her dress was green, paler than her eyes, short, in keeping with the new fashion (Nancy got the *Delineator* from Chicago every month), its silk knotted fringe shimmering a good six inches above the floor.

The Grange was a fairly depressing place. Somebody had decided to paint it gray inside as well as out, so that you always had the feeling you were stepping into a smoke-filled room, even though smoking wasn't permitted at any of the dances except in the men's room down the hall. The window trim was supposed to be a sort of salmon color, I guess, but it looked more like a faded red which, together with the green window shades and the hanging red-and-green crepe paper decorations, gave the room the look of a discarded Christmas. There were eight

32

windows on each long side of the room, and a tiny stage at the far end of the room, used by speakers whenever there was a meeting, but occupied now by Red Reynolds and his band. They were playing as we came in, but I recognized the tune as one of those new fox trots and I still didn't know how to do that damn dance. I'd had enough trouble keeping up with Nancy and trying to learn all the steps that had come in with the war, as if everybody was trying frantically to dance away all the world's troubles, a new dance every week: the bunny hug (Shall we bunny? No, let's just sit and hug), the turkey trot (Everybody's doin' it), the grizzly bear, the snake, the kangaroo, the crab, and now the fox trot and the tango. What I wanted to know was what had happened to the waltz and the two-step which my older sister Kate had taught me to do before she'd run off with her Apache or whatever the hell he was? I was a very good waltzer, and a fair two-stepper, but this new stuff was all pretty much beyond me, and so I sat on my folding chair beside Nancy and took her hand in mine and began talking about the colored band which was getting ready to relieve Red's boys on the stand. I asked Nancy if she knew where the expression "jazz" had come from, and she said she did not. So I told her it was originally a dirty expression, and she said, Bert, it was not. And I said, Really, Nancy, it was an expression used in Chicago, it was originally "jass," spelled with a double-s instead of a double-z and she said Well what does jass mean, and I said It was an expression used in the red-light districts of Chicago, and she said What's a red-light district? So I said It's where, well, the prostitutes work, and Nancy said You're making it up, and I said No, really, Nance, jass means to do it to a woman, and she said You always make up these things because you know they embarrass me.

The colored band came on about then and played something with a lot of clarinet and trumpet work intertwined, it was very difficult to keep track of the melody, I think it was "Tiger Rag" or maybe "Bugle Call Rag." I couldn't dance to the music *they* were making, either, so we sat through the next three or four tunes, and then Danny Talbot came over to say hello and to give Nancy the eye. Danny thought he was extremely handsome, which I guess he was, though I couldn't stand the flashy way he dressed. Nancy didn't pay him much attention, well not *too* much attention, though she did keep staring up at him all the while he told the latest Ford joke, which I'd only heard a thousand times already, the one about the man who was making out his will and insisting that the old Model T be buried with him when he died. "Jed," his wife finally said, "why do you want the Ford buried with you, for land's sake?" and the man answered, "Because I've never been in a hole yet but what that flivver couldn't pull me out," very funny, ha-ha, though Nancy did laugh more than politely, it seemed to me. Talbot finally wandered off, and I figured this was as good a time as any to tell her what I'd done that morning, but the jazz band stopped playing just then, and Red and his boys came back onto the stand, and began playing a waltz, thank God. So I asked Nancy to dance, and I led her out onto the floor and took her into my arms.

I got dizzy whenever I held that girl in my arms.

"Nancy," I said to her, "there's something I've got to tell you."

"What is it, Bert?" she said, and then immediately said, "No, don't tell me. I don't want to know. It's something terrible."

"How can you know it's something terrible?" I asked.

"Because the cream whipped stiff this morning," she said.

"Oh now, Nancy . . ."

"That's a bad sign," she said.

"Well, this isn't anything so terrible."

"What is it?" she said. "No, don't tell me."

"I joined the Army this morning," I said.

She was silent. Her hand tightened in mine, and she looked up into my face, her green eyes wide with shock and disbelief, and then she just sighed and rested her head on my shoulder and still didn't say anything. I wished she would say something.

"When the clouds roll by I'll come to you," Red sang in his deep baritone, the megaphone throwing his voice out into the small hall as couples whirled by us, "Down in lovers' lane, my dearie," girls in velveteen and tricolette, frocks of satin veiled with chiffon, crepes and jerseys, brocades, young men in flannels and tweeds, a few uniforms here and there among the crowd, "So wait and pray each night for me, till we meet again."

"Nancy?" I said.

34

"Why'd you do it, Bert?"

"It's a changing world," I said.

"Don't you love me, Bert?"

"I love you, Nance, but it's a changing world, everything's changing. They're talking about renaming Eau Fraiche, did you know that, Nance? They're talking about calling it Freshwater."

"What's that got to do with your getting killed?"

"I'm not going to get killed, Nance."

"But, Bert, why?" she insisted. *"Why?"*

"Because I have to do my part," I said. "I owe it to America."

"It's no use," she said, "men are but children of a larger growth," using a tried-and-true family expression, handed down from generation to generation together with a trunkload of proverbs and maxims that Nancy pulled out every so often like cherished relics from another age. I loved her for it. I loved everything about her. I loved the way her hand rested so lightly on my shoulder now, trembling just the tiniest bit, I loved the curve of her waist where my fingers spanned the sash of her gown, I loved the sweet scent of her, and the solemn look of her, the deadly serious look on her face as she raised it to mine, never missing a step, her eyes filming, glittering, caught in the red and blue rotating lights of the hall, Red Reynolds' voice behind her distorted through the megaphone.

"Don't die," she said. "Bert, please don't die on me, promise me you won't die."

The band stopped playing.

I stood with Nancy my love in the middle of the floor. We didn't say anything for the longest time, we just kept looking into each other's faces, and finally there was music again, and I smiled at her, and pulled her close, and we danced.

February ❦ ❦ ❦

I was at the center of all that sound, the sound buffeted me in successive electronic waves, I felt exhilarated and dizzy and confident, certain now that we'd win the battle. Standing behind my Farfisa organ, I banged out the chord progression of "Louie, Louie," A,A,A, and D,D, and E minor, E minor, E minor, and D, and D again, and heard Nelson to my left crashing away at the cymbals in rising crescendo. The name of the group was lettered in a psychedelic circle on Nelson's bass drum, DAWN PATROL, and the drumskin vibrated now with each successive thumping whap of Nelson's right foot on the pedal. This group is flying tonight, I thought, we are flying high above it, that's what this old group is doing, and exuberantly shouted "Haaaaaah," as Rog went into the final chorus. The sound was incredible. Connie was working the volume on his amp, building the feedback so that he had it sounding like a fifth instrument, Rog whapping away with the fuzz tone up full, Nelson beating the drums to death. My own fingers felt sore and swollen as I struck chords on the organ, sprinkled organ dust into the harmony of lead and bass guitar, threw crashing organ blasts out into the crowd there milling around the school gym. I saw Cass Hagstrom from the corner of my eye, and zocked a big E minor straight at her, and then grinned, and hit the volume pedal as we went into the last four bars.

I was sweating like a pig when we finished. Nelson was wearing a wild flushed crazy look on his face, "I think we took them, Wat," he said, "Jesus, we sounded great!"

Connie came over, unstrapping his guitar, his big round face broken in a toothy grin. "Hey, how about that?" he shouted, and slapped both me and Nelson on the back, almost sending poor skinny Nelson through his own bass drum. Rog meticulously turned off the amps, put his bass down on the seat of the folding chair, and walked over, looking very serious and pale and worried.

"What do you think?" he said.

"We sounded great," I answered.

"You think so? I think The Four Ducks were better."

"Never," Connie said.

"I think so. They had a better mix."

"Man, did you hear what I was doing with the feedback?" Connie said, still grinning, still very excited.

"Oh, man, that was tough," Nelson said.

"Man, we don't take first place . . ." Connie started.

"We've *got* to take first," I said. "We don't take first, the hell with any more battles. Who needs them?"

"We'll take first," Nelson assured us both.

"The Ducks were better," Rog said solemnly, and then took a handkerchief from his back pocket and wiped his forehead. "Did I sound okay on 'Rising Sun'?"

"You sounded great," I said.

"There's Mr. Jaegers," Connie said.

"Shhh, shhh."

Mr. Jaegers, the president of the Talmadge Lions' Club, which had sponsored this battle of the bands, adjusted the microphone, blew into it, and then said, "Can you hear me back there?" One of the kids standing at the back of the gym shouted, "Yeah, we hear you!" and Mr. Jaegers said, "How's that?" and a lot of kids this time shouted, "Great, crazy," and Mr. Jaegers blew into the microphone again, and said, "Our three judges are now deliberating, but before we give you their results, I'd like to make a few acknowledgments. I want to thank, first of all, the ladies of the church Altar Society for providing tonight's refreshments, and especially Mrs. Peggy Greer, who contacted the Coca-Cola Company and had them deliver the dispenser set up in the hall outside. I want to thank Mr. Teale, your principal, who gave the Lions' Club every cooperation in making the school and the gymnasium available tonight for the battle. And I want to thank our three judges—Mr. Coopersmith, who, as you know, is in broadcasting, and who was kind enough to come over here tonight, and also Mr. Isetti of the Clef and Staff Music Shop in town, and our third judge, who, like yourselves, is a teen-ager and a member of The ..." Mr. Jaegers paused, consulted the slip of paper in his hand again, turned away from the microphone, and asked, "What does this say?"

"The Butterfly Push," I said.

". . . a member of The Butterfly Push," Mr. Jaegers said into the microphone, "that's the name of his band. But most of all, I would like to thank Mr. Kevin Price of the Lions' Club, whose idea it was to have this battle, and who worked so hard co-ordinating all the various elements that have gone into making it a success."

"Come on, already," Nelson whispered. "Who *won* the damn thing?"

"Now, to reiterate," Mr. Jaegers said into the microphone, "and before our judges read off the results, there were five bands playing tonight, and they played for you in this order, first was Sound, Incorporated, second was Phase Nine, third was The Morse Code, fourth was The Four Dukes, and last, the band you just heard, was Dawn Patrol. Now, if Mr. Coopersmith will come to the stand, I'm sure we're all anxious to know who the winners are. Mr. Coopersmith?"

I waited patiently while Leon Coopersmith, who lived in Talmadge and who was a radio executive in New York, his desk job there presumably making him an expert on rock and roll, what with rubbing elbows with Cousin Brucie and Dandy Dan Daniel and the like all day long; waited while Leon Coopersmith, whom I had seen drunk on many an occasion at parties in our own living room, waddled to the stage weighing two hundred and ten pounds bone-dry, clasped the microphone in a pair of meaty hands, backed away from the sudden feedback, big radio executive that he was, removed one hand from the mike to consult the slip of paper in his hands, cleared his throat, and said, "Okay, kids, want to quiet down for just a few seconds?"

A hush fell over the gymnasium. Out on the floor, I could see Scott Dundee putting his arms around Cass from behind. I watched, hoping she'd move away from him, but she didn't move, she just let him circle her waist from behind, and then she folded her own arms over his, very cozy, I thought, while I played my brains out and my fingers to the bone.

"Taking third prize of twenty-five dollars," Mr. Coopersmith who was in broadcasting said in his whiskey-snarled voice, "is The Morse Code, will a member of that group please come up to the stage to accept the check?"

"So far, so good," Connie whispered.

There was applause from the kids, but not too much applause because The Morse Code was John Yancy's group, and he lived over in Wilton and didn't even go to Talmadge High. Yancy came up wearing a scrub beard and a bright red vest—all the guys in his group wore red vests, in fact, like Guy Lombardo or one of those big bands of the forties, though Kenton wasn't too bad, I'd heard my father playing some of his Kenton collection on the hi-fi just the other night; pretty far out, I guessed, compared to the other stuff they were playing in those days. Anyway, I shouldn't have been knocking my father's taste, I supposed, since it was he who'd suggested the

38

name "Dawn Patrol" when we were first starting the group. He'd initially come up with some names that were supposed to be comical, like The Sound and The Fury or The Intolerable Boils or The Noisemakers, horsing around when all the guys were seriously considering names for the group, making a pest of himself until he finally suggested Dawn Patrol, which none of the guys except Connie realized was a reference to a movie about World War I (Connie being a movie buff and also an avid watcher of old-time crap on television), but which all of us liked, anyway. "You mean I actually gave you an idea?" my father said. "Will miracles never?"

So Dawn Patrol it had been, and Dawn Patrol it still was, though many of the other groups changed their names constantly, like The Four Dukes, affectionately known far and wide as The Four Ducks. They once used to be called The Four Barons, nobly elevating themselves only after they'd been around for three months, and putting a sign up on their very next job, the sign reading THE FOUR DUKES, FORMALLY THE FOUR BARONS, which gave everybody but the illiterate Ducks a great big laugh.

Yancy was nodding and offering profuse thanks to everyone for the dubious honor of having placed third with his inept group. Mr. Coopersmith shook his hand with genuine enthusiasm, as though congratulating John Lennon, and Yancy finally sidled off the stage, all grins and embarrassment. Mr. Coopersmith gripped the mike again, leaned into it, and said, "In second place, winning a prize of fifty dollars ..." He hesitated here, and I held my breath, figuring if we didn't take second, we were *sure* to take first, and Mr. Coopersmith said, "In second place ... Phase Nine!"

Nelson gave a short nod as the crowd burst into applause, confirming my surmise: we were sure to take first now. Only Rog looked his usual sallow gloomy self, chewing on his fingernails as Peter Drew come up to the stage to accept the fifty-dollar check for Phase Nine. There was more applause, and a few catcalls ("You got robbed, Pete!") and Mr. Coopersmith clutched Drew's hand in both his own meaty hands and grinned approval from that great big world of radio broadcasting, and then Drew looked at the check, and nodded, and folded it, and put it into his wallet, and walked off the stage to where Donna Fields was waiting for him. She gave him a big hug, and I automatically glanced out over the gym floor to see how Cass was doing with Dundee's arms still around her, and Mr. Coopersmith held up one of his hands for silence again, and then said, "Now . . . before I announce the winner of the first prize, I'd like to tell you that the winning band'll be playing for an additional half-hour, and I hope you'll all stay around to listen and dance. So . . . in first place . . . for a prize of one hundred dollars . . ."

Again, Mr. Coopersmith paused. He grinned out at the audience. I glanced at Rog, who was busily chewing his fingernails.

"In first place," Mr. Coopersmith said, "Sound, Incorporated!"

"Sound, In—" Nelson started, and then turned to me with an enraged look on his face, gripping my arm fiercely just below the elbow, and then turning to gape at Mr. Coopersmith, as though certain he had made some terrible mistake. Rog, expecting disaster all along, merely nodded his head knowingly. Connie sat abruptly in one of the folding chairs and slapped his hand to his forehead. The response from the teen-age audience was mixed, some of them cheering and applauding, some of them booing and shouting at the stage. Mr. Coopersmith, unperturbed in his broadcasting tower, waited blandly for Gerry Haig to come up onto the stage for Sound, Incorporated, and collect the group's ill-gotten hundred bucks.

"That's the last time," I said. "I swear to God, that's the last time we play a battle!"

"Sound, Incorporated!" Nelson exploded. "They're the worst group here!"

"It figures," Rog said gloomily.

"Let's pack up," Connie said.

"You want to congratulate the winners?"

"The winners *suck*," Nelson said.

Angrily, convinced that there was no justice in the world, we began unplugging our leads, winding them up, covering the amps, taking our mike stands apart, unscrewing the organ legs, packing the guitars and drums. Danny Boll, who had been one of the judges, and who prior to this January had been the rhythm guitarist of the best group in the area, The Butterfly Push, most of whom were now away at college or in the Army, came up onto the stage while we were still packing. "If it's any consolation," he said, "I voted for you guys."

"Thanks, Danny," I said.

"You guys are really coming along fine," Boll said. "I can remember when you first started, and there's been a tremendous development."

"Thanks," Nelson said. "Thanks, Danny."

"I mean it."

"Thanks," I said.

But we were still angry and bitter, especially me, because I had a few other choice items bugging me besides. My father, for example, had refused me permission to drive the station wagon that night, his point being that there'd be a lot of heavy equipment in it, and it was dangerous to be lugging two tons of amplifiers and instruments on a Friday night, when half the population of Connecticut would be drunk and zigzagging all over the roads. I personally could not see the difference between driving heavy equipment around during the day or driving it around at night, and I'd informed my father that I'd shuttled the loaded car all the way to Stamford just last weekend, with six kids packed into the damn thing besides, and I was a very careful driver, and what dire thing did my father expect to happen, would he mind telling me? (This isn't a locker room, my father had said, watch your language.) I'd lost the battle with my father, and I'd lost the band battle, and now it looked as if I were losing the battle of Cass Hagstrom as well, to no less a hood than Scott Dundee, who ran around with a bunch of boozers, the dumbest asses in the school. How could you expect to ask a girl if you could take her home when you knew your *father* would be waiting in the parking lot? What was the sense of taking Driver's Ed a whole damn six months, what was the sense of having night lights if your father never let you *drive* the damn car at night?

As I carried Nelson's snare drum out to the loading ramp near the school commons, I heard Cass telling Dundee that she would just *love* to see *Dr. Strangelove*, she had heard it was a perfectly marvelous film, but she knew that *Love with the Proper Stranger* was playing in Westport, and Steve McQueen was her absolute favorite, so couldn't they go *there* tomorrow night instead? "Hello, Cass," I said as I went by, and she said, "Oh, hello, Wat, you were terrific," and I said, "Yeah," and walked off. Nelson was waiting outside on the ramp, the big bass drum in his hands.

41

"Where's your father?" he asked.

"I don't know, don't you see him?"

"No."

"Well, let's get the rest of the junk," I said. "He'll be here."

Cass was heading for the phone booth when I went inside again, undoubtedly to give her mother a ring, tell her she might be delayed as she had run into one of the school's intellectuals and they wished to discuss the satirical content of *Dr. Strangelove*.

"Hey," I said.

"Oh, hi," she said, "did I tell you you were terrific?"

"Yeah, you told me," I said. "What's with Dundee?"

Cass shrugged. She was a slender, diminutive girl with straight blond hair falling to her shoulders, dark brown eyes, a frightened smile that tentatively budded on her mouth even when she was deliriously happy, as she seemed to be now. "He's very nice," she said, and I immediately said, "He's a hood."

"Well, I have to make a phone call," Cass said. She was wearing a gray flannel jumper over a white turtleneck sweater, and she tossed her long blond hair now, and smoothed her skirt, and went clicking off down the corridor to the phone booth while I glared at her with something less than masked hostility. Nelson helped me lift the organ, and we carried it together out to the ramp. The Ford station wagon was waiting at the curb, but my father was not behind the wheel. Instead, my mother was sitting there, staring straight ahead through the windshield.

"Hey, hi," I said in surprise. "Where's Dad?"

"Stuck in the city," my mother said. "How'd it go?"

"We didn't even show."

"We got robbed," Nelson said.

"You want to lower this back window, Mom?"

"Who won?"

"Sound, Incorporated."

"Which group is that?"

"You don't know them, Mom."

"They stink, Mrs. Tyler."

"I thought Rog was going to start crying," I said from the tailgate of the wagon.

"We should have taken it, I mean it, Mrs. Tyler."

"Am I dropping you off?"

"If it's okay," Nelson said.

42

"Sure."

"Something wrong?" I asked her.

"No," she said. "No."

"You seem . . ." I shrugged. "Give me a hand here, will you, Nelson?"

I could see the back of my mother's head as we loaded the drums and organ into the car. She wore her brown hair short, the collar of her beige car coat high on the back of her neck. She was sitting very stiff and straight, staring through the windshield, puffing on a cigarette even though she'd given up smoking more than a month ago.

"I see you're back on the weed again," I said.

"Oh," she said, "I just . . ." and didn't finish the sentence.

"Shove the bass drum all the way back," I said.

"Why don't we put the organ in first? I'm getting out before you."

"Good thinking, Maynard."

We arranged the equipment with meticulous care, stacking it in tight to prevent it from sliding or bouncing on the rutted country roads. My mother sat silently smoking as we heaved and pushed and adjusted. The radio was on, classical music, QXR, I supposed, her favorite station. The engine was running, a bluish-gray exhaust rising lazily and steadily on the brittle air. At midnight, the news came on, and I listened vaguely as I worked, the words floating back through the heated car and out over the lowered tailgate, ". . . three months after the assassination of Diem and his brother, General Minh's regime was itself overthrown tonight in a coup that took most Saigon citizens totally by surprise. Lieutenant General Nguyen Khanh, thirty-six years old, considered by United States military advisers to be one of South Vietnam's ablest corps commanders . . ."

"Where's that other mike stand?" I asked.

"I'll get it," Nelson said.

"We ought to mark them, you know? I'm always afraid somebody'll walk off with them."

"Yeah," Nelson said.

". . . five miles from the Cambodian border, inflicting the worst toll upon South Vietnamese troops to date: ninety-four dead, and thirty-two wounded. Three American advisers were also killed in the bloody battle."

We shoved both mike stands in alongside the organ,

43

wedging the heavy metal bases in solidly against the covered hump of the spare tire.

"You can roll it up," I said to my mother.

". . . won't expire until March of next year. Mayor Wagner, though, apprehensive after New York's 114-day siege, has already begun talks . . ."

The roads were deserted. The newscaster's voice gave way to recorded music, Stravinsky, I guessed, though I wasn't sure. We passed the university, where lights still gleamed in the new science building, and the three chapels sat like snow-cowled nuns, and then drove past the old campus on Fieldston Street, where buildings erected in 1876 rose in turreted stillness against a sky dusted with stars. On the other side of the wooden bridge near the university's western gate, the car's headlights illuminated a mole who stopped dead still for just an instant and then waddled clumsily to the side of the road. We climbed the hill over Corrigan and then took the short cut through Pleasant, my mother handling the wheel expertly around each hairpin turn, although she looked somewhat like a gun moll, with the cigarette dangling from her mouth that way.

"You're going to lose that ash," I said, annoyed.

"Thank you," she answered, and took one gloved hand from the wheel, flicked the long ash into the ash tray, and immediately put the cigarette into her mouth again. She did not put it out until we were in Nelson's driveway. I helped him unload the drums and then carried them in with him through the garage entrance.

"We rehearsing tomorrow?" Nelson asked.

"I don't know," I said. "I'll buzz Connie in the morning and let you know."

"Okay," Nelson said. He paused for a moment, idly worrying a pimple near his mouth. "We got robbed," he said, almost to himself, and then from the open garage door called, " 'Night, Mrs. Tyler. Thanks a lot." In the idling automobile, my mother raised her hand in farewell. By the time I got back to the car, she had lighted a second cigarette. I glanced at it but said nothing.

She smoked silently as she drove, her face alternately illuminated by the green light of the dash and the glowing coal of the cigarette whenever she puffed on it.

"We should have taken it," I said.

"Well," she said, and gave a slight shrug.

"You okay?" I asked.

"Yes, I'm fine."

"You seem down."

"We were supposed to go to a dinner party. I had to cancel."

"Oh."

"I suppose I could have gone alone. They asked me to." She shrugged again.

"How'd Dad get stuck?"

"The De Gaulle book," she answered.

"They still working on that?"

"Apparently so."

We were silent the rest of the way home.

My father must have been watching for the car. The minute we pulled into the driveway, the kitchen door opened, and he came out without a coat, grinning, walking swiftly to the driver's side as my mother rolled down the window.

"Hi," he said, and leaned through the open window to kiss her on the cheek, and then looked across to me and said, "How'd it go, Wat?"

"We lost," I said.

"What does Leon Coopersmith know about good music?" my father said. "You want a hand with that organ?" He was very excited. His eyes were glowing, and his face was flushed, and I knew he was bursting to tell us something, and I felt the energy of his secret flowing through the open window and suffusing the automobile. I loved him most when he was this way. He seemed to me in these moments to be very tall and powerful. I half-expected him to reach into the car and pick me up and hold me out at arm's length and then clasp me suddenly to his chest, laughing, the way he used to when I was very young. I found myself grinning with him.

"Will," my mother said, "I thought . . ."

"Man of surprises," my father said, "man of surprises," and kissed her again in punctuation, on the mouth this time. "Do you still want to go to that party?"

"Well, I . . ."

"Let me help Wat," he said, and opened the door for my mother, and gave her a hug when she stepped out of the car, and then came to the tailgate with me. We

45

carried the organ into the house, and then brought in the amplifier and the mike stands and the two speakers. My father kept putting down Leon Coopersmith all the while we worked, telling me he had a tin ear, telling me the people who selected judges for these band battles should make certain they picked someone attuned to the sound of youth, all the while bursting with his own secret, but taking the time and the trouble to console me about Dawn Patrol's loss. As we made our last trip inside, he said, "Well, you'll win the next one," and then shouted, "Dolores, do we *have* to go to that damn party?"

My mother, still looking bewildered, said, "I suppose not, I've already called to . . ."

"Then let's forget it," he said. "Let's all go over to Emily Shaw's and celebrate."

"What are we celebrating?" my mother said. She was excited now, too. The energy he radiated was positively contagious. We stood by the kitchen sink, the three of us, grinning at each other idiotically, my father savoring the moment when he would tell us his secret, my mother and I relishing the suspense. When he finally revealed his coup—he had made arrangements with a French photographer named Claude Michaud to take a series of candid shots of De Gaulle, with the general's permission and cooperation—it hardly seemed as important as the buildup had been, but we showered him with congratulations nonetheless, telling him how marvelous it was, and agreeing that we had good cause for celebration. My mother looked radiant. As my father spoke, her eyes never left his face. She listened to him intently, proud and pleased, shining with adoration.

"Okay," he said, and jabbed a finger at me, "tie and jacket, on the double," and then turned to my mother and said, "Do you know what they say in France?"

"What do they say in France?" my mother asked.

"In France, they say 'This Will Tyler, he is one lucky son of a bitch!' " and burst out laughing.

"Hey, watch the language," I said, "there are little kids around."

"Who wants a drink?" my father asked. "*I* want a drink," he said. "Dolores? Would you like a drink?"

"All right," she said, "if you're . . ."

"Hey!" he said, and snapped his fingers. "He knows *Linda!*"

"Who knows Linda?"

"Michaud. He met her and Stanley when they were in Paris last year. Do you think I should call her?"

"Sure, if you want to," my mother said.

"The rates go down after six, don't they?"

"Last of the big spenders," I said.

"Ha-ha," he said.

"Debating a phone call to Chicago."

"Put-down artist," my mother said to me, but she was grinning.

My father went to the telephone. "Come on, come on," he said, "what's everybody standing around for?"

"I thought I was getting a drink," my mother said.

"I'll bring it up, hon," my father said, and lifted the receiver, and waited for a dial tone. My mother was watching him from the steps leading upstairs. "Hey," he said to her.

"Mmm?"

"I love you," he said.

My mother smiled and gave a brief pleased nod. Then she turned and went up the steps.

"Hello," my father said into the telephone, "I'd like to make a person-to-person call to Mrs. Linda Kearing in Chicago. The number . . ."

March ❦ ❦

It was my kid sister Linda, of all people, who clued me in. I had met her completely by accident outside the bio lab on the fourth floor, and casually asked what it was all about. To my surprise, she blushed and said, "I can't tell you, Will," and then went right on to tell me. That was when the bell sounded for the air-raid drill.

She made me promise upon pain of death and torture that I would never reveal my source of information, and I kissed her swiftly on the cheek and then raced back to my home room, which was what we'd been trained to do like robots whenever those three successive gongs sounded. A fire drill was a single steady repetitive gong, and an air-raid drill was three gongs in quick sequence, and then a long pause, and then three gongs again. For the fire drills, we always marched out of the school silently and solemnly and looked back at it from four blocks away, near St. Chrysostom's Church, presumably to witness the old brick building crumbling in flames.

I thought of what my sister had told me outside the bio lab, and I began planning and scheming all the way back to home room about how I would break the news to Charlotte Wagner. This was, of course, the eighth period, which was the last period of the day. We had never had an air-raid drill in the history of Grace School that did not take place during the eighth period. The routine was unvarying. Sometime between three-thirty and four-fifteen, the successive gongs would sound sharply and insistently, and we'd all rush back to our home rooms, crouch under our desks, clasp our hands behind our heads, and wait in cramped silence for about ten minutes until the gong sounded for the all-clear. Our teachers would then dismiss us, since by that time the last period would be almost over, the school day practically ended. It was my theory that this imaginative approach to protection against enemy attack was based on secret information delivered to our city officials by the Japanese themselves, who had doubtless promised that any bombing of the school would come sometime during the eighth period.

It was no different this time, except that this time I knew what "Keep 'Em Flying!" meant. I could hardly wait. The whole thing with Charlotte Wagner had started about two weeks ago, on the way home from school. Charlotte, like myself, was a senior at Grace, which had not been named after God's greatest gift to the soul, but merely after a man named Jeremiah Grace who had founded the school back in 1891. Grace was a private school, the nearest public school being Robert A. Waller High over on Orchard Street, which was quite a bus ride from the Gold Coast, where we lived. Our house was on East Scott, and Charlotte lived on Banks. Most of the other kids going to Grace lived in the immediate neighborhood, too, so we usually walked over to Division after school, for sodas. The only kid in our crowd who drove to and from school, in a black '39 Buick, was a guy named Dickie Howell, whose father was supposed to be in "essential industry," and therefore in possession of valuable C

48

coupons which entitled him to an unlimited amount of gasoline. *My* father was in the paper industry, but Uncle Sam did not consider that essential enough to rate anything better than a B ration. Besides, he actually used the car to go back and forth to work at his mill in Joliet every day, and we only had the one car, so I couldn't have driven even if I'd wanted to.

Actually, I enjoyed that walk home after school every day. Linda sometimes came with us, but I tried to discourage that because she was only fifteen and a lot of the jokes and kidding around were over her head. We were, after all, seniors. Michael Mallory had, in fact, enlisted in the Air Force just before his eighteenth birthday, and was expecting to be called right after graduation. His move, of course, was the only sensible one. Nobody in his right mind wanted to be drafted into the Army just then, because it was an almost certain bet that the Infantry would grab you, and you'd wind up in the invasion of Italy, which was definitely coming as soon as North Africa fell. Michael had thought of enlisting in the cavalry, having always been fond of horses, but then he'd learned that cavalry meant *mechanized* cavalry, which meant tanks, and we both knew a kid named Sal Brufani who had been burned to a crisp in a tank outside Bizerte, just before Christmas. Michael furthermore got sick even riding a boat on Lake Michigan, which eliminated the Navy as a possibility. So, unless he wanted to have his ass shipped to Italy or, worse yet, to the Aleutians or the Solomons, the only logical open choice (I convinced him) was the Air Force.

In any case, our language on the way home from school each day was inclined to get a bit salty, and I didn't like Linda hearing such stuff. For example, just last week, Michael had come up with a new Confucius Say joke, which broke everybody up, but which made Linda— *and* me—very uncomfortable. He'd told it without any warning, just popping it out of the blue, "Confucius say, 'Girl who marry basketball player get gypped; he always dribble before he shoot.'" Charlotte Wagner had thrown back her head and opened her mouth wide to let out one of her horse bellows, delicately feminine and designed to knock over the Wrigley Building. The other girls all followed suit, of course, except Linda. She started to laugh, and then quickly glanced at me, and blushed, and smiled

49

only tentatively and in a frightened way, and then put on a very grave and serious look when she saw I wasn't laughing at all. Sarah Cody had meanwhile knocked Michael's books into the gutter and called him a dirty slob. He laughed wildly and said, "Who? Me? What'd I say?" and began wrestling first with her and then Charlotte, with a lot of indiscreet cheap feeling going on, and with Linda walking very silently beside me, her eyes lowered. I later warned Michael to be a little more careful with his language when my sister was around, and he promised he would.

I was surprised by what my sister had told me outside the bio lab, not because it was really so dirty, but only because she'd told me at *all,* though with a blush. As I crouched under my desk now and listened for our punctual eighth-period Japanese raiders, I thought of how much pleasure it would give me to break the news to Charlotte as soon as this drill was over. The whole thing had started about two weeks ago when Charlotte, climbing the steps of her house on Banks, had waved to the other girls and said, "Well, girls, keep 'em flying," causing all the girls to burst into hysterical laughter which none of the boys understood.

"What's so funny?" Michael asked.

"Oh, nothing," Charlotte said breezily, and then turned to the girls again, and again said, "Keep 'em flying, girls," and went up the steps and into her house. Nor had that been the end of it. Every day since, the girls had given each other the same mysterious farewell, "Keep 'em flying!" They were obviously delighted by our puzzlement, and the harder we pressed them for an explanation, the sillier they became, giggling and exchanging sly glances, and shoving at each other, and generally behaving as though they were carrying around the ultimate secret of the female universe. Up to now, or more accurately up to the minute Linda had let me in on the secret outside the bio lab, I had always thought the slogan was a patriotic reminder to the folks at home, urging them to do their share in the war effort by respecting rationing and the like, and buying war bonds, and keeping silent about troop shipments. But now I knew. And whereas the slogan had a great deal to do with the war effort, it had nothing to do with pilots (although the silk was probably needed for parachutes—that *was,* in fact, the point) but only to do with the selfless contribution busty Charlotte and her girlfriends were being asked to make in these trying times.

I could hardly wait to let her know I knew.

A single gong sounded into the stillness.

"Okay, kids," Mr. Hardy said, "drill's over. You can all go home."

Outside the school, I looked for Charlotte. I found her just as she was climbing into Dickie Howell's black Buick and, wouldn't you know it, I didn't get a chance to say a word to her.

The house we lived in was the third one we'd owned since I was born, each larger than the one preceding it. It was on a street of similarly old houses, most of them built around the turn of the century, when Chicago's moneyed landholders were reconstructing after the Great Fire. The street ran from North State to the Drive, and had been surrounded for years by huge modern apartment buildings. It was my guess that the only thing sparing it now was wartime building restrictions. If we won the war—and I couldn't conceive of our losing it—I was certain that within ten years' time, East Scott would succumb to the bulldozer as well, and all these lovely old homes would give way to glass and concrete towers.

I loved that old house.

It reminded me, in style though not in grandeur, of what used to be the old Kimball mansion on Prairie and Eighteenth. My father said the Kimball house had been modeled after the Château de Josselin in Brittany, and had cost the old piano manufacturer a million dollars to build. Standing on the sidewalk and looking up at it one day, I could well believe it. The house was made entirely of Bedford stone, with turrets and gables everywhere, balconies and stone chimneys, a roof crowned with ornamental ironwork. There were more windows than I could count, flat windows and rounded windows, an oriel window on the north façade. A high fence of iron grillwork surrounded the entire house, and whereas I could have gone in, I suppose (it was then headquarters for the Architects Club of Chicago), I think I was too awed to move from my spot on the sidewalk. My father later told me there were beamed ceilings inside, walls paneled in oak and mahogany, onyx fireplaces in most of the rooms, and even onyx washbowls in the bathrooms, which were tiled from floor to ceiling.

Our house was built in the same French château style, but of course was neither as sumptuous nor as large. The entry hall and dining room were paneled in mahogany, but none of the other rooms were, and there were only three bedrooms in the house, not counting the maid's room, which was on the ground floor behind the pantry. My father's library was on the second floor at the top of a winding staircase with a banister Linda and I used to slide down daily. The top panel of our front door was made of frosted glass into which my father had had inserted a sort of Tyler family crest he'd designed, beautifully rendered in stained glass, leaded into the original panel: two green spruce trees towering against a deep blue sky. The doorknob was made of brass, kept highly polished by the succession of colored maids my mother was constantly hiring and firing. (My father said to her one day, "Nancy, you just don't *want* another woman living here, now let's face it.") From the time I was seven, however, I don't think we ever went for more than a month without a maid (and sometimes *two*) in the house. Whether this was at the insistence of my father or not, I couldn't say. I did sometimes get the feeling, though, that my mother often longed for the simpler existence she had known in Freshwater, Wisconsin.

She was in the kitchen when I got home that afternoon, but she barely looked up when I came in, being very used to air-raid drills by now. Though, come to think of it, she'd hardly paid any attention to our first air-raid drill, either. That first one had been very exciting to me, because it had come about two weeks after the Japanese attack on Pearl Harbor, and half the kids in the school thought the enemy was really over Chicago. The sense of impending disaster was heightened by the fact that the teachers sent us running home, none of that hiding under desks, just *run straight home,* they told us. So naturally we expected to see a Japanese Zero or two diving on the school, or perhaps a few Bettys unloading their cargo of bombs, it was all very thrilling. Coincidentally, a few Navy Hellcats from the training station winged in over the lake just as we were pouring out of the school, and this nearly started a panic, what with our high expectations for obliteration. I ran all the way home that day, and when I

52

got into the kitchen, out of breath, my mother said, "What is it, Will?"

"The Japs are coming!" I said.

"Don't be ridiculous," she said.

"I saw them," I answered. "Four of them in formation, flying in low over the lake!"

"On earth are no fairies," my mother said calmly. "You probably saw some planes from the Navy base," which of course was the truth, but which I wasn't yet ready to accept. She was standing by the kitchen sink, shelling peas and listening to the radio on the window sill, and her attention never once wandered from her slender hands, a thumbnail slitting each pod, the peas—almost the color of her eyes—tumbling into the colander. The radio was on very loud. My mother was a little hard of hearing in her right ear, and she favored the other ear now, her head slightly cocked to the side, as the trials and tribulations of "Just Plain Bill" flooded the kitchen the way they did every afternoon at four-thirty, the indomitable barber desperately trying to turn his lively daughter into a lady, while simultaneously fretting over her stormy marriage to the lawyer Kerry Donovan. I think if the Japanese had really been overhead, my mother would have waited till the end of that day's installment before running down to the basement. I had never seen her rattled in my life, and she was certainly as calm as glass that day of the first air-raid drill. Honey-blond hair behind her ears, reading glasses perched on top of her tilted head, eyes gazing down at the tumbling peas, she said, "If the Japanese were in Chicago, I'd have heard it on the radio. They'd have interrupted the program. Where's your sister?"

"On her way home," I said dejectedly.

I kept watching her in fascination, admiring her calm in the face of certain destruction, yet resenting it as well. She was not a tall woman, five-three or five-four, but whereas I was almost six feet tall, I had the feeling I was looking up at her; it was very unsettling.

"They told us to come *straight home*," I said ominously, but my mother went right on shelling peas.

We naturally had a maid living in at the time, a colored girl from the Washington Park section, but my mother never allowed her to prepare meals, mindful of a Wisconsin homily about two women in the kitchen being akin to a horse with a head on both ends, or something to that effect. My mother was a great one for proverbs. Sometimes, when she reeled off one of her homespun sayings, absolutely unsmilingly and with a sense of discovery (as if she hadn't said the very same thing a hundred times before), my father would roll his eyes heavenward and sigh deeply, and I would remember that she had been his childhood sweetheart and that he'd probably been listening to her words of wisdom since almost the turn of the century. The thought was frightening. She had a proverb for every occasion, the same ones in fact for totally different situations, and I lived in fear of the day she'd come up with a new and entirely fresh one because I knew I'd die of a heart attack on that day and *never* get into the Air Force.

"Would you like some milk?" she asked me now.

"Another air-raid drill today," I said, going to the refrigerator.

"I gathered," she answered.

There was some leftover icebox cake on the second shelf, and I cut a small slice of it. Then I poured myself a glass of cold milk, and took everything over to the round kitchen table under the Tiffany lamp. We generally took breakfast with the fork (one of my mother's expressions, translated from the English to mean a breakfast including some kind of meat, usually sausage), and since I didn't get to school each day until nine o'clock, I wasn't hungry enough to eat very much of the school lunch at noon. But neither did I dare eat anything substantial when I got home in the afternoon because dinner was at six-fifteen sharp and my mother was a stickler for eating everything put before you. So I usually just took the edge off my appetite with a little milk and maybe a chocolate pudding, or a few cookies, and then went into the living room to do my homework. We had a new Philco floor-model radio there, complete with push buttons, and as I worked I would listen first to "Terry and the Pirates" and "The Adventures of Jimmy Allen" in breathless succession on WENR, than a quick flick of the dial at five-thirty for "Jack Armstrong" on W67C, and then back to WENR for "Captain Midnight" at five forty-five. At six on the button, I'd hear my father's key in the latch, and the front door would open, and he would call his customary greeting, "Hello, anybody home?"

At dinner that night, I decided to reopen the Air Force issue.

My father seemed to be in a very good mood. He was talking about a recent War Production Board memo that eulogized the paper industry and made the printed word sound as important to the war effort as bullets. I always listened in fascination when my father talked about paper. I could never visualize him doing anything but work of a physical nature; his lumberjack background seemed entirely believable to me. When he came home from work each evening wearing a gray fedora and a gray topcoat and a pin-striped business suit, I was always a little surprised that he wasn't wearing boots and a mackinaw and a turtleneck sweater. He was a big man, still very strong at forty-three, with penetrating blue eyes and a nose I like to consider patrician (since I had inherited it). The table in the paneled formal dining room was eight feet long without additional leaves, and whereas my father always sat at the head of it, my mother did not sit at the opposite end but instead took a chair on his right, closest to the kitchen. She refused to keep a bell on the table ("Never count the number a bell tolls, for it'll bring you that many years of bad luck") and would more often than not rise and go into the kitchen herself if the maid didn't respond to her first gentle call. My sister Linda always sat on my father's left, and I sat alongside her, which was not the happiest of arrangements, since she was left-handed and invariably sticking her elbow in my dish.

"Well," I said, subtly I thought, "it looks as if Michael Mallory will be leaving for the Air Force soon."

"And here I thought we were actually going to get through a meal without hearing Will's enlistment pitch," my father said.

"The wheel that does the squeaking is the wheel that gets the grease," my mother said. "Don't you know that, Bert?"

"If I wait till my eighteenth birthday," I said, unrattled, "and then get drafted, I'll end up in the Infantry."

"Let's wait till your eighteenth birthday and find out, shall we?" my father said.

"Sure, I'll send you letters from Italy. Written in the mud or something."

"You spent six summers at camp without writing a single letter," my father said. "I have no reason to believe you'll be changing your habits when and if you get to Italy."

"That wasn't my point," I said.

"Your father knows your point," my mother said.

"I'll be eighteen in June," I said.

"We know when you'll be eighteen."

"Well, for crying out loud, do you *want* me to go into the Infantry?"

"I don't want you to go *anywhere*," my father said flatly.

"Well, that's fine, Pop, but Uncle Sam has other ideas, you know? Whether you realize it or not, there *happens* to be a war going on."

"Living in the same house with you, it'd be difficult not to realize that," my father said, and picked up his napkin, and wiped his mouth, and then looked me in the eye and said, "What's your hurry, Will? You anxious to get killed?"

"I'm not in any hurry," I said.

"You sound like you're in one *hell* of a hurry, son."

My sister glanced up at him quickly; it was rare to hear my father using profanity, even a word as mild as "hell."

"I'm only trying to protect myself," I said.

"Yes, by rushing over there to fly an airplane."

"Yes, which is a lot safer than . . ."

"No one's safe in war," my father said. "Get that out of your head."

"Look," I said, "can we talk reasonably for a minute? Can we just for a minute look at this thing reasonably?"

"I'm listening," my father said.

"It's reasonable to expect that I have to register when I'm eighteen, and it's reasonable to expect I'll be put in 1-A, and it's reasonable to expect I'll be drafted."

"Yes, that's reasonable. Unless the war ends before then."

"Oh, come on, Pop, you can't believe the war's going to end before June!"

"It may end before you're trained and sent overseas."

"Okay, then you should be very happy to let me join the Air Force. It takes longer to train a fighter pilot than it does an infantryman."

My father was silent. I felt I had made a point.

"Isn't that reasonable?" I asked.

"It's only reasonable for my son to stay alive until he becomes a man," my father said.

"*You* stayed alive, didn't you?" I said.

"I was lucky," he answered.

April ❦

I didn't know what I was doing on a troopship in Brooklyn. I wanted to be with Nancy. Instead, I was sitting in the blacked-out hold of a British vessel, on the edge of a bunk which was the bottom one in a tier of four, waiting to sail for Brest. I couldn't believe it. Nor could I even understand how I had got here.

My father was fond of saying that all of America's troubles had started with the assassination, a premise I couldn't very well argue, since I was only a year old when McKinley got shot. And even though the shock of the murder seemed to sift down through the next ten years or more, as if the idea of something so primitive happening in a nation as sophisticated as America took that long to get used to, it was never more than a historical event to me, vague and somehow unbelievable. I was, frankly, more moved when the Archduke Ferdinand and his wife got killed. Not shaken to the roots, mind you (I was fourteen, going on fifteen, too old to be carrying on like an idiot) but frightened and excited by everything that happened in the month that followed: Austria-Hungary declaring war on Servia; Russia moving 80,000 troops to the border; Germany declaring war on Russia; Germany declaring war on France; Germany invading Belgium; England declaring war on Germany; everybody declaring war on everybody else—except the United States.

We were neutral.

We were sane.

To me, in Eau Fraiche, Wisconsin, the war was something that erupted only in newspaper headlines—I didn't know where Servia was and I couldn't even pronounce Sarajevo. England was the only country with which I felt any real sympathy, but that was because both my parents were of English stock; my father, in fact, had been born and raised in Liverpool. But even then, I think my own attitude about the war in those early days was a reflection of what the rest of America was thinking and feeling, or at least the rest of America as represented by the state of Wisconsin. It wasn't our battle. We were determined to stay out of it. We had headaches enough of our own—all that mess down there in Mexico which we *still* hadn't resolved, and people out of work everywhere you looked, and southern Negroes causing even bigger job problems by moving in batches to the north and the midwest—we didn't need any war. And anyway, even though Germany's march into Belgium had caused us to sympathize momentarily with the underdog, it was really pretty hard to believe that people related to gentle Karl Moenke, who ran a dry-goods store in Eau Fraiche, could be even remotely capable of sacking Louvain, and shooting priests and helpless women there. The war for us was fascinating but remote. We didn't want involvement. We said we'd remain neutral, and that was our honest intention.

And yet—there was something. There's always something about war, a contagious excitement that leaps oceans.

I couldn't look at the battle maps printed in the Eau Fraiche *Record* without visualizing gallant armies massed beneath those tiny flags:

for French,

for Belgian,

for German.

By the nineteenth of August, the line stretched from Antwerp in the north to Mulhausen in the south, passing through towns with names like Charleroi and Bastogne and Bitsch (which gave me a laugh), but it was a fluid front that changed from day to day; you could follow it like a general yourself and discuss it with other generals— here's where I'd break through, here's where I'd try to outflank them. In addition, you could be a general for whichever side you chose, because in the months that followed each side certainly gave us reason to believe *it* was right and the other was wrong. If the Germans were cutting off the breasts of Belgian women and the hands of Belgian babies, then the French were firing on ambulances and killing doctors; if the English served coffee laced with strychnine to German prisoners, then the Huns were shipping corpses back home to be made into soap. We suspected both sides were lying, of course, but the Allies' stories were more inventive and entertaining in a horrible way than the ones the Germans concocted, so I guess even then we were beginning to lean in their direction—though we had no real quarrel with Germany and, if anything, distrusted the French who, we'd been told, "fought with their feet and fucked with their face." Wilson said in his address to Congress that year that this was "a war with which we have nothing to do," and we believed him, I suppose, even though we were already singing "It's a Long, Long Way to Tipperary" in the streets of Eau Fraiche, Red Reynolds' orchestra having introduced the song in November—"the favorite of the first British Expeditionary Force," he had proudly announced.

But if we identified (and I think we did) with the Tommies who were marching into France, we sure as hell did *not* appreciate what the British Navy was doing: seizing American ships and removing from their holds contraband items such as flour, wheat, copper, cotton, and oil; mining the North Sea; blacklisting dozens of American firms suspected of doing business with the Germans (none of *England's* damn business, since we were, after all, neutrals); or even—and this really galled—raising the American flag on her own ships whenever German submarines were in hot pursuit. A lot of the German-American people in Eau Fraiche felt, and probably rightfully, that our diplomatic restraint in dealing with British violations of our neutrality merely indicated we weren't neutral at all; we had, in effect, cast our lot with the Allies as early as the beginning of 1915. Well, maybe so. I myself was pretty confused, though I have to admit that by February, I began to lean toward the Allies again; that was when the Germans said they'd sink any enemy ship in the waters around the British Isles, and maybe a few neutral ships, too, if they couldn't determine their national origin, which was sometimes difficult to do through the periscope of a submarine. Not only did they *say* they'd do it, but they actually *did* do it, and whereas searching ships and seizing merchandise was one thing, sinking them was quite another. I don't think anybody in Eau Fraiche, not even those whose sympathies were with the Germans, condoned the actions of the U-boat commanders, who were already being pilloried in the press for their "wanton disregard of American life."

I guess the sinking of the *Lusitania* could have been the last straw if President Wilson hadn't kept his head. For me, it *was* the last straw; I was ready to go downtown with some of the other kids and smash Mr. Moenke's store window (we had begun calling him "Monkey the Hunkee" by then), but my father got wind of the scheme and told me if I left the house he'd beat me black and blue when I returned. I don't know if it was my father's warning or Mr. Wilson's restraint that changed my mood of black rage to one of patience. In a speech on May 10, three days after the sinking, the President said, "The example of America must be a special example. The example of America must be the example not merely of peace because it will not fight, but of peace because peace is the healing and elevating influence of the world and strife is not. There is such a thing as a nation being so right that it does not need to convince others by force that it is right. There is such a thing as a man being too proud to fight."

I liked what he said.

It reminded me of something my father had once said when I'd been having a lot of trouble with a skinny kid who was a head shorter than me. I told my father I was going to knock the kid cold the next time he said anything nasty to me, and my father said, "What pleasure will you get from killing a cripple?" So I never did fight with that kid because after that I felt sorry for him whenever he picked on me. I *knew* I could beat him up, and I realized my father was right; there'd be no pleasure at all in taking him apart. I didn't know whether or not the United States *could* beat Germany (the idea of going to war with people who were cutting off babies' hands was frankly terrifying) but it seemed to me nonetheless that President Wilson was correct in saying there was such a thing as a man being too proud to fight. If we knew that war was wrong, then we were only compounding the crime by reacting to warlike acts in a warlike manner. If we *really* believed the world had gone insane, then behaving insanely ourselves was no way to effect a cure.

Later, when Wilson's exchange of notes with the Germans got stronger and Bryan resigned as Secretary of State, I didn't know what to think. I admired Wilson, but now he seemed to be saying that he was ready to risk war if respect for human life was at stake. This seemed to me contradictory. If you respected human life, if you were protesting so strongly against the drowning of the 114 Americans who had sailed on the *Lusitania* (even *after* the Germans had taken out a newspaper advertisement warning they would sink any vessel carrying the flag of Great Britain or her allies), then how could you risk sending *more* Americans to die in a war which was none of our business in the first place? Wilson said he was for peace. Okay. But when Bryan refused to sign the President's second strongly worded note to the Germans, he said "I cannot go along with him in this note. I think it makes for war." All right then, *Bryan* was for peace. But the Eau Fraiche *Record* reprinted an editorial from the New York *World* which said that Bryan's resignation was "unspeakable treachery not only to the President but to the nation." Meanwhile, Teddy Roosevelt, who was for preparedness but *also* for peace, mind you, said, "No man can support Mr. Wilson without at the same time supporting a policy of criminal inefficiency," and in almost the very next breath said, "I am sick at heart over the actions of Wilson *and* Bryan."

I'm telling you, it was difficult to know what to think.

And to make matters worse, we Tylers began having a few internal problems of our own along about then. My older sister Kate had run off with a drummer from Arizona, a swarthy slick-haired character who everybody said was part Indian. The local opinion was that he had made her pregnant during the month of July while trying to sell tractor parts in town, and whether this caused my father's heart attack or whether the suspicion that he was part Indian did it, I can't say. The attack came in August, a massive pain knocking him to the forest floor as he brought back his ax, six smaller pains shuddering through his body as he tried to call for help. They got him over to the hospital in Eau Claire just in time, the doctors said, because the next two spasms would have killed him if he hadn't been in bed and close to medication.

I was only fifteen and still in high school, but I was the oldest of the two boys in the family, my brother John being four at the time, so naturally I had to take a job. The doctors said my father needed at least six months' rest (turned out to be eight months after all was said and done) but that afterward he could once again lead a "healthy, productive life"—those were their exact words. They took me on at the lumber camp immediately, even though I couldn't tell a bow saw from a pile of sawdust; my father had been working for them for twenty years, and they were more than willing now to come to his assistance.

In the midst of everything that was happening in America and in the world, there was a tranquillity to those woods, a calming regularity to the monotonous *chok* of ax against trunk, the rasping of the saws, the laughter of the men, the chittering of the forest animals. At night, I would sit outside on the steps of the bunkhouse and, deprived of my helpful newspaper battle maps, try to sort out what was happening over in Europe; but I found I could hardly even sort out what was happening over in Eau Fraiche. I think that at that point in my life, fifteen years old and going on sixteen, there were only two things of any importance to me: the fact that I could step in and support Mama and my brother and sisters; and the fact that a girl named Nancy Ellen Clark was madly in love with me.

I had met Nancy on the Fourth of July, just about when my sister was getting herself pregnant, I suppose. The occasion was the opening of the first Dodge car agency in Eau Fraiche, on Buffalo Street. Anthony Clark, Nancy's father, had moved his family to town in the middle of June, and then had spent the next two weeks getting his showrooms ready for a gala opening. And a gala it was! We had all heard about the new Dodge car, of course, and had studied pictures of it in the newspapers and magazines, but this was our first opportunity to actually *see* it. Mr. Clark had hung bunting over the entire front of the building, and three young girls wearing red, white, and blue in keeping with the spirit of Independence Day, were serving doughnuts and coffee at one side of the showroom. Mr. Clark himself was giving what amounted to an automotive lecture near the right front fender of one of the two new cars on display, a bright green beauty. The girls serving refreshments ranged in age from thirteen to seventeen; the one who caught my eye was the little blond in the middle, about my age, with eyes the color of the touring car Mr. Clark was describing.

"She's a four-cylinder automobile," Mr. Clark was saying, "with an L-head engine and a bore stroke of three and seven-eighths by four and a half inches . . ."

The blond girl with the green eyes looked at me.

". . . thirty-five horsepower," Mr. Clark was saying.

I looked back at her, and she blushed and dropped a doughnut.

"The piston displacement is two-twelve point three cubic inches, and she weighs twenty-two hundred and fifty pounds. The wheelbase is a hundred and ten inches . . ."

I walked over to where the three girls were serving. The stand had been decorated with red, white, and blue bunting, the same as the outside of the showroom. The girls were all wearing ruffled white hats on their heads, like Revolutionary ladies, white blouses with red silk sashes at the waists, and blue skirts.

"Is the coffee free?" I asked.

"Yes," all three of them said together.

I looked directly at the one with the green eyes. "Is it free?" I asked her.

"Yes, it is," she said, and again she blushed.

". . . tire size is thirty-two by three and a half. Now here's something you may not be able to discern with the naked eye . . ."

"My name is Bert Tyler," I said.

"I'm Nancy Clark," she answered.

"Nancy *Ellen* Clark," one of the other girls corrected.

"She's my sister," Nancy said, and smiled into my eyes.

". . . first car in the history of America, in fact, the history of the world, to have an all-steel body. Now let me show you the upholstery . . ."

I thought of nothing but Nancy Ellen Clark all that winter and through the next year. Mr. Wilson's policy with the Germans seemed to be working, and even Bryan supported him in the election of 1916, saying, "I agree with the American people in thanking God we have a president who has kept, who *will* keep, us out of war." I myself favored Hughes, but I wasn't old enough to vote, and anyhow I was in love. The election seemed remote, the war seemed remote, only Nancy danced through my head as I felled trees in those silent woods. In December, the Germans made a peace offer to the Allies, and the war seemed all but over. Besides, like a baseball game that had run into far too many extra innings, it had lost all interest for me. Even when President Wilson disclosed his plan for aiding the belligerents in securing peace, I couldn't have cared less. Peace would be nice, yes, I certainly wanted peace—but more than anything else in the world, I wanted Nancy Ellen Clark.

And then, I don't know what happened—it had all seemed so close, it had all seemed within reach—I don't know what suddenly happened to change it. The Germans weren't interested in Wilson's assistance, it seemed, nor were the Allies interested in Germany's peace offer. A few weeks after my seventeenth birthday, Wilson told the Senate all about his League for Peace and while in Wisconsin we were still talking about what he'd called "peace without victory," in Berlin the Germans announced that beginning February 1, they'd once again pursue a policy of unrestricted submarine warfare.

In the woods, the days were short, the sun glared through leafless branches, glazing the crusted snow. Word trickled back to us day by day. The wagon crew would return from Eau Fraiche to report that Wilson had severed diplomatic relations with the German Empire; Wilson would soon ask that America arm its merchant vessels; a note from a German minister named Alfred Zimmerman had been intercepted and decoded, and it proposed to give Texas, New Mexico, and Arizona to the Mexican people if they accepted alliance with Germany in a war with the United States—stories we half-believed, like the atrocity tales back in 1914. But then the wagon came back one Friday with a story we knew was true, a story we did not *want* to believe because it was far worse than the sinking of the *Lusitania* had been: the Germans had sunk *three* American ships, and Wilson had asked for a special session of Congress to discuss "grave matters."

We declared war against Germany on April 6.

I was seventeen years old and in love.

I wanted no part of it, I truly did not. And yet, less than a year later, I enlisted in the United States Army. If you'd asked me why at the time, I couldn't have told you. Oh sure, I'd given Nancy a big patriotic recital that night of the Grange dance in January, man's duty to his country, do my bit, make the world safe for democracy, all that, but I really hadn't known *why* I was so anxious to get to where the fighting was. Now, not four months later, in the hold of a ship that would be sailing for Brest within hours, I thought I knew.

There's a killing time.

There's a time when you need to kill and must therefore kill.

That time had come for me early in 1918, and I had acted impulsively on the burning itch inside me, the desire to move into action, to strike, to hurt, to kill. Now, in April, the bloodlust was all but gone, and I knew only that I was leaving Nancy for God knew how long, maybe forever, and I wanted to weep.

Timothy Bear found me in the darkness and put his huge hand on my shoulder.

"How goes it, Bert?" he asked.

"Lousy," I said.

"Ever think you'd see this day?"

"No," I answered honestly.

There was comfort in his presence beside me in the darkness. I had known him all through sixteen miserable weeks of preliminary training, weeks of repeating the manual of arms, weeks of formation drills and setting-up exercises and recruit instruction, lectures on the care of clothing and equipment, military discipline and courtesy, orders for sentinels, personal hygiene and care of the goddamn feet, Articles of War, the obligations and rights of the soldier (all obligations, no rights!), weeks of inspections, drills, and more inspections. I had suffered with him through courses on rifle sighting, rifle nomenclature and care, rifle aiming, and trigger squeeze; I had endured first-aid drills with him, gas-warfare drills, grenade and bomb drills, waking at 5:45 each and every day of the week, eating swill my mother wouldn't have allowed in her garbage can no less her kitchen, and tumbling exhausted into bed at ten each night, already dreading the sound of the bugle the next morning, *damn* Irving Berlin and his rotten song!

I think the company would have fallen apart in those sixteen weeks if it hadn't been for Timothy Bear (his last name was really Graham, but somebody had dubbed him "The Bear" in the first few weeks of cantonment at Camp

Greene, and the name had stuck). He was six feet four inches tall in his naked toenails, as wide across as any tree I'd ever felled in the woods north of Eau Fraiche, the Army uniform fitting him like a sausage skin strained to bursting across his powerful chest and shoulders. He could lift the rear end of a weapons carrier with his bare hands, unassisted, and his endurance was equally phenomenal; returning once from a twenty-mile forced march with full pack, Timothy Bear had wanted to go dancing in town. He never complained, not about anything, nor was his attitude faked—his face was as open as a child's, his brown eyes totally guileless. He had blond hair which he'd worn straight and long back on his father's Indiana farm, but which the Army barbers had cropped close to his head, heightening his resemblance to a big, affable grizzly. Lumbering, genial, inexhaustible, he became the kind of man and soldier we all wished we could be. He was eighteen years old.

Now, sitting beside me in the darkness, he understood my gloom, and reached into the pocket of his tunic for a folded sheet of paper which he handed to me. Shielding a flashlight with his cupped palm, he threw a beam of light onto the paper and said, "Have you seen this yet, Bert? A clerk from B Company ran some off on the ship's mimeo. It's from the *Dodger*."

"The *what?*" I said.

"You know, the Camp Dodge newspaper."

In the light of Timothy's shielded flash, I unfolded and read the mimeographed sheet:

If the war doesn't end next month, of two things one is certain: Either you'll be sent across the great pond or you'll stay on this side.

If you stay home, there's no need to worry. If you go across, of two things one is certain: Either you'll be put on the firing line or kept behind the lines.

If you're behind the lines, there's no need to worry. If you're at the front, of two things one is certain: Either you're resting in a safe place or you're exposed to danger.

If you're resting in a safe place, there's no need to worry. If you're exposed to danger, of two things one is certain: Either you're wounded or you're not wounded.

If you're not wounded, there's no need to worry. If you

66

are wounded, of two things one is certain: Either you're wounded seriously or you're wounded slightly.

If you're wounded slightly, there's no need to worry. If you're wounded seriously, of two things one is certain: Either you recover or you don't.

If you recover, there's no need to worry.

If you don't recover, you can't worry.

When I reached the bottom of the page, Timothy, who had been reading silently over my shoulder, began chuckling. I laughed with him. In the hold of a foreign ship waiting to sail across thousands of miles of ocean to a foreign battlefront, we laughed softly in the darkness, and I wondered if we'd ever in our lives see New York City again.

May ✝ ✝ ✝

I loved that city.

It took an hour and a half to get there from Talmadge, but ever since we'd organized Dawn Patrol, one or another of us guys would go in almost every Saturday to shop Forty-eighth Street or to catch whichever of the groups were downtown in the Village. My mother said I was a native New Yorker, which wasn't quite true in spite of the fact that I was born in New York; at Lenox Hill Hospital, in fact, on Seventy-seventh and Park. At the time, my father was attending NYU on the GI Bill of Rights, and living with my mother in a run-down apartment in what was then considered a terrible slum but was now euphemistically called the East Village. With a little help from my grandfather (or perhaps from *both* my grandfathers, since Grandpa Prine was still alive at the time) my father started his own business in November 1946, at first publishing stuff like street maps and industrial pamphlets, and then bringing out a series of one-shot, newsstand exploitation magazines, and then finally moving into hardbound books. We moved to Talmadge just before Christmas that year, two months after I was born, to the same house we still lived in on Ritter Avenue. So I hardly felt honest calling myself a native New Yorker, although it was technically true. Nonetheless, whenever I went into that city, I felt as if I were going home.

I didn't feel quite that way today.

I had come in to see my father because there was something important I wanted to discuss, and I had learned over the years that the best place to talk business with him was in *his* place of business. This was Wednesday, and Talmadge High was having teachers' conferences, so I'd caught the 9:34 out of Stamford, and was in the city by 10:19. I'd spent a half-hour in Manny's on Forty-eighth, looking over some of the new Japanese amplifiers, and then I'd called my father to ask him if I could come up. He sounded surprised but pleased, which was at least one point for our side. Still, I was scared.

I walked over to Forty-second and spent an hour or so in Bryant Park, where a fag tried to pick me up. I never knew what to say when a fag approached me. This one looked especially sad and uncertain, as if it were the first time he'd ever done anything like this, though that was probably his style. Anyway, I just said "Sorry," and got off the bench and walked away. I was unhappy about leaving the park because it had been a good place to think; I still hadn't come up with an approach to my father. I stopped for a hot dog and a Coke in a place on Forty-fourth and Sixth, and then ambled down to Fifth Avenue as if I didn't have a care in the world. It was a great day for walking.

We'd once had a man from California visiting us, a publisher my father was anxious to do business with, and he'd said the only time he really enjoyed New York City was "when they started taking their coats off." This was that kind of a day, with a blue sky stretched tight between the buildings, and bright sunshine spanking the sidewalks, and people walking along with their coats off, grinning. By the time I reached the Doubleday's on Fifty-seventh, I'd worked out a plan, so I immediately headed back for my father's office on Forty-eighth and Madison.

All the way up in the elevator, I rehearsed my scheme.

He's too smart to con, I told myself, though why I should even have to *think* of conning him is certainly a matter for speculation, considering the fact that I'll be eighteen in October—well, suppose he says no? Well, he can't say no if I get him to agree with me in principle first. Because if he concedes in *principle,* he can't refuse permission on any valid moral ground, that'd be hypocritical, he certainly isn't a hypocrite, whatever else he is. Anyway, I've never won a frontal assault against him in my life, why try now? Logic, that's the thing. Get him to yield intellectually, and then zing in the fast ball. It should work.

I hope.

The elevator doors opened. I took a deep breath.

Tyler Press occupied the entire sixth floor of the building, and so the company colophon and the company receptionist were the first things anyone saw when stepping out of the elevator. Of the two, I infinitely preferred the colophon, my father's taste in receptionists running rather toward the motherly type. This particular mother, one of a long line who had sat behind this selfsame desk since the company's formation in 1946, was in her fifties, a gray-haired dignified lady with pleasant blue eyes and a warm, helpful smile, ample mother breasts in a white blouse, gold chain hanging, semi-precious purple stone cradled, "Hello, Wat," she said, "how nice!"

"Hello, Mrs. Green," I answered. "Is my father in?"

"Let me check," she said, and smiled again, and lifted the telephone.

The company colophon was on the wall behind Mrs. Green's desk, a circular blue disc upon which were three spruce trees of varying heights, their towering tops protruding from the upper rim of the circle. There was a strong sense of growth and tradition inherent in the colophon, and I felt oddly moved each time I looked at it. Whatever the Tylers were, we had all most certainly descended from my grandfather Bertram Tyler, the lumberjack, and this heritage was clearly the intent of the colophon. Studying it now, though, I wondered for the first time which of those three spruces represented me—the shortest one in the foreground, or the tallest one reaching for the sky.

"You can go right in, Wat," Mrs. Green said.

"Thank you. Is he in a good mood?"

"Why, Wat dear, your father's *always* in a good mood," Mrs. Green said.

"Oh yes, certainly," I said, and went past her desk into the corridor. A brunette secretary in a tight woolen dress swiveled out of one of the offices, smiling at me as she went by. Neck craning, I knocked on my father's door.

"Come in," he called.

I went into the office. My father was standing behind his desk, shirt sleeves rolled up, tie pulled down, desk top covered with photographs. His attitude of concentration seemed posed, as though he had hastily rushed behind his desk, rolling up his sleeves the moment he heard the knock on the door, anxious to present to his son an image of a working publisher. If such were truly the case, he needn't have bothered; I'd always had enormous difficulty imagining my father at work, and each time I came to his office the task became perversely more difficult. I shouldn't have expected Tyler Press to be a mirror image of our own house in Talmadge—a man was, after all, entitled to decorate his offices to suit his own taste. But the difference here was so startling that it was difficult to imagine the man Will Tyler being comfortable in either place.

Our house was an early eighteenth-century colonial, white clapboard and slate, paneled doors and chimney architrave, leaded casements and molded panels. My mother, presumably with my father's assistance and blessing, had decorated in the style of the period, creating a warm and welcoming shelter that nudged the side of a hill from which you could sometimes see Long Island Sound. Crewel-embroidered curtains, blue-green with a touch of red, draped the living room windows. The walnut sofa was upholstered with blue-green damask, the cabriole-leg wing chair with tapestry. There was an oriental rug before the fireplace, which was flanked by two Hogarth-type side chairs and a tall-back wing chair, also done in red tapestry. The house was rich with brass and burled walnut, needlepoint and marble, the faint lingering aroma of woodsmoke.

In contrast, the first thing you saw when you entered my father's office was the huge gray Formica-topped work desk dominated at its far end by a wooden piece he had bought in a First Avenue shop, an African mask resting on a stainless steel cube. Two walls were a pristine white, a third wall was covered floor to ceiling with bookcases, their jacketed spines adding a patchwork quilt of color to the room. The fourth wall framed a window view of New York City, mocha-colored drapes hanging at either side of the glass expanse. The chairs were upholstered in brown leather and tweed, the carpet was beige. Out of a bosky glen of plants in the corner opposite the desk, there rose like some metallic woodland sprite, a joyously leaping Giacometti imitation. On one of the white walls, there hung an original Larry Rivers, and on the other a Goodenough. The lighting was hidden in walnut coves, except for two hanging white globes. The over-all effect was hardly similar to that in our home, and it made me believe that perhaps there were *two* Will Tylers, neither of whom I understood or even came close to understanding.

I went behind the desk and kissed him on the cheek without embarrassment; I could never understand those guys who have hangups about kissing their own fathers. He said, "Hello, son," and then spread his hands wide over the desk top. "What do you think of it?"

There were perhaps two hundred photographs of different sizes on the desk. All of them were of General De Gaulle, whom I had never considered a particularly photogenic subject, handsome though he may be.

"I thought it was further along than this," I said.

"Well, this is the final selection. What do you think?"

"It's hard to say. I mean, without any text . . ."

"Yes, but what do you think of the pictures?"

"Oh, they're great," I said.

"We'll be laying it out sometime this week," my father said.

"Great. When's publication?"

"God knows," he said, and waved the question aside. "Have you had lunch?"

"I grabbed a hot dog," I said.

"I thought . . ."

"Actually . . ."

"What time is it, anyway?"

"Close to one. Pop, the reason I stopped by . . ."

"I thought we were having lunch together. I purposely kept lunch free."

"Well, I've got to get back, you know. We're rehearsing this afternoon . . ."

"How come no school?" he asked suddenly.

"It's teachers' conferences."

"Oh."

"I mean, I'm not cutting or anything, if that's what you thought."

71

"Why would I think that?"

"Anyway, Pop, there's something I've got to discuss with you."

"Shoot," he said, and sat in the brown leather Eames chair behind his desk. He took a cigar from the humidor near the African mask, sniffed it the way I'd seen Adolph Menjou do in a thousand old movies on television, lighted it with a wooden match, blew out an enormous cloud of poisonous smoke, laced his hands across his chest, and looked at me expectantly. I cleared my throat.

"Well," I said, "as you know, I'll be graduating this June."

"Yes," he said.

"And this is May," I said, "and I thought I should be making some plans for the summer now. I mean, before it's here, you know. Because I'll be leaving for Yale in September, and I wanted to make some use of the summer, you know."

"Where do you want to go?" my father said.

"Well, that's what I wanted to talk to you about."

"Well, that's what we're doing is talking," he said, and smiled, and puffed on the cigar, and said, "I have a feeling this is going to cost me money."

"No, no," I said, "no." I cleared my throat again. "You see, these are, you know, changing times in America, and I thought, you see, I didn't want to just lay around on some beach all summer, though that would be nice, still . . ."

"You don't want to come to Fire Island, is that it?"

"I love Fire Island, it isn't that."

"It's some girl."

"No, no, I'm not serious about anybody right now. But the idea of just laying around all summer isn't too appealing to me right now. I want to *do* something."

"Like what?"

"You agree these are changing times?" I said, figuring I'd start my buildup now, get him to agree in principle the way I'd planned it, and *then* ask him for permission.

"Yes, these are changing times," he agreed.

"Okay," I said, "I want to go south this summer and help with voter registration. Negro voter registration."

My father puffed on his cigar.

"A guy I know from school is going," I said, "and I

want to go with him. They pay a salary. I can earn between fifteen and twenty-five dollars a week."

"Is he colored or white?" my father asked.

"He's colored." I said. "His name is Larry Peters, I think you met him once."

"I don't remember meeting him," my father said.

"After one of the dances. He was helping us load the wagon."

"I don't remember."

"Well, that's who, anyway. He's leaving for Mississippi in July. If I'm going with him, I've got to sign up as a task force worker right away. That's why I wanted to discuss it with you first."

"A task force worker, huh?"

"That's right."

"And that's why you came into the city today?"

"No, I looked at a new amp at Manny's too. But while I was in, I figured I'd call you and we could talk about it here. I haven't told Mom yet, I wanted to clear it with you first."

"She'll say no."

"Well, not if you've already given permission."

"She'll say no because it's dangerous down there. You can get hurt down there."

"Pop, you can get hurt crossing the street right here in New York."

"Why do you want to go down there, anyway?"

"I already told you. These are changing times . . ."

"Yes, yes . . ."

". . . and I want to help."

"You can help right here. If you want to do something for the Negro, why don't you get a job in Harlem this summer? At a playground or a youth center. Help them start a band, coach them in some sport, you're good at those things, Wat, you could be very useful in an area like Harlem."

"I can be more useful in the South."

"Your friend can be more useful there."

"No, I think it's important that some *white* people go down there."

"Why?"

"To show them we're interested. I mean, Pop, this isn't just *their* problem, it's *our* problem, too. If we care enough about what the hell's going *on* in this country."

73

"All right, don't get excited," my father said.

"Well, this means a lot to me."

"Did I say no?"

"You're *going* to say no, I can tell."

"I didn't know you were a mind reader."

"Anyway, I think I ought to tell you I'll be eighteen in October . . ."

"July isn't October. When did you say? You said July, didn't you?"

"Well, when school ends."

"That's not October."

"I *know* it's not October. Anyway, I may not even *need* your permission. I haven't really looked into the requirements yet, but I think . . ."

"I would imagine you'd have to be eighteen," my father said.

"Maybe and maybe not," I said. "Larry has all the information, I'll have to check . . ."

"If you're so serious about this, why haven't you checked already?"

"I am serious about it. I didn't think I was going to get such static here, that's all."

"I wasn't aware . . ."

"I'm not asking for your permission because I *need* it, Pop."

"No? Then why are you asking?"

"As a goddamn courtesy."

"This isn't a locker room," my father said.

"Okay, it isn't a locker room."

"I'm sure your mother wouldn't want you traipsing all over the South where you can possibly get your head busted by some rednecked farmer!"

"The reason I *want* to go traipsing all over the South is so that people *can* traipse all over the South without getting their heads busted."

"And if you run into trouble?"

"I won't."

"Suppose you do?"

"I can take care of myself."

"That's another country down there."

"Is that supposed to be a pun?"

"What?" he said. "I'm telling you that's a foreign country down there. I was there during the war, and it's worse

74

now. You'll need a passport to get in, it's a foreign country."

"It's America," I said.

"Don't give me any of that patriotic bullshit," my father said.

"This isn't a locker room," I said, and tried a smile.

My father picked up his cigar and began puffing on it. He didn't say anything. One of De Gaulle's pictures caught his eye, and he moved it over next to another lovely shot of the general.

"Well," I said, "how about it?"

"The answer is no," he said flatly.

"I figured."

"You figured correctly."

"Why?"

"Because voter registration in the South is a dangerous occupation for a seventeen-year-old boy."

"I'll be eighteen in October."

"Then go in October."

"Pop, I have to be in New Haven on September fourteenth, you know that."

"Right. So spend your summer on the beach, take it easy. You think Yale's going to be a lark?"

"What about Larry?"

"Who the hell is Larry?"

"Larry, Larry, my friend. How can I spend the summer sitting on my ass when I know he'll be down South fighting for his *life!*"

"Invite him to the beach."

"Pop!"

"It's not your battle," my father said.

"Will you at least think about it?"

"I've already thought about it."

"I'll go without your permission, you know. If I have to be eighteen, I'll lie about my age, I'll get a phony draft card, there're millions of them around."

"Then why'd you ask me in the first place?" my father said.

"Because I thought you'd be proud to say yes."

I went out of his office and down the corridor to the elevator, angry as hell. Mrs. Green came from behind her desk and fluttered up to me.

"Oh, Wat," she said, "your father told me about your being accepted at Yale, that's just wonderful."

"Yeah," I said.

"I guess you're all excited about graduation."

"Yeah," I said.

"Do you have something in mind?" she asked.

"Huh?"

"Something special?"

"What do you mean?"

"For graduation. A present."

"Oh," I said, and suddenly realized she was here on a specific mission, she had been told earlier that I'd be coming up, and had been instructed by my father to find out what I wanted as a graduation gift. In what she had doubtlessly considered a subtle manner, she had led the conversation to the point where she could pop the big question, and now she stood studying my face eagerly, hoping against hope that I would reveal my desire before the elevator arrived. I did not want to disappoint her, and yet I could not think of a single thing I wanted or needed. I began wishing that something extravagant would occur to me, but nothing did, and I stood in mute embarrassment as the approaching elevator whined up the shaft, feeling terribly sorry for Mrs. Green, but feeling even sorrier for my father, who could not *personally* ask his own son what he wanted most for graduation.

"There *is* something I want," I said.

"Yes?" Mrs. Green said, nervously fingering the purple stone on her bosom. "What is it?"

"Get him to say yes," I told her. "Get him to say I can go to Mississippi."

June 🌱 🌱

My father said yes at the beginning of June, but Michael and I did not celebrate until the night before he left for Keesler Field, when we both went over to the colored section in Douglas. It was one of those rare Chicago nights, with a full moon hanging over the lake, and people swimming off the sand beach at Oak Street, portable radios going everywhere along the shore.

I don't know what led us over to Douglas. I don't think we intentionally *started* to go there, and we certainly weren't looking for any trouble. There was rioting in Detroit that Sunday, we had heard all about it on the radio. But the trouble there was understandable because Negro sharecroppers had been coming up north by the hundreds of thousands, lured by the higher wages being paid by the wartime automobile industry, and the city just didn't know how to cope with its new mixed population of two million people. A white man and a Negro had begun hitting each other, and before you knew it whites and Negroes were battling it out all over the city, and a cop got shot six times with his own gun, and dozens of other people, Negro and white, had been killed. I kept expecting it to spread to Chicago—we were only two hundred and seventy miles or so from Detroit, and we had a colored population of more than 275,000, most of which was clustered in Grand Boulevard, Washington Park, or Douglas. But nothing had happened. Nothing *ever* happened in Chicago.

The whole point of that Sunday, June twentieth, nineteen hundred and forty-three, was that I had been accepted by the United States Air Force, hallelujah! Moreover, it seemed likely that I'd be inducted sooner than I'd expected, in which case I might somewhere along the line just possibly catch up with Michael, who was set to leave Chicago tomorrow morning for five weeks of basic training in Mississippi. We had every reason to celebrate, and we began celebrating early that afternoon, there being three of us at the beginning of the spree that eventually led us into Douglas. Ronny Booth was a pain in the ass, but he was twenty-one years old and therefore entitled to buy alcoholic beverages in our antiquated state. Here were two red-blooded American boys, Michael and myself, who had already been accepted by the Air Force, but we weren't permitted to drink in Illinois, right? On the other hand, Ronny Booth, who was 4-F because of a heart murmur (but who also happened to be twenty-one) was permitted to buy all the whiskey he wanted; which he had done the day before, and which the three of us now consumed happily on the edge of the lake while someone in a rowboat on the water strummed a guitar and lazily sang, "I'll Be with You in Apple Blossom Time."

Ronny Booth kept saying, "Men, we are getting drunk."

He was a tall skinny guy with straight black hair and brown eyes that looked enormously offended. He had begun growing a mustache, doubtless to assert his manhood in defiance of his 4-F classification, but it was coming in patchy and sparse, and it gave him the appearance of a skinny, comic Hitler.

"*Ja,* Adolf," Michael said, "ve are getting plastered."

"Please don't call me Adolf," Ronny said.

"*Jawohl,* Adolf," Michael said.

"I have seen more hair on a strip of bacon," I said, and Michael laughed.

"Men," Ronny said, "I tell you we are getting drunk."

"Let's go find some pussy," Michael said.

"Shhh," Ronny said. "There're ladies present."

"Where?" I said.

"Out there on the water plucking their guitars."

"Let's find some pretty pussy to pluck," Michael said, and laughed and threw his arms around me. "You know what I'm going to do, Will?" he asked.

"What're you going to do?"

"Pee in the water," Michael said.

"Men," Ronny said, "we are getting drunk."

Michael had, with considerable difficulty, already unzipped his fly, but he judiciously allowed me to lead him away from the water's edge and into one of the underpasses where he urinated against a wall that had been chalked with the legend SLAP THE JAP!

"Rat-tat-tat-tat-tat," Michael said, drilling the wall with a steady stream of urine. "Rat-tat-tat-tat."

"Behold the yellow menace," I said.

"The yellow *peril,*" Michael corrected. "I am going to tell you something about this war," he said, slopping onto his trouser leg as he tried to maneuver himself back into his pants, "Will Tyler, here's the thing about this war." He put a scholarly finger alongside his nose, tilted his head to one side, blond wood shavings spilling around his ears, grinned cherubically, and said, "This war will soon be over oecause two brave and stalwarts are going over there to *zap* them!" and triumphantly zipped up his fly.

"Men," Ronny said, and slid down the sloping concrete wall and passed out, chin on his chest.

"Men," I said, "Ronny Booth is unconscious."

"Fuck him," Michael said. He threw his arm around my shoulder, and we crossed under the Drive at Division Street, and began walking downtown, away from Ronny and the lake, singing "Jingle Bells" because it was clever in June, and "Over There" because it was corny at *any* time, and "Mairzy Doats" because it was crazy like us, and then trying to hum "Holiday for Strings" because it was difficult especially when intoxicated. The Loop had never been too terribly exciting on a Sunday night, but ever since the war began and the lights were dimmed, it had become positively ghostly, with servicemen milling around the streets as if searching for a party that had somehow been canceled. In defense against the gloom, Michael and I began singing the Army Air Force song, mindful of the unamused glares of the servicemen all around us, but marching bravely along anyway, arm in arm, as we belted out the lyrics.

Douglas was four and a half miles from downtown Chicago, and nobody in his right mind would have chosen it as a nighttime destination. We were not precisely in our right minds that Sunday, though, nor were we consciously heading for Douglas. We were, instead, heading into the skies above where brave fighter pilots plunged their war machines into fat billowing clouds, Or, to be more precise, we were heading for Wentworth Avenue, which was the main street of Chinatown, where we hoped to get some egg rolls and chow mein. Carried along by the spirit of our rousing song, *off we go,* we marched past Marshall Field, *into the wild blue yonder,* grabbing a subway train at State and Randolph, *climbing high,* all the way to Cermak Road where we disembarked and staggered into the Sun Shu Chinese Restaurant, in which establishment we consumed four egg rolls apiece and two orders of chow mein, not to mention huge quantities of Chinese tea, none of which made us any soberer than we'd been at the start of our journey. Mistily shrouded by the warm Chicago night and the alcohol fumes that blurred our vision, we lurched out of the restaurant and instead of turning back toward Cermak and the subway station, turned in the opposite direction instead and, singing, misgaited, giggling, and bellowing, made our way into the colored section of Douglas.

As we came into Douglas, we felt at once, Michael and

I, and communicated it without speaking to each other, that we had been shot down by Messerschmitts or worse and must now through courage and guile, through wile, women, and song somehow find our way back to our own friendly lines, which were either the Douglas or the Jackson Park Lines of the Rapid Transit.

"Shhh," I said.

"Shhh," Michael said.

There was in this contorted drunken landscape a conglomerate architecture sprung from poverty, rooted in need, that had transformed a once-affluent residential area into a congested slum within the space of forty years. Tarpaper shacks, squatted cheek by jowl with barrackslike structures, spindly wooden staircases rising to rickety second- and third-story porches. Rusted parts of washing machines, sewing machines, bedsprings, tricycles, bicycles, abandoned automobiles sprouted everywhere, a jagged, disintegrating crop. Monumental heaps of moldering garbage rose like undisputed bunkers against soot-streaked crumbling brick buildings—Fuck You painted on a wall in shrieking white, sheets and bloomers and blouses and skirts flapping on clotheslines, trying to escape the backyards below, a dog squatting and shitting outside the entrance doorway to a shack, a little girl idly dragging her doll through the mud. We had come down Wentworth, I guess it was, and then State, and then turned east on Thirty-first, and now we threaded our way with fallen-pilot care through a populace sullen in blackface, men in undershirts and trousers throwing sidelong slitted glances as we passed, women in flowered housedresses, hair up in pieces of rag, remnants of the Old South only four and a half miles from downtown Chicago, only a hundred years away on the underground railway. A group of men sat playing dominoes outside a ramshackle tottering structure, one of them wearing only patterned Bermuda shorts, another drinking beer from a pitcher, *Fat black bucks in a wine-barrel room,* you could hear that towering Illinois voice reverberating through this crouching slum as the breeze from the lake ahead, blowing fresh and clean onto the Drive five miles north, here brought in a stench as strong as that of Michael's piss in the underpass.

I was suddenly filled with rage.

My anger had nothing to do with sympathy for an oppressed minority or any of *that* crap. I didn't feel any democratic principle was being violated here, is wasn't anything like that. There was too much *real* democracy at stake everywhere else in the world; I wasn't about to start crying over a bunch of poor bastards living in the asshole of Chicago. Actually, I didn't know *what* caused my anger. But I suddenly did something very strange and dangerous.

I picked up a brick and threw it.

I happened, in fact, to throw it at a first-floor window which smashed with amazing alacrity, not for nothing had I been a star third baseman with the Grace School Blues. A fat Negro man sitting on an upturned garbage can and fanning himself with a folded copy of the *Tribune* didn't quite appreciate either my anger or my throwing arm. "You sumbitch white bastard!" he shouted, and jumped off the garbage can and came racing after Michael and me, brandishing the folded newspaper like a hatchet. Michael, who was not as sober as I yet, even though he'd reacted to my window-smashing in absolute astonishment, stumbled and fell, and I ran back to help him, and then looked up to discover that seven thousand men and boys of varying sizes, shapes, and shades were coming down the street after us, led by the *Tribune*-swinging fat man.

I was terrified.

I thought how ignominious it would be for a future fighter pilot to be squashed into the pavement by a rioting band of black men who had surely misunderstood why I'd thrown a brick through one of their windows, even though I myself didn't yet understand why I'd done it. Michael, the idiot, was laughing! I thought, Oh my God, please don't let these boogies, niggers, Negroes, NEGROES hear this madman laughing! Clutching Michael's hand in my own, running like the track star I once had been, though burdened by Michael, who giggled and lurched and stumbled and cursed, I heard the sudden sweet sound of the train rumbling along the tracks on Michigan Avenue and miraculously found the platform at Thirty-first, it must have been, or Twenty-ninth, or Twenty-sixth, God knew where, while Michael laughed insanely, and behind us the Negroes shouted bloody murder just because I'd hurled one lousy little goddamn brick. The train rolled in to a screeching stop.

I never thought we'd get out of there alive.

July ❦

There was, I had not expected, there was, the German guns had started shortly after midnight, star shells erupting in the moonlit sky over the Marne, the river itself a curve of molten silver winding through poppy-dotted wheatfields, I had not expected. The shells came screaming at us from twenty miles away, Holy Mother, Mary of God, and we crouched trembling in trenches we had deepened the day before when the papers on a captured German major revealed Von Boehn's plan of attack to us. The trenches faced Varennes and Courtemont, which the French were defending and which we expected to be overrun, our own plan being to wait until the German bombardment had abated, at which time we would scramble out of these deeper trenches and move forward into the echeloned slit trenches that would form our line of defense against a flanking attack.

I was Private Bertram Tyler in Captain Reid's F Company of the 38th Infantry Regiment, 3rd Division, with our backs to Hill 231, wooded, higher than the plain, our bayoneted rifles pointed toward the curving right flank of the Marne horseshoe, the toe caulk of which was Jaulgonne to the north, the two heel caulks being Mézy to the west and Sauvigny to the east. The Paris-Nancy (*Nancy!*) railroad tracks paralleled the river, passing through H and E Companies massed on the bank, skirting behind the 28th's L Company facing Jaulgonne, and then disappearing out of sight to the east.

I was Private Bertram Tyler, and I had never been in battle before. As we waited now for them to come across the river in pontoon boats, as I lay with my face pressed to the dirt wall of the trench, there was insinuated into all the smells around me—the smell of men vomiting, the smell of phosphorus, the smell of earth suddenly exploding, richly, darkly turning loamy interior to the midnight air, the oppressive biting stink of cordite, the rancid aroma of sweat produced by fear, the smell of the waist-high

82

wheat gold and silver in the moonlight, splashed with blood-red gilded poppies—into all these contradictory smells came the stench of human flesh burning and entrails exposed, the horrible sickly scent of death.

I tried to move away from Timothy, I did not want him to know how terrified I was. I was weeping into the earthen wall of the trench, ashamed of myself, frightened beyond sanity, the Germans would be coming soon, they would cross the river and storm our position.

"Easy, Bert," Timothy said beside me.

"I'm scared," I said. "Oh God, I'm so scared."

"I am, too."

Trembling, crouching, weeping, I flattened myself against the side of the trench as another shell exploded. I had not expected, there was nothing to prepare, I did not imagine, could not have, the noise. I wanted to cover my ears, but I was afraid to let go of my rifle. There was no small arms fire as yet, only the heavy steady pounding of our own guns firing northward across the river, unrelenting, and the muted faraway counterpoint of the big German guns, a steady rumble on the horizon. The sky flickered with light, erratic and unsettling, as though the eyes were out of focus. Shells exploded in the distance, adding to the muted enemy percussion, and the air shivered with the high whining whistle of incoming artillery fire, the deafening explosions everywhere around us, the shrapnel adding its own deadly high whistle to the air, clods of earth growing wheat and poppies landing with lifeless thuds, soil sifting in a whisper into the trenches, the sound constant, until at last the barrage stopped and we knew they were coming across the river because we heard the clacking of machine guns and the popping of the rifles and the irregular louder explosions of grenades along the bank. Someone was shouting, the shout streaked the comparative silence like a smear of blood, a whistle shrilled into the midnight expectancy, a doughboy whispered "Jesus save us," sibilant and scared, and we came out of the trenches and ran in waist-deep wheat like children in a dream summer on a star-drenched night— It's really only another July, I told myself, and firecrackers are popping for independence by the river.

There was, you could not, all order was gone, the troops retreating on our front were French, their uniforms, you could, the Bois de Condé was where they would hold, the reserves of the 28th were waiting there, French at first, you could see their uniforms. And then the color changed, the landscape changed, the army coming over the railroad tracks and into the fill was German, fierce against the summer sky, bayonets glinting in moonlit pinpricks, machine-gun carts hauled by barking dogs, horse-drawn batteries rumbling into place. They wished to go to Paris, and we were there to stop them, but Paris was not the prize to defend, Paris was not the immediate goal. The prize was Hill 231, where a strategically placed machine gun could control the entire plain, a knoll worthless for anything but artillery now, perhaps a good site for a small French château in another time and in another place, but not here and not now. Here, with the German batteries in place and beginning to pound shells into the slit trenches, now with the machine guns adding their staccato ululation to the din, we understood very little, and cared less, about over-all strategy or logistics. We did not know where the 4th or the 7th were, did not even fully comprehend whether Château-Thierry was to the east or the west across the Marne. We knew only Hill 231. This was our reason for being here, Hill 231, this was why we crouched and waited to kill, crouched and saw Fritz come over the horizon with identical intent, to kill for that elevation of ground behind us, from which our own guns were now firing over our heads.

I knew I would remember Hill 231 forever.

The rest was chaos.

Fear, excitement, and incredibility waged a war within me as fierce as the one that lurched across that disputed plain.

I had never known such terror. It came in successive waves of shock, the same tingling crack of surprise accompanying it each time, a sharp spasm jerking the neck and causing the eyes to pop wide open, a hot rush of blood to the head, a loosening of the bowels, a weak drained feeling in the crotch, but no time, no time to think or feel because new white tremors erupted almost at once, like unexpected slaps to the face in a pitch-black room.

The excitement rode over each exploding peak of horror, a curious wild and heady sense of adventure, a feeling of absolute maleness contradicting the terror, the rifle in my hands as enormous as a penis on the edge of ejaculation. Dodging, running, crawling, I *felt* like a soldier, and

I regretted that no one was there to see me behave so courageously (even as fear rocketed into my skull again), no one but other men exactly like myself experiencing the same crude mixture of emotions, no one there to take my picture and shout exultant praise.

I could not believe what was happening. In my terror and excitement, a logical tiny section of my mind kept asking what I was doing here, was I insane running a zigzag course through exploding grenades, were my eyes actually witnessing a man's body being cut in half by a shell, his head and torso flying off in one direction, his legs standing lifelessly erect for an instant before they toppled over like twin sandstone columns, was I dreaming? A grenade exploded some ten feet ahead of me and a German fell back into the wheat with a gushing hole in his abdomen. A machine gun instantly opened fire, and I leaped sharply to the left, eyes straining, the terror was back, the fear had a stench of urine I could smell in the crevices of my brain, I threw myself headlong through the rustling wheat, and watched the slender golden stalks dancing fitfully as the bullets whined through, and began to weep in fear and ecstasy and open incredulity.

I did not kill a man until four o'clock that morning, I think it was four o'clock, they told me later that was when Captain Reid made me a corporal in the field, but I have no recollection of being promoted, I can only remember the first time I killed a human being.

He was, I could not, I was exhausted, we had been fighting since midnight, there had been no letup. Endless corridors of wheat, running, why was I running? Explosions everywhere, the feeling that I alone was the quarry, a desperate skittering figure in a moonwashed landscape, some unseen force trying to obliterate me, hurling salvo after salvo of lethal steel wherever I turned, however I maneuvered. I was tired enough to fall flat to the earth and hug the trampled stalks to my mud-stained tunic, but too frightened to rest because machine guns relentlessly chewed the night and new bomb craters opened everywhere, spewing fresh legs and arms, sodden mannequin limbs dripping human blood, a severed helmeted head rolling, rolling, rolling, and coming to a stop at last, black with powder, red with blood, startling white where bone fragments had come through the cheek.

He appeared, he suddenly, I had expected someone like

85

myself, young and frightened, the German equivalent of an Eau Fraiche lumberjack, with a girl back home in Dusseldorf, a *fräulein* writing the equivalent of Nancy's letters, someone who perhaps had listened to our own barrage this past midnight and trembled as I had, someone who had never slain and who now, because of a numbered hill behind us, was ready to kill for the first time. But he, the wheat shifted in a sudden wind fresh off the river, I raised my head and jerked my eyes to the right and then rapidly to the left, every sound was terrifying, every movement cause for fresh panic, and he, he rose, he suddenly stood before me in the undulating wheat. For a moment brief and static, for a frozen moment brittle enough to shatter with a heartbeat, we looked at each other, our eyes met and we stood on the edge of homicide in a foreign wheatfield while machine guns clacked like distant farmyard fowl.

He was very big, I thought Why, he's a *man*, they're asking me to fight a *man*. Not a boy, not someone like myself, but a grown man who looked at me in shocked surprise from beneath a helmet certainly more formidable than my own, new leather boots and belt, gas mask slung and hanging from a strap on his massive chest, rifle clutched in both hands, his finger inside the trigger guard. I looked at him, this all took place in a tick of time, there was a sudden hush as the machine guns stopped for only an instant, and we looked at each other, and I thought Say something to him and I thought What are we doing here? and I wanted to giggle. I was possessed of an uncontrollable urge to giggle, I could feel my face cracking with an overriding need for laughter. And then the machine guns near the railroad fill began again, and I knew that one of us must kill. *I* knew, *he* knew, we faced each other in that foolish instant of nonrecognition, and we were both murderers in our hearts long before one of us became a murderer in fact.

As my finger groped for the trigger of the rifle, the notion that this stranger would want to kill me seemed idiotic, we did not *know* each other. And yet my finger moved of its own volition, it seemed, found the trigger with practiced ease, those weeks and weeks of pulling off shots at lifeless targets paid off now in a moonwashed field south of the river Marne, and I raised my rifle even as my finger tightened and the gun recoiled sharply, the butt hitting me in the ribs, so that I was aware only of my own sharp pain at first and did not see the German's face burst open. I winced, I must have cursed, he was falling away from me, falling back straight and stiff, already dead, the force of the bullet knocking him back some three feet. I watched as he fell, fascinated by his face spurting blood, and wondered if he, like me, had wanted to giggle at our unexpected confrontation.

And then I turned away.

Feeling nothing.

Only later that day, when Captain Reid told us we'd broken the back of the German attack and with it their hopes of taking the Surmelin Valley and the Rocq Plateau, only then did I say to Timothy Bear, "I killed a man, Tim."

And he said, "Yes, Bert."

"I didn't feel anything," I said.

We looked at each other. We were eating horsemeat goulash in a trench stinking of pulp and gristle; overhead, four Spads were engaged with a flight of red-nosed Fokkers. We looked at each other and were silent. I studied Timothy Bear, his face, his eyes, and knew I would never again see the Indiana farmboy who had cajoled us through sixteen weeks of training at Camp Greene. In his place, there was someone as alien to me as my German victim had been, and I realized as he stared back at me, that he too was seeing someone other than the Bertram Tyler he once had known. Friendly strangers, we sat and chewed on horsemeat and watched the aerial acrobatics overhead, and in a little while we were telling stories about what had happened to us separately that night, and a short time later we were laughing together.

August ✿ ✿ ✿

We had come all the way from the campus of the Western College for Women in Oxford, Ohio, following the same route the three slain civil rights workers had taken at the end of June, stopping in Meridian, Mississippi, and then going on to visit the charred ruins of the Mount Zion Methodist Church in Longdale, the heat a sentient adversary, dust and mimosa mingled, the taste of death and the scent of fuzzy pink, the insects rattling in the scrub pine, the scorched iron bell lying mute in unforgiving ashes. We had then gone through Philadelphia, namesake of another town in another place where another bell had once sounded for liberty, and driven twelve miles northeast on State Highway 21 to the Bogue Chitto Swamp where the charred remains of the Ford station wagon had been found, three of its hubcaps already stolen by Choctaw Indians from the reservation, a final piece of irony. And then we had traveled in shimmering Mississippi heat, our pilgrimage taking us in the opposite direction to the Old Jolly Farm where the three men had been found six weeks after they'd disappeared, buried twenty feet deep in red clay, each of them shot to death. Chaney, the Negro, had first been viciously beaten. The New York pathologist who examined his body said later, "I have never witnessed bones so severely shattered."

Now we rode westward toward the Louisiana border and a town called Clayton, where we hoped to continue our voter registration work. The man driving the car was a twenty-three-year-old named Luke (no relation to the saint, but a divinity student nonetheless) Foulds from Brewster, New York, who had been one of the eight hundred students indoctrinated at Oxford during the week Chaney, Schwerner, and Goodman were there. He wore rimless eyeglasses, and he had a pale pinched face, a rather sharp nose, thin unsmiling lips. A humorless man by nature, he had become positively dour after learning that the three workers—he had known Schwerner casually— had indeed been killed. A rumor had circulated in the beginning, you see, that the disappearance of the trio was a hoax, a stunt concocted by CORE to call attention to the voter registration drive. I knew right away they were dead, however, and I told my father that their murders only strengthened my resolve to go south with Larry Peters.

I was sitting alongside Luke on the front seat of his old Chevy, and Larry was in back with a girl named Jennifer Scott, who was a sophomore at Vassar, and who never let anyone forget it. Blond hair cut close to her head, busty in a white peasant blouse, thick-hipped in a pale denim skirt, meaty thighs flashing whenever she crossed her legs, she sat barefoot beside Larry and tried to convince him she had not been frightened when a gang of kids in Philadelphia had yelled "Nigger lover!" at the car. I knew she was lying because I myself had been scared half out of my wits. The only one of us, in fact, who had maintained his cool against the approach of what looked like impending disaster was old dour Luke. Which was perhaps proper and fitting, since Luke was our mentor and our boss, and the three of us were here only to serve as his assistants, having symbolically joined him on the Fourteenth of July, Bastille Day.

It had been some July.

I was willing to bet there had never been a July like it in the history of the United States.

"This July started in June," my mother had said, and I think she was right, but I also think she was referring only to the temperature, which was the highest ever recorded in Talmadge for that month. Lake Abundance (ha!) fell a good four feet (which wasn't very comical to the people who owned summer homes around it) and there were more brush fires in town than ever before, the siren on the firehouse roof erupting some two or three times a day, volunteers popping into their cars and rushing all over the countryside, invariably arriving too late to save anything but the plumbing. Elsewhere, though, July had also started in June with the resignation of Ambassador Lodge in Saigon, and the disappearance of Goodman, Chaney, and Schwerner in Mississippi. Of the two events, the one unquestionably most important was the disappearance of the rights workers. Immediately following the passing of a massive civil rights bill by the Senate, the scent of violence rising from that snake-infested southern swamp caused most thinking citizens to wonder what would happen when the bill passed the House and became the law of the land. The war, or whatever the hell it was, in Vietnam had been meandering along through four administrations now, and there seemed little danger of it changing its course for the worse, even with the appointment of an Army general as the new ambassador. In fact, President Johnson had told the press that Taylor's appointment in no way indicated a change of policy in Vietnam. "The United States intends no rashness," he said, "and seeks no wider war," and there was every reason to believe him. We had our hands full right here at home without worrying about a limited commitment eleven thousand miles away. In fact, by the time the civil rights bill became law in July, we had lost only a hundred and forty-nine American advisers in Vietnam, which was not a bad average considering the fact that we'd been actively involved there since December 1961, when our first helicopter company went over to assist the Vietnamese army.

In Mississippi—where for the first time in history Negroes were protected by law when entering such heretofore exclusive places as polling booths, classrooms (though I had thought they'd settled *that* one back in 1954), factories, hotels, restaurants, movie theaters and even barber shops—they were dragging the Pearl River and trying to find the body of a Negro named James Chaney, who together with the two white men Schwerner and Goodman ("Are they Jewish?" my father asked) had disappeared on June 21. It made for confusion.

It even made for confusion in a place like Talmadge, which in all modesty had more than its proportionate share of intellectuals and influentials: professors, writers, editors, art directors, critics, performers, publishers, all of them eager and willing to tell the rest of the nation what to read, eat, wear, watch, enjoy, drink, feel, and think. Even the Talmadge brain trust, as exemplified by such sterling exhibits as Professor Robert Fitzhugh who taught film and film techniques at the university and who only the week before had reviewed *Harlow* for *The New York Times Book Review,* and who had written oh just *countless* critiques of other books for *The New York Review of Books* and anonymously for *Time;* or Leon Coopersmith, he of battle-of-bands fame, not to mention fortune in radio broadcasting earned through the popularity of his most ambitious show, a gem titled *Hello, Mrs. America,* which was beamed daily from a restaurant somewhere in downtown Pasadena; nor even the television producer David Regan, who had created a half-hour teen-age comedy show entitled *Wing It!,* doubtless inspired by his beauteous wife Katherine Bridges Regan, acquired not four years ago, he being almost forty at the time, and she having practically gone through elementary school with me (I had, in fact, once had a terrifying crush on her); even *those* towering intellectuals—but no, seriously, even the *really* intelligent and creative people in Talmadge didn't know quite what to make of that July.

Goldwater did nothing to help the confusion. Talmadge was a Republican town but essentially sensible, anyway, except for the Lake Abundance crowd and the four faggots on Javelin Road and the wife-swappers who had lived in brief discreet bliss on Caramoor Way. So now the Party in conclave high and solemn had nominated for its presidential candidate a man who had: 1- Voted *against* the civil rights bill (there were only three Negro families in all Talmadge and perhaps a bushelful of Jews, but everyone in town nonetheless liked to think of himself as highly democratic, small d), and 2- Advocated the defoliation of Vietnam (the people in Talmadge. tree-worshipers all, visualized a vast unsightly parking lot in Southeast Asia, probably in a two-acre residential zone) and 3- Promised to give his commanders in the field all the support they needed, even if it meant the tactical use of nuclear weapons (that giant mushroom specter rose over the twin steeples of the First Congregational Church—wherein David Regan had taken for his bride the young and doubtless giggling Katherine Bridges—and scared the population witless).

The British publisher who was bringing out my father's De Gaulle book in London, visiting our house at the end of June, solemnly asked, "You people aren't serious about this Goldwater person, are you?" and my father had pooh-poohed the Arizonan's chances, figuring even then that Scranton would surely get the nomination, especially now that Lodge was coming home to help him campaign. But in July, there was Goldwater, boasting—as the current joke had it—that come November he would ride triumphantly into Washington in his coach and four. And nobody in Talmadge knew *what* the fuck to think.

My mother's daily letters to me in Mississippi were a form of cursive whistling in the dark. She had told my father that he owed it to me to grant me my manhood, but now that I was actually in the South and violence was breaking out everywhere around me, her courage was beginning to falter and she filled page after page with Talmadge's reactions to the nomination, gossipy, endearing, her tiny precise handwriting only inadvertently betraying the fears she later confided to me. The situation was not helped when she received a letter from the very

91

organization I was serving, warning of the dangers I might encounter, and announcing that because of the "tense situation," they were not accepting any further volunteers for their program. Then, to put the maraschino cherry on it, a New York detective shot and killed a fifteen-year-old Negro boy, and a cry of police brutality roared all the way from Yorkville into black Harlem where full-scale rioting erupted on the loneliest night of the week, which also happened to be hot and sticky like most July nights in New York, there *has* to be a connection between heat and violence.

In July, Talmadge pondered the Republican platform promising "full implementation and faithful execution of the Civil Rights Act of 1964," while brick-throwing, looting, burning Negroes in Harlem were passing out leaflets that proclaimed: "We don't have to go to Mississippi because Mississippi is here in New York."

And in August, I was *in* Mississippi in a moving car on a deserted highway as dusk deepened the sky and birds chittered wildly in the treetops.

(Wat Tyler, nattily dressed for travel in southern climes, rests his weary head against the back of the seat. In black-and-white, the sun glancing through the trees casts a leafy filigree upon the windshield.)

The automobile was parked at the side of the road ahead, the headlights on even though it was not yet dark. A man stood casually leaning against the side of the car as we approached. Seeing us, he stepped into the middle of the road and held up his hand. He was wearing gray trousers and a white shirt open at the throat. A gun was slung in a holster on his hip, and there was a deputy sheriff's star pinned to his shirt pocket. Luke stopped the car. The man walked over. His hair and mustache were the color of his dusty boots. His eyes were a bright blue.

"Evening," he said.

"Good evening," Luke said.

"Mind if I have a look at your license and registration?"

"Is something wrong?" Luke asked.

"Nothing at all," the deputy answered, and glanced into the back seat. "You coming from Philadelphia?" he asked.

"That's right," Luke said.

The deputy accepted Luke's license and registration. In the beam of his own headlights, he studied both and then walked back to our car. "This's a New York driver's license," he said.

"That's right," Luke said again.

"You from New York?"

"Brewster," Luke said.

"That in New York?"

"Upstate New York."

"Guess that's how come you ain't familiar with the law here in Miss'ippi."

"What law is that?" Luke said.

"Lights on at dusk," the deputy said.

Immediately, Luke reached for the dashboard switch and turned on the headlights.

"Well, it's a little late now," the deputy said. He glanced at his watch. "Close to seven o'clock," he said, "that's a long way past dusk."

(Wat Tyler, sitting beside Luke on the front seat of the silent automobile, feels a sudden lurch of fear. He wets his lips. The deputy stands motionless outside the car. In the woods lining the road, an owl hoots and falls silent.)

"Want to come along with us?" the deputy asked.

"What for?"

"I jus' tole you. Lights on at dusk." The deputy smiled pleasantly. "Yours were off."

"Well, they're on now," Luke said.

"But too late."

"Look, officer . . ."

"I jus' think y'all better come along with us, huh?" the deputy said, still smiling. "For your own p'tection, huh?"

"We're supposed to be in Clayton by . . ."

"Oh, were you heading for Clayton?"

Luke was silent for a moment. Then he merely nodded.

"Huh?" the deputy asked.

"Yes," Luke said.

"What you going to Clayton for?" the deputy asked.

"We're going there on business," Luke said.

"What kind of business?"

"Personal business."

"Nigger business?" the deputy asked. Glancing at Larry

in the back seat, he grinned and said, "Oh, 'scuse me, boy. Didn't see you sitting there in the dark and all." Turning his attention back to Luke, he said, "Been a lot of agitation down this way, maybe you heard about it. I think y'all be safer with us tonight, 'stead of cruising the roads."

"We're not cruising the roads," Luke said. "We're driving directly to Clayton."

"No," the deputy said, and shook his head. "Maybe you *was* driving to Clayton, but you ain't driving to Clayton no more. What you're doing is you're letting my partner there take the wheel, and you're coming along with us. Now *that's* what you're doing, you see?" The deputy smiled again. "I think you see," he said.

Casually, he sauntered over to the other car and whispered a few words to his partner behind the wheel. The front door opened. His partner, wearing identical gray trousers and white shirt open at the throat, came out of the car and tugged at his undershorts. He was almost entirely bald, a fringe of reddish hair circling his tanned pate. A dead cigar stub was clamped between his teeth. He ambled over to our car, smiled at Luke, and said, "Evening. My partner says I'm to drive you into town."

"I guess so," Luke said, and sighed.

"It's for your own p'tection," the second deputy said, almost apologetically, and then looked into the back seat. "Nigger," he said, "you mind getting out?"

"What for?" Luke asked.

"I don't like riding with niggers. He'll have to walk."

The first deputy, who had come back to the car and was standing casually and angularly near the fender, the heel of his right hand resting lazily on the butt of his revolver, said, "Come on now, Fred, be democratic."

"Oh, I *am*, Curly," Fred said, "I am that. It's just I can't stand the stink of niggers, that's all. You mind getting out boy?"

"You stay where you are," Luke said, without glancing into the back seat.

"Now that's not wise," Fred said chewing on his cigar. "Not wise at all. You don't want to be adding a more serious charge to a tiny little traffic violation, now do you?"

"What's the more serious charge?" Luke asked.

"Resisting an officer."

"No one's resisting an officer."

"Well now, I just heard you advise that black nigger back there to stay where he is, whereas I asked him to get out of the car." Fred leaned into the open window and said, directly to Larry, "Nigger, didn't I ask you polite and nice to get out of that friggin' heap? 'Scuse me, miss," he added, and touched his index finger to his eyebrow, as if in salute.

"Well, what do you say, fellas?" Curly asked.

"If *he* gets out, we *all* get out," Luke said.

"It's a long walk to town," Fred said.

"Close to four miles," Curly said.

"Past dam sites and everything," Fred said.

(Another jagged lance of fear. Wat Tyler remembers the farm where the bodies of the three workers were discovered, bitterweed and scrub pine, the hole left by the dragline in the earthen dam, the men buried in shallow graves while the dam was still in construction, and week after week the unsuspecting builder had covered them with yards of red Mississippi clay.)

"He's not getting out of this car alone," Luke said.

"Suit yourself," Curly said. "You want to *all* get out? *Please?*"

We got out of the car. We all stayed close to Luke. The one called Curly (though his hair was as straight as my own) seemed the least menacing of the two deputies, and our eyes kept wandering to his face for reassurance. Jennifer was petrified. The stench of fear rose from her body as though emanating from her crotch, strong and female and feral. She was not a pretty girl, but there was a look of ready availability about her, combining now with the fear on her face and in her eyes, to create an impression of extreme vulnerability, the willing rape victim. I sensed it was a dangerous look to be wearing on this deserted highway, and I felt my own fear rising again as Fred's eyes traveled over the outline of her full white brassiere beneath her white cotton blouse. Jennifer turned slightly sideways, into my shoulder, to avoid his gaze.

"You ain't afraid, are you, miss?" Fred asked.

"What's there to be afraid of?" she asked, intending the words to come out boldly and with just the proper touch of Vassar hauteur, surprising even herself when she heard the tremulous sound that issued from her mouth.

"Nothing," Fred said. "Any white girl who ain't afraid

95

of riding with a nigger sure ain't got nothing *else* to be afraid of, has she, Curly?"

"Nothing at all," Curly answered.

"You just trot your sweet little ass up ahead of the car there," Fred said, and grinned around his cigar. "We'll drive nice and slow all the way to town."

(In Wat Tyler's camera eye, the eye of a generation, he sees himself in a filthy jailhouse, winos and bums holding kangaroo court over his sodomized form inert on an insect-ridden, excrement-befouled floor. Courageously he bears the weight of a bearded redneck who calls him nigger lover and screaming faggot pansy while outside a deputy holds a water hose at the ready and the black-and-white film cuts fitfully in orgasm not his own.)

The holding cell I occupied with Larry and Luke was perhaps eight feet long by five feet wide, a washbasin in one corner, an exposed toilet bowl in the other. The cell, the corridor outside were scrupulously clean, smelling of disinfectant; even the water in the toilet bowl was tinted green and smelled of pine. A deputy sat at the far end of the long corridor, reading a magazine under a caged light bulb. An air conditioner hummed somewhere serenely.

(An old Negro condemned to death for raping a white girl strums on his guitar while next door Jennifer sobs out her fears to the two Negro girls from Howard who share the cell with her. She is afraid that the deputies will force her to strip and stick their fingers into all her apertures. On black-and-white film, Wat Tyler sticks his fingers into at least one of her apertures. Her milky white breasts, nipple-tipped, fill the screen, and Larry Peters' black face is superimposed on them while the offscreen Negro strums his guitar and mournfully laments the fact that he was caught in *flagrante delicto*.)

A television set was going at the far end of the corridor, the turnkey alternately dozing and glancing up at the movie which had come on at eleven-thirty. Luke was asleep in one of the hanging berths against the right-hand wall of the cell. I was sitting on the lower berth, and Larry was on a straight-backed chair opposite me. I had had to move my bowels from the moment the deputy stopped us on the highway, but now I was embarrassed to do so on a toilet bowl that could be seen from the corridor outside the cell. They had officially charged us

96

with the motor vehicle violation, as well as with resisting a public officer in the discharge of his duty (the judge had said something about willfully delaying and obstructing) both of which heinous crimes were probably only misdemeanors but apparently serious enough to warrant the setting of bail for each of us at a hundred dollars.

"The idea is to keep us here long enough to miss the Clayton meeting tomorrow night," Larry said. "Everybody'll arrive at eight o'clock, waiting for the fearless rights workers from the North, but the fearless workers won't show. So they'll all drag their asses back to their shanties, and shake their heads, and mutter in their pone about how there isn't any hope for the Negro in this country, they jes' ain' no *hope* for us pore ole niggers, Amos," he mimicked in a thick watermelon dialect, and then scowled in despair.

He was very black, no, that's not true, he was very brown, a good chocolate fudge brown color, with thick lips showing pink inside, and wide nostrils, and a huge brow, and hair cropped very close to his skull. You could not mistake him for anything but a Negro. I mean there was not the slightest possibility that he would have been cast as Santa Claus in a high school play. Considering his somewhat obvious coloration (he was one of two Negroes at Talmadge High, the other being a sort of mocha color, like the drapes in my father's office), I should have noticed him sooner. The fact is, however, that I was busy with my own friends and my own pursuits and didn't become aware of him until *he* made the approach.

He introduced himself on the steps outside Main one day, and told me he was a piano player and was interested in getting himself an organ, did I think he could come over to the house to try mine out before he bought one. I said sure he could, and he came over one spring day after school, we were both juniors then, the forsythias lining the drive were in full flower, I remember how rich his skin looked against the riotous yellow as we went into the house.

I took him up to my room and he fooled around with the Farfisa a little, and then hesitantly asked me how much it had cost. When I told him, he nodded solemnly and then said maybe he ought to take a few lessons before he spent that kind of money. Then, unexpectedly, he asked if *I* would like to give him lessons, and offered to pay me for them. I told him I'd be happy to teach him what I knew (I wasn't happy at *all*) and that he certainly didn't have to pay me, which pleased him enormously and which doubtless qualified me for membership in the NAACP. Anyway, I gave him three lessons and discovered he was absolutely without talent. He didn't even have a sense of rhythm, which sounds like a sick joke, but which happened to be absolutely true. After the fourth lesson, I told him he was a hopeless case, and he got mad as hell and didn't speak to me for a month afterward. Then, I forget what happened, I think we were working together on the junior variety show, that's right, Dawn Patrol was playing and Larry was running the switchboard, and we got to talking again, and he admitted he couldn't even *hum* in tune in the shower, and that was how we got to be friends.

Well I say friends, but we weren't really friends, not then.

I don't think I was using Larry as my Show Nigger, but I do think he became my Guinea Pig Nigger, and I'm sure now that my curiosity was a bit overbearing at times, yes, I'm positive. There were too many things I wanted to know about Negroes, and Larry was the only Negro I knew, so I pursued him relentlessly, asking him whatever came to mind, even if I felt or knew the question would embarrass him. That sounds terrible now, I'm really quite ashamed of it, like superior white massa asking bare-ass pickaninny do he stand when he pee like de white man do. But I had the idea then (or at least this is what I told myself in defense of my own position) that the only way Larry and I could explore our samenesses was to understand our differences. We had to do this, I told him, because the Negro as we had invented him in America simply was *not* the equal of the white man.

The first time I told Larry he was not my equal, he punched me in the mouth. That was when we were still getting to be friends. The second time I told him was when we were both seniors and feeling like big shots with our orange-and-black senior beanies, the big T for Talmadge on the front superimposed with the hopeful date of our graduation, '64. We were coming past the playing field where the soccer team was practicing head shots, Coach Lambert throwing the ball repeatedly at the skulls of his players, and they dizzily batting it back to him. It was a bright fall Connecticut day, clear and sharp and invigorating. Larry was wearing his team sweater (he was on the swimming team and had earned his varsity letter as a freshman) over a white turtleneck—brown skin, black sweater, orange arm stripes and letter T, orange-and-black beanie, and behind him the riotous plumage of autumn, red, orange, gold, tan—color was everywhere around us, and very much on my mind.

I opened the subject cautiously this time; he had a devastating right jab, and I was very fond of my teeth. I also opened it guiltily, wondering whether all my talk about equality or the lack of it wasn't merely a coverup for what was actually prejudice. Was I, in effect, simply taking an unpopular position (You are not my equal, Larry, and I will explain why) to screen an even less popular position? (I do not like the color of your skin, Larry, nor the way you talk, or walk, or smell. In short, I envy the size of your cock.) I had, for example, never been able to stand the complexion of Indians (not *American* Indians; I had never seen one—but *Indian* Indians) who always seemed to me to be the color of dried anemic dog shit.

Well, I said, and Larry listened, ready to take offense, what I meant when we talked about this in June, you see, is that the white man has forced this goddamn peculiar situation . . .

Oh, peculiar, Larry said. Is that what it is? Peculiar?

Yes, because it's unnatural. Well, you know what I mean, Larry, all the business, for example, of not allowing slaves to marry. How can we expect the Negro male today to accept responsibility if his ancestors . . .

He's lazy and shiftless, right? Larry said.

Look, I said, I'm trying to be serious here. I'm talking about not allowing the Negro to get a good education or a meaningful job, I'm talking about *all* the crap the white man's forced upon the Negro in order to create an inferior human being.

Here we go again, Larry said.

Larry, I'm trying to say that the white man's task in the next generation . . .

The white man's burden, you mean.

I mean *our* task, all right, yours and mine, not only the white man's, *ours*, okay? *Our* task in this next generation'll be to cut through all that crap and create a new American Negro who . . .

By selective breeding, right? Like livestock, right?

Fuck you, I said.

Fuck *you,* Larry said. You're a bigot like all the rest. You're just a smarter bigot, is all.

Okay, I said.

You don't *want* me to be your equal, Larry said.

I *want* you to be my fuckin' equal, I said.

Then get me a date with a white girl, he said.

Get *yourself* a date with a white girl, I answered.

He didn't tell me until much later, when we trusted each other enough to talk openly about girls (and I honestly believed *that* was the last barricade) that he had taken my advice and got himself a date with a white girl named Patricia Converse from Stamford, who was no prize, but who had sucked him out of his mind. I felt an initial flaring of anger, don't tell *me* prejudice doesn't die hard. Don't tell *me* my aversion to the color of *Indian* Indians (not *American* Indians, mind you) had nothing to do with Negroes. I visualized Patricia Converse as a very fair blonde with blue eyes, I saw Larry's ugly black cock in her mouth, and I felt violently protective of *all* my women, big white massa standin in de doorway guardin Missy Annabelle home fum Atlanta, don't tell *me,* man. Don't tell me I didn't have to step on something inside me and crush it that day, smashing what I thought was the final barricade, and seeing a small flash of triumph in Larry's eyes, knowing he savored the image of White Womanhood Defiled that flitted through my mind, and wanting this time to punch *him* in the mouth because he *was* my equal now or at least I thought he was. What I understand was that I was not yet *his* equal.

To become his equal (and I didn't learn this until we arrived in Mississippi), I would have to stand with him on a red clay dam, and be shot to death by white men to whom my color meant nothing, shadowed as it was by my Negro friend beside me.

I was not willing to die for Larry Peters.

I sat opposite him in a very clean cell in a very clean jail, both of us tired and depressed, neither of us speaking. From the far end of the corridor, we recognized Lyndon Johnson's voice coming from the television set, and Larry said, "What's that?" and I said, "Shhh."

"My fellow Americans," Johnson said, "as President and Commander-in-Chief, it is my duty to report that renewed hostile actions against United States ships on the

100

high seas in the Gulf of Tonkin have today required me to order the military forces of the United States to take action in reply . . ."

"What does he mean?" I asked Larry.

"Those PT-boats a few days ago," Larry said. "The ones that attacked our destroyer."

"That reply," Johnson said, "is being given as I speak to you tonight. Air action is now in execution against gunboats and certain supporting facilities in North Vietnam which have been used in these hostile operations."

"There it is," Larry said. "The son of a bitch is declaring war!"

"How can he do that without an act of Congress?" I asked.

"He's doing it, isn't he?" Larry answered.

"Our response for the present," Johnson said, "will be limited and fitting. We Americans know, although others appear to forget, the risks of spreading conflict. We still seek no wider war."

The turnkey, apparently bored by these events in Southeast Asia, clicked the set to another channel. Robert Mitchum's unmistakable voice superseded Johnson's in the jailhouse corridor as he urged his men into combat against the Japanese.

"Maybe they're just testing us," I said.

"Maybe," Larry said.

"Like . . ."

"Like what?"

"Like . . . I don't know . . . when they put those missiles in Cuba."

"Testing our resolve, huh?"

"Yeah, our resolve."

"Yeah," Larry said. He sighed deeply. "You think we'll ever get out of this joint?"

"Sure," I said. "My father should have got the telegram by now, don't you think?"

"Oh sure," Larry said. A troubled look crossed his face. He hesitated a moment, as though not certain he wished to reveal what he was thinking. Even when he started to speak, he said only, "Jesus, I hope . . ." and then shook his head.

"What?" I said.

"I don't want to go to war, do you?" he said.

"No," I said.

It was not my father who came down to bail us out.

The man who stepped through the doorway at the far end of the corridor the next morning, ducking his head under the lintel, rising to his full height again as he followed the turnkey to my cell, tall and powerful-looking for all his sixty-four years, was my grandfather.

"Hello, Walter," he said.

"Hello, Grandpa," I said, and smiled.

"Have they been treating you well?" he asked.

"I guess so," I said. "Grandpa, these are my friends, Luke Foulds and Larry Peters."

"How do you do, boys?" my grandfather said.

"And there're some more in the next cell," I said.

"How many all together?" my grandfather asked.

"Well, the three girls and us," I said.

"I'll make out a check for six hundred dollars," my grandfather said to the turnkey.

"I got nothing to do with money," the turnkey said. "You see them upstairs about that."

"I will," my grandfather said.

"Sir," Luke said, "this is very kind of you, but I've sent home for money and . . ."

"My grandson's wire indicated you were all in a hurry to get somewhere."

"Yes, sir, we are. But . . ."

"Well, you can reimburse me later," my grandfather said. "Meanwhile, let me get you out of this place."

"Grandpa?" I said.

"Yes, Walter?"

"Couldn't my father come?"

My grandfather looked at me for what seemed like a very long time. At last, he said, "No, Wat, I'm sorry, he couldn't." He hesitated only an instant. "He has an important business meeting in New York tomorrow morning." And then, before I could read the truth in his eyes and be hurt by it, he turned swiftly and walked down the corridor.

September ✝ ✝

My mother died on the second Sunday in September, four days after Italy surrendered to the Allies. The Air Force gave me an emergency furlough and a lift on a C-47 to the Orchard Place Airport in Park Ridge. From there, I took a train and arrived in Chicago shortly after dusk. I did not want to go home. I was certain there would be a black wreath on the door, and I did not want to see it.

The chaplain had called me into his office at ten o'clock that morning and said, "Cadet Tyler, I'm afraid I've got bad news for you. We got a call from Chicago just a few minutes ago. Your mother had a heart attack and passed away last night."

I looked at him and hated him instantly, the gold-rimmed eyeglasses and the echoing gold cross on his collar, the harsh grating sound of his Bronx speech as he told me my mother was dead—no, "passed away," he had said, "passed away last night," the euphemism somehow making the fact more intolerable. I nodded and fastened my eyes on a bayonet letter opener on his desk, refusing to look into his face, afraid that I would begin crying here in the presence of this goddamned pious fool from Baychester Avenue.

"I'm sorry, Cadet Tyler," he said.

"Thank you, sir."

"I've already spoken to the C.O. about leave."

"Thank you, sir."

"He'd like a few words with you when we're through here."

"Yes, sir."

"My own mother died in childbirth," he said, as if somehow that exonerated him.

The barracks was empty as I packed my duffle and tried to sort out in my mind what I would need for my four-day furlough to Chicago. They would be burying her on Wednesday, and this was Sunday—no, that was only three days, I was due back by formation Thursday morning. The C.O. had told me he'd have to put me back a class unless I returned in time. As it was, I would have to make up two hours of code, two hours of sea-air recognition, and an hour each of math and physics, the C.O. telling me all this as though the possibility of washing out was the foremost thing in my mind on that Sunday my mother died. I told him I would be sure to be back by formation Thursday, sir, and he said I had better, because whereas it was permissible for me to miss three days of my intensive and arduous ten-week training program (though I *would* have to make up those lost hours, I understood that, didn't I? Yes, sir, I said. I understand that), it was inconceivable that I could miss anything more than that without getting chased into the class behind mine. It's for your own good, Tyler, he told me, we can't put a man in the air without the training he needs to survive, all of this while the knowledge of my mother's death sat behind my eyes and I wanted to cry but could not.

I could not cry on the transport, either, because there were twenty-five other guys in the plane, all headed for the Chicago Army Air Base. The train into the city was packed with civilians and soldiers, and I sat stiffly erect by the widow and listened to the wheels and thought of movies I had seen where a guy is sitting by a train window and the wheels are clacking and the sound triggers a flashback, but there seemed to be nothing I could remember. I could not remember what my mother looked like, I could not remember a single one of her homespun sayings. And, of course, I could not cry because a member of the United States Army Air Force does not cry on a public conveyance, not when he is wearing on his garrison cap that winged propeller, no.

I could not cry in the taxicab, either. The driver, watching me in the rear view mirror as we worked our way east down Washington Street from the station, said, "Well, it looks like the Cards and the Yankees again, huh?"

"I guess so," I said.

"Same as last year."

"Yes."

"Probably be a lousy series."

"Mmm."

"Well, how can you have a good series when half the guys are already in the service? You know where Di Maggio is? In Santa Ana. Where's that, that Santa Ana?"

"California."

"Yeah, California. Remember the pitching Johnny Beazley done for the Cards in last year's series? You know where he is this year? In the Air Force, that's where he is. It's gonna be lousy, how can it be good? You think it'll be good?"

"I don't know."

"Naw, it can't be good," the driver said, and fell silent until we pulled up in front of the old house I loved on East Scott Street. Then all he said was, "That's seventy cents, soldier." I paid him and tipped him and got out of the cab and hesitated on the sidewalk because I suddenly felt like a stranger here. I had left Chicago on June 27, and had spent five weeks in basic military training in Nashville, Tennessee, proceeding at the end of July, directly and without furlough, to Maxwell Field in Montgomery, Alabama, for pre-flight schooling—a stranger here now, and more a stranger because my mother was dead.

There was no wreath on the door.

I thought at first that someone had made a mistake, perhaps that cockeyed preacher from the Bronx had given me a message intended for a Cadet Taylor or Wylie or some other unlucky bastard, but *not* for me, Will Tyler, whose mother could surely not be dead, she was only forty-two years old. The brass doorknobs were polished, the twin spruces climbed into the blue stained-glass sky, everything seemed the way it always had. And then the door opened, and I looked at my sister Linda's face, and knew there had been no mistake. My mother was dead.

They had placed the coffin in the living room, and I thought at once they had put it in the wrong room. It should have been in the kitchen, with the radio going, and with "Just Plain Bill" filling my mother's calm universe with fictitious turmoil. There were wooden folding chairs arranged in rows before the coffin, and my father sat on one of them beside my Aunt Kate and her Apache husband, Oscar, who looked more and more like an Indian the older he got. There were banks of flowers heaped beside the open coffin; I suddenly wondered if I should have sent some. My father's eyes were red-rimmed.

I had not yet looked at my mother.

I went to my father, and he embraced me and kissed me on the cheek, and said only, "Will," and my Aunt Kate turned to Oscar and said, "Oscar, it's Will," and Oscar nodded, his seamed and wrinkled face impassive. There were other relatives in the room, they came slowly into focus, my father's younger brother John, who now lived in Milwaukee, and my mother's two sisters, who still lived in Freshwater, and cousins I had never seen, hordes of relatives, how had they managed to assemble so quickly? I had the strangest feeling they were all waiting for me to go to the coffin, that this was the part in the movie where someone would turn to someone else and say, "It's her son," the way Aunt Kate had said, "Oscar, it's Will," and then their eyes would follow me, and they would carefully gauge my reactions when I saw my mother dead, calculating my grief, sympathizing with my loss, and yet somehow detached, as though denying the presence of death by forcing only the immediate family to become its reluctant hosts. Perversely, I would not go to the coffin, not while their eyes were upon me. I saw the question on my father's face, *Aren't you going to pay your respects, Will?* and I ignored it and chatted with my Aunt Clara, who was my mother's oldest sister, and whose son was with the Marines somewhere in the Pacific. Do you think you'll be heading out that way, Will? she asked, and I said I didn't know, I still had almost seven months of training ahead of me, and my aunt said, Maybe it'll be over before you get there, and I said I certainly hope so, Aunt Clara, not meaning it.

I did not go to the coffin until I was alone in the room.

My sister had made sandwiches and coffee, and everyone had gone into the kitchen, Oscar asking my father if there was anything to drink in the house, the old Injun seeking the white man's firewater, and my father took him into the dining room where the locked liquor cabinet stood against one wood-paneled wall. I listened to the voices floating through the corridors of the house that could never seem home to me again, drifting toward the kitchen (the image of my mother, head tilted to one side, favoring her good ear as she listened to the radio, peas as green as her eyes tumbling into the sink colander), and I was alone with her, and she was dead.

I knelt by the coffin, and I looked into her face.

And her eyes closed gently by some undertaker's thumbs were sightless, and I noticed white strands in her golden hair, and I remembered in a painful rush that brought fresh tears to my eyes this gentle woman I had loved so dearly, this humorless country girl who could explode into sudden laughter, this comforting, guiding, devoted woman who had been my mother. I reached out to touch her cold and lifeless hand folded across her bosom, and sobbed my grief against the padded altar railing before the coffin and could think of no prayer to send her out of my heart and out of my mind.

I felt my father's hand on my shoulder.

He said something to me, and I nodded and turned to him, and held him close as though fearful I would lose him too in the very next moment, held him fiercely and tightly while the voices whispered in the other rooms.

We buried her on Wednesday morning.

I went directly from the cemetery to the Northwestern station on Canal and Madison, and from there by train to the Orchard Place Airport where I hitched a ride on a C-54 going to Montgomery. We developed engine trouble on the way down, and landed for repairs at a small airport someplace in Tennessee The pilot told us we would not be ready to take off again until eleven that night, and were free to leave the airport if we wanted to. I checked my duffle bag and took a bus into the nearest town.

There was a sense of anonymity in those wartime streets. The sidewalks were sticky with a gelatinous khaki-colored mass that seeped in and out of bars and shops, arcades and luncheonettes, an eyeless seeking protoplasmic ooze that sucked from every Army town in the country whatever juices it possessed. Souvenir shops and shooting galleries, hot-dog stands and honky-tonks, movie theaters and greasy spoons boomed with the coming of the GI dollar, fifty dollars a day once a month for the lowliest buck private, ten million men in khaki searching for pleasure on their hours away from camp. I was grateful for the loss of identity, and resentful when two farmer-type MPs singled me out to ask for my furlough papers. There was nothing in them to indicate that my mother had died. The MPs studied them leisurely, noting when I had left Montgomery and when I was due back, and then the tallest of the pair said, "Okay, soldier," and I put the folded papers back into the pocket of my blouse, and continued walking up the street.

There were the sounds of approaching night, a tenor saxophone and trumpet in B-flat harmony, a woman's laughter, wire brushes on a snare drum's head, a soldier swearing, a bass fiddle pulsing like an exposed heart in a laboratory jar, a piano tinkling with a whorehouse beat, New Orleans twice removed, automobile horns and the clatter of high-heeled pumps ankle-strapped, the shuffle of GI boots along streets already cooling, the amplified blare from a record shop, "It seems to me I've heard that song before, It's from an old, familiar score," and across the way a sidewalk hawker shouting out the starting time for *Stage Door Canteen,* which was supposed to be a good movie and which I had not seen. I walked past him resplendent in his blue uniform and gold braid (wondering why he wasn't in a *real* uniform) and studied the glossy black-and-white stills in the display cases, and then stood decisionless near the box office, and finally moved on again, merging with the sidewalk soldiers.

I didn't know what I wanted to do.

Whiskey was scarce as hell, but by asking around, I managed to get onto a GI who had brought a case back with him from a weekend home, and who was selling the stuff at premium prices. I tucked the bottle into the waistband of my trousers, under my blouse, and walked into a little park on the edge of town where a Civil War general spread his quivering buttocks astride a rearing stallion, his sword pointed toward Washington, D.C., no doubt. I found a bench far from the sidewalk noises, uncorked the bottle, and began to drink. I drank steadily and deliberately. In a little while, I began crying.

The girl came lurching out of the darkness, as drunk as I was, as black as the darkness, black skin and black eyes, black chiffon dress tight across small high breasts, stumbled clickingly out of the darkness on high-heeled patent leather pumps, black, as sudden and as shocking as death itself, and stopped before me and put her hands on her hips and squinted me into focus and whispered, "What's the matter, so'jer?"

"Nothing," I said.

She stood above with the professional tilt of a sidewalk whore, pelvis angled toward me, black dress clinging to a certain nakedness beneath, the promise of a tangle of black pubic hair, a pink nigger twat as ripe as the thick lips smiling at me now in open invitation. There was a small knife scar on her right temple. She smelled of perfume and perspiration.

"Why you cryin' then?" she asked.

"My mother's dead," I answered.

"Tha's too bad," she said, and sat beside me with some difficulty, and put one plump widespread hand on my thigh. "Give me a drink, so'jer," she said.

"Sure," I said, and handed her the bottle.

She wiped the lip of the bottle before drinking from it, and then tilted it to her mouth and took a long burning swallow, and gagged, and wiped the lip again and handed the bottle back to me.

"Where you get that stuff?" she asked. "Taste jus' like piss."

"Bought it," I said.

"Taste jus' like piss," she said again. "Give me some more of that stuff," she said, and reached for the bottle. She drank again, said, "Whoo, man, that's jus' awful," and then said, "What's yo' name?"

"Will."

"I'm Daisy. How's that?"

"That's fine," I said.

"No, it ain't, it's dumb. Dumb ole nigger name."

"No, it's fine," I said.

"Listen. I'm sorry 'bout your mother," she said.

"That's okay."

"I got two li'l kids my own," she said, "I know wha's like to be a mother. I'm real sorry, man."

"That's okay," I said.

"Sorry," she said, and shook her head. "Listen, Bill," she said, "there one thing . . ."

"Will," I said.

"Will," she said, "one thing Daisy know how to do, it's take the miseries out a man, you hear?"

"I hear," I said.

"You want me to?"

"Got no money. Spent it all on this piss here."

"I know you got money, Bill."

"No, cross my heart."

"How you 'spect to get a fancy lady 'thout money, Bill?"

"Got none though."

"Show you a real fine time, Bill."

"Got no money though."

"Listen, Bill, tell me the truth."

"That's the truth."

"You got money, Bill?"

"No money."

"Pore Bill," she said. "Mammy gone, money gone, whiskey 'most all gone. Give me some of that whiskey there, Bill." She took the bottle again and, without wiping the lip this time, tilted it to her mouth and drank. "Oh, man," she said, "like to burn a hole clear thu me."

She handed the bottle back to me. We sat silently on the bench.

"Well, Bill," she said at last, "what we goan do 'bout you?"

"Nothing," I said.

"You wanna go back there in the bushes?"

"Got no money," I said.

She rose unsteadily and stood swaying before the bench, her head tilted, her eyes squinted, a single gold earring dangling from her left ear, the other doubtless lost in some GI's undershorts. She held out her hand to me then, the white-pink palm suddenly revealed, and said, "Come on, Bill, we goan to church."

She led me stumbling drunkenly off the path to the spreading cover of an oleander, and then she guided me gently to the ground and pulled the black dress up over her long brown legs and put my hand between them. "You got a rubber, man?" she asked, and I said, "Mmm, yes," and she said, "Doan you come inside me 'thout one," and I thought, Minister's daughter or whore, all anybody thinks about these days is getting pregnant. What would be so wrong about getting pregnant, Daisy-girl, what would be so wrong about shooting some hot white seed into you? You want to be a whore with a twat of gold? Okay, make a baby for me, Daisy, make a baby girl with long blond hair and honey molasses skin to take the place of the one we laid deep in the ground today. "You goan be able to get this up, Bill?" she asked, and I said, "Take it in your mouth, honey," and she said, "How I know where you had it last?" but she put her head into my lap and her lips gently parted over me, soft and wet and thick, and she sucked deep dizzying draughts and then abruptly moved her head away and whispered soberly, "Where's the rubber, man?" I rolled onto my side, her hand dropping to cover me and coax me while I fumbled with my wallet and extracted from it the Trojan the United States Army Air Force had so thoughtfully provided. She smoothed it onto me with professional agility, and said, "You goan put that thing real deep inside me, Bill, you goan fuck this mother clear out of your head," and I thought she had somehow got the sentence wrong, and then she was on her back again, her legs bent and spread, holding me in both deft guiding hands as she pulled me into her. "Now give it to me, Bill," she said, and I thought, Honey, it's *Will*, can't you get that straight, and she said, "Tha's right, baby, give it to me, fuck me out of my head, baby, give it to me, Bill, *give* it to me," repeating a litany she had probably learned in the cradle, changing nothing but the name, and even *that* was wrong. *All* of it's wrong, I thought, I'm choosing the wrong memory, *this* is what I'll remember for September 15, 1943, and not an open grave receiving my mother's body! I tried desperately to recall what my father had said to me as I knelt beside the coffin because it seemed to me all at once that my mother was in danger of being instantly forgotten, of disappearing forever into an urgent brown void beneath a spreading oleander in a Tennessee park. I could remember my father's presence suddenly behind me, could remember the weight of his hand on my shoulder, and then, at last, his words came back to me, and I repeated them in my head as Daisy wrapped her legs tight around me and pulled my orgasm into her slippery vault, not knowing what all the words meant, but taking solace from them anyway.

"I almost lost her years ago," he said. "We were lucky," he said. "I loved her, Will. I won't know how to live without her."

October ✠

My darling Bert,

How are you, my dearest? I've just received four of your letters in today's mail, dated September 16, September 17, September 20, and September 21. It certainly does take long for them to get here, doesn't it? I think maybe there are German spies at work. Have you been getting mine?

I took them all up to my room and read them one at a time with Clara making a big fuss trying to get in the door. She sometimes behaves like nine instead of nineteen! This time, she claimed I had hidden her *Vanity Fair,* which I hadn't even *seen!* All she wanted to do, of course, was read your letters. You *do* seem to have got pretty passionate over there in France, my dear. I sometimes blush myself when I read them. (Maybe you ought to go see the chaplain, if there is one.)

Bert, do you wear your gas mask around your neck at all times? I read a story in the Record that said too many of our boys over there have been throwing away their respirators or whatever you call them, and then when the Germans shoot their gas, it's quite unfortunate. Be sure to keep yours and not throw it away. Did you get the socks I sent you? I think it's terrible that your feet are always wet. Don't they ever give you any time at all to dry them off? Don't you have two pairs of boots?

Bert, I miss you very much.

Things are about the same here in Eau Fraiche, except that you aren't here, and of course most of the other boys are gone, too. It's very quiet and strange. The Chenemeke was playing *Lest We Forget* with Rita Jolivet this week, and I took Meg to see it. She is quite a little pest, even though she's my sister. Whenever a love part comes on, she starts squirming and fidgeting, which I think odd for a girl going on fifteen, don't you? I hope you are not making goo-goo eyes at any of those mademoiselles, by the way. I hear they are really something, those French girls. You be careful, Bert, because I love you very much, and am of course being true to you.

Clara is right this minute making a terrible racket on the Pianola in the parlor because she knows I'm up here writing to you, and she can't let anyone live in peace, naturally. Bert, I worry about you day and night, please be careful.

I shall have to end this before I start crying.

All my constant love,
Nancy

Dearest Bert,

We have had our first four cases of the Spanish influenza, which I think is a pretty romantic name for a *disease,* don't you? Do you know about it? Has it reached there yet? The Record says it has gone into the trenches because infected boys going over there have taken it with them. I pray to God it does not come to where you are.

It has been terrible here in the States. We were very lucky up to now in Eau Fraiche. It's like a regular plague, Bert, nobody can understand it. Apparently, you get sick all at once, with pains in your eyes and ears (all over your head in fact) and your back and belly, and with a very high fever of 101 or 102 that can last for up to a week or so. A lot of people have been dying from it. Bert, they turn bluer than a whetstone when they die! It's really ghastly! Nobody seems to know whether they die from the flu itself (that's another word for it) or from pneumonia, which can be one of the complications.

Anyway, the Record had a headline in this morning's paper, and also a story about the four bona fide cases that were discovered in town yesterday. I don't know any of the people who were stricken. Two of them live over on Mechanic Street, and one is over on Beaufleuve near the furniture factory, and the last one (the name sounds familiar, do you know anybody named Victor Meining?) is out toward the peninsula (but nowhere near your house, Bert). I guess they must have had some wind of this as early ago as last week, because that was when Mr. Humphries, the county health officer, ordered all the theaters and saloons shut down. (Quite unfortunate, too, because the Dolly Sisters were supposed to be coming to The Wisconsin.) Apparently crowds are very dangerous, and enclosed places are to be avoided, though I can't understand how this fits with what the Record said we should do, namely Stay Home And Close All The Windows. There's a poem we were reciting here in Eau Fraiche even before these four cases were reported, and it goes like this, Bert—

> *I had a little bird*
> *Its name was Enza*
> *I opened the window*
> *And in flew Enza.*

(Do you get it? It's influenza.)

I do hope this does not become an epidemic like in other parts of the country. But most of all, I hope it does not reach *you*, my darling, because you have enough on your mind, and you must stay strong and well and come back home to me when this terrible war is over.

You are of more value to me than many sparrows, so please be careful.

Your Nancy

October 4, 1918

Dearest Bert,

I have not had any mail from you since your letter of September 21st. I know you are not permitted to tell me where you are (and they do a very nice job, I must say, of making your letters almost unreadable) but I got the feeling from your last letter that you were in training again someplace, and now I don't know what to think. Please do be careful, wherever you are, and tell your buddy Timothy that my prayers go up for him as well.

Did you get the candy I sent? Clara and I made it one Saturday morning, and then went downtown to the Red Cross center on Fifth Street, where we rolled bandages all day. Bert, I hate to tell you this, but Montgomery Ambrose was killed in France two weeks ago, his mother still doesn't know where or how, all she got was notification, poor woman. You remember him, he was always doing imitations of Eddie Foy, he was a nice sweet person. Oh Bert, I worry all the time about you. Please, please, *please* be careful.

Things have not been too good here in Eau Fraiche, though we still hope and pray the flu will pass over us quickly, the way it has in some other towns. There were seven new cases in the past two days, Bert. The Board of Health has taken over the row of empty stores on Buffalo Street, where my father used to have the agency, do you remember? (There is talk, by the way, of changing the name of the street to Pershing Street. I think it comes up at the town meeting next Thursday.) Anyway, they are going to use those buildings, which were supposed to be condemned for the new mall and town administration offices, as an emergency hospital until the flu is gone. Dr. Wheeler has been appointed the whole team and the little

114

dog under the wagon, which is pretty good since he's an eye, ear, nose and throat man, who has had a lot of experience with bronchitis, laryngitis, and the like. The first thing he did was to ask the Town Board to pass an ordinance against expectoration (which is spitting—I didn't know myself until I looked it up!) with a fine of fifteen dollars if you're caught doing it.

In addition, Mr. Larsen, the superintendent of schools, has ordered the elementary school and also Juneau High closed until further notice, and nobody will be going to church this Sunday because all the churches have been shut down, too. This "preparedness" may sound silly, Bert (we were "prepared" for the war you're now fighting, too, and yet you're thousands of miles away from me today) but the situation could become very serious. In Chicago last week, according to the Record, ninety-two people died of the flu. And at Camp Grant in Rockford, more than ten thousand soldiers are supposed to be sick with it. As you can see, this is not just a tempest in a glass of water.

Please write to me soon. I am forever,

Your Nancy

October 6, 1918

Bert darling,

What excitement!

We caught a spy!

Last night, Mr. Breier was making his rounds at the rubber plant when he came upon this small man carrying a satchel. Well, he challenged him, and the man ran pell-mell for a cat race. Mr. Breier, who's got very weak eyes, fired two shots after him and miraculously hit him in the leg. It turns out that the man's name is Heinrich Schumann, and he was carrying *bombs* in the satchel, Bert, obviously to sabotage the plant! And what's more, they say he was also carrying *influenza* germs in that bag of his, probably in little bottles or something! Can you beat that!

Actually, and thank God for this, the flu seems to have quieted down here in Eau Fraiche. We have had only two deaths from it, and luckily only three new cases in the entire county. They had put signs up all over the city telling us to keep our bedroom windows *OPEN* (!) now, to prevent influenza, pneumonia and tuberculosis, but I guess the new advice is working because, as I say, we seem to be over the worst part of it. We have been quite fortunate, Bert. The rest of the country is just devastated by this germ or whatever it is, God forgive me for gloating over our own good luck.

Guess what? Your sister came home from Arizona with her husband yesterday, and he's not half so bad as everyone made him out to be. Actually, he's sort of handsome (though not as handsome as you) in a dark mysterious way. There's no doubt he's an Indian, Bert; in fact, Kate seems quite proud of his Apache background. She had her little boy with her, and he's a good-looking child with Kate's good nose and mouth, and his father's brooding eyes. She is pregnant again, I don't know whether you knew that or not. We all had a marvelous supper at your house last night. Your father was a little surly toward Oscar at first, but he came around after a few drinks, and they began swapping stories about lumber camps. Oscar used to sell harnesses on the road, so he naturally got to visit a lot of the camps, including those in Eau Fraiche. Your father is in the best of health, by the way. He told me he gained seventeen pounds in the past three months, which I can believe because your mother is such a marvelous cook! Oscar and Kate and their little boy were staying at the United in town, and they dropped me off on their way in. Oscar has a brand-new Reo, so I guess selling tractor parts is very good business these days.

Bert, are you writing to me? I have not received a single letter since yrs of September 21. I love you with all my heart. Do be very careful.

Your Nancy

Tuesday, October 8

Dearest Bert,

You may drive out nature with a pitchfork, yet she will come back.

The epidemic is full upon us. Since I wrote you Sunday there have been six hundred cases reported, with thirty deaths in the last twenty-four hours alone. The furniture factory has been closed, and there is talk of shutting down the rubber plant as well, even though everyone knows how important it is to the war effort. A new emergency hospital has been opened at the empty McIver mansion on the peninsula, and Mayor Hutcheson has ordered ten big Army tents set up on the lawn outside. There are seven Eau Fraiche policemen riding horses around town, Bert, to keep people away from the saloons, where the fools have been trying to sneak in through the back doors. Everyone in town must wear a gauze mask over the nose and mouth, and you can be fined fifty dollars if you're caught without one in public. Everything is closed, my dearest, schools, churches, saloons, theaters, even most of the restaurants. (Claude Rabillon died Sunday night, and the county health officer ordered the Lorraine to shut its doors at once.) Even the library is closed because it's feared the flu can be spread by the public circulation of books. We do not know what it is, Bert, and we do not know what to do.

There are some who say it is carried by dust, there are others who say it is not a disease at all but really a contamination of the air caused by the use of so much poison gas in Europe. Some say it is caused by a bacillus, and others say by a virus. I don't know what either of those are, Bert. I only know that people are dying, and I am scared out of my wits. It is as if God has sent a scourge to punish His foolish creations who insist on destroying each other and the human race.

Oh my darling, please forgive me. I know you are in constant danger, and I must not trouble you further. Please be careful. I love you.

Your Nancy

P.S. I took some cookies to the Post Office yesterday, but Mr. Aubrey asked whether I was sending foodstuffs to you, and when I said I was, he told me he could not permit it because the contamination might spread further among the troops. Are you well, my dearest? Please, please, *please* write to me, I am frantic with worry.

N.

October 9, 1918

Dear Bert,

My father was stricken with influenza today. He had been complaining of a headache all day Monday, but he has frequent headaches, you know, and we thought nothing of it. (Actually, I think we were all too frightened to

117

accept it as the possible beginning of something.) But then, oh Bert, he just began to *look* so sick, I've never seen him look that way in my life. His eyes got red, and his nose was all stuffed up, and he had this terrible backache, and then of course the fever came and we sent for Dr. Henning who could not come until six o'clock tonight. There are only three doctors in town, as you know, and they've been making calls to other parts of the county as well. People have been taking turns driving them, and they've been sleeping in the automobiles between patients, and working around the clock Dr. Henning told us on the phone to give Daddy quinine and aspirin, but that didn't help at all, and when he finally arrived, poor Daddy was burning alive with fever. He had him removed at once to the McIver place down-peninsula, and we will not be allowed to see him until he's better because the house has been quarantined.

As I write, I can see through my window to the Emerson porch across the street, where funeral services are being conducted for Louise Emerson, who died last night. It is forbidden now to keep the bodies of victims in a closed room where others might become infected.

I am so frightened.

I have to make this short, my darling. Meg is in tears, and I must go to her.

I love you,
Nancy

Friday, October 11

Oh my darling!

A treasure trove of mail today! Fourteen letters from you, only two of them dated, and the same postmark on each of the envelopes, so that I had to read them all through once, and then sort them out as best I could and read them through a second time in sequence. (One of your letters said you had no idea what day it was. Just keep safe, Bert, and keep writing to me, and I won't care if they're all dated September 31st.)

I know you're in the Meuse-Argonne, even though you're not permitted to say. The newspapers are full of nothing else. There is talk here that the war will be ending soon, that this offensive will be the one to break the German resistance. I pray day and night that this is so. I have bought a huge map of France, and I have been trying to follow the advance, figuring out loud to myself—Nantillois is where Bert must have been when he wrote this letter and this one was written in Cierges, and this is where he fell into the stream, Gesnes, trying to be with you, my love, trying to share it with you.

We have not been allowed out of the house since Daddy took sick, but we have been in telephone contact with the emergency hospital. It is so difficult to get through because so many families have sick people there, but we managed to talk to Dr. Henning early this afternoon. He said there has been no change in Daddy's condition. The fever is still with him, and there is nothing we can do but wait and pray. What cannot be cured must be endured, my dear Bert. When they took him away Wednesday, Meg began screaming and yelling, which didn't help matters at all. We are very much aware of death in this town, it has become a frequent caller. As they carried Daddy out of the house unconscious, I think all of us felt we might never see him alive again, God forbid. And Meg gave voice to our fears, hitting at the men who were carrying him out on a stretcher, their faces masked, silent in white, while across the street we knew Louise Emerson, thirty-two years old and pregnant, was dead. We gave Meg some hot milk and put her to bed, but I heard her whimpering in her sleep all night long, and the sound was a reminder of what we all had felt when we saw Daddy so helpless that way.

I am absolutely exhausted, my darling. It has been a difficult few days. Thank God I've heard from you at last, and know that you are safe and well. I am going to take some aspirin now, and then go upstairs to read your letters through again before I go to bed.

I love you,
Nancy

Sunday, October 13

Dear Bertram,

I am writing this in Nancy's stead, and with great trepidation. I know you will begin to worry if you do not hear from her as usual, but at the same time I don't want to add to your burden by bringing you bad news. I must

119

tell you, however, that Nancy has been taken sick with influenza.

It was quite sudden, Bertram. She went to sleep with a headache Friday night, and yesterday morning we had to send her to the hospital as her fever had gone up to a hundred and three degrees. She is still very sick, Bertram, and we are all praying for her recovery. I will write to you daily. I pray God that you are safe.

Yours truly,
Clara

October 14, 1918

Dear Bertram,

There is no improvement in Nancy's condition. She is still feverish, and Dr. Henning fears that the influenza may lead to pneumonia. My father is recovering. It is our hope that he will be out of the hospital very shortly. This is his third day without fever, and Dr. Henning says he is no longer in any danger. We hope and pray that Nancy will have the strength to overcome this terrible disease as he did.

God keep you safe, Bertram.

Yours truly,
Clara

Tuesday, October 15

Dear Bertram,

Dr. Henning was here just a short time ago, and I'm afraid the news is neither good nor bad. Nancy's fever went down to a hundred and one yesterday, but is up to a hundred and three again today. Her lungs seem clear, with no symptoms of either bronchitis or pneumonia, but Dr. Henning is afraid the influenza may have caused some other infection which he cannot as yet diagnose. I will of course let you know as soon as there is any further word.

My father came home today. He is still a bit weak, but seems anxious to get back to work.

God keep you safe.

Yours truly,
Clara

I received all three of Clara's letters on the same day, October 21. It was the day after Timothy Bear got killed in the Clairs-Chênes woods. He had been lying not three feet away from me when the German shell exploded. We had both thrown ourselves headlong into the dirt seconds before it hit. Timothy did not get up after the explosion. He lay silent and motionless with one hand still clasped over the base of his skull, just below the protective line of his helmet. There was no blood on him, no scorched and smoking fabric to indicate he'd been hit. I thought at first he was merely taking a longer time than usual to get to his feet again. I crawled over to him, and I said, "Timothy? Are you okay?" and he did not answer. And then I saw the steel sliver that had pierced the top of his helmet, sticking out of the metal and the skull beneath it like a rusty railroad spike. "Timothy?" I said again, but I knew that he was dead.

The next day, the 33rd Division on our right was relieved by the French 15th Colonial, who brought in mail for us, and with it Clara's three letters. I had not cried when Timothy Bear was killed. There is something in war, you do not cry, it is almost as if the person never existed. But now, reading Clara's letters, I began to weep because I was certain I would lose Nancy, too, and then nothing in the world would matter. They thought I was shell-shocked at first. I cried all during the attacks on La Mi-Noel and the Bois de Forêt and the small woods southwest of Clery-le-Grand, cried throughout the mopping-up operations on October 24. I did not stop crying until we were relieved by the 5th Division on October 27, and sent back to Montfaucon, leaving our artillery behind in support.

A letter from Eau Fraiche was waiting for me upon my arrival there.

Sunday, October 20

Hello, darling,

Clara says she's been afraid to write to you for almost a week, so let me assure you here and now that I am alive and well and back home again and in receipt of two letters from you, so I know that you're safe, too, and that's all that matters to me.

They thought I was dying.

I'll tell you something, Bert, *I* thought so, too!

Oh boy, Bert, what a time it was! I guess Clara told you

121

it started with an awful headache which I didn't pay any mind to because I figured it was caused by all the worry over Daddy and everything. But the next morning I tried to get out of bed and almost fell on the floor, I was so dizzy. And there was a terrible knife pain behind my eyes, as if someone was inside trying to cut his way out! Mother took my temperature, and I seemed to be all right, but that night it shot up from normal to a hundred and three and Dr. Henning packed me off to McIver. (They are now calling people like Daddy and me, who go to the emergency hospital and manage to get out of it alive, "McIver Survivors.") I didn't think I would make it, Bert. I kept having terrible nightmares, all about Hell and being burned alive at the stake, and this went on for more than a week, which is quite unusual since if you're going to get well at all it usually takes three or four days for the fever to pass. Dr. Henning tells me, though, that I also had a touch of encephalitis, and that I'm "a very lucky little girl."

I have to tell you something, Bert.

I can't hear too well in my right ear. Dr. Henning says this was caused by the infection in the auditory center, and may be temporary or permanent, but that in any event it is a small price to pay. I feel terrible about it because I don't think it's exactly feminine to be saying "How's that?" all the time, do you? Will you still love me if I have to carry around a horn?

Clara is here with some aspirin and some hot milk, so I'd better take it and close the light. She has been an absolute dear all through this. I may even let her read your next letter (if you promise not to say any of those *awful* things in it!) Seriously, Bert, I think it might be a good idea if you wrote to her personally, if you have the time, that is. She was so worried that she'd done the wrong thing in telling you I was sick, and I know a reassuring word from you would set her mind at ease.

Keep safe and well, Bert, and let's hope the war will soon be over as they say it will be. Then you can come home and marry me, and we will live happily ever after, okay?

I love you,
Miss Nancy Ear-Trumpet

122

November ❦ ❦ ❦

The train had come down from Boston, and it was jam-packed when it stopped at New Haven. She had her crap spread out all over the seat, two valises, a guitar, and a duffle bag, as if she were going on a grand tour of the Bahamas instead of probably just home for the Thanksgiving weekend. I had come through three cars looking for a seat, and when I spotted her living in the luxury of this little nest she'd built, I stopped and said, "Excuse me, is this taken?"

She had dark brown eyes and long black hair parted in the middle of her head, falling away straight on both sides of her face, framing an oval that gave a first impression of being too intensely white, lips without lipstick, cheeks high and a bit too Vogue-ish, a finely sculpted nose and a firm chin with a barely perceptible cleft. The look she gave me was one of extreme patience directed at a moron, her glance clearly saying *Can't you see it's taken?*

"Well, *is* it?" I asked.

"I've got my stuff on it," she answered. Her voice sounded New Canaan or mid-Eighties Park Avenue. It rankled immediately.

"I see that," I said, "but is anyone *sitting* here?"

"*I'm* sitting here."

"*Besides* you."

"No."

"Then would you mind putting your stuff up on the rack?"

Her look of patience turned instantly to one of annoyance. I was forcing her to move her furniture out of the apartment just after she'd painted and settled in. She turned the look off, got up without so much as glancing at me again, lifted the guitar onto the rack and then reached for the heavy duffle.

"I'll get it," I said.

"Don't bother," she said.

She was wearing sandals and tight chinos, and I discov-

ered her backside as she lifted the duffle up onto the rack
with a great show of delicate college girl maidenhood being
strained to its physical limits. The gray sweatshirt she had
on over the chinos rode up as she lifted one of the valises,
revealing a well-defined spine, the halves of her back
curving into it like a pale ripe apple into its stem. She
turned to pick up the other valise, and I saw MIT's seal on
the front of the sweatshirt, flanked by a rounded pair of
breasts too freely moving to have been confined by a bra.
She saw my goofy leer, made a face, hoisted the valise up
onto the rack, slid back into the seat, cupped her chin in
her hand, and stared through the window.

"Thank you," I said.

She did not answer.

"Look," I said, "your *bags* didn't pay for a seat, you
know."

"I moved them, didn't I?" she said, without turning
from the window.

"Okay," I said.

"Okay," she said, but she still did not turn from the
window.

"You coming down from Radcliffe?" I said.

"What gives you *that* impression?" she said, and turned
from the window at last, and assumed again that patient
expression of someone talking to a cretin.

"You sound like a Radcliffe girl."

"And just how do Radcliffe girls *sound?*" she asked, *so*
annoyed by my presence on her turf, and *so* confident of
her own allure in sweatshirt and chinos, brown eyes burning with a low, angry, smoky intensity, white face pale
against the cascading black hair, completely stepping
down several levels in the social strata by deigning to utter
in her New Canaan nasal twang anything at all to someone like *me,* who should have been up a tree someplace
eating unpeeled bananas instead of trying to start a conversation with the WASP princess of the western world. I
was already half in love with her.

"Radcliffe girls sound rude and surly and sarcastic," I
said.

"So do Yalies," she said.

"*Are* you from Radcliffe?"

"No, I'm from B.U."

"Is that a school?"

"Ha-ha," she said. "You're from Yale, all right."

124

"How can you tell?"

"I can tell," she said in dismissal, and turned to look through the window again, pulling her long legs up under her.

"Must be fascinating, watching all those telephone poles go by," I said.

"Yes, it is."

"My name's Wat Tyler," I said.

She turned to me with a reproachful look. Certain she had tipped to a put-on, she said, "Mine's Anne of Bohemia."

"Hey, how'd you know that?" I said, surprised.

"How'd I know what?"

"About Wat Tyler. Not many people do."

"Luck," she said.

"Come on, how'd you know?"

"I had to do a paper on the Four Horsemen of the Apocalypse."

"What's that got to do with Wat Tyler?"

"Nothing. But that's how I got to him."

"How?"

"Well . . . can *you* name the Four Horsemen?"

"Sure. Plague, Pestilence . . ."

"Wrong."

"You're not talking about the Notre Dame foot . . ."

"No, the Bible."

"Plague . . ."

"Wrong."

"I give up."

"I'll give you a clue."

"Give me a clue."

"They're on different colored horses—white, red, black, and pale."

"Pale what?"

"Just pale."

"I still give up."

"Death's on the pale horse," she said. "War's on . . ."

". . . the black one."

"Wrong, the red one. *Famine's* on the black one."

"Then Plague's on the white one."

"There *isn't* any Plague."

"*Has* to be a Plague."

"That's what I thought, too. But there isn't."

"Then who's on the white horse?"

125

"Christ. At least, a lot of people *suppose* it was Christ. Nobody really knows for sure who John the Divine meant."

"But *you* thought it was Plague."

"Yes. That's why I went to the library to see what they had."

"What'd they have?"

"Plagues, epidemics, blights, *everything*. But there was a very *popular* plague back in 1348 . . ."

"Popular?"

"In that it was widespread. The Black Death, you know?"

"From the Tony Curtis movie of the same name," I said.

"It was bubonic."

"It certainly was."

"Killed a third of England's population."

"Sound of Music was even worse."

"Anyway," she said, and raised her eyebrows and quirked her mouth as though in exasperation, but it was clear she was enjoying herself now, feeling comfortable enough with me to be able to make a fleeting facial comment on my corny humor, and then move right on unperturbed to the very serious business at hand, which was how she happened to know anything at all about Wat Tyler who had been killed by the mayor of London in 1381, lo, those many years ago, when both of us were still only little kids. "Anyway," she said again, and turned her brown eyes full onto my face, demanding my complete attention, as though knowing intuitively it was wandering to other less important topics, never once suspecting, heh-heh, that I was lost in thought of her alone, of how absolutely adorable she looked when she struck her professorial pose, relating tales of poxes and such, and stared back into her lady-hypnotist eyes and wanted to bark like a dog or flap like a chicken, *"Any*way, when I was looking *up* all this crap, I learned that a couple of the labor statutes put into effect around the time of the plague were thought to have caused the great peasant rebellion of 1381, do you see?" she said.

"You have a tiny little beauty spot right at the corner of your mouth," I said.

"Yes," she said. "Listen, are you sure *you* know who Wat Tyler was?"

126

"Oh sure," I said. "He led the great peasant rebellion of 1381. Against Richard II."

"So what did I just say?"

"I don't know, what *did* you just say?"

"I said that certain labor statutes . . ."

"That's right . . ."

". . . caused the rebellion of 1381."

"So?"

"So Richard II was married to Anne of Bohemia."

"I know."

"So that's why when you said you were Wat Tyler, I said I was Anne of Bohemia. Because when I was looking up *plagues* in the library . . . the hell with it," she said. "What's your real name?"

"That's my real name."

"Wat Tyler, huh?"

"*Walter* Tyler. Everybody calls me Wat, though. Except my grandfather sometimes. What's yours?"

"Dana. Don't laugh."

"Dana what?"

"Castelli. Guess who *I'm* named after?"

"I can't imagine."

"You *can* imagine."

"Oh no! Really?"

"Really. I was born in 1946, right after my mother saw him in *The Best Years of Our Lives*."

"When in 1946?"

"Was I born, or did she see the picture?"

"Born."

"December. Two days before Christmas."

"So what did you find out about him?"

"Dana Andrews?"

"No, Plague. On the white horse."

"I told you, there was no Plague. Only War, Famine, Death, and Jesus."

"Then all your research was for nothing."

"I didn't mind. I like libraries." She smiled again. "Besides, it gives me something to talk about on trains."

"Listen," I said, "I'm really sorry I asked you to move your bags."

"Don't be silly. I was being a hog."

"Would you like a beer or something?"

"I don't think there's a bar car."

"*Has* to be a bar car."

127

"Had to be a Plague, too, but there wasn't."

"You watch the seats," I said. "I'll check it out."

In the next to the last car on the train, I ran into Scott Dundee who was now a freshman at Tufts and who was sitting with a girl he introduced as "Gail Rogers, Simmons '67," the same asshole he'd always been. He asked if he could give me a lift home from Stamford, but I lied and said I was being picked up, preferring a taxi to his Great Swordsman company, and then hurrying into the last car, knowing by then of course that Dana Castelli had been right, there *was* no bar car. I lurched and staggered my way forward again, the New Haven Railroad performing in its usual glassy-smooth style, and when I got back to where she was sitting I nearly dropped dead on the spot. The guitar, the duffle bag, and both suitcases were piled onto the seat again, and Dana was turned away from the aisle, legs up under her, one elbow on the window sill, staring out at the goddamn telephone poles. I felt, I don't *know* what, anger, rejection, embarrassment, stupidity, clumsiness, everything. And then, suddenly, she turned from the window, whipping her head around so quickly that her black hair spun out and away from her face like a Revlon television commercial, and her grin cracked sharp and clean and wide, confirming her joke, and we both burst out laughing.

That was the real beginning.

We talked all the way to Stamford.

She told me her father was Italian and her mother Jewish, this WASP princess of the western world. They had met while he was still a budding psychoanalyst in medical school, an ambition that cut no ice at all with her mother's father, who objected to the marriage and who threatened to have this "Sicilian gangster" castrated or worse by some gangster friends of his own, he being the owner of a kosher restaurant on Fordham Road in the Bronx and therefore familiar with all kinds of Mafia types who rented him linens and collected his garbage. Joyce Gelb, for such was her mother's maiden name, was then a student at Hunter College and running with a crowd the likes of which had only recently signed petitions for the release of the Scottsboro Boys. She wasn't about to take criticism of her Sicilian gangster, who in reality was descended from a mixture of Milanese on his mother's side and Veronese on his father's and who anyway had blue

128

eyes which she adored. Joyce told her father he was a bigot and a hypocrite besides, since he hadn't set foot inside
a synagogue since her mother's death eight years ago, when
he had said the Kaddish and promptly begun playing
house with his cashier, a busty blond specimen of twenty-
four. The couple, Joyce Gelb and Frank Castelli, eloped in
the summer of 1941, fleeing to Maryland, where they
were married by a justice of the peace in Elkton, Frank
constantly glancing over his shoulder for signs of pursuing
mohelim. In 1942 the Castellis bought a small house in
Hicksville, Long Island. Secure from the draft (he had
been classified 4-F because of his asthma) he began an-
alyzing the neurotics in Hempstead and environs.

"Do you know the kind of town Hicksville was?" Dana
said. "When I was still a kid, the suggestion came up that
they should change the name of the town to something
better, you know? Like there are some towns on Long
Island with really beautiful Indian names—Massapequa,
Ronkonkoma, Syosset—and even some very nice, well,
suburban-sounding names like Bethpage and Lynbrook
and, well you know. So guess what? The town fathers
objected! They actually preferred *Hicksville,* can you
imagine that? Which is just what it is, of course—
Hicksville, U.S.A., I lived there until I was thirteen years
old; the most thrilling thing that happened was the erec-
tion of a shopping center, you should pardon the expression."

At the age of thirteen, as she was entering puberty
("and beginning to *blossom,*" Dana said, and winked and
gave me a burlesque comic's elbow), Dr. Castelli moved
his practice and his family to Park Avenue . . .

"In the mid-Eighties, right?" I said.

"Seventy-ninth," Dana said.

"Close," I said.

"No cigar," she said.

. . . and Dana began attending the Dalton School, no
mean feat for a kid whose Italian grandfather still ran a
latticeria on First Avenue, and whose Jewish grandfather
made a good living keeping the fleishedig plates from the
milchedig. She was now, she told me, an English major at
Boston University, and she hoped one day to write jokes
for television comedians, which I might think a strange
and curious ambition for a girl, but after all some of the

funniest people in America were women, witness Lady Bird Johnson, she said, without cracking a smile.

We began talking about Kennedy then, both of us realizing with a sudden shock that he had been killed just a year ago, and then doing what people inevitably did when talking about that day in November remembering with almost total recall exactly where they were and what they were doing when the news broke ("I could hear them saying, 'The head, the head,' and I listened in bewilderment and fear because I was sure now that something terrible had happened to *me,* that they were all talking about *my* head, that maybe my neck was twisted at a funny angle, maybe there was a line of blood trickling from under my white helmet."). Dana had been in her father's office, necking on his couch with a boy from CCNY, Friday being Dr. Castelli's day at Manhattan General, where he worked with addicts on the Narcotics Service. The radio had been tuned to WABC, Bob Dayton spewing machine-gun chatter and canned goodies from The Beatles, when the announcer broke in to say that Kennedy's motorcade had been fired upon, the news causing Dana to leap up from the couch not a moment too soon, being as she was in a somewhat vulnerable position just then.

"What do you mean?" I said.

"You know," she said.

"Oh," I said, and felt violently protective all at once, ready to strangle the snot-nosed, pimply-faced City College rapist who had dared put his hand under her skirt or whatever it was he'd been doing.

"Well, you know," Dana said.

"Sure," I said.

Which led us into talking about the MIT sweatshirt she was wearing, and how she had come into possession of it so early in her college career, the fall term at B.U. having started only in September.

She told me that she had met this dreamy boy at the Fogg Museum one rainy Saturday (Oh, please, I said, where are the violins?) and he'd turned out to be a very sensitive young man who had managed to get out of East Berlin immediately after the Russians lifted their blockade in 1949. (A German, I said, that's real groovy. What was his father during the war? A baker?) His father, Dana promptly informed me, was Jewish and in fact a survivor

130

of Auschwitz, which, I might remember, was a German concentration camp, in fact *the* camp where four million Jews were annihilated, in fact. His father had chosen to continue living in Germany . . .

"What's this guy's name?" I said.

"I don't see what difference that makes," she said.

"I like to know who we're *talking* about, that's all," I said.

"His name is Max Eckstein," she said.

"He *sounds* like a Max Eckstein," I said.

"The way *I* sounded like a Radcliffe girl, right?" she said.

"All right, go on, go on," I said.

. . . his father had chosen to continue living in Germany, Dana told me, rather than emigrating to Israel or America because he felt that Hitler had almost succeeded in destroying the entire German Jewish community, and if there were to be *any* Jews at *all* in Germany, some survivors had to elect to stay and raise their families there. But whereas he had been slow to recognize what was happening in Germany in '38 and '39, he immediately realized in 1949 that the Communists were constructing in Berlin a state not too dissimilar from Hitler's. He had packed up his wife Dora, his seven-year-old daughter Anna, and his five-year-old son Max, and together they had fled to America. Anna had since married a football player for . . .

"A what?" I said.

"A football player. For the New York Giants," Dana said.

"How'd a German refugee get to meet a . . . ?"

"She's quite American," Dana said. "She was only *seven* when she came here, you know."

"Yes, and little Maxie was five."

"Little Maxie is now twenty," Dana said. "And not so little."

Her relationship with Max, she went on to say, was amazingly close, considering the fact she'd known him such a short time, actually only a month and a half, she'd met him in the middle of October on a . . .

"Yes," I said, "a rainy Saturday, I know."

"He's a very nice person. You'd like him."

"I hate him," I said.

"Why?"

"Just how close *is* this relationship?" I asked.

"Close," Dana said.

"Are you engaged or something?"

"No, but . . ."

"Going steady?"

"Well, we don't have *that* kind of an agreement. I mean, I can *see* anybody I *want* to, this isn't the Middle Ages, you know. I just haven't *wanted* to go out with anyone else."

"Well, suppose I asked you out?" I said.

"Well, I don't know," she said. "I mean, I don't know what you have in mind."

"You mean you want to know where I'd take you?"

"No, no. I mean the relationship between Max and me is very close, and I haven't really any *need* for what you might have in mind, *if* it's what you have in mind. *That's* what I mean."

"*What* do you mean?" I said.

"I mean Max and I are very, well, *close,*" she said, and shrugged. "Do you see?"

"No."

"Well, I really don't think I need spell it out," she said.

"Oh," I said.

"So if you want to just go to a movie or something, or maybe take a walk if you're in the city one weekend . . ."

"Gee, thanks a whole heap," I said.

"Well, there's no sense being dishonest."

"You're sure Maxie won't disapprove? I certainly wouldn't want to get him upset."

"His name is *Max,*" Dana said.

"Say, maybe the *three* of us could go to a movie together," I said. "You think Max might be able to come down one weekend?"

"He's carrying a very heavy program," Dana said.

"Then I guess we'll just have to go alone," I said. "How about Thursday?"

"Thursday's Thanksgiving."

"Friday then."

"All right. So long as you understand . . ."

"I understand only one thing."

"Which is what?"

"Which is that I'm going to marry you."

132

December ✤ ✤

My instructor at Gunter Field in Montgomery, Alabama, was a man named Ralph Di Angelo, who had been a civilian pilot before the war, and who—because of the extreme need for trained pilots—had been taken into the Army with a first lieutenant's commission and immediately assigned to Gunter, where he taught what the Air Force called Basic Flying. Di Angelo was a Service Pilot, and because there was a tiny letter S on his wings, we all called them Shit Wings.

I had gone from Preflight School at Maxwell Field to Primary Flying School in Orangeburg, South Carolina, and from there had reported directly and without furlough to Gunter Field. There were six flying squadrons on the field, each with about a hundred cadets in them. I was in the 379th School Squadron, Class 44J, the 44 designating the year I was expected to be awarded my silver pilot's wings, the J designating the month and date this event would take place, the first half of May, hopefully.

This was my third day at Gunter, and nobody including myself was feeling too terribly happy just then because we had not been given any leave after Primary and we'd already been told there'd be no Christmas furloughs, either. My father had made plans to come down to Montgomery to visit with me on Christmas Day, but Montgomery was a far cry from Chicago, and besides, I was getting very very tired. At Orangeburg, I had flown the PT-17, which was possibly the most rugged plane ever built, strong enough for aerobatics like snap rolls and Immelmanns, with a fixed-pitch prop and a 225-horsepower Lycoming engine, blue with yellow wings—my instructor called his plane "Yellowjacket," the name stenciled onto the fuselage just back of the cowling, with a sting-tailed bee, blue with black stripes, yellow-winged like the plane itself, hovering over the black lettering.

I'd had a total of seventy hours in that plane, my instructor being a man who had once run a small airport in

133

Iowa and who was now doing his bit for the Army by making life miserable for aviation cadets. His name was Captain Felix Burmann, and he was a son of a bitch down to his boots. It was rumored that the obstacle course at Maxwell Field (where he had also taught) was named "The Burma Road" in his honor, it being a tortuous winding exhausting piece of real estate that snaked its way around the officers' golf course, and then down by the river as cadets jogged their little hearts out around it. Son of a bitch or no, he had taught me to fly, and I was feeling like a pretty hot pilot by the time I got to Gunter and was introduced to the biggest damn airplane I had ever seen up close in my life, the BT-13, which was fondly, ha, called the Vultee Vibrator, or so Lieutenant Di Angelo told us the first day we marched out behind him to the flight line.

The lieutenant was olive-complected, with curly black hair, dark brown eyes, and a black mustache. Short and somewhat chunky, he kept a dead cigar stub clamped between his teeth at all times, reminding me of Mr. Fornaseri who ran the candy store on Division and Dearborn back in Chicago and who would not be caught dead without his guinea stinker in his mouth. Mr. Fornaseri was from Palermo, and it was reasonable to believe that Lieutenant Di Angelo could have easily blended with the population there—though how he would have fared in Milan was another matter. He came, he told us, from Elmira, New York, and had quickly added, *"Not* the prison there," a quip we were all too frightened to laugh at. He had then gone on to say that we five cadets would be taught personally by him during our stay at Gunter Field, and that we would be doing all our flying in the BT-13, "this airplane here, which is fondly called the Vultee Vibrator, as you will soon find out."

"It's got an unpleasant reputation," he had said, "but you'll learn to develop a great deal of respect for it. I know it looks enormous to you, but that's only because it is; the engine under that housing's got four hundred and fifty horses in it. I realize you're all aces already, but you've never flown anything with a controllable pitch propeller, or mixture controls, and this is also going to be the first time you're flying without a helmet and goggles because there's a canopy to close over your head, as you may have noticed. You'll be wearing earphones instead

134

because you'll be in constant radio contact with the tower —that's another first, you've never flown a plane with a radio in it before.

"Now you all heard what the squadron commander told you a little while ago, and I'm going to repeat it now because he was absolutely right, and you might as well understand it. Nobody's going to coddle you here at Gunter. Both me and this airplane are going to be a lot less forgiving of your mistakes. In Primary, you learned how to take an airplane up and how to bring it down, but here in Basic we're going to teach you to use it as a tactical weapon, and I can tell you the pressure's going to be a lot tougher than it was in Primary, no matter *where* you went to Primary—we get them here from all over, believe me, and even the best of them have been known to bawl in their second week. The C.O. asked you to look at the man on your left and then at the one on your right because one of you was sure to wash out of here and end up in navigator or bombardier school. Okay. I'm telling you now that out of you five cadets, there's a strong possibility only three of you will make it through Basic, and out of those three, only *one* of you might get through Advanced. So you'd better listen hard and keep your heads moving at all times because you're here to learn to fly and not to fool around. You'll notice that there's a little picture of a burning pitchfork painted behind the cowling of my plane there, and that the name of the plane is 'The Eighth Circle,' and whereas I don't want to *frighten* any of you aces, I also want it clear that I'm going to make life *hell* for you if you don't learn to fly the way I *want* you to fly.

"Now I want one of you to get into the front cockpit and the rest of you on the wings there, and I'll try to familiarize you with the instruments and controls, after which you can feel free to climb into any plane on the field and learn that cockpit inside out and backwards because you'll be talking a blindfold test on it day after tomorrow. You, what's your name, you get in the cockpit. It's going to feel a little strange at first, but don't let that bother you."

That was our first-day introduction to Lieutenant Ralph Di Angelo, who seemed about as pleasant as Captain Burmann, the terror of Orangeburg. (I wondered, in fact, which obstacle course had been named after *him*.) Yester-

135

day, my second day at Gunter, I had gone up for my orientation flight, and today Lieutenant Di Angelo gathered the five of us around him at one of the long tables in the squadron building and chewed on his cigar and said, "Cooper, you want to pay some attention here, or do you want to wash out on your third day?" to which Cooper replied, "No, sir, I'm listening, sir," and Di Angelo said, "Yes, then keep your head moving," and cleared his throat, and in his lovable gravelly Elmira, New York, voice said, "Today we're going to have a demonstration of take-off with the stabilizer back. You'll remember that yesterday I showed you how to fly with the power off, and the stabilizer trimmed for a glide, and you'll remember how hard it was to hold your nose down in flying position when we turned the power on again and rolled the trim-tabs back. As a final check before we fly over to Taylor Field today, we're going to deliberately take off with the stabilizer rolled back about three-quarters, that's approximately the position for landing. I want you to remember that this is what might happen if you forget your cockpit procedure before take-off or are shooting follow-through landings and aren't quick enough to neutralize your trim-tabs.

"Remember that you've got to keep the *attitude* of the airplane constant when you're climbing out of the field, never mind the position of your stick, you're going to have to *fight* that stick in order to keep your nose down. Until I decide to zero the trim-tabs and trim up the ship, you'll be working your right rudder to correct the torque, and you'll be keeping that heavy forward pressure on the stick to compensate for the stabilizer being in the wrong position. Any questions?"

"Yes, sir," Cadet Bollinger, a fuzzy-cheeked boy from Pennsylvania said in his high, almost girlish voice, blue eyes opened wide as if in expectation of a religious miracle. "What happens if we let go of the stick, sir?"

"Bollinger," Lieutenant Di Angelo said, "if you're by yourself, you're dead. I'll be back there today, so presumably nothing will happen. Seriously," he went on, though I hadn't honestly caught any joke, "the nose'll rise, you'll do a snap roll at fifty feet, and you'll end up in the ground. Any other questions?"

Nobody had any other questions.

"Okay," Di Angelo said, "after we've each had a chance

136

at trying to kill ourselves, we're going over to Taylor and shoot some more landings. Murphy, I want them at the ground today, and not three feet in the air. Jacobs, I want your head moving all the time. There are a couple of hundred airplanes in the air around here, and I want you to keep track of all of them whenever you're up there. Okay, Tyler, let's go."

It was a bleak, gray day, penetratingly cold and damp. I was wearing a zippered jump suit over my underwear, fleece-lined leather flying pants and jacket, fleece-lined gloves and boots, but I was still chilly. My parachute tucked up into the small of my back so it wouldn't bang against my ass with each step I took, I followed Di Angelo out to his plane, silvery against the gray day, the blue cowling indicating our squadron, the ramp crowded with planes from all the other squadrons as well, yellow cowlings, red ones, white ones. The Eighth Circle, very funny, I thought, and Di Angelo said, " 'Morning, Harris," to the T-3 who was his crew chief, and who was standing near the propeller. "All right, Tyler," he said to me, "get the log book, and check the red-line entry," the red line being a diagonal mark across a small box, to the right of which were listed all the Army tech orders not yet complied with. If a red cross was marked in the box instead of that diagonal line, it meant the airplane was unsafe to fly and was not to be taken up under any circumstances.

Sitting on my parachute in the front cockpit, with Di Angelo behind me, I fastened my seat belt, and then took off the control lock and verified the freedom of the stick and rudder. I turned on the master electrical switch then, put on my earphones, and tuned in the tower. The radio-interphone switch was on RADIO. I kept watching it from the corner of my eye because I knew that whenever Di Angelo snapped it to INTER from his controls in the rear cockpit, I'd be getting an interphone bleat about something or other I was doing wrong. Nor was a cadet supposed to say anything to his instructor from the moment they got into the airplane to the moment they got out; all the radio squawks would be one-way, from the rear cockpit to the front. I verified that my propeller control was in full-low pitch, set my mixture control full-rich, cracked the throttle, and then hit the primer three or four times.

The switch clicked over to INTER.

"Let's go, Tyler, we haven't got all day here, there's a war waiting."

I pulled the stick back against my belly, and then put my toes on the brakes to make sure they were locked. With my right hand on the magneto switch and my left on the throttle, I stuck my head out of the cockpit and yelled, "Clear?" to Harris.

"Clear!" Harris shouted back.

I moved the magneto switch through 1 and 2, *click, click,* and heard the third *click* as I moved it to BOTH, and hit the starter. The propeller spun and caught. I yanked the stick against my belly again, added throttle, and then pulled back to idle. Picking up the mike in my left hand, I said, "Gunter Tower, this is 0934, over."

"0934, this is your instructor in the rear cockpit," Di Angelo said. "How about switching back to RADIO before trying to contact the tower?"

I immediately turned the switch to RADIO, and said again, "Gunter Tower, this is 0934, over."

"0934, this is Gunter Tower, go ahead."

"0934 on the line, ready to taxi."

"Roger, 0934. You're clear to taxi to runway 27."

"0934, Roger and out."

I signaled to Harris to pull the chocks, my toes on the brakes, the engine ticking over. He yanked them and gave me the thumbs-up signal. I began adding throttle, and the stick suddenly came banging back hard into my belly, jerked by Di Angelo in the back seat, who immediately cut the throttle and snapped the switch to *inter* and shouted, "You forgot to keep your stick back, Tyler! You were adding too much throttle! Keep that damn stick back!"

Rattled, I released the brakes and managed to roll the plane out correctly, turning left past the parked planes on the ramp, and moving straight out onto the taxi strip. Di Angelo's voice erupted into my earphones again.

"Zigzag her down the line, Tyler, how else can you see anything over that big humping engine? Do you want to get us killed before we're off the ground? Keep your head moving!"

Trembling now, hating that goddamn RADIO-INTER switch and wishing it would break off in his left hand, I waited for the other planes to clear, zigzagging down the line past the maintenance hangars and the squadron building, and finally moving into the number-two position for take-off, parked at a ninety-degree angle to the runway.

"All right, Tyler, I've rolled the stabilizer control three-quarters of the way back," Di Angelo said, "and it's going to stay there until I roll it to Neutral when we get up in the air."

I nodded and wet my lips.

"You're about ready for take-off, aren't you?" he said, and I looked ahead to see that the number-one plane had already left. "Is your head up and locked?" he shouted. "Let's keep it moving at all times, Tyler, on the ground as well as in the air, let's see what the hell's *happening* around us, shall we?"

I checked the two mags, my eyes on the tachometer, and moved the prop control all the way to the rear, the engine straining, the sound changing as the prop blades cut the air at a greater angle, and then I put it back into low pitch and returned the throttle to idle. I switched to RADIO, picked up the microphone in my left hand and said, "0934, ready to take off."

"Roger, 0934," the tower said, "clear to take off."

I could not get used to the feel of the stick. I was adding throttle, and the plane was roaring down the runway, but I couldn't get the tail off the ground, and the pressure on the stick was completely strange to me. The huge engine pounded and pulled, the whole plane seemed to be vibrating with the need to break free of gravity, but the tail woud not rise, I could not get her to lift. I remembered what Di Angelo had said about the *attitude* of the plane, concentrate on the *attitude* and never mind what the *controls* are telling you, so I pushed harder on the stick and felt the tail come up only slightly, still refusing to rise completely off the runway, pushed even harder, my arm trembling, the muscles straining, my hand wrapped tight around the resisting shaft of metal that controlled the elevator, pushing, pushing, *What happens if you let go, sir?* The tail was beginning to rise slowly, I could feel her coming up, I kept both feet working the rudders to keep the plane straight, "You're doing well, Tyler," Di Angelo said, "keep the pressure on that stick, keep your nose down, you're getting her off the ground now, there you go, hold her hard, Tyler, don't let go of that stick, keep the pressure on it!" We were making eighty or ninety miles an hour now, the plane was leaving the runway, rising steadily, fifty feet, climbing smoothly into the air, a hundred feet, still climbing, we had *not* done a snap roll, we had *not* flipped over and hit the ground. From the tail of my eye, I saw the trim-tab control move forward as Di Angelo shoved it into the Neutral position.

"All right," he said, "climb out of this traffic and level off at 1500 feet, we'll be flying southeast to Taylor Field. You're still not looking around enough, Tyler. Close your goddamn canopy. And stop feeling so fucking proud of yourself," he added, even though he could not see my grin from the rear cockpit.

We walked around the field on Christmas Day, my father and I.

We did not talk much at first. A noisy wet wind was blowing in fiercely off the highway, discouraging conversation. We walked briskly, our strides almost identical, somewhat duckfooted, frankly unattractive. I was an inch shorter than my father, with the same angular build, the same blue eyes and high cheekbones, the same nose my mother used to call "the beak of Caesar, the Roman greaser," the same thin-lipped mouth. To the single hardy cadet who approached us from the north, we must have looked like differently dressed twins skirting the edge of the parade grounds there, my father with one gloved hand clutching his Homburg to his head, the other in the pocket of his black coat; I with my garrison cap tilted jauntily, the collar of my short overcoat pulled up high around my ears like a raunchy ace.

When my father began talking, his first words were carried away by the wind. I turned toward him and squinted into his face, straining to hear him, because I thought at first he might be saying something important. But he only wanted to know how my training was going, whether or not they were really teaching me to fly because what would matter most when I got over there was how well I knew my job. I told him that my instructor in Primary had taught me all sorts of combat tricks, and then I explained how much I was enjoying Basic, where I was flying the 450-horsepower trainer, and how I was looking forward to Advanced, where I hoped to start flying two-engine planes in preparation for the P-38, assuming of course that the Army didn't have other plans for me—like perhaps training me for a single-engine fighter plane or, fate worse than death, one of the big four-engine bombers. Ferrying a bomber over Germany, I told my father, wasn't exactly my idea of fun.

My father said that none of it was fun, and the sooner I learned that, the better off I'd be. Oh yes, he said, he knew how anxious I was to get over there, a young man likes to be where the action is, likes to feel he's helping to make history. He could understand my frame of mind, he said, because he'd felt exactly the same way back in 1918 when he'd hurried off to join the Army and do his share in winning the Great War. Of course, he said, we don't call it that any more, do we, Will, the Great War? Which may indicate *some* measure of maturity on the part of the American people since there's no such thing as a *great* war, is there?

I didn't enjoy the fact that he'd stooped to punning to make his point, which I found dubious to begin with. I was also beginning to feel very cold and wet, the Alabama rain coming in hard against my face, driven by a fierce northwest wind. Nor was I looking forward to one of the little lectures my father had been fond of delivering before I'd enlisted in the Air Force. I really thought we'd settled *that* question once and for all on the day he said he'd sign. So I figured I'd put an end to any further discussion right then and there by simply stating that the Nazis were *bad* and that fighting them was therefore *good,* period.

Yes, my father said, but only three months ago the Italians were bad, and fighting *them* was good. It now appears they were only poor misguided victims of Mussolini, who couldn't wait to get rid of him, ignoring for the time being a heritage of fascism that went all the way back to the Roman Empire. But then, Will, this is all about fascism, dictatorship, totalitarianism, and enslavement versus liberty, justice, freedom, and Abraham Lincoln's mother's dog, isn't it?

I was about to tell him I didn't particularly appreciate the note of sarcasm in his voice because I happened to believe that's *exactly* what this war was about, and I was willing to defend with my life if necessary the very principles he seemed to be mocking. But he wasn't expecting an answer, and he wasn't waiting for one. He brought his hand up sharply to clamp the Homburg tighter onto his head as a fresh gust of wind threatened to send it skimming across the railroad tracks to where the Negro troops were billeted. We're saving the world for democracy all over again, he said, speaking louder than the wind and with the same angry sarcasm, his head turned toward mine, his face wet, his blue eyes demanding attention. We're assuming, of course, that what the world *wants* or even *needs* is democracy, he said, and we're assuming that our great American experiment—which is now only in its hundred and sixty-eighth year—will succeed one day, will come to full maturity one day. I wonder just when that's going to be, though, don't you? We came through our puberty when we fought the Civil War, Will, and we might have made it safely into manhood if only the world hadn't involved us in another war so soon afterward. But the very young are always expected to solve the problems of the world, and God knows we were the youngest nation around just then. Europe had thrown some sixty-five million men into the meat grinder and solved nothing at all, so I guess it seemed only proper for us to throw in another four million and set everything right. Well, who knows? Maybe Europe's getting too old and too wise to ever fight another war after this one. Then again, I thought she was too old even after the *last* one—which didn't turn out to be the last one at all, did it, but merely the *first* one.

I wish you'd stop making puns, I said.

And now we've got the *second* one, my father said, and after we win it—oh yes, I'm fairly certain we'll win it, we're a strong and determined nation—after we win it, I'm not too sure we won't make the same errors all over again, the errors we made last time, the ones that led inevitably to what we've got now. The sad part, Will, is that we've never really been permitted to grow out of our adolescence. You could write the history of our country through the eyes of a teen-ager because that's exactly what America's been for as long as I can remember—an impulsive, emotional, inexperienced adolescent, who, I'm beginning to suspect more and more, enjoys action, enjoys violence, enjoys, yes, murder. It's murder, son, don't look so outraged. I don't care if you've got a Nazi boy pulling that trigger, or a Jap, or a sweet apple-cheeked lad from New Hampshire, it's murder, it's killing another human being without anger and in cold blood, it's the worst *kind* of murder.

My face, wet and raw from the rain and the wind, was burning now with anger besides. If he was trying to prove to me that the adolescent was a murderous animal, he had certainly succeeded because I was ready to strangle him now, father or no. I mean, what the hell, *I* was working my ass off training to be a pilot so that I could go over there to help *end* this damn thing, and *he* was telling me, in effect, that I was being trained to commit murder. That was a good way to build somebody's morale, all right, especially your own son's, especially when he was in Basic and was hoping to get his wings come next May and be in Europe or the Pacific by July. That was a nice way to send your son off, by telling him he was a murderer for wanting to kill the people who were trying to enslave the goddamn world. Look, I said, nobody *wants* to fight a goddamn war, but sometimes you have to defend yourself, can't you understand that?

Yes, he said, I can understand that. We all had to defend ourselves last time, too. France had to defend herself because she'd lost Alsace-Lorraine when the Germans beat Napoleon III. England had to defend herself because Germany was becoming a very big maritime power, and was grabbing off too much of the world's commerce. Germany had to defend herself because tariff barriers were going up against her everywhere she turned. Russia had to defend herself because getting the Balkans would have satisfied her historic itch for an outlet on the Mediterranean. Even America, an ocean's width away, had to defend herself because of her own expanding importance; if we had let the most powerful nation in Europe win the war, we'd have lost too much of the world's trade, and our prestige as a rising power would have plummeted. We all had a lot to defend, Will. It just wasn't what they *told* us we were defending, that's all. And now we're justifying yet another war—the Japanese attacked us, so of course we have to defend ourselves— striking our familiar adolescent pose and pretending we're motivated only by high ideals and lofty principles.

He looked me straight in the eye then and said, Go fly your airplane, Will, and convince yourself it isn't all bullshit. I'm afraid I can't do that any more.

I was genuinely shocked because my father rarely swore, even in anger, and he did not seem to be angry now, he seemed only to be overwhelmed by an intolerable

143

grief. I wanted to reach out suddenly to touch him. I wanted to say It's okay, Pop, I'll take care of you, please, Pop, it's okay.

We forget, my father said. In July of 1918, I killed a man for the first time in my life, Will, I shot him in the face because we were defending an important hill overlooking a strategic plain.

I can't remember the number of that hill now.

I can't for the life of me remember it.

II

January ❧

Eau Fraiche hadn't changed much.

My division had moved into Germany shortly after the Armistice, and I'd stayed with them as far as Simmern, where the Army doctors decided they couldn't get my feet to stop itching and recommended me for discharge. That was all right with me.

I arrived in New York on January 10, 1919, almost two weeks after my nineteenth birthday, and then went by train to Milwaukee. Everybody there was talking about Victor Berger, who was of course a Socialist and one of our state's congressmen, and who had been convicted of conspiracy in December (while my division was proceeding into Germany via Luxemburg, to Saarburg, to Morbach, and then to Simmern where the doctors gave up on my feet). The conspiracy trial had taken place in Chicago under the Sedition Act, which meant that Berger had either said or written or done something tending to upset the authority of the government; when arrested, he was charged with obstructing the draft. He had been sentenced to twenty years in prison, and Milwaukee was still all abuzz with the verdict. I guess most civilians at the time were feeling fiercely protective of our freedom, and weren't about to let the Bolsheviks take over America the way they'd done Russia in 1917. To me, it looked like a lot of fuss over nothing; all I knew was that the Great War had given me itchy feet.

But the issue was very real to the people in Milwaukee, and also to those in Eau Fraiche when I finally got there. Berger had been released on bail, naturally, and everybody was wondering whether Congress would deny him the seat to which he'd been reelected just this past November, and also whether the verdict would be reversed once the case came up for appeal. Even Nancy, who hardly ever troubled herself over politics, kept talking about the Victor Berger case, the Victor Berger case, and I got the feeling that almost everyone in town had seized upon it as a topic of interest only because the war was over now and they didn't have death and dying to worry about any more.

Nancy seemed changed.

I don't mean physically, except for the way she tilted her head now, favoring the ear that hadn't been damaged in her battle with the flu. She was developing a vocal tic as well, an automatic and irritating "Pardon?" whenever she didn't quite catch a word. "Pardon?" she would ask, and tilt her head to one side, and raise her brows ever so slightly over eyes that seemed a deeper green than I remembered them, "Pardon?" Until finally one day after I'd been home about a week, I guess it was, I said, "Nancy, with all these pardons you're throwing around, they should make you warden of Waupun State Prison," and she burst into tears.

"I *knew* you'd hate my infirmity," she said.

"It isn't your infirmity I hate. It's that damn *pardon* all the time."

"Well, what shall I say?" she asked, sobbing. " 'I can't *hear* you, sir, I'm a little *deef?*' "

"That might be better," I said.

"Pardon?" she asked, not having heard me, the word escaping her lips before she could catch it. A look of startled dismay crossed her face, and then she burst into fresh tears. She was still not eighteen. I held her in my arms as she sobbed against my chest, and I felt too old. That was how Nancy had changed. She was so very young.

Not too much had happened to the town, though, it looked almost the same as it had when I'd left it a year before. Oh yes, they had changed Buffalo Street to Pershing Street, and had begun breaking ground for the new mall and administration building, and there were two new automobile agencies on Beaufleuve, and a new movie house on Seventh, but for the most part, there were very few differences. I walked the town alone the first night I got back. I had taken Nancy home at about eleven, and then had sat around the kitchen talking to my family, though I couldn't think of much to tell them—should I have said I once stepped into a German's guts? Along about midnight, I borrowed my father's flivver again, and drove into town and parked it outside the courthouse, and then just began walking along Chenemeke Avenue. I finally turned left on Mechanic, and went on down behind the rubber plant. Nothing had changed much. I could hear a locomotive chugging along the siding on the plant's west end. I was home. Nothing had changed.

The town was silent and deserted.

I walked up to Chenemeke again, and stopped in the center of the avenue. For only an instant, I thought I could hear the sound of muted artillery fire across some distant river. In my mind's eye, but only for an instant, the reality of that cobblestoned street in Eau Fraiche, Wisconsin, merged with memory to become a narrower street in some unremembered town where a horse reared back in fright as a shell exploded, and the white wall of a house suddenly collapsed.

Only for an instant.

I started walking back toward the courthouse.

Karl Moenke's dry-goods store was on the corner of Third and Chenemeke, same as always. Alongside it was the Coin de Lorraine, a sign in the window announcing that it was Under New Management. The marquee of The Wisconsin was dark, but you could still make out the names of the acts playing there that week, all of them familiar, business as usual. I suddenly wondered whether there had ever truly been a horse bleeding from the mouth in a French town, the name of which I'd already forgotten, ever truly been a young girl shrieking in the upstairs bedroom of a gutted house, ever truly been someone named Timothy Bear who had worn a shell fragment in his helmet like a Saint Davy's Day leek.

I started the car and drove home.

We went down-peninsula on the last Sunday in January, Nancy and I.

It was a bitter cold day and Lake Juneau was frozen shore to shore. Nancy was wearing a dark brown motoring turban and a grayish-brown cape with a little fur collar, moleskin I think she said it was. She kept her hands inside her muff. There was a strong wind, and she leaned close to me so that she could hear everything I said. We were on a rock overlooking the icebound lake, surrounded by enormous pines. The picnic tables were below us in the distance, but no one was on the grounds, and the entire place had a forlorn look to it. I didn't know why I'd taken her there.

I had been back for almost two weeks.

I thought at first I wanted to tell her how I'd felt on my first night home when I'd walked the deserted town and listened to the chugging of the railroad train behind the plant and later imagined gunfire, but I realized there was nothing to say about it, or at least nothing she would understand.

I wanted to tell her I didn't love her any more, I guess.

She sat with her hands inside her muff, the muff resting on her lap, her eyes wide on my face, listening as I told her what it had been like on the troopship back to New York, where I'd been berthed with a lot of strangers because I'd been separated from my own company, of course, and how I had lost seventy-four dollars playing poker with some fellows from San Francisco, and how my feet still itched, I would have to go to see Dr. Henning, I told her, though I doubted he could do anything for me, not if the Army medics couldn't. She listened with her eyes wide and expectant, straining to catch every word I uttered, while all the time she knew I was leading up to saying I didn't love her any more.

I couldn't bring myself to tell her.

The wind came roaring in over the lake, blowing snow devils across the ice, and Nancy shuddered deeper into her cape, the fabric hanging in loose folds around her so that she blended with the rock, her green eyes never wandering from my face, her feet together, her muffed hands resting in her lap.

At last she said, "Bert, we hardly seem to know each other."

I did not answer her.

"Bert," she said, "were there other girls? French girls?"

I shook my head.

"Is it that you don't love me any more?" She turned away suddenly and looked out over the lake. "If it's that, you can tell me."

"I don't know what it is," I said.

"Pardon?" she said, and turned swiftly toward me, her eyes brimming, and said, "I'm sorry, Bert, I didn't mean to say that, I know you don't like me to say that. But I . . . I didn't hear you, Bert."

"I said I don't know what it is."

"When I saw you at the station," she said, "I didn't know who you were."

"I recognized you right away."

"I've lost so much weight. I lost twelve pounds when I had the flu."

"You look fine," I said.

"I'm too skinny. I never *did* have a bosom, but now . . ." She shook her head. "I didn't know who you were, and I thought to myself That isn't Bert, that isn't who I love. But then you kissed me and I looked up at you, and I thought, Well of *course* it's him, you can cover the sky with clouds, yet still there'll be the stars and the moon above. But now I think maybe it's *me* who's changed, maybe I'm not what you thought I was or how you imagined me to be when you were over there."

"You're how I imagined you to be, Nancy."

She was about to cry. I wished she would not cry. I put my gloved hand on her shoulder and tried to tell her with a slight pressure that Please, I did not want her to cry, I was not worth crying over.

"What . . . what do you suppose it is, Bert?" she asked.

"Nancy," I said, "it's just that I don't know where I belong any more."

"Maybe you belong with me."

"Nancy . . ."

"Because I love you."

"Nancy, I wake up in the middle of the night, and I don't know who I am."

"You're Bertram Tyler."

"Or where I am."

"You're home."

"That's just it. I don't *feel* as if I'm home." I took a deep breath. "Nancy," I said, "I think I want to leave Eau Fraiche."

"All right," she said.

"Yes," I said, and nodded.

"But why?"

"I don't know why."

"Where would you go?"

"Milwaukee," I said. "Or Paris."

"Paris?" Nancy said, as surprised as I myself was, and then suddenly she burst out laughing. "What in the world would you do in Paris?"

"Well," I said, "I guess I'd sit and drink wine or something," and then I grinned, and then I began laughing, too.

"Paris," she said, "well, well."

Her laughter trailed. She took one hand from her muff, wiped at the corners of her eyes, and then quickly tucked it away again. We sat silently on the huge rock overlooking the frozen lake.

"Bert," she said, "if it's because you don't love me, please don't feel ... please don't go away because of that."

"No, it isn't that."

"Bert," she said, "please don't go to Paris."

"I wouldn't go to Paris."

"Please don't go anywhere."

"Well ..."

"Without me," she said. "I'm so embarrassed," she said. "I thought ..." She shook her head. "Here I am being so forward and you've ... made all sorts of plans that don't include me." She reached up suddenly with one clenched hand and pressed it to her cheek. "Forgive me," she said.

"Nancy," I said, "I killed seven men."

"Pardon?"

"I killed ..." She lifted her face to mine, her eyes immediately seeking my lips. I took her naked hand in both my own, and very softly said, "I killed seven men."

"Yes, Bert," she said.

"I shot one of them in the back."

"Yes, Bert."

"I stole from dead soldiers. A ring from one German

and a pair of boots from another. I threw away the ring."

"Yes."

"In a town one day, I can't remember the name of it, we ... Nancy, there were five of us on patrol, and there was this dead horse in the courtyard and a French girl standing in the doorway, and we ... we took her upstairs to where one wall of the house had been blown away, and they, on a straw pallet up there, they did it to her, Nancy. *J'ai treize ans!* she screamed. *Une vierge!* But they forced her, Nance, and ... I ... I didn't try to stop them, I didn't do anything to stop them. And then we left her there and walked down the wooden steps and out into the courtyard again where the horse lay dead in bright sunshine with flies buzzing around his bleeding mouth, and a soldier named Kerry showed us a silver pendant necklace he had taken from the second bedroom upstairs where the girl's mother was dead on the floor from the shell that had hit the house, and which he said would bring him luck, I didn't try to stop them, I didn't even try."

I was out of breath. I bent and put my forehead down on Nancy's hand. She sat unmoving.

Then she said only, "Yes, Bert."

"Did you hear me?" I said.

"Yes, Bert," she said. "I heard you."

February 🌳 🌳 🌳

On the weekends I had to play, I would die from wanting Dana.

I had got together with three other freshmen guys at Yale, one of whom was in pre-med and who had suggested the name for the group, a great name, The Rhinoplasticians, a rhinoplastician being a doctor who does nose bobs. We didn't sound as great together yet as the old Dawn Patrol had, but we were getting there, and also we were beginning to play a lot of local jobs, especially at preppie parties in the vicinity, where college MEN made a big hit with all the little girls from Miss

Porter's. We usually pulled down about twenty-five bucks a man whenever we played, and we played approximately once every other weekend, which meant that I was earning between fifty and seventy-five dollars a month, more than enough to pay for the apartment in Providence. I was living on a tight allowance from my father, and I didn't think it was fair to ask him for additional money to pay for the apartment, so the new group was a godsend. But at the same time, whenever I played to earn money to pay for the apartment, I couldn't get up to Providence to *use* the apartment; it was something of a dilemma, not to mention painful besides.

The apartment belonged to a guy named Lenny Samalson, who was studying graphic design at Risdee. Lenny had a girlfriend in New York, and her name was Roxanne, and she went to Sarah Lawrence but her parents were very strict, making it necessary for Lenny to go down to the city each weekend if he wanted to see her. Roxanne lived in the same building as Dana, on Seventy-ninth and Park, and when Dana casually mentioned, you know, that it would be convenient if she and I had, you know, a place where we could be alone together on weekends, Roxanne said, Well, how about Lenny's place in Providence? and we grabbed it. Lenny was delighted to let us have it because I paid him thirty dollars a month for using it only on weekends, and not *every* weekend, at that. On the other hand, we were delighted to get it because it was only two hours from New Haven and an hour from Boston, which meant that Dana and I could both leave for Providence after our respective Friday afternoon classes, and get there for dinner, by which time Lenny was already on his way to New York and the carefully guarded Roxanne, who, Dana said, had lost her virginity at the age of fourteen on the roof with the boy from 12C.

I had very little difficulty getting away from Yale for weekends, but our trysts involved a certain amount of subterfuge on Dana's part. Dana was but a mere female freshman living in Shelton Hall and blanket permission (pun unintended by the administration of B.U., I'm sure) for overnights had to be in writing from her parents. With permission, she was entitled to unlimited weekends, provided she signed out before the two a.m. curfew, and left a telephone number where she could be reached.

Dana had little difficulty convincing Dr. Castelli that blanket permission would be far simpler than having to call home each time she was invited to spend a weekend with a girlfriend. And the telephone number she left at Shelton each Friday afternoon before putting her check in the overnight column was of course the one at Lenny's apartment.

Providence was a singularly grubby town, but Lenny's apartment was really quite nice. I had always thought artists were sloppy people who left twisted paint tubes and dirty rags all over the place, but Lenny was very tidy. In fact, since he was in Graphic Design rather than Fine Arts, he hardly ever worked in oils, and the place was miraculously free of the aroma of paint or turpentine, which could have been disastrous in a one-room apartment with a screen separating the kitchen from the bedroom-living room. Lenney had hand-decorated the screen himself, using the Nuclear Disarmament symbol in various sizes as an over-all black-and-white pattern. The symbol, Dana informed me, was a composite of the semaphore signals for the letters N and D, this information having incidentally been garnered by her in library research for a paper she was doing on William Shakespeare, figure it out. The screen stood at the foot of the bed, and tacked to it was a very decorative poster Lenny had painted in blues and reds, advising everyone to MAKE LOVE, NOT WAR, though actually we didn't need any reminders.

I loved Dana very much.

Before Dana, I had only had a relationship with one other girl in my life, and that had been Cass Hagstrom. The time with Cass had been very exciting for me because she was the first girl who had let me do anything substantial to her and I was overwhelmed and grateful. That was also when everything else was really going great for me —Dawn Patrol was playing almost every Friday and Saturday night, I was the football team's captain and quarterback, and I was maintaining a ninety average at Talmadge High. I was as much in love with *life*, I guess, as I was with Cass.

But even the most exciting times with Cass, and there were some, did not compare with what I experienced with Dana. I loved everything about Dana, and this wasn't a matter of a first sex experience, nor were things going so great at Yale, either, because they weren't. In fact, to be

153

perfectly truthful, I was having a very difficult time adjusting to college life, being burdened with two creepy roommates, and carrying a full program of English, French, History, Economics, and Physics. Moreover, I was confused about a lot of things.

I had dutifully registered for the draft in October 1964, within five days after my eighteenth birthday, aware that I owed the Army two years of compulsory service, and ready though reluctant to pay my debt to the country. Well, that's corny, banners waving and bugles blowing and all that crap. But I *believed* in freedom, you see, I *believed* in the concept of self-government, and I recognized that a great nation *did* have responsibilities to the rest of the world, and I was committed to sharing those responsibilities. I knew my Army duty would be postponed so long as I kept up my grades at Yale and continued to be classified a student, but I knew that eventually I would have to serve, and whereas the idea was a pain in the ass, patriotism aside, I was nonetheless ready to do what had to be done.

In February 1965, I began to get confused.

I don't think Dana had anything to do with my confusion, though perhaps she may have. She was a very opinionated beautiful young lady, and her contempt for President Johnson was something monumental. Like a lot of girls, she had accepted Kennedy as a sort of father-image with whom incest was not only thinkable but perfectly acceptable. And then, out of all cuts, this positively groovy guy had been replaced by a real father-type who had a stern demeanor and a disapproving down-turned mouth, who wore eyeglasses when he read his speeches, who whooped it up with all the ladies at the inaugural ball, and who spoke in a lazy Texas way designed to alienate every kid on the eastern seaboard, if not the entire world. Dana's favorite nickname for him was "Ole Flannel Mouth," though she also began calling him "Loony Bins Johnson" shortly after the inauguration. In Lenny's apartment one night, she performed for me a ten-minute argument between LBJ and his daughter, which ended with him shouting, "Well, I reckon *Ah'm* the Pres'dent, and y'all kin *not* have the automobile tonight!" When I told her that he was a good administrator who could goose Congress into giving us some much-needed legislation, Dana said, "Oh, crap, Wat," and tacked another anti-

Johnson Feiffer cartoon to Lenny's Ban-the-Bomb screen, and then did a devastating take-off of Johnson collaring unsuspecting senators in the cloakroom and twisting their arms to vote for legislation on new bird sanctuaries, her imitation developing to the point where I'm positive it was slanderous (though I have to admit it was funny as hell, too).

February got confusing.

I'm not trying to say that everything wasn't pretty confusing to begin with. I had two roommates in Edwin McClellan Hall. One was named Alec Kupferman, and he was a spooky kid with a beard who hardly ever said a word to anyone, wandering around the campus and the room immersed in whatever private thoughts consumed him day and night. I don't think he attended classes. He would appear like a sudden hallucination in the door-frame, and merely nod, and go to his bed, and put his hands behind his head and stare up at the ceiling. I felt very uneasy whenever he was around, which thank God was not too often. My other roommate was a winner, too. He was a kid named Abner Nurse from Salem, Massachusetts, who claimed that he was a direct descendant of Rebecca Nurse who had been tried and hanged for a witch in 1692. I believed it. If ever there was a warlock in the world, it was Abner Nurse. He had red eyes. I swear to God, they were red. Not fire-engine red, of course, but a brown that was so close to orange it was red, especially when he sat at his desk late at night with the single lamp burning, probably reading up on evil potions and deadly brews from a witch book hidden behind his copy of *Playboy*. He had black hair that stuck up on his head in two spots, *exactly* like horns. I had never seen him naked because he was very shy about taking showers when anybody else was around, but I think that's because he had a long tail he kept tucked up inside his underwear. He changed his underwear every day. He always left his Jockey shorts in a corner of the room, like a neat little burial mound, until there was a week's supply piled up there, and then he would pick them up and carry them down the hall to the john where he would hand-launder them as though they were dainty delicate unmentionables. I once heard him talking in his sleep, and what he said was "Hanna-Kribna" over and over again in rising cadence, which I'm sure was authentic Salem witch talk.

When I caught him reading a rather personal letter from Dana to me, I told him I would bust him in the mouth if he ever did it again, and he rooted me to the spot with his red-eyed satanic gaze and shouted, "Descend in flames, turd!" and then laughed maniacally and stalked out of the room. I didn't hit him because he was somewhat larger than I, measuring six feet four inches from the top of his head to the tips of his cloven hoofs, and weighing two hundred and twenty pounds in his Jockey shorts.

So the room situation at old Eli was somewhat confusing, as was the situation with the Rhinoplasticians (Jesus, I really *dug* that name!) because we were trying to develop a unique and original sound that was far-out and divorced from hard rock, but at the same time we knew we couldn't get *too* experimental or we'd never get any jobs, and I needed the job-money to keep up the Providence apartment, but I couldn't get to use the apartment if we played too *many* jobs, which we *wouldn't* play if our sound got too shrill or unintelligible.

"Now *this* is what I call providence," Dana said the first time we used the apartment, and then sat shyly on the edge of the bed, her hands folded in her lap, as demurely and expectantly as a bride. And though we had made love before, several times in the back of the station wagon and once in her bedroom on Park Avenue, while Dr. Castelli and his wife were at the opening of *I Had a Ball*, this was in a sense the first time for us.

She studied me with a solemn brown-eyed look, as though aware that something memorable was about to happen, that we were *really* about to commit to each other here in Lenny Samalson's apartment on Lenny Samalson's bed, about to share an intimacy that would be infinitely more binding than our previous hurried and awkward couplings had been. She stared at me for several moments, as though trying to read on my face the knowledge that I, too, knew this was extremely important. And then she rose silently and fluidly from the bed and walked toward the john at the other end of the apartment, near the kitchen, and came back to me naked not five minutes later.

Her body was a contradiction, I observed it at first with all the professional aloofness of a gynecologist. She had large breasts with pink-tipped nipples. I had touched her often, I knew the feel of her by memory, but this was the

156

first time I'd seen her naked, and now she seemed too abundant somehow, as though her mother-earth ripeness, her bursting fullness had been designed for another girl and not her. The triangle of her pubic hair was thick and black. An equilateral tangle of Neapolitan density, it sprang from the whiteness of her belly and thighs like some unexplored jungle, promising fecundity, combining with the lush womanliness of her breasts to deny the girlishness of her narrow hips and long legs. She did a self-conscious model's turn for me, and her backside came as another surprise, hinted at before in skin-tight jeans, but nonetheless startling now in its swelling nakedness, an unsubtle echo of her breasts. Her body advertised its erogenous zones in billboard blatancy, refusing secrecy to her sexuality, brazenly inviting what her downcast nun's eyes sought to conceal.

She had learned some things from Max that I had never learned from Cass, but she taught them to me only subversively in the weeks that followed, never once indicating they were skills acquired in another man's bed, pretending we were learning everything together for the first time ever on earth. There was a gleeful exuberance to the way she made love. Cass Hagstrom had approached sex with all the joy of a mortician, her brow covered with a cold sweat, a tight grim look on her face, her eyes widening in frightened orgasm as though she were looking into her own open coffin. But Dana entered our Providence bed with nothing less than total abandon, an attitude I naturally and mistakenly attributed to my own great prowess until I learned she took the pill religiously each and every morning and, thus liberated, could fearlessly express and expose herself. When we began making love each time, a small pleased smile would light her face and her eyes, lingering as we crossed those separate male-female boundaries to that suspended genderless territory where we each became the other. It was then that something else moved onto Dana's face to replace the smile, drifting into her eyes and swiftly, smokily stretching them out of focus. Reason, intelligence, conscious will drained from her features as an utterly wanton look took complete possession, flushing onto her face, rising there directly from the hungrily demanding slit between her legs. In those few mindless moments before she came, she was totally and recklessly female, completely trusting my maleness, paradoxically fortifying our oneness, our commingled identity, receiving and demanding and responding and succumbing until everything surrounding me and containing me was Dana, this cloud, my love, this sweet sweet Dana. In January, we found each other, and in the discovery found ourselves as well.

But in February, the confusion began.

In February, the way Dana and I later reconstructed it, everybody in Vietnam decided it was time for a little truce, little wine-rice break in the heat of battle, get these troops out of the hot sun, Captain, don't you know it's time for the Year of the Dragon to become the Year of the Snake? Let's get some of these lads back to Saigon for some fun there, hey Captain? Charlie wants a seven-day cease-fire, why, fine, we'll *give* him a seven-day cease-fire.

Dana: Oh, Colonel, it was nasty! Those wily Orientals, they was all the while hiding ammunition and putting up they mortars, sir, while we was guzzling beer in Saigon bars with Hello, Joe, you likee fig-fig girls, oh, sir, I can tell you it was terrible. Where they was heading for, sir, was Pleiku, down around Quinhon, Phumy, Kontum and Hanna-Kribna, I swear that boy is a witch, sir! And what they done, they pound the *hell* out of us, sir.

Me: Well, sir, the cease-fire ended at midnight, and we was sitting around having a last smoke 'fore we hit the sack when all of a sudden Charlie come running out of the high grass either side of the air strip, musta cut a sizable hunk thu the barbed wire to get thu that way with them satchel charges, sir, and he begin blowing up everything he could lay his hands on, he hits the choppers, he hits the recon planes, he just determined, sir, to blow Camp Holloway clear off the map.

Me again, different voice: They opened up with the 81s along about the same time, they musta been hiding oh six or seven hundred yards from the compound, and them mortars come banging in, man, they musta fired fifty, sixty rounds of them. Knocked down a quarter of the goddamn billets, killed seven of our guys, and wounded about a hundred.

Dana, doing her now world-famous President Johnson imitation: The worst thing we could possibly do would be to let this go by. It would be a big mistake. It would open a door to a major misunderstanding. I want three things: I want a joint attack. I want it to be prompt. I want it to be appropriate.

She got what she wanted.

Or rather, *he* did.

The United States aircraft carriers *Ranger, Hancock,* and *Coral Sea,* cruising in the South China Sea launched forty-nine Skyhawks and Crusaders twelve hours after the Vietcong attack on Pleiku. The planes roared over Donghoi, a hundred and sixty miles above the seventeenth parallel, and bombed and strafed the staging area there. The next day, Vietnamese Skyraiders joined United States jets from the Danang base and flew north to bomb Vinhlinh, a Red guerilla communications center.

Dana: He come striding across the field, you dig, man, and he ain't bad-looking for a gook, he got this real pretty girl gook with him, she look like the Dragon Lady. He got this black mustache and these six-guns slung on his hips, man, he look like a real marshal, 'stead of a gook marshal. His name Nguyen Cao Ky (man, I'm *positive* now that boy a witch!) and he wearing this all-black fly suit and a white crash helmet, man, he going to shoot every motherless Cong clear off the face of the earth.

Me, assuming the role of the President's Press Secretary: Today's joint response was carefully limited to military areas which are supplying men and arms for attacks in South Vietnam. As in the case of the North Vietnamese attacks in the Gulf of Tonkin last August, the response is appropriate and fitting.

I honestly did not know how appropriate or fitting it was because I honestly did not know just what was going on over there. Nor did anyone seem anxious to tell me. There were rumors that Maxwell Taylor, our ambassador to South Vietnam would soon be recalled because of differences with General Nguyen Khanh, the current head of the Saigon government, not to be confused with Nguyen Cao Ky, the Vice Air Marshal, he of the black jump suit and white crash helmet, Nguyen apparently being a Vietnamese name as common as Tom. I had no idea what Khanh looked like because the South Vietnamese seemed to change their leaders as often as Abner Nurse changed his underwear, very often leaving *them* in little piles in the corner, too. Our new man who'd been sent to Saigon to investigate the developing situation was called McGeorge Bundy. (I didn't believe *his* name, either.) He was the President's top White House foreign relations adviser. To show how important he was, it was shortly after he arrived in Saigon that the Vietcong decided to kick hell out of us. General Westmoreland, who I guessed was running the whole shooting match for us over there, was shocked by Charlie's audacity. "This is bad," he said, "very bad."

I, too, was beginning to think maybe it wasn't so good.

On the other hand, President Johnson assured the nation that there had been no change in the position of the country in regard to our desire or our determination to help the people of Vietnam preserve their freedom. "Our basic commitment to Vietnam," he said, "was made in a statement ten years ago by our President Dwight Eisenhower, to the general effect that we would help the people of Vietnam help themselves." Dana's respect for Eisenhower was exceeded only by her respect for Johnson, but she doubted that our policy of containing Communism had originated with dear old Ike, preferring to believe instead that we'd been chasing Reds at home and abroad for such a long time now that anyone becoming President was duty-bound to continue the pursuit, the present echoing the past, the course already charted, the future preordained, and all that jazz. Ten years ago, when Eisenhower made the statement to which Johnson now alluded, I was only eight years old and thought the President was that nice bald man who sounded a lot like Sally Lawrence's grandfather. I had no idea what he was saying about the country or what he was doing for it. ("Nothing," Dana insisted.) What I *did* remember about ten years ago was being led into the basement of the Talmadge Elementary School, which had been stocked with food and water and blankets and battery-powered radios, and being told by Mrs. Weinger that this was a practice air raid and that we would remain in the basement until we heard the all-clear sounding from the firehouse roof. She then went on to tell us a little about radiation, all of us sitting wide-eyed and fearful, and I could remember wondering aloud what would happen if my father was caught in New York when the bomb fell (Shhh! Mrs. Weinger warned me) and my mother was at our house on Ritter Avenue, and I was here at school—would we ever get to see each other again? I was terrified.

Now, everyone seemed to have forgotten all about shhhh the bomb, everyone seemed to have passed it off as just another nasty little weapon no one in his right mind would use, the way no one in his right mind would have used gas in World War I, the way no one in his right mind would even *think* of waging war in this day and age, because war was hell (we had been taught to believe), war was foolish, and war was suicidal. Yet we were waging war in Vietnam. Or so it seemed.

Something was happening, and I didn't know what. But whereas I was confused, I did not begin to get *frightened* until Sunday, February twenty-first.

Dana had an old beat-up straw hat she used to wear whenever she was studying for an exam. She had bought it six years ago when she'd gone to Nassau with her parents, and it was just about falling apart now, its red ribbon faded and torn, its edges jagged, its crown full of open holes. But it was her "study hat," and she compulsively pulled it down over her ears before cracking a book, as though isolating herself from the outside world within its tattered straw confines. She was wearing the hat and nothing else that Sunday, sitting cross-legged and naked in the center of Lenny Samalson's bed, surrounded by open French textbooks. She was in the midst of intoning some Baudelaire out loud, *Ma jeunesse ne fut qu'un ténébreux orage,* when the news announcement interrupted the music, this must have been, oh, a little past three in the afternoon, *Traversé ça et la par de brillants soleils,* and the music stopped, and the announcer said that Malcolm X had been shot to death by a man with a double-barreled sawed-off shotgun at the Audubon Ballroom on upper Broadway in Manhattan. The announcer went on to say that Malcolm's murderer had been a Negro like himself (small consolation to the dead man) and that he had been immediately apprehended by the police and charged with homicide.

I don't think either Dana or I experienced any great sense of loss. But sitting in the center of Lenny's bed, wearing only her study hat, she began to weep softly, and I went to her and took her in my arms, and we huddled together, suddenly chilled, as the radio resumed its program of recorded music.

March ✤ ✤

Columbus, Mississippi, in 1944 was hardly a service-man's paradise, so I guess we were all moderately grateful that a dance was being held on the post that Friday night. Besides, the propwash around the field had insisted that girls from places as exotic and as distant as Memphis, Tennessee, were being brought in by the busload as Colonel Chickenshit's big St. Patrick's Day gift to the cadets. (It was later rumored that the colonel had initially decided to limit the festivities only to those men who, like himself, were of Irish descent. But it had been pointed out to him by a tactful Chair Corps officer that Purim had come and gone only eight days before with scarcely a nod of recognition to the Jewish cadets, so maybe it would be a better idea to give *all* the men a well-earned and much-needed opportunity to dance till dawn with southern belles from far and wide, eh, Colonel? The colonel had reluctantly agreed.)

I had been sent to Columbus Army Air Field on February 27, to begin flying twin-engine AT-9s in preparation for the P-38. Michael Mallory, who was in Advanced Flying School at Luke Field in Arizona, had postulated the theory in one of his letters to me that both the quality and quantity of nookie in any given American community diminished in direct ratio to the quantity of servicemen there. His observation certainly applied to Columbus. I went to the dance that night only in desperation, hardly believing that Old Chickenshit was *really* bringing in girls from all over Dixie. As it turned out, I was absolutely right.

The mess hall had been decorated with green crepe-paper streamers, green cardboard cutouts of leprechaun hats and shamrocks, white cutouts of clay pipes. A make-shift bar had been set up on sawhorses in front of the steam tables, and bottles of 3.2 beer were being handed over it as I came into the building. A seven-piece Air Force orchestra was playing at the far end of the hall near the doors leading into the kitchen, with an inept lead trumpet player struggling vainly to imitate Ziggy Elman in "Opus Number One." There were perhaps two dozen couples dancing. Some thirty girls lined the walls, sitting in ante-bellum splendor, easily recognized from previous sorties into town as nothing but local talent. Fifty hungry aviation cadets ogled these beauties, entertaining lewd thoughts of getting them out behind the PX, fat chance. Fifty more crowded the bar (similarly decorated with pipes, shamrocks, and hats) laughing a lot and telling stories in loud voices of their aerial exploits that day. "Opus Number One," clumsily modulated into "Tuxedo Junction." A cadet, already drunk on the mildly alcoholic beer and in imminent danger of washout, kept striking his hand on the scarred piano top in time to the music, throwing the trumpet player off beat, as if that poor soul *needed* an additional handicap. The band droned on interminably against a counterpoint of girlish southern voices clacking away in augmented fifths, mingled and mixed, bouncing off the high-ceilinged room, echoing, streaked with the sharp aroma of tomorrow's chow being stewed in tonight's kitchen. The whole scene looked dismal and sounded bleak, an entirely unsatisfactory substitute for a weekend pass, which privilege was undoubtedly forbidden by some secret Air Force regulation to the effect that no aviation cadet be permitted to have any fun whatsoever during his training period, lest this somehow diminish his effectiveness as a fighting unit of the United States Army. I decided to have a beer before leaving, and then I decided the hell with the beer, I'd just leave. I was turning to go when I heard someone just behind my shoulder say, "Beautiful, absolutely *gorgeous*," with such dripping sarcasm that I imagined for a moment I'd spoken my own thoughts aloud. I turned to find myself looking directly into the amused eyes of a cadet I recognized as Ace Gibson, reputed to be the hottest student pilot at Columbus. He was shorter than I, about five foot eight, and he looked like one of Walt Disney's little forest animals, with wide wet brown eyes, a pug nose, and slightly bucked teeth. I would have disliked him immediately even if I had not been jealous of his reputation or prejudiced by his nickname.

"Nothing in town," he said to me, "and nothing here, either. What's a man supposed to do?"

163

"*I'm* going to sleep," I said, and started to take a step around him.

"No, hold it," he said, and gestured with a slight jerk of his head to where a girl sat alone on the side of the room. "The chaperone," Ace said. "A sweet young mother. Come on."

She was sitting some thirty-five feet from where we stood near the entrance doors, a blond girl wearing a white piqué dress and brown-and-white spectator pumps. Her long legs were tanned, and she kept them primly crossed, but one foot was jiggling in time to the music. She looked to be about seventeen or so, and I could not understand how Ace had figured her to be a mother, young or otherwise. Besides, a revised quick count of the available nookie had downgraded my original estimate to perhaps forty girls in all (*including* the blonde in the white dress) meaning that the odds tonight were approximately three to one, more than I felt like coping with after a hard day's flying. But Ace Gibson clapped me on the shoulder, which I didn't like, and burst into a chittering sort of expectant laughter, which I also didn't like, and then hooked his arm through mine and led me over to where the girl was sitting.

"Good evening, ma'am," he said to her, "my name is Ace Gibson. This is my buddy . . ." and paused.

"Will Tyler," I said.

"How do you do?" she said. "Ah'm Hattie Rolfe."

"Hello, Hattie," Ace said, "would you mind if we joined you?"

"Ah'm not permitted to dance, you know," she said. "Ah'm one of the chaperones."

"Well then," Ace said, as I stared at him in amazement, "we'll just sit and chat, if that's all right with you, ma'am."

"Thet'd suit me jes' fine," she said, and smiled.

Up close, I was beginning to notice a few things about her that Ace must have spotted immediately from the doorway. She was definitely not seventeen, though how he had been able to tell that from a distance of thirty-five feet was beyond my understanding. Could he have seen the crow's feet around her eyes, could he have possibly noticed the wedding band and small diamond ring on her left hand, could he have detected from such a distance that the knitting in her lap was a partially completed khaki-colored sleeveless pullover. (Was there a soldier husband overseas someplace, Rooms for Rent, the possibility of a permanent-party arrangement with an experienced woman of at least twenty-seven or -eight years old?) How could he have surmised all this from thirty-five feet away? I looked at him appreciatively. He was now telling the girl that he had spent some time in Mississippi before coming here to Columbus, having taken his Basic Training in Biloxi, and suddenly he asked me where *I'd* gone through Basic, and almost before I could say, "Nashville," he turned again to Hattie and said, "Not much of a crowd here tonight, is there?"

"Well, it ain't much to holler about," Hattie said. "I'll allow that."

"Will and I were hoping for something a bit more gaysome," he said, which I assumed was a southern expression because Hattie reacted just as though he'd served her a heaping full platter of chit'lins and pone, laughing helplessly, and all but slapping him on the knee. They were certainly off to a fine roaring start. So promising, in fact, that I decided to go back to the barracks, and was waiting to make my break, when Ace brought me into the conversation again. I realized all at once that the inclusion was deliberate. He truly wanted me to stay. He was not using me as a straight man, the way some guys did while they worked their points with a chick. I felt suddenly and oddly touched.

"Will and I both like Columbus a lot," he said, "but it's really difficult, you know, to get to understand a place, isn't that right, Will?"

"Oh yeah," I said, "it's really difficult."

"Especially when we get into town so infrequently, huh, Will!"

"We don't get in too often," I said to Hattie, and grinned stupidly, entirely mindful of how little I was contributing to the discussion, and grateful for Ace's efforts, and hopeful that he would not think I was a moron.

"Though Sundays are usually free," he said.

"Unless there's a cross-country scheduled," I said.

"Yes, they come up every now and then," Ace said.

"Yes," I said.

"What do *you* do on Sundays?" Ace asked Hattie, and nodded almost imperceptibly to me, signaling that *this* was where we were supposed to lead the conversation, get it, Will? Around to where we could find out what this delicious piece of pecan pie did with her Sundays, get it?

"Oh," I said, and Ace smiled and raised his eyebrows approvingly at the coming of the dawn.

"I work on Sundays," Hattie said.

"What kind of work do you do?" I asked.

"She must be a movie star," Ace said.

"Oh," I said. "Yeah."

"No, I'm not," Hattie said seriously.

"Of course not," Ace said. "She's a fashion model."

"Not that either," she said.

"A designer?" I said, and looked at Ace.

"Of what?" Ace asked.

"Dresses?" I said.

"Ladies' dresses?" Ace said.

"Third floor," I said, and he burst out laughing.

"No, no," Hattie said, shaking her head.

"Well, I give up," Ace said.

"So do I," I said.

"I'm a waitress," Hattie said, and shrugged.

"Days or nights?" Ace asked immediately.

"Days. I go on at eight in the morning, and I'm off at four."

"Look at this little girl," Ace said. "Slaves all week long in a restaurant . . ."

"A diner," Hattie said.

". . . a diner, and then comes here on her own free time . . ."

"I'm off Mondays," Hattie said.

". . . to do her part for the war effort by providing a little bit of cheer for servicemen far from their homes and their loved ones."

"I'm only here by accident," Hattie said. "We had to have six chaperones for the girls, and they called me yesterday because one of the women supposed to come got taken to the hospital."

"Oh, the poor woman," Ace said.

"What was wrong with her?" I said.

"Nothing," Hattie said. "She was pregnant, and it got to be her time."

"Do you know what we're going to do this Sunday when Hattie leaves the diner?" Ace asked.

"Yes," I said. "We're going over to the hospital to visit

that poor little old woman who was supposed to chaperone tonight."

"Wrong," Ace said. "We're going to wait on Hattie."

"You're going to *what?*" Hattie said.

"*Wait* on you."

"What do you mean?"

"We're going to buy a big steak, and then me and my buddy here . . ."

"Will Tyler," I said.

". . . are going to bring that steak over to your place, Hattie—you *do* live in Columbus, don't you?"

"Oh, yes," she said, "but . . ."

". . . where we'll cook it and serve it and clean up the kitchen and do the dishes afterwards, without your having to lift a finger all night long. How does that sound to you, Hattie?"

"Okay, I guess, but . . ."

"No buts, Hattie," Ace said.

"Well, I guess he wouldn't mind too much."

"Who?"

"My husband."

"I'm sure he'd be pleased to know you're being so well taken care of," I said.

"Oh yeah, it isn't that," Hattie said.

"Then it's settled," Ace said.

"It's just that he's usually so tired," Hattie said.

"Tired? Who?"

"My husband."

"Tired?" I said.

"When he gets home at night."

"Home?"

"My husband."

"Home?" Ace said. "Home from where?"

"He's a sergeant in the Medical Corps. He's stationed at Northington General in Tuscaloosa. He gets home every night about six o'clock. Unless there's an epidemic or something."

"I take it there is no epidemic right now," Ace said.

"No," Hattie said.

"Nor one expected for Sunday."

"No. I really don't think he'd mind, though, if you fellows came over. He likes steak."

"Might be difficult to find an open butcher on Sunday," I said.

"Mmm, yes, hadn't thought of that," Ace said. "And what about ration coupons?"

"What about that Lycoming radial?" I said.

"What about it?" Ace said.

"That faulty horse. Supposed to be two ninety-five," I said.

"He's talking about the Curtiss AT-9," Ace explained to Hattie.

"Oh," Hattie said.

"We're supposed to check the red-line entry," I said.

"There're these two Lycoming radial engines, each two hundred and ninety-five horses."

"Oh," Hattie said.

"One of them's missing," Ace said.

"One of the horses," I said.

"Dangerous to fly her that way."

"Have to tend to the horses."

"Supposed to do it before tomorrow morning."

"Almost tomorrow morning now," I said.

"Better be going," Ace said, and rose. He executed a courtly bow, lifted Hattie's left hand with the wedding band and small gleaming diamond to his lips, brushed a gentle kiss against it, and said, "Until next time, Hattie."

"Goodnight, Hattie," I said.

"Charmed," Hattie said.

Outside the mess hall, Ace took off his hat, wiped the sweat band, and replaced it on his head at a precariously jaunty angle, but not before I'd noticed that his thatch of brown hair was already beginning to thin at the crown. On the way over to the EM's Club, he told me he would be nineteen years old in a few months, and that his real name was Avery Gibson. The nickname, he explained, had nothing whatever to do with his flying prowess. It was instead the result of an inventive WASP father who, in fine *Saturday Evening Post* tradition, had bestowed "Ace" on Avery at the age of three, and "Skipper" on his older brother Sanford. The older brother was now in the Pacific with a PT-boat squadron, his rate being Gunner's Mate/ Third, his nickname apparently causing no end of conflict with the lieutenant (j.g.) who commanded the boat. Ace said he hated his own nickname because it gave him all the renown of a Western gunslick; everyone was waiting to shoot him down long before they met him. But I noticed that he walked with a cocky rolling gait, as though he were carrying an invisible swagger stick in one clenched fist, and he wore his uniform with all the authority of an already commissioned officer.

In the club, we sat drinking beer and talking.

Ace was from Reading, Pennsylvania, where his father, Stuart Gibson, was a stockbroker. His mother, Miriam, whom everyone called "Mims," kept horses. Six horses. Ace hated horses, an aversion directly attributable to the fact that he had been thrown from the saddle at the tender age of ten and then dragged, foot caught in the stirrup, for some twenty feet before Mom-Mims caught the horse's bridle and brought the beast to a stop. His father kept a forty-four-foot ketch on the Schuylkill, and he could be found out on the sailboat most good weekends, though it was Ace's estimate that he was lucky if he got to use it twenty days all summer. It was apparent from what Ace said that he had as little love for boats as he had for horses.

Surprisingly, I said out loud, "Don't you like your parents?"

"Do you like *yours?*" he asked.

"My mother's dead," I said.

"I'm sorry."

"She died last year. I liked her, though. I think I liked her."

"What about your father?"

"He's okay," I said, and shrugged. "He sure gave me a lot of static about joining up."

"Mine was eager to get me out of the house," Ace said, and smiled.

"It's just he's so *dumb* about some things," I said. I guess I felt a little guilty saying it; he was, after all, my father. So I quickly told Ace how much I respected a man who had started as a lumberjack in Wisconsin and had gone on to become a very important man in the paper industry. I sketched in his early days as a trainee at Ramsey-Warner, relating the story the way I'd heard my father tell it so many times at the dinner table, and then explained how he had taken a job as salesman for the Circle Mill after he'd lost his first job, and how after fifteen years of tough in-fighting he had become Executive Vice President, from which position he was finally able to challenge the company's president, an older party who was slowly becoming incapable of making tough business decisions. The challenge had involved two vital points, and perhaps my father would have lost the battle if he hadn't convinced the board that he was right about both. One was a takeover offer from Ramsey-Warner, the company he'd once worked for, and the other had something to do with wallpaper, either with severely cutting production of it, or increasing production, I'd forgotten which. But the board sided with him, and almost eighteen years to the day he'd started at Circle, my father became president of the company, which was certainly something to admire. Ace admitted that it was certainly something to admire and then, probably shamed by his own earlier references to old Stu, told me how *his* father, too, had been an uneducated man who took it upon himself to learn the workings of the market and then had amassed a fair fortune playing with stocks, which was certainly nothing to sneeze at. It certainly wasn't anything to sneeze at, I agreed. Thus having coped with our separate heresies, we went on to discussing more pleasant matters, namely Ace's brother Skipper, of whom he seemed genuinely fond, and whom he described as "a really handsome guy, Will, the original golden boy." I told him a little about Linda then, and what a great crazy kid she was.

We finished our beers and walked over to the flight line, where the planes sat in a moonlit row, ready for the morning flight. Ace told me he couldn't wait to begin flying that old P-38, which was only the best damn fighter plane ever built. I told him that the way the war was going, we might not get over there in *time* to fly one, and he said, "Don't you worry, Will. This war ain't going to end till I get there to end it," and then laughed his chittering little laugh, which I still found annoying.

There were several *other* annoying things about him.

I discovered, for example, that he had a remarkable sense of humor and a truly enormous stockpile of jokes for every occasion. (That wasn't the annoying thing.) The annoying thing was that whenever he saw or heard something that nudged his joke file, he would automatically recall the punch line out loud, "Yeah, but *last* time we were taking movies," and then would say, "Do you know that joke, Will?" and whether you knew it or not, "Yes, I know it, Ace," he would go right on to tell the entire joke, anyway. So if you'd heard it, you would have to sit through it again in Technicolor with Ace relishing each hilarious syllable. And if you *hadn't* heard it, you had in *effect* heard it because he'd already given the punch line before telling the joke. The result was mind-numbing. Then, in a luncheonette later that night, after we'd taken a jitney into Columbus, and after Ace had told seven jokes, three of which I'd already heard, the punch lines to the other four already delivered, I discovered another of his little faults, and this one *really* bothered me.

When the waiter, a tired old man dragging ass after probably twelve hours of labor, shuffled over to the booth and gave us our menus, Ace said, "Bacon and eggs, please," and then politely inquired, "Is the bacon nice and soft?"

The waiter said, "Oh yes, sir, the bacon is nice and soft, very tender bacon, sir."

Ace instantly said, "Then I don't want it. I like my bacon crisp."

The waiter looked puzzled for an instant, and then said, "Well, we can make it crisp for you, sir, if that's the way you like it."

Ace considered this, and then asked, "You won't burn it, will you?"

"Oh *no* sir, of *course* we won't burn it."

"I like it burnt," Ace said.

"Well, if you like it burnt . . ."

"Never mind, I'll have ham instead."

"Ham and eggs, yes, sir."

"No, ham on rye with a slice of pickle. Are the pickles very sour?"

The waiter, wary now, asked, "How do you *like* your pickles, sir?"

"How have you got them?"

"However you like them."

"I don't like them."

I should not have been surprised by his waiter-baiting. Ace had removed the wire grommet from his hat the moment we left the field, giving it a raunchy fifty-mission crush, and on the darkened streets of the town he'd been thrown at least six highballs from soldiers mistaking him for brass. He had returned each salute unblinkingly, as if they were only properly his due; there had been no mistaking his cruel enjoyment of the ruse. But I guess I was dazzled by his flow of confidences that night, and overwhelmed by his enormous ego, even though I was not completely taken in by his fancy patter and sleight-of-hand. I knew, for instance, that whereas he claimed to hate the name "Ace," he nonetheless enjoyed his reputation as a hot pilot and felt the name, however acquired, was entirely appropriate. I suspected, too, that his boasting desire to get overseas and "shoot down a thousand Germans" may have been masking a fear of actual combat with real enemy airplanes. And yet, I felt pleased and flattered to be in his presence.

A friendship was beginning that night in Mississippi, and I think we both recognized how slowly and carefully it needed to be explored, both respected how easily it could have been destroyed before it even truly started. I was willing at once to forget whichever of his small inadequacies rankled, and ready to trust that he would forgive my own annoying defects in return.

It was a good beginning.

April ❦

We had come from the vestry into the chancel, where we stood now and waited for the wedding to begin, though I suppose it had properly begun the moment I made my entrance with the minister and my best man. It had been raining all day Saturday, and the ground outside West Presbyterian was soggy and riven, mud running off the sloping lawn down to Indian Street. I stood before the red-carpeted steps to the left of Danny Talbot, who was my best man, and watched the slow Sunday drizzle that pressed the high arched windows of the church. I did not want to look at the open wooden doors through which Nancy Ellen Clark would come on her father's arm within the next few moments. I did not want to get married. Rosalie Hollis in the organ loft was playing "Claire de Lune," and I could see from the tail end of my eye, as I steadfastly watched the oppressive drizzle, my family sitting in the first three pews on the right side of the church, Nancy's family on the left, all of them there to witness a

172

wedding that should not be taking place, I did not love her.

Yes, I loved her.

No, I did not love her. I was nineteen years old, there was too much yet to do, too much yet to see, to experience, to feel. I did not want to marry Nancy Ellen Clark and take her to the apartment we had rented in Eau Fraiche on Mechanic Street, the apartment I had painted last week in colors Nancy chose from Mr. Eckert's sample book, our furniture arriving on Wednesday from Talbot's, an unreal shelter that apartment, unlived in, unused, waiting empty for the bride and groom to return from their two-week honeymoon in Chicago, where we would be staying at the Blackstone Hotel, I did not want to go.

I wanted to go. I wanted to make love to her, I wanted to take off her dress and her petticoat, hold her naked in my arms, tell her secrets about myself, whisper them in her good ear, hold her close and confide everything because I loved her so much I could die.

They sat in anticipation, the wedding march was beginning, my mother and father in resplendent Sunday-wedding best, and beside them my sister Kate with her half-breed stud, no feathered headdress on his proud Apache skull, but wearing instead a white man's dark suit probably bought second-hand in an Arizona beer hall, arms folded across his massive chest. And on his right, my sisters Harriet and Fanny in georgette chiffon, and my brother John, all of eight now, probably longing to pick his nose, but worrying the flap of it instead with his forefinger as Rosalie Hollis pounded the keys and Lohengrin reverberated in the wooden church and the gloomy drizzle pressed against the windows.

Too much to see and do, I wanted to devour worlds, every universe there was, the ushers starting down the aisle, two by two in black, why did men dress alike for weddings and for funerals? The ground upon which Timothy Bear had lain exposed in death, his mouth open, his eyes open, his skull open to the shell fragment that had drained his maleness and left him there for friend and enemy alike to see, a limp geometric tangle of lifeless limbs, my best man dead while flashy Danny Talbot stood next to me by default and the four ushers joined us, sealing off escape, I could not run, I wanted to bolt.

And in Paris, what would I do? In Paris, I would learn

to say *"Je vous en prie,"* and I would roam Montmartre in search of fancy ladies, gartered and laced, perfumed and rouged, who would lift their skirts and French me, would Nancy Ellen Clark do that, would I dare to ask her in the secret dark of our bedroom on Mechanic Street to do things she had never once conjured in her wildest fantasies? I would become the Paris correspondent for the New York *Tribune,* I would send daily dispatches on the progress of Mr. Wilson's efforts to quell the land-hungry appetites of the British, the French, and the Italians, my byline would read Bertram A. Tyler, the A for Alfred, though Nancy perhaps herself did not know this, another secret to tell in our midnight cloister, my middle name is Alfred, is that not amusing, *mon gamin,* let me take off your garter and press it to my lips. Or I would become a translator once I became fluent in the language, I had learned to say *Voulez-vous couchez avec moi ce soir, mademoiselle* with considerable ease in far too many French towns, what a laugh when Timothy Bear tried to cope with the language, what a laugh that boy was. And once fluent with the tongue (I beg you *mademoiselle,* be more careful with your tongue, eh?) once fluent with the language, I would translate novels, perhaps pornography, I would walk along the Champs Élysées wearing a black derby and a long black coat with a black velvet collar, carrying a walking stick, and they would whisper about me in every sidewalk café, not knowing who I was, but surmising I was terribly important, fluent as I was in four languages, and able to translate Marcel Proust's most complicated writings, I, Bertram A. Tyler, the amazing nineteen-year-old American who had set the continent abuzz, tall and handsome and oo-la-la *quel homme!*

The bridesmaids were coming down the aisle singly now, somewhat drizzle-dampened in peach-colored gowns, each carrying small bouquets of tea roses and baby's breath, Nancy's younger sister Meg first, a silly bewildered grin on her face, followed by Adelaide Moore, who had been voted Dairy Queen of the state three years back, before we'd entered the war, but who still hadn't caught herself a husband. Behind her, in the identical peach gown was Brigitte Rabillon, who was keeping steady company with Danny Talbot, it was said they would be married in June as soon as he became executive sales manager of his father's furniture company. He had already asked me if I would do him the extreme honor of being his best man, but by June I would be in the Loire Valley, one of France's most discriminating wine tasters, but he is an *American*, they would say! Ah *oui, monsieur,* but he knows wine like no other man on earth, it is said he can tell a good vineyard from the road as he approaches in his automobile, ah *oui monsieur,* he drives one of those Stutz Bearcats, he is *très formidable, vraiment.* Then came Felice Clark (no relation to my intended bride), who, it was rumored, had had numerous exciting things done to her down-peninsula during our great American adventure, while all the town bloods were away in Europe, the party having been thrown by several forty-year-old members of the Republican Club, who decided in private smoke-filled conclave that this might be a good time to explore the virtues of some of the younger ladies around, they being deprived of company of their own age and all, hence the sad story of Felice Clark, who had lost it repeatedly down-peninsula one starless night last October on the back seat of a flivver, and who now marched down the aisle looking hardly sullied or blemished, had Nancy ever done anything with anybody anywhere anytime? Suppose, no, the thought was unthinkable, not here with Reverend Boland at my side, but suppose, ah *suppose,* well, are we any of us perfect? but suppose in that Chicago hotel room tonight (will we be there tonight, did I check the train schedule?) suppose there is no blood? the blood on the straw pallet under the thirteen-year-old girl in that French farmhouse and the blood of her mother on the floor of the second bedroom and the blood of the horse in the courtyard outside, the flies eating blood, suppose there is no blood from my Nancy, will it matter? I do not love her, how can it matter?

Clara, Nancy's older sister and her maid-of-honor, came through the doors radiantly happy in a pale blue gown, yellow roses crushed in a bouquet against her bosom, dear Clara who had written to me of her sister's illness during those dread weeks so many centuries ago, I must have loved Nancy very much then, I cried for days when I thought I might lose her.

Oh Jesus God, I love her now, too, with all my being! I love her desperately, I would kill any man who touched her, who even dreamt of touching her. I pledge to you,

175

Nancy, my life, my troth, my undying devotion, I love you, Nancy, I will never stop loving you!

Or perhaps an automobile agency on the Avenue Neuilly, strictly American cars, bring the old Ford over there, put the nation on wheels. Ah, *oui, madame,* you may well ask who that strikingly handsome American is! He is Bertram A. Tyler, he is the man who brought the Ford automobile to France, ah, *oui,* and put the nation on wheels. (Has someone *already* brought the Ford automobile over there and put the nation on wheels?) I'll drive him out of business, I'll fluently make speeches in the Bois de Bologne, I will stand on the equivalent of a French soapbox, make speeches the way the Bolsheviks are doing here in America, only I will extol the merits of buying a Ford automobile from the Bertram A. Tyler Agency on the Avenue Neuilly, where the owner himself, the proprietor, the boss, *mesdames et messieurs,* speaks fluent French, why even colloquial French, and where you will get the squarest little deal on the continent, bar none, buy your car from *me,* my friends, make me rich, I want to be a rich American bum, I want to gamble the night away at Monte Carlo, and dance the waltz in the grand ballroom of the Alhambra in Cimiez, and take my yacht to Cannes, I want to be Bertram A. Tyler, the notorious American bachelor tycoon, *bachelor,* do you hear? I don't *want* to get married, not today, not any day, not ever, ever, *ever!*

She came through the doors on her father's arm.

My heart stopped.

Her hand rested ever so delicately on the sleeve of his black coat, her eyes behind the veil were downcast as though she were carefully watching the toes of her white slippers, the white lace gown seeming to float of its own slow volition down the church aisle, suspended around her tiny figure as she came closer to me and the organ notes floated from the loft in fat and mellow accompaniment, my Nancy's triumphal music. She was beside me now, standing on my left, the minister before us, her father having stepped back and away, symbolically mine already though her father had not yet given her in marriage, not really mine as yet because the words had not been spoken. "Dearly beloved," Reverend Boland said, "we are gathered together here in the sight of God," perhaps not even mine *after* the words were spoken, perhaps not to be

176

mine for a long long time to come, "to join this man and this woman in holy matrimony, which is an honorable estate." We were both so very young, I felt our exposed youth glaringly out of place in this old people's church, they who knew so very much, but who watched this ancient ritual in silence now, saying nothing, eyes wet, watching, "not to be entered into unadvisedly, but reverently, discreetly, and in the fear of God. Into this holy estate these two persons come now to be joined," Nancy's eyes still downcast behind the veil, I wanted to see her eyes, I wanted to read what was in her eyes, did she want this marriage any more than I did?

I thought of a forest at dusk and the lone barking of a dog against the approaching night, the laughter of a lumberjack booming from the bunkhouse, "or if there be any present who can show just cause why these parties should not be legally joined together, let him now speak or forever hold his peace."

I wanted to say Yes, *I* can show very just and reasonable cause why we should not be joined. I hardly know this girl. I've known her forever, but I don't know her at all, why are you all rushing us into this? Why are you insisting that I become a man when I'm still not done being a boy, a father when I want to remain a son? Stop them, somebody, I thought, *stop* them! Papa, tell them I'm still your son, tell them there are still a boy's worlds to conquer, there are still hoptoads to catch.

"Who giveth this woman to be married to this man?" Reverend Boland asked, and Nancy's father said, "I do," gruffly, his two seconds on stage after eighteen years and one month of caring for his Nancy, feeding her, clothing her, loving her, all finished in the two words, "I do," I give her to be married to this man, I do, his chance to stop it gone, wasn't *anyone* going to stop it? Reverend Boland put Nancy's right hand into my own right hand, and suddenly looked very solemn and frightening.

"Bertram Alfred Tyler . . ."

(My secret gone, he had given away my secret, he had given me one less thing to confide to Nancy, to bind her to me in the night.)

"Wilt thou have this woman to be thy wedded wife, to live together in the holy estate of matrimony? Wilt thou love her, comfort her, honor and keep her, in sickness

177

and in health, and forsaking all other keep thee only unto her, so long as ye both shall live?"

"I will," I said.

"Nancy Ellen Clark, wilt thou have this man to be thy wedded husband, to live together in the holy estate of matrimony? Wilt thou love him, honor and obey him, in sickness and in health, and forsaking all other keep thee only unto him, so long as ye both shall live?"

"I will," Nancy said.

"The ring," Reverend Boland whispered.

The ring was in my hand, Danny Talbot immediately pressed the ring into my hand. Reverend Boland again said, "The ring," and gently pried the golden circle loose from my fingers, and said, "The wedding ring is the outward and visible sign of an inward and spiritual bond which unites two loyal hearts in endless love," and then gave me the ring again. I took Nancy's left hand in my own, and repeated what I had learned at yesterday's rehearsal, "In token of the pledge of the vow made between us, with this ring I thee wed," and quickly slipped the ring onto her finger.

Reverend Boland stood still and tall and majestic for a moment, a pleased awed smile on his face, as though he had been privileged to witness a miracle. Then, as I stood before him with Nancy's trembling hand in my own, he intoned in a rich and solemn and echoing voice the words we were in this church to hear, the words that had taken less than ten minutes (I had met her in the summer of 1915!) to reach, "Forasmuch as Bertram Alfred Tyler and Nancy Ellen Clark (it was still not too late, I could bolt for the doors at the rear of the church, run west for California and the Pacific Ocean) have consented together in holy wedlock, and have witnessed the same before God and this company (get a boat to Hong Kong, become a rich silk merchant there, wear a little black hat on my head) and have declared the same by joining hands (and have a dozen concubines, Lotus Blossom, Peach Tree Honey) and by giving and receiving a ring (it's not too late, I thought, run, I thought, run!) I pronounce that they are husband and wife together, in the name of the Father, and of the Son, and of the Holy Spirit." Reverend Boland paused and raised his face heavenward. "Those whom God hath joined together," he said, "let not man put asunder." He paused again. He looked at us both. "Amen," he said.

Nancy lifted her head and her eyes and her veil, and I brushed my lips against hers, embarrassed to be kissing her here in public, even though she was my wife now, my *wife!* And I said, not knowing if I meant it, "I love you, Nancy," and she tilted her head to one side and, eyes glistening, said, "Pardon?" and I knew that I had meant it.

May ⚘ ⚘ ⚘

There was pot in the apartment, of course, provided by Lenny as matter of factly as he provided the silverware and the sheets, nothing to write the Federal Bureau of Narcotics about, just enough for a little smoke every now and again. Actually, it would have been just as simple for Dana and me to have bought our nickel bags in Cambridge or New Haven, but it was more convenient to have the stuff waiting there for us in Providence each weekend (not to mention a good deal safer besides, what with all those state lines being crossed). Lenny would leave it in a little plastic bag in the refrigerator ("Oregano, in case anyone asks; livens up the cuisine") and we would pay him for it on a consumer basis, using an honor system Dana and I scrupulously respected. Neither of us were potheads. We'd bust a joint on Friday night when we got to the apartment, and maybe have oh at the most two or three more over the weekend, something like that. It was good.

Everything was good that spring.

Dana said that nobody in Hollywood would have been interested in Our Love Story because it was so plebeian; we had not met cute, and we didn't do any kookie offbeat things like buying red onions on Olvera Street, the commute being a long one from Providence. I informed her, however, that she possessed a couple of natural attributes long considered viable commodities on the Hollywood mart, and that perhaps we could approach a movie sale under the table, so to speak, Our Romance being weak on plot, true enough, but at least one of the characters being well-developed, if she took my meaning. ("Oh *yes*, sir," she trilled, "I *take* your meaning, and I *do* so want to be a star!") But I suppose our relationship *was* singularly lacking in spectator interest. We did not, for example, walk barefoot in the rain even once that spring. We walked— yes, sometimes when the sky over that old city was an unblemished blue, and the spring air came in off the Atlantic with a tangy whiff of salt and a promise of summer suddenly so strong it brought with it the tumbled rush of every summer past, the lingering images of crowded vacation highways and white sand beaches, fireworks and beer, hot dogs, lobster rolls, children shrieking, weathered oceanfront hotels, last summer crowding next summer in that Providence spring—we walked hand in hand and told lovers' secrets no more important than that I had cheated to win a prize in the third grade (and had not been found out) or that Dana had lettered in eyebrow pencil when she was twelve years old, on her respective budding breasts, "Orangeade" and "Lemonade."

But we had no favorite restaurant, and we did not discover a great Italian joint with red-checked tablecloths and candles sticking in empty Chianti bottles dripping wax, where Luigi whom we knew by name rushed to greet us at the door (*"Mama mia,* you no binna here long time!") and led us to a table near a cheerful fire that dispelled whatever winter's bite still hovered, though spring was surely upon us and we were in love. We had no such rendezvous where jealous patrons watched as Luigi fussed over our glowing romance and waited while we tasted the rubious wine, and kissed his fingers and nodded and went out to the kitchen to tell his wife that the young lovers loved the wine, our personal Henry Armetta, while we ourselves grandstanded to the crowded cozy restaurant, I staring deep into Dana's eyes, she touching my hand on the checked tablecloth with one slender carmine-tipped forefinger, we had no such place.

We had instead a hundred places, all of them lousy. We ate whenever we were hungry, and we were hungry often. Like frenzied teeny-boppers we became instantly ravenous, demanding food at once lest heads roll, and then were instantly gratified by whatever swill the nearest diner offered—until hunger struck again and we became wild Armenians striding the streets in search of blood. Dana was at her barbaric worst immediately after making love. She would leap out of bed naked and stalk through the apartment, a saber-toothed tigress on a hunt, heading directly for the refrigerator where she would fling out food like the dismembered parts of victims, making horrible sounds of engorgement all the while, and then coming back to me to say, "Shall I make us something to eat?" She was an excellent cook, though a reluctant one, and she sometimes whipped up ginzo delights learned from her father's mother, and unlike anything even dreamt of by *my* mother, Dolores Prine Tyler, with her Ann Page pasta.

The games we played were personal and therefore exclusive, lacking in universality and therefore essentially dull to anyone but ourselves. The Tyler-Castelli Television Commercial Award was invented one Saturday night while we were watching a message-ridden late movie on Lenny's old set, wheeled to the foot of the bed. The judges for the TCTC Award (Dana and I) gave undisputed first prize to the Wrigley Spearmint Chewing Gum commercial as the best example of freedom from complexity, pretentiousness, or ornamentation; the coveted runner-up prize went to the Gallo Wine Company, whose handsome baritone actor-vineyard owner on horseback was forced to sing "wine country" as "wine cun-*tree*" for the sake of the jingle's scan. In similar fashion, there was the Tyler-Castelli Award for Literary Criticism (first prize went to Martin Levin of the New York *Times* for having reviewed ten thousand books in five months, somehow skipping only the novels of Styron, Salinger, Bellow, Roth, Malamud, and Updike); the Tyler-Castelli Award for Athletic Achievement (first prize went to Sonny Liston for his recent one-minute performance in Lewiston, Maine); and the Tyler-Castelli Award for Quick Thinking (which went to Lyndon Baines Johnson for his speedy dispatch of the United States Marines to Santo Domingo, his second such award in three months).

There was (I knew, Dana knew) nothing very special about our love, except that it was ours and it was good. We floated, we drifted toward a limbo of not-quite-irresponsibility, lulled by each other's presence and the soporific vapors of spring. I was protected from the draft by my student status at Yale, and I was smart enough (Wat

Tyler on black-and-white film asserts to his own high intelligence while assorted professors and scientists applaud his modesty) to be able to grapple with whatever old Eli threw at me in the semester to come, confident in short that I could preserve my deferment. Dana was a bright girl and an honor student, and if we slouched through most of our courses, it didn't show in our grades. We bathed regularly. We wrote or called home even when we didn't need money. We were a pair of passionate isolationists who sought neither followers nor converts, involved in a love we knew was genuine and true. And since it was ours alone, and since it was so good, we naturally felt free to abuse it.

(This is Wat Tyler's first screen appearance in color, idol of millions, and he is disturbed by his red-faced image, did he look that way in the rushes? Apart, he wonders how Dana can have caused such rage in him. The flickering flames of film reveal the camera coming in for a tight close shot of his fists clenching and unclenching. The audience Wat Tyler watches the star Wat Tyler as the sound track shrieks under the tense, homicidal hands, "I can't get no satisfaction.")

Dana was sitting in the center of Lenny's bed, eyes averted the way they'd been that first night here in January, partially turned away from me, hands in her lap. She was wearing faded blue jeans and a green sweater. Her hair was pulled back into a ponytail. There was no lipstick on her mouth. It was ten o'clock on a Friday night. She usually caught the five o'clock train from Boston and was at the apartment by six-thirty.

"Why are you so late?" I asked her.

"I ran into someone."

"Who?"

"An old friend."

"Where?"

"In Boston, where do you think? My God, Wat, it's only . . ."

"Why didn't you call?"

"I wasn't anywhere near a phone."

"Well, where, what do you mean, there're phones all *over* Boston, how could you possibly not be anywhere near a *phone?* Didn't you know I'd be worrying?"

"No, I didn't know."

"Well, I was."

"I'm sorry."

"Where were you?"

"By the river."

"What river?"

"There's only one undergraduate river in Boston, which river do you think?"

"I'm not that goddamn familiar with Boston."

"The Charles," Dana said softly.

"With who, whom?"

"With Max."

(The close shot of Wat Tyler's eyes reveals jealousy, fury, fear, unreasoning black rage, all represented by a superimposed fireworks display erupting in each pupil. The soundtrack features his harsh breathing. The Stones's "Satisfaction" has segued into The Yardbirds' "I'm a Man." It is wintertime in the film, the window behind Wat Tyler is rimed with frost, there is the distant jingle of Dr. Zhivago sleigh bells on the icebound street outside. In the room it is May and Lenny Samalson has put flowered Bonwit Teller sheets on the bed in celebration of spring, but it is a dank winter in Wat Tyler's mind; her body will hardly have deteriorated at all when they find it naked in the snow a week from now.)

"Max," I repeated.

"Yes. Max."

"You ran into him."

"Yes."

"Where?"

"I didn't exactly run into him. He called."

"When?"

"This afternoon. I went back to the dorm to pick up my bag, and Max called."

"To say what?"

"To say how was I, and it had been a long time, and all that."

"So how'd you end up by the river?"

"He said he had a few minutes and would I like to go for a walk or something? So I said I was on my way to catch the train to Providence, and he said Oh, in that case. So I felt sorry for him and I said Okay I'll take a walk with you, Max."

"So you went by the river for a few minutes, and now it's ten o'clock at night when you should have been here by six-thirty."

183

"We didn't stay by the river."

"Where'd you go?"

"Wat, I'm very tired. I really would like to put on my nightgown and go to bed. Can't this wait until morning? Nothing so terrible happened, believe me."

"What *did* happen?"

"We went up to Max's room, and we had a drink."

"And then what?"

"And then we had another drink."

"Did he try to lay you?"

"Yes."

"Did you let him?"

"No."

"Why'd you go up there, Dana? Didn't you *know* he'd try?"

"No, I *didn't* know he'd try. I wanted to *see* if he'd try."

"You were sleeping with the guy for a month before we met, did you expect him to get you up to his room and discuss the weather?"

"I didn't know what to expect. I hadn't seen him since December, when we ended it, and I was surprised when he called and ... I was curious, all right? I wanted to see."

"See what?"

"I wanted to see if . . . there was anything there any more."

"What did you expect to be there?"

"Damn you, Wat, I loved him once!"

"The way you love me."

"Yes. No. Right now, I hate you."

"Why? Because I don't like you kissing around with your discarded boyfriends?"

"We didn't ... oh, all right, *yes,* he kissed me, all right? He kissed me several times, all right?"

"Good old trustworthy Max."

"You're a riot, do you know that? You even expect *Max* to be faithful to you!"

"I expect Max to get run over by a bus!"

"Go make a little doll, why don't you?"

"I'll make two while I'm at it."

(The image on the screen, the Victorian strait-laced stuffy impossible image of Walter Tyler, Esquire, is amusing even to himself. He cannot believe the

184

soundtrack, he cannot believe that these words are issuing from his mouth, and yet the camera never lies, and he can see his lips moving, he can hear the words tumbling sternly from his prudishly puckered mouth, what does he expect from her?)

"I expected more from you."

"More? Than what?"

"Than . . . whatever you want to call it. An *adventure* in some guy's room. Kissing you and . . . getting you drunk . . ."

"Oh, crap, Wat, I'm not drunk. Do I look drunk?"

"You look like a cheap cunt."

"Thank you," she said, and rose suddenly and swiftly from the bed, and walked immediately to the lone dresser in the room where she began pulling out slips and bras and nightgowns and stockings, flapping each garment angrily into the air like a battle flag.

"Where do you think you're going?" I said.

(The words are familiar and clichéd, they suddenly reduce this love affair to the absurd, taking from it even its dullness, its lack of uniqueness. His face in closeup is clichéd, too, it expresses the emotional range of a stock company James Garner. He looks by turn indignant, terrified, self-righteous, and a trifle ill.)

"I'm going back to Boston," Dana said.

"You just got here," I said.

"Yes, and I'll get back, too."

"I thought you loved me."

"You don't own me," Dana said.

"I don't own you, but I thought you loved me."

"I do love you, but you don't own me."

"Well, stop flapping your goddamn clothes around like that."

"They're *my* clothes, I'll flap them however the hell I want to flap them, you silly bastard," she said, and burst out laughing.

In bed there was no quarrel, there was never any quarrel.

(There is no film, either. There is no second Wat Tyler when he is in bed with her, no alter ego, no schizophrenic super-image hovering somewhere in the air-conditioned spectator darkness.)

The long limp line of her lying still and spent against the rumpled sheet.

185

I came out of the bathroom and was surprised anew by her, each fresh glimpse a discovery. One arm raised above her head, elbow bent, hand dangling, she lay on her side with eyes closed and lips slightly parted, distant, oh so distant from me and the apartment and Providence and the world, cloistered in whatever sun-dappled female glade we had led her to together. I stood with the bathroom door ajar behind me, one hand still on the knob, and watched her quietly, and knew something of her selfsame mood, felt it touch me from across the room to include me in a sweet and silent private peace.

The first time she blew me, I yelled when I came and the guy next door banged on the wall.

"Who taught you that?" I whispered later. "Max?"

"Oh no, sir," she said. "That was my very first time."

"Sure," I said and smiled. Max could not have mattered less. We were still discovering each other, Dana and I. We were falling in love over and over and over again.

June ❦ ❦

Dear Will,

I met a girl last night who said she knew you. (Actually, what she said was "Your brother and I are acquainted.") Anyway, I gave her your address, and she said she might write. Her name is Margie Penner, are you "acquainted"? She seemed a bit *fast*, brother dear.

So now what? I swear, Will, I'm having the darndest time trying to keep up with your meanderings. You left Mississippi on the sixth of May, and this is only June 11th, so I guess you're still in California. But when do you go into the pilot pool, and where *is* the pilot pool (Are enlisted men allowed to swim with you guys, hee-hee) and does this mean you'll be going overseas before long? (Daddy says I shouldn't ask you about when you're going overseas because you can't answer me, anyway, but how about a little hint, huh?)

I guess you're just panting to know what's new here in the Windy City, ho-hum. Iris and I went to see Vaughn

Monroe at the Chicago Theatre Tuesday night, he of the gravelly tonsils and the lunar speed contest. He's got a pretty good band, though I must say I's reactions were largely glandular, swooning and flopping all over the place like a salmon going upstream to lay her eggs. (Oh my! Naughty naughty Lindy!) She's been dating a boy who works in the grinder room at Daddy's mill. Actually she met him here one night when we had some kids over listening to records and he came to deliver some papers Daddy had left at the office. He's 4-F because of a heart murmur. It's my guess that I is developing a heart murmur of her own, though, judging from the way she talks about him all the time. But V.M. gave him a little competition Tuesday night.

I am now busily reading *A Tale of Two Cities* in *Classic Comics* for a test coming up next week in Miss Lougee's English class. (I think you had her when you were a junior, she's the one with the long nose and the teaspoon figure, a charmer altogether.) She marks on a curve, and the highest grade on the last quiz she gave was a 47! I guess that gives some indication of the wisdom she's distributing to us little adolescent minds, huh? Speaking of little adolescent minds, Dumbo, how about writing once in a while? I know you're a very big officer now in charge of Air Force personnel, planes, landing fields, bases and parachutes (not to mention that big pool where you won't let the enlisted man swim, shame on you!) but perhaps you will now and then think fondly of your bratty little sister back here in Chicago and drop her a line other than those change-of-address cards you're always shooting off.

Guess who's home?

And guess who went out with him?

Me!

And I won't tell who.

> Your mysterious sister,
> Lindy

P.S. Who's Ace Gibson, he sounds a dream! Bring him home on your next furlough! *That's an order!*

6/12/44

Dear Will,

Remember me? I'll bet you don't. We met at Michael Mallory's house one New Year's Eve, and spent a little time together, remember? I guess you're wondering how I got your address. Well, I'll tell you.

The U.S.O. on Michigan and Congress has this system where girls who want to help out can give private parties in their houses. There has to be a chaperone, of course, and whoever's giving the party has to provide for refreshments and all that. It's a very nice way for servicemen to meet people in a homey atmosphere. There are so *many* servicemen in Chicago these days. Anyway, I have a week's vacation (I'm working at The Boston Store now, and my mother said it would be all right if I contacted the U.S.O. and arranged for such a party, which I did). But I was short of girls because I needed around a dozen, so I asked the U.S.O. if they could help me get some nice girls for the party, and they gave me a list of about ten names, three of which came. Well, one of the girls was an attractive little blonde, seventeen years old, with a very cute figure and blue eyes that reminded me of a fellow I had met one New Year's Eve. We got to talking and her name turned out to be Linda Tyler. Anybody you know? It was, naturally, your sister, and when I told her I had once met you, she said you might like to hear from me, and she gave me your address. I hope she was right.

Well, well, so you're a lieutenant now! That's very exciting. What kind of airplanes do you fly? Your sister wasn't sure. She said a P-38, I think. Is there such a plane? She also told me you'd be spending some time in California, you lucky thing. I'll bet you're as brown as a berry. I've never been to California. I'll bet it's very nice out there, though the weather here in Chicago is pleasant just now. Even got over to the lake for a little swimming the other day.

Before I forget, I'm not sure this will reach you at the address your sister gave me because she didn't seem to know how long you would be in Transition Training before you were shipped overseas, so I'm just taking a chance sending this to you at the Santa Maria Army Air Base, and hoping it will be forwarded to you if you've already left there. There was a boy I was corresponding with in the Marine Corps before he got killed, and they were very good about forwarding his mail to him wherever he went, though he had an F.P.O. address, and I see that you don't have an A.P.O. yet. Well, I'll just hope you get it, that's all. I'll hope, too, that your sister was mistaken about your being sent across. Now that we've landed in Normandy, the war should be over soon, don't you think?

Do you hear from Michael Mallory? Your sister said that he was a pilot, too. Well, I don't seem to have much more to say. I hope you receive this letter, and I hope you'll remember me, and answer it if you can.

Yours truly,
Margaret Penner

P.S. We don't live on Halsted any more. My new address is:

Miss Margaret Penner
5832 South Princeton Avenue
Chicago, Illinois

I can't wait for you two guys to get together. My brother's about as big as you are, Will, maybe an inch or so taller, with blond hair and brown eyes and *my* dumb buck teeth, only on him they look good. Are you an athlete? He was an athlete back home, a four-letter man, his sports were baseball, basketball, soccer, and track. Baseball was really his game, though; he pitched a no-hitter in the Little League when he was only ten years old, I'll never forget that day as long as I live.

My mother came over to the field in the seventh inning, wearing jodhpurs and flicking her riding crop against her boot. I told her Skipper had a no-hitter going, and she said, Really, what's a no-hitter? She was there to pick us up after the game, and she was pissed off because it wasn't over yet. She kept telling me about a dumb mare named Peony who'd developed a capped hock. I wanted to say Listen, go to hell, you and Peony both, my big brother's got a no-hitter going, can't you understand that? They carried him on their shoulders after the game, he was all covered with sweat, his face all flushed, and he looked around—he was on his back, you know, legs up in the air, arms waving for balance—he twisted his neck and spotted me in the crowd and yelled Hey there, Ace, we did it, huh? *We* did it.

He was in college when this thing started, you know, he could have gone in as an officer, but he didn't want to. I told him he was crazy. Look, I said, get the most out of it, Skip, get the good chow and the broads and the easy times, why knock yourself out? No, he couldn't see it my way. He enlisted in the Navy, so now he's a big deal Gunner's Mate/Third, what's that the equivalent of, Will? A buck sergeant? He's wasting himself, he really is. And with that Navy officer's uniform, he could be getting more tail than he'd know what to do with, not that he's making out too badly as it is. He's got himself a little nurse off the hospital ship out there, she's risking decapitation for fraternizing with an enlisted man, but she just can't keep her hands off him. She goes around in a fog all day long, just waiting to get ashore to be with him, No, no, Miss Abernathy, I told you to prick his boil, do you know that one? You do? There's this new nurse at a hospital, you see, and on her first day the intern tells her . . .

Dear Will,
The picture on the front of this card is me at Cape Cod. (Ha-ha) Here with Mommy alone just now, but Daddy will join us on the Fourth. How come the Air Force never sends you home? They sure are keeping you flying, lieutenant. (Ho-ho!) Our address here is: c/o Lambert, Truro, Massachusetts. Write, right?
Love & stuff,
Charlotte Wagner

Dear Will,
I'm writing again because I thought my last letter might not have reached you.
I guess you're wondering how come all this activity when we haven't seen each other for almost a year and a half now, and hardly knew each other even then. Well, I found you very interesting to talk to that night, and I thought it might be fun for both of us to start a correspondence. There are no ulterior motives involved here, Will, as I have a boyfriend at the University of Ohio who is in the Navy's V-12 program there, and he knows I'm writing to you. I told him so when I spoke to him on the telephone last night. His name is Frederick Parker, Freddie for short. He's from Edison Park, perhaps you know him.
Well, enough about Freddie.

I'm dying to know what it feels like to fly an airplane, Perhaps, if you have the time, you might describe it to me as I'm truly interested. I would imagine a person would be scared to death up there. Suppose you run out of gas or something? Do you fly with another person in the airplane with you, or are you all alone up there? Is it difficult to read all those instruments? In pictures I have seen, it looks like there's a hundred of them.

I suppose you're very handsome in your lieutenant's uniform, though Freddie would kill me if he could read that. (I won't tell him if you won't.) In case you've forgotten what I look like, I'm enclosing a picture I took at the lake a few Sundays ago. (Don't mind the girl clowning around in front. She's my girlfriend Louise.) I got a terrible burn the day the picture was taken, you should have seen me. I'm a redhead (I *guess* you remember) and it's true what they say about redheads having very fair skin that boils in the sun.

Well, I guess that's all for now. *I Love A Mystery* goes on in about ten minutes, and I don't want to miss it. Please tell me all about flying.

Fondly,
Margie

I've always had a thing about names, Will. When I was twelve or thirteen, I used to dream of dating girls with names like Connie or Grace or Wendy or Gail, they were all lovely blond dolls with long hair blowing. I guess I must have fallen in love with a dozen Connies later on, but only because I was already in love with the name. Even now, if someone says, Listen there's this great girl you have to meet, her name is Gladys or Adelaide or Hannah, it's simply not the same as April or Deborah or Diane. Okay, it's a quirk. But *you* try living with Avery for a while. All I'm trying to say is that the *name* got me even before I saw the actual airplane. Even the *number* got me. What are you laughing at? You think P-38 is the same as P-40 or P-47? Well, it isn't. There's something sexy about P-38, stop laughing, will you? P-38, *listen* to it! It rolls off the tongue, P-38, it's got a nice easy flow to it—you jackass, I'm trying to tell you something about this *airplane* we're flying!

You know what the Germans call her? *Der gabel-*

schwanz teufel, I think that's how it's pronounced. It means fork-tailed devil. Now, Will, that's a pretty fair reputation to have up there with you, the fork-tailed devil, the Lockheed Lightning. You can't tell me that Curtiss Warhawk or Republic Thunderbolt sound anywhere near as exciting as Lockheed Lightning, that's like saying Minnie is as exciting as Fran. I'm not even talking about *looks* now, I'm talking about the *name* of this bitch, the P-38 Lightning, it makes you want to hop into her and ride her up against whatever they've got!

The first time I glimpsed her, Will (I know you felt exactly the same way because I saw you when you landed, I saw that look on your face) the first time I glimpsed her sitting out there on the field in a long line of silver beauties in the sun, I thought You can't ask me to fly that sweet precious thing, you can't ask me to risk taking her off the ground where she might get hurt, you've got to build a big plexiglas bubble all around her and just let people come to gape at her the way I'm gaping now. I could have written a poem about that piece, well, what the hell's so comical, would you please tell me? I happen to be *serious* here.

No, the hell with it. Never mind. No, never mind. Just forget it. If you want to go through life an ignorant, insensitive clod, that's your business. Why don't you go over there and sit with old Hotshot Horace, let him spit on you when he talks, maybe you like guys who use their hands when they tell how they dove at the screen, rat-tat-tat-tat-tat, pwwwwwwwwssssssssshhhhhhhhh, all over your blouse, go ahead, Will, never mind the people in this world who've got a little feeling for things.

I know that airplane has the same effect on you, I *know* she has.

Will, did you ever *see* anything so gorgeous in your life? I could've kissed that whole long shining silver line of her, right from that sweet thrusting nacelle, cannon and all, machine guns, every tooled part of that beautiful machine, kissed both those booms and traveled down her belly under those majestic wings—did you ever *imagine* such a wingspread? I thought, God, she's the biggest fighting airplane I've ever seen, she's going to *swallow* me, this bitch, and make me a part of her. When I climbed inside her, Will . . .

Dear Will,

I haven't heard from you as yet, but I thought I'd write anyway, just to see how you were getting along. It is now two o'clock in the morning, and I just got home from a dance at the U.S.O. The dance ended at twelve-thirty, but some of us girls went over to Wabash for hot dogs afterwards, and so I just got here. It is very quiet and still here in the house, you could hear a mouse squeak. (Not that we have any.)

I had a dream about you the other night, it was a very strange dream, I don't even know if I should tell it to you. Louise says I shouldn't, but I'll take a chance. She thinks I'm crazy writing to you, anyway, even though my boyfriend Freddie knows all about us. (I mean, about my writing to you and all. I have never told him about how we met, do you think I should? I will do whatever you advise. He's a very jealous person.) Anyway, about the dream.

It took place in Michael Mallory's house, but it wasn't on New Year's Eve, it was Christmas morning instead. And it seemed I was living there or something because I woke up in the bedroom upstairs, and I was in my nightgown, and I came down the steps into the living room wearing only my nightgown. There was a big Christmas tree in the center of the room, all lit up with lights, and there were a lot of Christmas presents all around the tree, and all of the presents were for me. They all had these little cards on them saying "To Margie."

So far it's a funny dream to be having in the middle of the summer, don't you think, when the temperature here in Chicago was ninety-four degrees yesterday!

Well, naturally, I started opening all the presents (this is the part Louise says I shouldn't tell you) and in each one of the presents there was *YOU!?!* Even the tiniest present, when I opened it there was *YOU!?!* inside. You were wearing your uniform and a flying helmet and goggles and a white scarf and you had grease marks on your cheeks and around your eyes when you lifted up the goggles. You also had a mustache. (You haven't grown a mustache, have you?) And each time I opened another present I was very happy to see that it was you, and I kissed you each time (I mean each time I took off the wrapping paper and there was another you). I got your grease all over the front of my nightgown. It was this pink nightgown I have, it's hardly anything at all. Finally the whole room was all full of these Will Tylers, some of them life-size, some of them smaller, some bigger, I was absolutely surrounded! Then you said, this was the first time you said anything in the dream, you said "Margie, you have my grease all over you," and I said, "Yes, my nightie got dirty," and I woke up.

That's some funny dream, don't you think? What do you think of it?

Well, here I am in the same pink nightgown I had on in the dream (but no grease on it) and I feel just miserable in this heat. I hate Chicago in the summer, don't you? As a matter of fact, I also hate it in the winter. I sometimes wish I could just leave this damn city and go someplace where nobody knows me. You fellows are lucky, though you don't realize it. You get a chance to travel all over the country and even the world with Uncle Sam paying for it. Maybe I will join the Wacs, do you think that's a good idea? Though brown isn't my color. Maybe the Waves.

The dance tonight was very depressing, I don't know why. I am a very moody person, Will, I guess you don't know that, but it's true. Sometimes, when Freddie calls me long distance from Ohio, I feel as if I have nothing to say to him because I'm in one of my moods. He's a very nice fellow and he wants to be an engineer when the war is over, which is why the V-12 program is so good for him. It is paying for his college education, and he will also be an officer when he gets into the Navy. He says the Navy is the best place to be because you always know where you're going to be sleeping that night, not like the Army, and also because you get hot meals. I think that's very sensible. I sometimes wonder what it would be like married to an engineer. I don't even know what it is engineers do. Do you plan to continue flying when you get out of the service? I guess all the airlines will be hiring you boys who have flying experience.

Did you get my picture? If so, what did you think of it? I know it's not a very good picture, but I am interested in your opinion. It's so damn hot here, you have no idea. I probably will go to the beach again tomorrow, and then tomorrow night it's into my little bed early because Monday morning I have to go back to work. I certainly hate to go back after such a nice vacation.

Well, I seem to be running out of words, so until I hear from you, I guess I'll sign off. Let me know what you think about my crazy dream, as I'm very interested in your opinion. Also about the picture I sent to you.

Affectionately,
Margie

6/25/44

Dear Will,

First of all, I hardly know the girl. As I told you, we met at a U.S.O. party, and she casually said (with a lot of coy arching of the eyebrows) that you and she were (little nudge of the elbow) very close (Get it, dearie?) and what a shame it was that she didn't have your address. So I gave her your address. So a week later, I had just come back from the beach with Iris (the weather here has been so beastly, you could die) and the phone rings and it's Margaret Penner. Margaret *who?* I said. Margaret Penner. Okay, hello, Margaret Penner, how are you? (Aside to I: Who the hell is Margaret Penner?) Margaret Penner explains who Margaret Penner is. She is the girl who gave the U.S.O. party at her house, remember? and she used to know my brother Will, remember? So I said Oh *yes,* Margaret Penner! Whereupon she told me she had sent you a letter at Santa Maria but now she wasn't sure you would get it because I had mentioned something about your perhaps going overseas soon, or into the pilot pool, or whatever, and did I think it would be all right if she sent you a second letter? So I said I certainly didn't think you'd mind, and it was very sweet of her and all that, our dear beloved boys in the service of this mighty nation being very greedy for mail. Goodbye to Margaret Penner.

Until tonight.

Tonight, I washed my hair and I was in my pajamas listening to Eddie Cantor and the telephone rings again. It is (guess who?) Margaret Penner again, and she's in tears. Apparently my dear brother Will wrote her some kind of filthy letter describing in detail all the things he would like to do to her, and Margaret Penner wanted to know from me whether I thought she looked like *that* kind of girl, the kind of girl you could write *that* kind of letter to. I assured her she looked every bit as sweet as Moll Flanders, and that you probably had written your letter in a drunken frenzy, the strain on fighter pilots being intolerable, and that you were probably sorry as could be afterwards.

I don't know what's wrong with you, Will, I think the Air Force has made you a little dotty. I don't mind straightening out your romances (like hell I don't) or handling nutty girls on the telephone right when Parkyakarkus is coming on, but I'm really disappointed that you could write a letter like that to *anybody*, really, Will! I might as well tell you this now while you're still in the States, because I guess once you're overseas I'll have to be very careful of what I say, otherwise some nasty Nazi will shoot you down in flames and I'll be sorry the rest of my life. I think it was a lousy miserable and not very comical thing to do, and you should be ashamed of yourself. There.

Besides, aren't there any girls out there in California?

Linda

We had driven down to Los Angeles from Santa Maria, and were sitting with a sodden captain from the Van Nuys Army Air Base in a bar called The Eucalyptus on Wilshire Boulevard. The captain's name was Smythe, and he had received a Dear John letter from his wife the day before. He was telling us that all women were tramps and that you could not trust them as far as you could throw them.

"To coin a phrase," Ace said.

"Absolutely," Smythe said, "to coin a phrase."

He had a red mustache, and he stroked it now and lifted his empty shot glass, tried to drain it all over again, realized there was no whiskey in it, and said, "Bartender, let me have another drink here, willya? My glass is empty here."

The jukebox was bubbling with red and blue and yellow lights and oozing "Harlem Nocturne" into the scented dimness of the bar. From the leatherette booths came the muted hovering whisper of men engaged in earnest negotiation with all the town whores, the clink of melting ice in whiskey-sodas gone two a.m. flat, the lamentable sound of

196

someone puking in the men's room behind the hanging flowered curtain.

Smythe sipped at his fresh drink with remarkable restraint, and then began to describe his wife's lover in far-too meticulous detail, it seemed to me, almost with reluctant admiration, almost as if he longed to poke us with an elbow now and then, and grin fraternally, and say, "How do you *like* that son of a bitch?" The son of a bitch was a real estate agent in Smythe's home town somewhere in Massachusetts. Naturally, he was 4-F, but apparently not too physically handicapped to have escaped Mrs. Smythe's attention. "Knew the fellow all my life," Smythe said. "Went to *school* with him. To *school*. With him. Her, too. Went to school with both of them."

"He could have had the decency to stop while you were talking," Ace said, and laughed, and said to me, "Do you know that one, Will?"

"Yes, I do," I said.

"You know him?" Smythe asked. "You know the man who womanized my wife?"

"Never heard of him," Ace said.

"Went to school with him," Smythe said.

"What school was that?"

"Saint Thomas Aquinas."

"Are you a Catholic?" I asked.

"No," Smythe said. "Saint Thomas Aquinas was a Catholic, but I am not a Catholic, no. My wife is a Catholic. *Was* a Catholic. The man who womanized her is a Catholic. I should never have gone to Saint Thomas Aquinas. That was my first mistake."

"That was your *second* mistake," I said.

"What was my first mistake?"

"What was his first mistake, Ace?"

"Getting," Ace said.

"Getting what?" Smythe asked.

"Born, married, drafted, screwed."

"Yes, sir," Smythe said, "that was my first mistake, all right."

"This is the best pilot who ever lived," Ace said.

"Thank you," Smythe said, "but I am not a pilot. I am in Supply."

"I was referring to my friend here, Will Tyler."

"Thank you," I said.

"Will Tyler owes the squadron thirty-seven dollars."

197

"Which I'll pay."

"Which he will of course pay because he's a trustworthy and decent human being."

"Not like that son of a bitch Andy, how do you like that son of a bitch?" Smythe said at last, and grinned and actually gave Ace an elbow.

"I take it that Andy is the guy who put the horns on you," Ace said.

"That's who he is, all right. Biggest mistake I ever made in my life," Smythe said.

"Would you like to know why Will Tyler owes the squadron thirty-seven dollars?"

"No, why?" Smythe said.

"Because he put thirty-seven bullets into the screen, and all thirty-seven of them made holes longer than the legally prescribed length of two inches. That's why."

"Thirty-seven holes, my, my," Smythe said.

"Thirty-seven holes at one dollar a hole equals thirty-seven dollars, if my addition is correct," Ace said.

"Your addition is flawless," I said.

"Are you boys fliers?" Smythe asked.

"We are very hot pilots," I said.

"Are you familiar with air gunnery, sir?" Ace asked.

"Oh no," Smythe said.

"There's a B-26 that tows a screen for us to shoot at," Ace said. "We use a B-26 because it's the only one of the bombers that can simulate the speed of an enemy fighter. The screen is made of woven wire . . ."

"Oh, I see," Smythe said.

". . . wrapped in thread, and we fire live bullets at the screen. Fifty-caliber machine-gun bullets."

"Oh yes."

"Each pilot has different colored bullets. So at the end of the day we can see how many hits he's made. Will's bullets today were red."

"Old Red Bullets Tyler," I said.

"Now there's an angle beyond which we are not supposed to attack because shooting down the bomber is *not* the objective, sir, definitely not the objective."

"No, no."

What he was trying to explain to Captain Smythe whose wife had run off with Andy the real estate man was that you came up on the screen (you usually *rose* to meet

198

enemy fighters because they tried to attack an escorted bomber formation from above, a position that gave them the advantage in speed and maneuverability) you came *up* on the screen in a flight of four airplanes, your bullets painted in one of the primary colors, red, blue or yellow, with green thrown in for good measure. Because the screen was constructed of tightly woven wire mesh, the bullets left a streak of paint behind them whenever you scored a hit. Now when you attacked the screen in a perpendicular pass, it was difficult to hit because you were traveling in different directions and had to lead it the way you would a flying duck. But if you fell *behind* the screen it became easier to hit because you were then traveling in the same direction at almost identical speeds and it was somewhat like firing at a stationary target instead of a moving one. At the same time, though, you were endangering the bomber because it was now *ahead* of you, say at one or two o'clock level, and there was the possibility of ripping its tail assembly to shreds with your enthusiastic slugs. The further you fell behind the screen in your pass, the more oblique was the firing angle, with the result that the slashes you put into the target got longer and longer. That was what Ace was trying to explain to the drunken captain from Massachusetts.

". . . costing the United States Government a considerable amount of money should a bomber get shot down by accident."

"Naturally."

"There is a fine of one dollar per bullet for each bullet that has left a telltale hole larger than two inches."

"Oh yes."

"Today, Fearless Will Tyler put thirty-seven such holes in the screen, thereby causing the pilot of the B-26 to have a screaming shit fit. I tell you, sir, Will Tyler is already a flier of renown, even though he has not yet shot down a single enemy plane. He almost got one of *ours* today, but that doesn't count. I ask you, Will, I ask you now in the presence of this grieving officer and gentleman . . ."

"That's me," Smythe said.

"I ask you why the hell you did such a dumb fool thing?"

"Because it was fun," I answered.

June 27, 1944

Dear Will,

Daddy and I will be leaving for Wisconsin on the Fourth to spend a few weeks with Aunt Clara in Freshwater. The address there is:

   c/o Edwin Mueller
   1110 Congress Street
   Freshwater, Wisconsin

If the Air Force has any plans for you, please let us know about them there. We'll be home again on the sixteenth or seventeenth, it's not entirely settled yet. Please take care of yourself.

         Lindy

June 29, 1944

Dear Will,

I showed your letter to Freddie and he thinks you're a pervert. I also showed it to Louise, and she says she never read such filthy language in her entire life. Freddie wanted to send your letter to the Air Force as he thinks you're unfit to serve this country in the uniform of an officer. I advised him not to bother.

I'm sorry you chose to abuse our friendship.

I certainly will never understand what got into you.

Goodbye, and I hoped you have a wonderful summer writing other dirty letters to other girls who did nothing to deserve them.

       Margaret Alice Penner

July   ❧

The temperature in Chicago on that Sunday, July 27, had reached ninety-five degrees by four o'clock that afternoon, and there was scant relief from the oppressive mugginess, even on the beach. In Eau Fraiche, on a day like this, we would have packed a picnic lunch and gone down-peninsula where the breeze blowing in off Lake

Juneau would smell of pine and the water would be as clear and as icy cold as a cut diamond. Here in Chicago (which Mr. Sandburg three years ago had called, "half naked, sweating, proud to be Hog Butcher," and I didn't know how right he was till now) we sat on a lakeside beach and wondered if we wouldn't anyway be basted in our own fat.

On days like today, when Chicago seemed out to destroy us personally, when her buildings crowded in too tight, and her people jostled and pushed and talked too loud, the thought would again cross my mind that maybe I'd been shell-shocked over there, otherwise why would I have done a crazy thing like sacrificing the eight-dollar deposit on the Mechanic Street apartment and paying all those freight charges to have our new furniture moved here? Nancy crying and saying she did not *wish* to go to Chicago, and my telling her there was opportunity for me there, *what* opportunity? A madman's dream I had caught in a butterfly net on our honeymoon?

The advertisement had appeared in the *Tribune,* asking for a man with some knowledge of the paper industry to start as a trainee at Ramsey-Warner Papers, which was opening a new mill on the waterfront at Kedzie and Thirty-first. The waterfront had turned out to be the West Fork of the South Branch of the Chicago River, and the new mill would not be completed until June 1921, but in the meantime they were willing to retrain experienced people in their own production methods, and were willing to pay twenty-two dollars a week besides, which was not exactly alfalfa where I came from. So I had gone to see a Mr. Moreland out at the Joliet mill, and I had told him that whereas I did not have any experience in the paper industry, I did know a considerable lot about timber, having worked in a logging camp from the time I was fifteen until the time I enlisted in the Army—

"Oh, are you a veteran?" Mr. Moreland asked.

"Yes, sir," I said.

"See any combat?"

"Yes, sir," I said. "I was with the Third Division at the Marne and later fought in the Meuse-Argonne offensive."

"We were hoping for somebody with at least *some* experience, though," Mr. Moreland said.

"Well, I haven't any experience, sir," I said, "but I'm a

hard worker. I've got a wife to support, you see, and . . ."

"Oh, are you married, Taylor?"

"Tyler. Yes, sir, I was married just last Sunday. I'm here in Chicago on my honeymoon."

"You're applying for a job while you're on your honeymoon?"

"Yes, sir."

"Well, well," Mr. Moreland said.

"Sir," I said, "I can't see any future for me in timber."

"Can you see one in paper?"

"Yes, sir, I can," I said.

"When's your honeymoon over, Taylor?"

"Tyler. On the twenty-first of April."

"Can you start on May first?"

"Yes, sir."

"Then I guess you're hired."

"Thank you, sir," I said, and that was that.

I was always having to break things to Nancy after I'd already gone and done them, it seemed. I told her that night about my taking the job, and she said she thought I was crazy, so I reminded her that not so long ago she had said she'd come with me even to Paris if that's where I wanted to go, and she said, Pardon? which she said a lot lately when she heard things she didn't want to hear.

The apartment on Springfield and Twenty-eighth was nice, even Nancy had to admit that, a far sight nicer than the one we'd agreed to rent in Eau Fraiche. But Chicago was overwhelming, and I thought I would never get used to it. In our first several weeks there, I imagined I would choke each time I walked out into the street, the soot and grime were so terrible. Smoke poured from a thousand chimneys, prairie dust billowed up from the sidewalks, filth seemed everywhere in evidence, despite the big iron litter bins on the curbs, two and a half feet long and eighteen inches high, but so positioned that you had to step into the gutter to lift the lid and drop anything into them.

The buildings were another thing, not as big as some I'd seen in New York but enough to make me dizzy anyway whenever I looked up at one of them. In Eau Fraiche, the tallest building had been the Wisconsin Trust over on Carter Street, six stories high and considered huge. Here in Chicago, the City Hall and County Building covered the entire square between La Salle, Randolph, Washington and Clark Streets. Even the post office filled a whole city block, a big slate-gray bulding with a huge dome in the center and openwork stone balustrades over the pillared wings on each of its four sides. Of all the architecture in Chicago, I think I felt most comfortable with the two lions outside the Art Institute, themselves enormous, but affectionately called "prairie dogs" by the people of the city. I was not yet a Chicagoan. I could not get used to the grime or the size, I could not get used to the lack of open space, and most of all, I could not get used to the noise.

Trolley cars rattled and clanked over countless switch intersections, iron wheels raising a din so loud you could hardly hear yourself speak, whether you were riding in one or walking alongside it on the sidewalk. There were more automobiles in two Chicago city blocks than there were in all of Eau Fraiche (well, maybe I'm exaggerating) and they made more noise with their honking horns and squeaking brakes and squealing tires and broken wheel chains than I had ever heard anywhere else except on the battlefield in France. There were still a lot of horses in Chicago, too, clomping along, pulling coal wagons that tumbled their clattering loads onto chutes into open basement windows, hauling wagons carrying jangling scrap iron and junk, drivers screaming at their teams, policemen blowing whistles, and over it all the elevated trains pounding in from north, south, and west, to add to the resounding cacophony that was the parallelogram of the Loop. I could not stand anything about Chicago.

Moreover, I was beginning to think in those first few months that the paper industry wasn't exactly for me. My job was to stand between the barker and the woodpecker, which did not mean that I was positioned between a dog and a bird, though the foreman did have a dog, a Welsh terrier who nipped at my heels and who went frantic each time the cranes piled up a new shipment of eight-foot-long logs. It seemed to me that a dog who went crazy at the sight of wood shouldn't have been hanging around a paper mill. I'd never liked dogs, anyway. (That's not true. I started disliking dogs when the Germans were using them in the war.) This particular little dog was called Offisa Pupp after the cartoon character, and he started hating me the day I reported to work. My partner on the job was a fellow named Allen Garrett, a strapping six-footer from Chicago's South Side, who, like me, was seeking to make a "future" in the paper industry. Allen worked with me at the far end of the barking drum where the peeled logs came out. We both held spiked picaroons in our hands, and we—well, I think I'd better explain what I was beginning to learn about making paper from wood.

Back in Eau Fraiche, we always cut a felled tree into eight-foot lengths, but the drum barker wasn't designed to take such big chunks of wood and also you couldn't make paper out of wood that still had the bark on it. So the first thing that happened was all the logs were piled up in these towering pyramids and then dumped into what was called the hot pond, which was a big concrete basin through which hot waste water from other parts of the plant flowed. This was done to soften the bark and get rid of leaves and ice and clinging forest dirt. Then they were carried up a jackladder conveyer to the circular saw where they were cut into four-foot lengths so they could be taken to the drum barker. I came in after the drum barker, some exciting job, I was not exactly an executive.

The drum barker, or the barking drum as we also called it, was a cylindrical steel tube open at both ends, close to fifteen feet in diameter and some forty-five feet long. Supported by rollers and enormous steel tires, power-driven by chain belts slung from overhead and spaced along its entire length, the drum received a tangle of logs on a conveyer belt from the hot pond and the cut-off saw, tumbled, tossed, and sprayed them for maybe fifteen minutes, and then plunked them stripped and white onto a conveyer belt at the other end. The drum made a lot of noise, as what wouldn't with thousands of logs banging into each other and shedding their skins, the loosened bark dropping through the open-rib construction onto another conveyer belt, to be whisked away as fuel for the steam plant. At the far end of the drum, Allen Garrett and I studied each of the logs as they went by on the conveyer belt. If we saw one with a section of bark still clinging to it, or a furrow filled with pitch, or a knot, we hooked it with our picaroons and rolled it over to the woodpecker, where the operator there would either drill out the knot or grind off the bark, after which we rolled the log back onto the conveyer belt. I knew nothing at all about what happened to the wood once it moved deeper into the mill. I was new in this business, and it was a bore.

I worked fifty-four hours a week, from eight o'clock in the morning to six o'clock at night. It took me almost an hour and a half to get to the mill in Joliet, which meant that I had to get up at six in the morning, wash and dress, go into the kitchen for breakfast with Nancy, and then run down to catch the #88 streetcar to Archer Avenue, where I transferred to the #74 to Cicero Avenue, and then caught a train. The train was run by the Chicago and Joliet Electric Railway, and the trip was thirty-one miles each way, morning and night. I would not get back to the apartment until close to eight o'clock. It was a long, grueling noisy day, broken only by the pleasant lunch-hour conversations I had with Allen Garrett. I naturally looked forward to my Sundays with Nancy.

It was therefore disheartening to wake up to a ninety-one degree heat that Sunday, and the promise of another suffocating Chicago day. We packed a picnic lunch, much as we might have done back in Eau Fraiche, took two streetcars to Twenty-ninth Street, walked the three blocks to the beach, and tried to enjoy ourselves despite the rising temperature and the throngs of people.

I was exhausted when the trouble started.

Nancy was lying beside me on the blanket, her blond hair curled into a bun at the back of her head, her black bathing costume striped horizontally at the skirt-hem and on the mid-thigh pants showing below, wearing black stockings that must have been unbearable in this heat, a fine sheen of sweat on her face and on her naked arms. A ukulele started someplace, and a man with a high whiny voice began singing all the old war songs, "Good Morning, Mr. Zip-Zip-Zip!" and "I'd Like to See the Kaiser with a Lily in His Hand," and finally got around to some of the newer stuff to which he didn't know the words, "Baby, Won't You Please Come Home," and "Let the Rest of the World Go By," Nancy trying to hum along with him, but the heat defeating everything, a stultifying crushing heat that made movement and even conversation too fatiguing to contemplate.

With considerable effort, I had raised myself up on one elbow in an attempt to locate the ukulele player with the nasal voice, scanning the beach and only chancing to look out over the water where I saw first a small raft, and then

205

noticed that the person on the raft, paddling it toward the beach, was colored. New to Chicago, I did not know at the time that the Twenty-ninth Street Beach was considered "white" territory, an improvised adjunct to the Twenty-fifth Street Beach which bordered the black belt, the section of Chicago known as Douglas. I only learned that later. What I realized now, signaled by the sudden cessation of the ukulele and a hush so tangible it sent an almost welcome shiver up my back, was that something was wrong. Something was terribly wrong. A man was running down toward the lakefront. Another man was shouting, "What's that nigger doing here?"

"Get back where you belong!" someone yelled.

"Get him out of here!" a woman screamed.

I rose to my feet and with my back to the sun (this was close to five o'clock, I suppose, but the sun was still strong behind me), I looked out over the lake and saw that the intruder was just a boy, fourteen? fifteen? it was difficult to tell from this distance, but a boy certainly enough, judging from the slenderness of his body and the quick eager way he lifted his head and broke into a grin that flashed white across his black face. Perhaps he had not understood the consternation he was causing here on this white beach, perhaps he had assumed the men and women running down toward the shore were there to greet him after his exceptional and extraordinary navigational feat, the brave sailor who had come halfway around the world, or at least the several hundred yards separating the white beach from the black beach beside it, he had surely misunderstood because he was still grinning when the first stone struck him.

"Get the little bastard!" someone yelled (they *knew* he was little then, they *knew* he was only a boy) and another stone struck the raft, and the grin vanished from the boy's face, he knew now that the people on this discovered shore were unfriendly, were perhaps even hostile, a volley of rocks and stones falling upon the raft and upon his shoulders now as he frantically paddled in an effort to get out of range, "What is it, Bert?" Nancy said, and I moved off the blanket and began running toward the shore as a rock struck the boy full in the face and he fell into the water.

And now, now a hush fell over the beach again, deeper than that initial shocked silence that had marked the boy's

206

approach, expectant now with an almost theatrical suspense. Would the boy surface, had the rock stunned him,
would his grinning black face pop suddenly out of the
water to the cheers of the onlookers and the applause of a
crowd mollified by his moxie, would he climb once more
onto his flimsy raft and paddle his way back to those
African shores from whence he had come? The question
hung suspended in stifling heat and tempers stilled but only
for a moment. There were colored men on the beach
now, "Let us through," they were saying, three or four
brave scouts probing this humid white no man's land, "let
us *through,* goddamn it! The boy's drowning!" and I
thought, Let us *through!* but we were not being let
through, the boy had not yet surfaced, the raft rotated in
aimless circles on the lake as still as death. A policeman
appeared, I heard a Negro say, "Officer Logan, there's the
man there who threw the rock," and a white man whispered, "Logan, the Cottage Grove Station," and I
thought, The boy is drowning, let's get to him.

But the motion of history moves away from minor
events toward those of succeeding importance, the minor
event here being an adolescent Negro who had paddled in
too close, who had invaded too deeply, drowning now
perhaps as some other Negroes still tried to get past the
barricade of white men who prevented them from entering the water, while behind them and slightly removed, the
voices continued in rising argument, the colored men
insisting that Officer Logan of the Cottage Grove Avenue
Station arrest the man who had thrown the rock which
had knocked the boy from the raft into the water where
he was now perhaps drowning as the voices continued
their tedious assault, Arrest him, arrest him, and the white
men complained that the boy had merely slipped off the
raft, and the debate went on, it being the major issue
now, and the boy did not surface, and Officer Logan did
not take action. The white man who had thrown the
possibly fatal rock stood apart from the angry bubble of
dissent, wearing upon his face the proud look of an
acknowledged marksman, knowing he was the center of a
debate of magnitude, the eye of the storm, basking in his
newly earned celebrity until suddenly the colored men
whirled upon him in fury (He's drowning out there, I
thought, O lord Jesus, he is drowned) and began to hit
him.

If one can say when any war begins, it was then that this war began, this was the firing of the first shot, so to speak. Forget the ancient festering ills, discount them as a possible cause—the 50,000 Negroes who had been coming from the South over the past two years, moving into previously white neighborhoods, crowding into already crowded sections of the city where the rents were lowest and the anti-black feelings were highest, taking jobs that white men felt were rightfully their own, often working for lower wages, many of them bringing back from the war a new sense of maleness—had they not slept with the same French girls, had they not drunk the same French wines, had they not faced the same German bullets—forget all this, discount whatever *real* reasons existed for this war, discount even the minor incident of a stray rock causing a boy to drown out there on the lake, and mark the *true* starting time of this war as seven minutes past five o'clock on the afternoon of July 27, 1919, when a crowd of angry indignant Negroes attacked a white man.

There were slats on the beach, pieces of weathered wood, rocks, empty bottles, all sorts of weapons for a ragtag army suddenly called into front-line action, whites and Negroes, all of them sweltering in the same Chicago blast furnace. Reinforcements were coming now from the Twenty-fifth Street Beach, black men running over the blistering sand to join the fray, driving the white men into the water where the drowned boy was all but forgotten now and the raft still drifted in idle circles, and then turning on Officer Logan himself to chase him off the beach and onto Twenty-ninth Street.

I tried to break away, to get back to Nancy. I saw a knife suddenly appear in a Negro's hand, I felt the same sense of futile confrontation I had felt in that Marne wheatfield so long ago, was I now to face another stranger, was I now to kill for another meaningless piece of real estate. The shouting, the noise, the insane chatter of sweaty combat filled the gravid air, a wooden club came down upon the man's brown forearm, a gash of bright red blood ran from his elbow to his wrist, there were other men upon him now, and more running from every corner of the beach, a white man's face pressed into the sand, a Negro stepped upon, a kick, more blows, cursing, I thought only Nancy, I must get to Nancy. I shoved my way through. She was on her feet when I reached her, I

208

had never before seen a look of such utter disbelief on her face as I seized her hand and yanked her to me and, leaving our blanket and our picnic basket behind, rushed her away from this frightening mass of struggling humans.

"Meanwhile, the fighting continued along the lake," I read to Allen Garrett from the Chicago *Tribune* on our lunch hour the next day. "Miss Helen Mehan and her sister, Marie, had been bathing with a friend, Lieutenant Banks, a convalescing soldier. A colored woman walked up to the trio and made insulting remarks, it is said. Banks attempted to interfere, but the colored woman voiced a series of oaths and promptly struck the soldier in the face. Negroes in the vicinity hurled stones and rocks at the women and both were slightly injured. In less than a half hour after the beach outbreak, Cottage Grove Avenue and State Street from 29th South to 35th were bubbling cauldrons of action."

That cauldron was still bubbling and would contine to bubble until the end of the week, when 6000 troops of the state militia and 3500 Chicago policemen managed to restore order. By that time, 23 Negroes and 15 whites had been killed, 537 people had been injured, and 1000 more had been left homeless.

The militia was withdrawn on August 8.

August ✤ ✤ ✤

When Dana and I got off the ferry at Fire Island Pines, my mother was waiting on the dock with a little red wagon upon which was painted the name of the people from whom we had rented for nine summers, ROSEN, the lettering expertly rendered, not for nothing was Sid Rosen an art director at Doyle Dane Bernbach.

My mother looked terrific.

She would be thirty-eight years old on the tenth of the month, Tuesday in fact, but summer did something for her each year, and from a distance I could visualize her as she must have looked as a young girl. She was wearing faded dungaree shorts and a blue tee shirt, her grin white against a deep tan, her brown hair windblown and curling somewhat from the salt air, legs and breasts still good (those *never* change, King Oedipus, sir, Your Majesty), moving swiftly toward the gangway with a nervous quick energy that made every step she took seem impulsive, almost impetuous. Summer robbed her of ten years each year; rob her of another ten gratuitously, and you had the eighteen-year-old girl Will Tyler, the returning fighter pilot ace, met in New York City in the spring of 1945. Not quite eighteen actually. I looked out over the dock. Will Tyler, ex-Air Force *Wunderkind* and current somewhat aging *enfant terrible* of the publishing world was nowhere in evidence. Home sulking, I thought, ruminating in his martini about the tastelessness of only sons who bring home girls with whom they are undoubtedly sleeping, for shame.

My mother embraced us both, lifting her cheek for Dana's kiss.

"You brought the sun with you," she said. "We've had nothing but rain for the past five days. Dana, you look lovely."

"Thank you," Dana said. She always seemed a bit shy in my mother's presence. I suspected she didn't like my father at all, but I knew she was genuinely fond of my mother, and I could never understand her reserve. We were coming away from the slip now, walking past the plumbing supply store, threading our way through the swarms of bicycles, wagons piled with luggage and groceries, summer people in shorts and swimming suits, all scattering off the dock and onto the narrow wooden walks. The Pines, when we had first begun coming to it in 1956 had been a quiet family community with one or two fags living in blissful silence far from the gay hectic life at Cherry Grove. It was now, I would guess, fifty per cent queer and fifty per cent straight, which was at least giving everybody a fair shot at equal housing oportunities. I still felt a little strange, though, whenever I was candidly appraised, as now, by a mincing boardwalk stroller ("Never take candy from strange men," my grandmother had told me in the fastnesses of her Tudor City apartment, she being my only living grandmother, a spry old dame of sixty-six, with the same quick energy as her daughter Dolores Prine Tyler), but the discomfort wasn't anything like what I had felt the first time my father took us to visit Cherry Grove. My embarrassment then, of course, had been caused only by deep insecurities about my own manhood, I being all of ten at the time. But I had not dug the scene, and I had never gone back.

My mother seemed excited to see us. She immediately told us all about the cocktail parties we'd been invited to during the next week ("Everyone's dying to see you, Wat, and of course to meet Dana") and the surprise birthday party being given for her on Tuesday night, and the possibility that we might be able to borrow a boat for a sail on Wednesday, but then assured us we could be by ourselves whenever we wanted (I thought at first she meant something other than she did) and that we were under no obligation to trail along with her and Dad.

"Where *is* Dad?" I asked.

"Back at the house," she said. "He's looking forward to seeing you both."

I wondered, in that case, why he had not been at the dock, hmmm? It was my guess that he was still wrestling with the problem of who would sleep where and do what to whom, a surmise that was immediately confirmed when he grabbed our suitcases at the door of the house. "Wat!" he said. "Dana! Hey, it's great to see you! How was the traffic coming out?"

"Oh, not bad," I said, and found Dana and myself being drawn in his wake to the bedroom at the rear of the house, where he quickly deposited Dana's bag. "This is your room, Dana," and then turned to take my elbow in a firm, fatherly, guiding grip, wheeling me around the bend in the hallway and leading me to the bedroom near the kitchen (where I knew the damn screen needed repairing) and saying, "This is yours, Wat, do you both want to freshen up, or would you like a drink first?" He was being very tolerant in his attitude, including us in his adult world where you offered grown-ups drinks if they didn't want to freshen up first after those tedious Long Island parkways, but he was also making it clear he didn't expect any adult hanky-panky under his roof for the several weeks Dana and I would be there, preferring us to fornicate on the open beach instead, I guessed.

I looked at the single bed against the torn screen, and then I looked at my father, and his eyes met mine and clearly stated, That's the way it is, son.

211

And my eyes clearly signaled back, Aren't we being a little foolish?

And his said, If you want my approval, you're not getting it, son.

And mine said, Okay, you prick.

Out loud, I said, "I see the screen's still torn."

Out loud, my father said, "I'll get John to fix it in the morning," John being the Pines idiot who went around fixing torn screens and putting bedboards under sagging beach mattresses.

I went back to Dana. She was still standing in the corridor around the bend, her hands on her hips. She looked totally forlorn. I took her in my arms.

"Drink, Dana?" my father called from out of sight somewhere, the liberal Spanish *dueña* sans mantilla or black lace fan.

"Yes, thank you, Mr. Tyler," Dana piped, and then whispered, "Listen, are we supposed to . . ."

"What are you having?" my father called.

"Whatever you've got!"

"We've got everything!"

"Just some scotch, please," Dana said. "With a little water. Wat, are we supposed to even *know* each other?" she whispered.

"I'll climb the trellis each night," I said.

"There *is* no trellis," Dana said. "Besides, what's that big bedroom right next door? That's the master bedroom, isn't it?"

"I think so."

"Wat . . ."

"In fact, I know so."

"Wat, do you want a drink?" my father called.

"Yes!" I shouted. "I think I need one."

"What?"

"Yes, a little scotch on the rocks please."

"Coming up," my father said.

"Did you get the kids settled?" my mother asked from the kitchen.

"Yes, Dolores, the kids are settled," my father said, not without a trace of smug satisfaction in his voice.

"I'll wither and die," Dana whispered. "Oh, Wat, it'll be just awful."

The first week was, in fact, absolute hell because it was the week my father was taking away from his office (ten days, actually—he had come out on Friday the sixth). The way he wanted to spend his vacation, it seemed, was by wandering around that old gray clapboard house like one of the queen's own guard, Dana being Her Majesty, and I being a surly peasant trying to break into her bedchamber. He scarcely ever left us alone during the day, and his snores from the master bedroom each night were an unsubtle reminder that the old family retainer was sleeping right *there,* man, ready to spring into action at the first hint of a footfall in the corridor outside. We finally *did* make love on the beach one night, but Dana was ashamed to take a shower after we tiptoed back into the house, because she said everyone (meaning Old Hawkeye) would know she'd got "sand all up her."

I couldn't understand my father at all. He was charming and pleasant to Dana, telling her really entertaining stories about the publishing field, spicing them with gossip about this or that literary celebrity, "Did you know that Jimmy Baldwin?" or "Were you aware that Bill Styron?" pretending to a vast inside knowledge that he honestly was not privy to; my father's list consisted largely of books of photographs. (It was as if, in allowing the Tyler evolution to follow its natural growth pattern, he had brought it from lumberjacking, through papermaking, into book publishing, and then had sophisticated it a step further by publishing books that were non-books; even as America itself had evolved from a nation where men first labored with their hands into a nation where machines did the work for men—and often did work that was utterly without meaning.) But despite what seemed to be his total acceptance of the girl I had chosen, he adamantly refused to let me possess her. I had the feeling more than once that he was actually coming on with her himself, that he looked too longingly at her breasts, leaped too hastily to light her cigarette, tried too hard for a cheap laugh to an old joke. I didn't want a goddamn sparring match with my own father; I wasn't attempting to turn the old bull out to pasture, but neither did I want him gamboling around with the young heifers. It was all very unsettling. I was having my own doubts about where I fit into the scheme of things just then (if my father's publishing of picture books was a logical development in the growth of the Tyler family, what came next? Where did I take it from there? Was I the comparatively stunted tree in the foreground of the colophon, or the giant spruce towering against a limitless sky?), and I did not need added aggravation from dear old Dad.

My mother's tactful intervention helped the situation somewhat. She was very careful to let me know whenever she and my father planned on being out of the house for more than a few hours, and on one occasion she managed to cajole him into taking her into the city for dinner. I even overheard her discussing the entire spectrum of morality with him one night, and whereas her admonitions did nothing to lessen his surveillance of the sanctum sanctorum, he at least quit hanging around Dana and me during the daytime, when all we wanted to do was lie on the beach together and talk quietly about my developing plans.

I found out about my father during our last week at the beach, so I guess you can say he had a lot to do with the decision I finally reached. But if there are endings, there are likewise beginnings, and my grandfather Bertram Tyler—the beginning—also had something to do with shaping my molten thought.

Grandpa, en route from Chicago to London where he was negotiating a contract for the export of clay-coated boxboard, came out to the beach unexpectedly, a few days after my father had gone back to work, amen. He had met Dana briefly at Christmas time, and was delighted to see her again. But he looked tired, his blue eyes paler than I remembered them, his face somewhat drawn. As it turned out, I was unduly worried about him; he had had a truly harrowing trip from Chicago, with his plane circling Kennedy in the fog for an hour and a half before finally being turned away to Philadelphia International. He had taken a train to Pennsylvania Station (which was in the throes of a massive overhaul) and then *another* train out to Sayville, and *then* the ferry to the Pines, and was now near total collapse. Dana mixed him a martini that would have curled the toes of an Arabian used to drinking camel piss. My grandfather said, "Dana, this is just what I used to drink in Chicago in 1920," and then called to my mother in the kitchen to come join us. "In a second, Pop," she yelled back, "I'm getting some snacks," and my grandfather put his feet up on the wicker ottoman and sighed and said, "It's good to be home."

We had our talk two days later.

The weather, heralded by the fog that had marked his

arrival, had turned surly and gray again; a fire was needed each morning to take the chill out of the old house. We had used up the small supply of shingles in the living room scuttle, and my grandfather and I volunteered to replenish it. It was a pleasure to watch him work with an ax. I always felt that unless I was careful I'd chop off a couple of my own fingers, but he used the ax without even looking at it, almost as if it were an extension of his right hand, talking all the while he worked, the way some men can play piano and smoke and drink beer all at the same time without once missing a beat. He would hold the shingle upright in his left hand, the ax clutched close to the head in his right hand, and *whick,* a single sharp stroke and the shingle was split, another shingle appeared in his left hand, another *whick,* "How are you doing at school, Wat?" he asked.

"Oh, great," I said. "Everything's great."

"Getting good marks?"

"Oh, sure."

"I like your Dana."

"I like her, too."

"When do you go back?"

I didn't answer him. He was looking directly at me, his left hand reached out automatically for another shingle, he felt sightlessly along its top for the true center, jabbed it with the ax once, sharply, raised his eyebrows and said, "Walter?"

"I'm not sure, Grandpa."

"Not sure when you're due back?"

"Not sure if I'm *going* back."

"Oh?"

We didn't say anything for several moments. My grandfather busied himself with splitting the shakes, and I busied myself with stacking them up against the chimney. The air was penetratingly bitter, tendrils of fog sliding in off the beach, a needle-fine drizzle cutting to the bone. I was wearing blue jeans and my Yale sweatshirt, but I was cold. My grandfather had not brought any beach clothes with him; he worked in pin-striped trousers and an open-throated white shirt with the sleeves rolled up over his gold cuff links, studiously bent over each shingle now, even though he could have done the job blindfolded. At last, he said only, "How come, Walter?"

"I'm just not sure, Grandpa."

215

"Don't you like school?"

"I like it."

"Having trouble with somebody there? One of the teachers?"

"No."

"Is it Dana?"

"No."

"Do you want to talk about it?"

"I guess not," I said.

"All right," my grandfather said, and smiled, and looked down at the shingles and said, "Think we've got enough to get us through the winter?" and smiled again, and put the ax back in the shed and then rolled down his cuffs, and I started piling the rest of the split wood in orderly rows against the chimney. I wanted to tell my grandfather what I was thinking of doing, wanted to get an opinion other than Dana's, but I was afraid he'd think I was a coward. So I worked silently, with my brow wrinkled, longing to communicate with him and knowing I could not. And finally, when I'd stacked all the wood, I said, again, "I'm just not sure, Grandpa," and he said, "Well, why don't we take a little walk?" and I looked at him curiously for just a moment because the last time I'd taken a walk with him was when I was six years old and we had gone up the hill behind the house on Ritter Avenue and looked out on a bright October day to where Long Island Sound stretched clear to the end of the world.

I had told him that day that there was a girl in the sixth grade whose name was Katherine Bridges, and I loved he, and she was the most beautiful girl in all Talmadge, even though she wasn't born there but was adopted and had come from Minnesota. But I did not want to tell him now that Dana Castelli was the most beautiful girl in the world; I wanted only to tell him of what I'd been slowly but certainly deciding to do come fall, and I didn't want to tell him *that*, either, because this was a man who had faced German bayonets in the trenches at Château-Thierry. Nor was it a particularly inviting day for a walk, the drizzle having grown heavier, not quite yet a true rain, but forbidding nonetheless.

We walked down to the ferry slip and watched the boat coming in through the fog, her horn bleating, and watched the passengers unloading. My grandfather suddenly said,

"Isn't that Will?" and I looked to where he was pointing and saw a tall man wearing a Burberry trenchcoat coming down the gangway and striding onto the dock in a duck-footed walk that could have belonged to no one but a Tyler.

(In Wat Tyler's camera eye, the man he sees striding toward him and his grandfather is simultaneously the villain who is keeping him from Dana and a rather impressively handsome gentleman with an expansive smile on his face. The images, double-exposed, are confusing. He wants to hate this man for his offhanded treatment of the Love Affair of the Century, and yet he cannot help but respect and admire him. For the first time in his life, or at least for the first time that he can remember, he wants to say, "Pop, I love you." The screen images dissolve.)

My father saw us immediately and came to us, embracing first my grandfather, kissing him on the cheek, and then going through the same family ritual with me.

"I didn't expect anyone to meet me," he said. "I caught an earlier boat."

"Actually, we were just going for a little walk, Will," my grandfather said.

"Well, good," my father said, and threw his arms around our shoulders, comrades three, and said, "I'll join you," which did not overly thrill me, because frankly I did not want him to know about the plan I'd been considering, and I was afraid my grandfather might mention the doubts I'd voiced about going back to Yale.

But we took off our shoes, all of us, and went onto the beach where the mist enveloped us, and walked close to the water's edge, the ocean seeming warmer than the air, and we talked. We talked about the weather first, it being omnipresent, I explaining to my grandfather that the summer people were divided into two factions, those who believed the best weather came in July, and those who favored August. And from there, as a natural extension of talking about the weather, we began to discuss the riots that had taken place in Watts the week before, Watts being a Los Angeles community I'd never heard of before it made racial headlines, and I said something about heat probably being a contributing factor, and my grandfather expressed the opinion that heat had very little to do with emotions that had been contained for more than a century.

"I can remember once . . ." my father started, and then shook his head and fell silent.

"Yes, Will?" my grandfather said.

"No, nothing," he answered, and shook his head again. He was walking between me and my grandfather, his shoes in his hands, his socks stuffed into the pockets of his trenchcoat, his trousers rolled up onto his shins. Together, the three of us skirted the sea's edge, silent now.

(The screen is suddenly filled with the image of three spruces against a sky certainly much bluer than the real sky over Fire Island. The trees are swaying lightly, there is the whisper of wind on the sound track. The film must be a foreign import, the first such in Wat Tyler's memory. There are English subtitles traveling along the bottom of the screen, as though blown there by the same wind rustling in the treetops. The titles are abominable. The first title reads HERITAGE, and the next reads GENERATIONS. Wat Tyler wishes to leave the theater of his mind, perhaps to buy some popcorn in the lobby.)

My grandfather began speaking again. He was a wise old bird, my grandfather, I don't think I realized just how wise until that day on the beach when the mist insulated the three of us from the world. He must have understood, long before I did, that my father was truly in the center of our solitary march along the beach, geographically and genealogically, the only one of our company who could lay claim to being a father to one of us and a son to the other. Because of this, because my grandfather must have sensed the strain of this double role being exerted on *his* son and *my* father, he led us gently into conversation, talking across my father to me, talking across me to my father, transforming our three-way discussion into something remarkably crazy.

(On the screen, the three spruces, one slightly taller than the next, have dissolved into the three Tyler men walking in the mist. But the men refuse to maintain fixed camera positions. One becomes interchangeable with another and yet another, so that it seems sometimes that Wat is talking directly to his father when he is really in conversation with his grandfather, seems at other times that Will is talking to Bertram when he is actually looking at Wat. The whole thing is very *avant-garde*. Wat is sure it will cop the Golden Lion Award at Venice.)

"You can't expect violence to be self-restrictive," my grandfather said.

"What do you mean?" my father said.

"The riots. Surely they're linked to what's happening in Vietnam."

"I don't see any connection."

"He's talking about our way of life," I said.

"I don't understand."

"Our way of *life*," I repeated, knowing I still had not made myself clear, and looking to my grandfather for help. But his attention seemed momentarily captured by a boat barely visible through the fog on the water, and as we walked on the edge of ocean merged with shore, equally lost in obliterating fog, he remarked how crazy it was for a boat to be out in this kind of weather and then abruptly mentioned that he had read about the forty-nine-year-old singer Frank Sinatra coming off his yacht, *Southern Breeze,* in the company of the nineteen-year-old actress Mia Farrow and two somewhat older actresses, for a Hyannis Port visit with the father of one assassinated President and two current United States senators.

"I grew up listening to that man," my father said.

"You don't have to tell me," my grandfather agreed, smiling. "You had that Victrola going day and night."

His archaic language suddenly rankled. I wanted to get the conversation back to Vietnam, back to the truly modern idea he had offered but only tentatively explored, the idea that this pointless war of ours was beginning to seep into every phase of our national life, the idea that violence as a solution for problems abroad was most certainly being emulated as a solution for problems here at home. I resented the digression. Without so much as a preamble, I said, "First they take the air war north of the Hanoi line, and bomb only eighty miles from the Chinese border, and then . . ."

"But of course, there's a great deal of violence everywhere you turn," my grandfather said, interrupting me, and causing me to frown momentarily. "Not only in Vietnam." There seemed to be a note of warning in his voice, as though he were anachronistically saying, Cool it, baby. You want to rap about this Yale thing, then let your wise omniscient venerable old guru lead us into it gentle-like, dig? I blinked my eyes.

(The screen conversation is taking a ridiculous turn.

The film is becoming even a bit far-out for the likes of *Cahiers*. Someone asks if anyone has read *Up the Down Staircase*, someone else—it sounds like Wat but it could just as easily be Foxy Grandpa—says that laughter is cleansing, it is good for America to enjoy a healthy laugh, not to mention a sob or two, over the problems of a teacher in a slum school, the same way it is good for America to enjoy the James Bond cinema spoofs.)

"They're *not* spoofs," I said. I was certain now that both of them, father and grandfather, had veered off on a tangent because they refused to discuss something that was terribly important to me. Together, father and son, they had decided in secret conspiracy to prevent an airing of my thoughts, thereby scuttling my plans even before they were fully formed. So I very loftily said something about the "spoof" label being a very handy way of alleviating our Puritan guilt over enjoying a sado-masochistic reaction to Bond's screen exploits, the same way we had felt it necessary to call *Candy* a spoof as well, so that it would then become acceptable reading for all the ladies of Garden City.

"Did *you* read *Candy?*" my father asked, surprised.

"Yes, didn't you?"

"Well, yes, but . . ."

"But it was a spoof, right?"

"No, it was pornography," my grandfather said.

"So what's wrong with pornography?" I said.

"Nothing," my grandfather said.

"I just didn't think you were reading pornography," my father said.

"What'd you *think* I was reading? *Tom Swift and His Electric Rifle?*"

"No, but not pornography."

"I've also read the Marquis de Sade," I said.

"Where'd you get hold of that?"

"From the top shelf of books in your bedroom," I said.

"Got to be more careful with your dirty books, Will," my grandfather said, and smiled.

"I guess so," my father answered, and returned the smile, and again I had the feeling they were excluding me, that their bond with each other was closer than mine with either of them. So I forced the conversation back to Vietnam again, because Vietnam was what was on my mind, and I wanted them to know this, while simultaneously wanting to keep my formative plans from them, telling them that first Ambassador Maxwell Taylor had informed the nation that the aggression was from the north, while 8000 of our Marines landed at Danang, bringing our total number of men in arms to 75,000 with experts predicting 150,000 American troops in Vietnam before the end of 1965. Then President Johnson had said, "What we want to do is achieve the maximum deterrence with the minimum danger and cost in human lives," and announced that 50,000 *more* men would be sent there right away, bringing our total to 125,000 with the estimate for year's end now being 200,000 and the draft quota more than doubled from 17,000 to 35,000 a month.

"Well, *you* don't have to worry about the draft," my father said.

"Pop," I said, "maybe we *all* . . ."

"He's a student," my father explained.

"I know," my grandfather said.

"Suppose I wasn't?"

"Weren't."

"Weren't. What then?"

"But you are."

"But a lot of kids *aren't*. And when the bomb falls, it's not going to ask who's a student and who isn't."

"There's not much danger of that," my father said. "Not with a hotline between Washington and Moscow."

"Assuming somebody has a dime to make a call."

"It's not a pay telephone," my father said, exhibiting monumental humorlessness.

"I once got a call in Chicago," my grandfather said, "from a man who told me, 'Mr. Tyler, this is your exterminator.' Scared me out of my wits."

"*You?*" my father said. "Scared you?"

"Sure," my grandfather said. "Turned out he really *was* the exterminator. Your mother had called about ants in the kitchen."

"We're *all* scared of the exterminator," I said. "We're like a gambler down to his last chip, down to his underwear in fact, with nothing more to lose. We're saying, 'The hell with everything, I'll take my chances,' and we're putting shorts and all on the next roll, figuring we'll either walk out naked or fly home in a private jet."

221

"Survival's *always* been a gamble," my father said. "Do you think you're saying something new?"

"Yes!"

"Well, you're not. The first time a caveman picked up a club ..."

(The screen is filled with the impressive image of William Francis Tyler, publisher and lecturer as he expounds his theories on *The Ultimate Weapon*, relating to a dozing audience the alarm felt in the civilian population each time a new weapon is developed, going on to explain while the camera zooms in on a busty blond co-ed picking her nose that mankind has always had the good sense, the camera is back on his face now, in close-up, to place restrictions on its own capacity to destroy itself, his voice droning on as the camera suddenly cuts away to a shot of the grandfather, Bertram Tyler, staring moodily out to sea, and then intercuts close shots of Will Tyler's face with those of Wat Tyler's, to emphasize the point that this is strictly between father and son now, the provocateur oddly removed. Nobody understands the film any more. The theater is half empty.)

"Yes, thank you very much, Pop," I said, "but that kind of thinking no longer applies. This Vietnam thing *is* new. It's new because a lot of kids aren't willing to *gamble* any more, don't you see? Why should we? So a hotshot Vietcong-killer like Ky can go on running his cruddy little country? Who the hell cares?"

"South Vietnam is important to our security," my father said.

"Whose security?"

"Ours. Yours, mine."

"How about the security of the five hundred Americans who've already wasted their lives there?"

"Some people would not consider that a ..."

"... or the God knows how many more we seem *ready* to waste?"

"Do you want all Asia to go Communist?"

"I don't give a damn *what* it goes, Pop."

"You don't mean that."

"I mean it."

"You don't."

"It's a bad war, and ..."

"There are no good wars," my grandfather said suddenly.

". . . and the only way to make it any better is to end it."

"How?" my father asked.

"By refusing to *fight* the goddamn thing," I said.

I was very close now. I was very close to telling him. We stopped walking for an instant, the three of us. I was trembling. My grandfather was suddenly standing between us, one hand on my shoulder, one hand on my father's. I was not aware that he had moved, but he was between us.

"These are different times, Will," he said gently.

"I fought my war," my father said.

"So did I."

"Then why . . ."

"And we also made our peace."

A strange thing happened then. We both turned to our fathers at the same moment, we were both sons at the same moment. Simultaneously, my father and I both said, "Pop . . ." and then fell abruptly silent. I no longer knew what I wanted to say, or even if I wanted to say it. My father shook his head. We began walking up the beach again. The air seemed suddenly dense, the fog suffocating. It was my grandfather who broke the silence again.

"Have either of you seen *The Sandpiper?*" he said.

Quickly, with a glance at my father, I said, "We gave Burton and Taylor the award for August."

"Award?" my father said. There was a dazed expression on his face, as though he had wandered into an alien world from a familiar and much-loved landscape. He had tucked his shoes under his arms, and he walked with his hands in the pockets of his trenchcoat, looking first to me, and then to my grandfather, as though he did not recognize either of us.

"The Tyler-Castelli Award," I said.

"Oh," he said, and nodded, though I was sure he did not yet understand.

"For the Most Convincing Performances in a Religious Film," I said.

"Supposed to be packing them in all over the country," my grandfather said.

"That's because truck drivers enjoy watching a man kiss his own wife," I said.

"In Metrocolor," my grandfather said.

"And Panavision," I said.

"It isn't always possible," my father said abruptly.

"What isn't?"

"Peace."

"I'm sure Hanoi wants peace every bit as much as we do," I said. "If we could just . . ."

"Do you mean Vietnam?" my grandfather said, and suddenly looked his son full in the face.

"Yes," my father said too quickly, and I suddenly realized he had not been talking about Vietnam at all, and was immediately ashamed of my own driving need to make clear my position on the war. I wanted to shout, No, please, Pop, *say* what you were about to say, *tell* us what you really meant, but I knew the moment was gone. I thought Oh, Jesus, if only I hadn't been here, he'd have told my grandfather, they'd have talked, they'd have *talked* together. And then I recognized that I was really thinking about myself and my father, and felt suddenly desolated, the way I'd felt that day waiting for the elevator, when he'd sent Mrs. Green to find out what I wanted for my graduation.

We walked the rest of the way up the beach in silence, my grandfather, my father, and I.

The bedroom Dana occupied was adjacent to the master bedroom and opposite the john. In the off-season, it belonged to the Rosens' little girl who, judging from the evidence arrayed around the perimeter of the room, was a child with a scientific bent. On bookshelf and dresser top, end table and vanity was a formidable collection of spiders in jars. The spiders were all currently dead, but this was no indication that they had not been alive and hale when little Dwight (for such was the darling's name—Dwight Rosen) had incarcerated them and fed them their wingless, legless flies, the withered carcasses of which now littered the bottom of each jar. As a homey touch (or perhaps as further nourishment—who knew the mysterious workings of the scientific mind?) Dwight had further provided a carpet of lettuce for each of her jarred prisoners, which leaves were now wilted, brown, and mildewed. Altogether, her collection was a little unappetizing.

Her room was an airless chamber, a single screened window facing the door, an opposition adequate perhaps for cross ventilation if the door were left ajar, but since Dana and I were naked on little Dwight's bed, I had not deemed it appropriate to leave the door ajar, or even unlocked. Yes, the pink door was locked, and the flowered window shade was drawn over the screened window, so that the groping and the writhing on the bed was contained within these four walls even as the spiders were contained in their jars, unseen by any eyes save those of the Walt Disney characters who cavorted on the wallpaper, they being only dumb forest animals who could register neither complaint nor surprise.

My mother, while not wishing to aggravate our tenuously resolved Oedipal situation by letting on that she knew Dana and I were, uh, ah, enjoying an, uh, ahem, sexual relationship, had nonetheless collared me in the kitchen on the Friday after my grandfather left for London and informed me that she had been invited to a party down the beach at the Stenquists' (Erik Stenquist being a closet queen with a wife who was apparently deaf, dumb, and blind) starting at five p.m. and that she'd be there until eight o'clock, at which time she planned to meet my father's ferry, it being his habit (now that his vacation had ended) to take the six-thirty p.m. boat from Sayville every Friday night, and the eight-ten a.m. back each Monday morning.

"So I'll be gone from five o'clock to a little after eight o'clock," my mother said.

I said, "Oh, okay, Mom."

She looked at me steadily, hazel eyes unwavering, and said, "I'll be leaving at about ten to five, and your father and I won't be back until a little after eight."

"Fine," I said.

"We'll have dinner then," my mother said, "Just some cold cuts, will that be all right?"

"Great," I said.

"At eight o'clock or a little after," my mother said. "When your father and I return."

"Right," I said, "you'll be gone from five to eight."

"Yes, from five o'clock to eight o'clock," my mother said.

"Okay," I said.

We nodded at each other like teacher and pupil who had just come through a particularly difficult educational experiment and were now anxious to march off to our just and separate rewards, hers being a few martinis at the Stenquists', mine being Dana.

It was about seven o'clock, I suppose (I don't really *know* because I had taken off my watch and put it on Dwight's vanity alongside a jar containing a very large black and, I was sure, poisonous and thankfully dead spider) but it was *probably* around seven or thereabouts because we had come into the bedroom at five-thirty, giving Mom a half-hour's grace period, and had made fast and furious love, and were now beginning to explore each other again, not truly explore because you cannot explore territories already claimed, but beginning to walk around our acquisitions like proud landholders with pleased smiles and small nods, appreciatively and gratefully, and beginning also to get a little excited in the bargain, all metaphors aside. It was about seven o'clock, then, when I heard footsteps in the hallway outside, and sat straight up in bed, and heard the bathroom door closing across the hall, and heard someone urinating. Dana had clutched the sheet to her naked breasts (it's true that girls do that, I had never believed it when I saw it on the screen) and had turned to me with her brown eyes wide, neither of us speaking, both of us listening to the interminable stream across the hall behind the closed bathroom door, and then the door opened again, and there were more footsteps, retreating, the floorboards creaking in the old seaside house, and I heard my father's voice call from the living room, "Dolores?" and hesitate and then call again, "Anybody home?"

I was, by this time, already out of bed and pulling on my blue jeans while Dana fumbled with bra and panties, neither of us speaking, listening for those footsteps that would bring Old Sherlock directly to the spider lab of Dwight Rosen, but hopefully not before we were both properly dressed and admiring all those lovely dead arachnids in their jars. The footsteps instead stopped outside the master bedroom next door. My father hesitated in the corridor again, called "Dolores!" again and then went into the bedroom. I heard the door whisper shut behind him. I heard the slip bolt being thrown. I looked at Dana. She was dressed now and frantically combing her hair. I heard the telephone being dialed in the bedroom next door, a toll call, judging from the number of times the dial was twirled, and I thought several things in tumbling succession. I thought first what a good thing it was that my father *hadn't* allowed Dana and me to share this bedroom next to the master bedroom because the walls were obviously paper-thin and he would have been able to hear every rattle and creak of every spring on Dwight's narrow bed, and I thought it odd that Dana hadn't mentioned hearing any of my parents' own nocturnal action, and suddenly wondered if they still engaged in such action (Oedipal wish), and thought also that my father was probably calling his office with some last-minute instructions, having undoubtedly left some time after lunch to catch an earlier boat than usual, forgetting for the moment that it was now seven o'clock or thereabouts and the office would be closed, forgetting *all* of these things in the next few moments because that was when my father's voice cut through the cardboard walls with their Disney characters cavorting, cut through my thoughts, cut through my life and made it abundantly clear that this my America was a phony bitch of a land where anything of worth or value was becoming buried under an overwhelming heap of garbage. All of this my father accomplished in less than twenty sentences.

"Hello," he said. "Everything all right?"

"I just got here," he said. "It's okay, she's out somewhere."

"I ache all over," he said.

"Oh, really," he said, and chuckled. "That's very interesting."

"Stop it," he said. "You're giving me a hard-on."

"Listen," he said, "I'd better go now."

"Will I see you Monday?" he said.

"I love you," he said.

"Goodbye," he said.

That was how my father honed the steel blade my grandfather had helped to pour and hammer. That was how my father—in a voice strangely unlike his own, coy, flirtatious, arch—convinced me that I would not go back to Yale in the fall, I would no longer use my student deferment as an excuse to avoid confronting the draft, I would instead drop out of school and do whatever I could in protest against this war that seemed to me representative of everything rotten in America, including my father.

I could not look at Dana.

We left little Dwight's bedroom and walked noisily out of the house, the fucking hypocrite.

September ✿ ✿

I was Lieutenant William Francis Tyler of the 94th
Fighter Squadron of the 1st Fighter Group of the 306th
Fighter Wing of the Fifteenth Air Force based in Foggia,
Italy. I had got to bed at two a.m. the night before after
having drunk myself into a stupor at the Allied Officers
Club in town. It was now six-thirty a.m. and the sergeant
who shook me awake kept saying over and over again,
"Let's go, lieutenant, let's go," and I mumbled in my
sleep, "You're kidding," even though I had seen my name
chalked onto the blackboard at Group Headquarters yesterday afternoon, and knew that I would be flying this
morning. "You're on, lieutenant," he said, "let's go."

"Okay," I said.

"You up?"

"I'm up."

"You sure?"

"I'm sure, goddamnit."

"Okay, lieutenant."

It was cold in the tent. I unzipped my sleeping bag and
heard the sergeant moving over to Ace's cot to shake him
awake, and then going down the line past Tommy Rodwin
and over to where Archie Colombo was snoring. There
were only four of us in the tent. For the past month, we
had been paying an Italian mason to build us a permanent
shelter out of tufa block and corrugated steel, but he was
working slowly and the house was not yet finished. I sat
on the edge of my cot, shivering on my air mattress even
though I was wearing long johns.

"What the fuck time is it?" Ace asked.

"Six-thirty," I said.

"Never let a fuckin' man *sleep* around here," he said,
and swung his legs over the side of the cot and stood up
and began waving his arms in big circles while running in
place.

"Hey, Colombo, you up?" I shouted.

"I'm up," Colombo answered.

228

"We'll all be up, you don't keep quiet," Rodwin mumbled from his cot, the only one of us who was not flying that day.

I pulled on a pair of coveralls, picked up my toilet kit, and stumbled out into the dawn, glancing automatically at the sky above, clear and blue, which was no indication it would be the same over the target, wherever that might be today. The autumn countryside was yellow and soft in the early morning light, a faint mist still clinging to the ground where the sun had not yet touched the shadowed hollows.

I had shaved the night before, so I just washed my face now, and brushed my teeth, and looked at my watch and tried to tell myself I did not have a hangover. The officers' area was adjacent to the flight line, and the P-38s were lined up with their noses facing the runway, catching glints of sunlight, crew chiefs and mechanics moving up and down the line as they coughed the airplanes into life, warming them up in case we would be flying today. I dropped off my gear at the tent and then walked diagonally out of the area into the officers' mess hall where I ate my usual breakfast of canned orange juice, oatmeal with powdered milk, powdered scrambled eggs, Spam, and coffee. If we flew, I would not be eating again until late this afternoon.

The Briefing Room was in an old church taken over by the Fifteenth as its headquarters. I took a chair alongside Ace, who had not shaved and who would probably eat after the briefing, as was his superstitious custom. Our Operations Officer, Major Dimple, who was second in command to Colonel Spiller, was standing behind a table at the front of the church, where the altar once must have been. An Air Force map of southern Europe, covered with a sheet of plexiglas, hung on the wall behind him. A crayoned red circle on the plexi located today's target, some place in Yugoslavia. Crayoned blue lines to the target area indicated our headings from Foggia. Crayoned red dots along our flight route indicated expected flak points. Major Dimple consulted the clipboard in his hand, cleared his throat, and said, "Good morning, gentlemen," and no one answered. It was still dim inside the church; the huge map was illuminated by a long fluorescent tube; the half-light of dawn pressed against the arched stone windows like faded silk. "Mission and target," the major

229

said. "Rendezvous with B-24s over Kraljevo, Yugoslavia, provide penetration, target, and withdrawal cover." This was hardly a surprise, since those crayoned blue lines led straight to Yugoslavia, but an audible sigh of relief went up nonetheless from the assembled pilots. It would be a short run. Our last raid had been deep into Germany, and we had lost eight B-17s over the target, a heavily defended synthetic petroleum plant, five of them to flak and three to mid-air crash. It was an incredible feeling to be sitting a thousand feet above the heavies as they flew into the box barrage put up by the Germans, knowing there was nothing you could do but wait until they had dropped their load and come off the target, at which time you would try to protect them from any fighters the Luftwaffe still had. You saw those poor bastards sailing directly into the black puffs of flak, each evil-looking blossom indicating the explosion of a shell, and even though you could not hear anything over the roar of your own engines, you knew that each of those unfolding black flowers was malign but oddly impersonal. The barrage the Germans laid up into the sky was in the shape of a box through which they knew with certainty the bombers *had* to fly if they expected to reach the target. It was as simple as that, no question of markmanship, no question of ground battery crews zeroing in. The flak exploded and the bombers flew through it, and each black puff was only objectively deadly. It was different when, flying unarmed through soup on a weather reconnaissance mission deep behind enemy lines, you saw nothing, no explosive puffs, but suddenly felt the airplane rock from a percussive blast behind you, and knew the ground radar was closing in on your tail, and suddenly swerved to the right in panic, and dropped two thousand feet and dodged to the left, knowing you could in your stripped-down state outrun any fighter they put into the air against you, but terrified of those invisible bursts tracking you in the eyeless night. Over the target on a bombing mission, you were safe if you flew a fighter plane because you veered up and away to wait while the B-17s or B-24s dropped their loads, unable to assist them in any way (the Luftwaffe would not send its own fighters into the teeth of a ground barrage) until the ordeal was over, and they broke from the target and headed home. And oh the goddamn pitiable sight of those poor bastards coming off the target, broken, smoking, losing altitude, limping away after they had arrived in such bold formation and suicidally rushed that wall of exploding flak. If you ever talked to a bomber pilot, you wondered how he managed to keep his sanity, and you felt oddly embarrassed when he told you the prettiest sight in the world was a P-38 coming down to cover him as he broke off target.

"Take-off time is 0845," the major said. "Your route is as follows: base to forty-four ten north, twenty twenty east to Kragujevac to Paracin to forty-three fifty-two north, twenty-one twenty-four east to last landfall at Albanian-Yugoslav coastal border to base. ETA at rendezvous is 1000 hours, altitude 21,500 to 22,000 feet. Radio silence, of course, until you're over the target," he said, which was the cue, as it was at every briefing, for the group's meteorologist to step up with the day's weather report. Captain Rutherford was a moon-faced little man with a pencil-line mustache and a high reedy voice. He invariably read the weather report like a radio announcer doing a thirty-second spot following the news, as if totally unaware that one or another of us had earlier flown a recon mission over the target to gather the information, the enemy being extremely chary about letting us know when it was okay to bomb. If the skies were clear, Rutherford sounded as though he were reporting the good news to thousands of housewives anxious to go out shopping, rather than to a collection of sleepy-eyed pilots who were dragging ass and hoping for fog over the target. When he said, as he did now, "Stratus at 2000 feet over Dubrovnik and the offshore islands," we ladies of Lake Shore Drive knew he really meant it was raining lightly there, "clearing rapidly inland approximately midway to target, cirro-cumulus at 24,000 to 26,000 over the Kragujevac-Paracin-Kraljevo area, ceiling and visibility unlimited." He smiled, pleased with his delivery; in a mimeographed Intops Summary, the weather would probably be reported later as simply CAVU. Rutherford nodded in dismissal, took a seat behind the table, and did not look up when Captain Schulz (who we all insisted was a Nazi spy, even though he was our own Intelligence Officer) came forward to give us our flak and enemy aircraft information. This was the part we always listened to very closely. With the back of his hand, Schulz brushed a hank of straight blond hair off his forehead, blinked at the assembled pilots, consulted a scrap of brown paper so tiny that we were certain he would swallow it as soon as he had read us the information on it, and then matter-of-factly said, "Flak reported on mission route week of September 10 as follows: Stolak and Bileca, light to medium; Pljevlja, heavy; Priboj, intermittent light; extremely heavy over target area and in Kragujevac-Paracin-Kraljevo triangle. Suggest alternate headings to avoid Pljevlja batteries. Very little E/A activity this past week, though eight Me 109s were sighted ten miles southeast of Sarajevo, at five thousand feet, no markings. Eighth Air Force has reported sighting jets again, but the possiblity of any in Yugoslavia is extremely slight; whatever comes at you from Belgrade/Zemun or possibly Novi Sad will be conventional aircraft. You'll probably have a lot of stragglers coming off the target, plenty to keep you busy on the way home. If you're shot down . . ." (We all stopped listening here, because this was the part we heard at each and every briefing, reiterated for all of us idiot pilots who were only flying an airplane that cost a quarter of a million dollars and who had been trained at an expense of another couple of hundred thousand dollars, but who were too dumb to know what we were supposed to do if we got shot down, unless it was repeated seven days a week) ". . . properly and with respect if you're picked up by the Luftwaffe, hostilely if the ground forces get you, and extremely badly if the Gestapo does. Check your sidearm before take-off, make sure you've got your packet of money, your first-aid kit" (ho-hum) "your emergency rations, and your knife. If you're forced down, you're under orders to destroy the airplane. If you bail out, get rid of your parachute." Schulz looked at his little brown piece of paper again, and then sat down. Major Dimple came forward.

"All right," he said, "here are your plane assignments," and began reading off the names of the pilots and the numbers of the planes they would be flying into Yugoslavia. Our group was always briefed together, which meant that there were forty-eight pilots assembled in the church that morning. The 94th Squadron had twenty-five pilots in it, but no more than sixteen of us went up on any mission, four flights—White, Red, Blue, and Yellow—with four P-38s in each flight. Today, only fourteen of us were going, in flights of four, four, three, and three. Not every pilot had the same plane assigned to him for every strike, but Ace and I were lucky in that respect, flying the identical plane each time, a privilege usually reserved only for senior pilots. (We naturally considered those airplanes our own, and were terribly annoyed when they were assigned to other pilots for a mission we were not flying.) On both nacelles of Ace's airplane, he had painted four spread playing cards, all aces, and the name *Aces High* stenciled in a semicircle above them. My plane was called *Tyler's Luck,* a bastardization of the comic strip *Tim Tyler's Luck,* and the design on my engines featured blond Tim and black-haired Spud, both grinning. Anyway, since Ace and I *knew* which planes we'd be flying we stopped listening again, until the major said, "Check your timepieces," and then hesitated, watching the sweep-hand, and then said, "It's oh-eight-seventeen, good luck, gentlemen," which we never felt he really meant.

Captain Kelper, who had been assigned squadron leader for this mission, gave us a brief talk outside the church, telling us what altitude he wanted to fly at to rendezvous, and setting our courses and speeds. He told us again that he didn't want any noise until we were over the target, and then he looked at his watch, said, "Okay, guys," and walked off to get a second cup of coffee in the mess hall. Ace and I went to the latrine because this would be our last opportunity to do so (we rarely used the pilot's relief tube) until sometime this afternoon. Then he went for his good luck cup of coffee, and I went back to the tent to dress.

The weather was still mild on the ground, but it would be something like eighty degreees below zero outside the airplane at 30,000 feet, and even though the P-38 was equipped with a heating tube, the temperature in the cockpit rarely rose to above fifty-five degrees. The Air Force also had a heated flying suit complete with an electric plug that fit into a cockpit jack, but the suit shrank when you washed it, and as a result only the smallest guys in the squadron flew in anything like heated comfort. So I always wore long johns, over which I pulled on a pair of khaki pants and shirt, and then coveralls, and then my leather fleece-lined jacket. I never wore the leather helmet because it got too uncomfortable on a long flight, preferring the poplin instead. I took very good care of my hands and my feet because those were the parts of the body that really began to ache after a while (those and the coccyx; you were sitting on the valve of a Mae West throughout the entire mission). I had bought a pair of fleece-lined boots from a British officer for twenty bucks, and those were what I wore on each raid, together with a pair of woolen, flannel-lined, sweater-cuffed GI gloves. Still, my hands and feet were always cold.

Sergeant Balson was standing alongside the plane when I came up to the flight line at about eight-thirty. He had already started her, and he stood listening to the engines now, bald head cocked to one side, the way my mother used to listen, though the crew chief was not the slightest bit deaf. Hands on hips, wearing coveralls and a wool cap, he kept listening to the engines as I approached, and then, without a word of greeting, said, "She seems to be warming up slowly, sir, missing a few times, but she's sound, don't worry. The left engine throttle lever is loose. And the trim-tab on the right is pulling a little hard."

"Anything else, Ballsy?"

"That's it, sir, have a good flight."

"Thank you. See you later."

"Right, sir."

I went up the ladder onto the wing. The P-38 was not a small airplane. It weighed 17,500 pounds combat-loaded and 14,100 pounds when the cannon and machine guns were taken out of the nose for an unarmed weather recon flight. Either way, it was a huge hunk of machinery for one man to take into the air, and I always climbed into that cockpit with a sense of apprehension, knowing that my full concentration would be demanded for the next several hours, and knowing that I would come back to the field with a pounding headache. The P-38 cruised at close to 270 miles an hour, as fast as the Mustang or the Thunderbolt, except at high altitudes, and even though I rarely experienced a sense of speed in the air (all of us were weaving over the bombers at the same speed, throttles set), I nonetheless recognized that I was hurtling through the sky at very high velocity, especially when we passed a stationary cloud mass and the point was suddenly and forcefully driven home, and I knew that the only things keeping me aloft were those twin 1600 horsepower Allisons and my own intelligence. So I constantly listened to every sound, reacted to every vibration, every alien ping, knowing instantly if an engine was missing or an instrument was off, preparing to deal with any malfunction that threatened to drop me to the ground—and that alone could give a man a goddamn headache, even if he didn't have the Luftwaffe and the flak to worry about.

On the ground, though, the airplane was nothing less than beautiful. Looking at her head-on, you saw three huge, thrusting silver bullets, the forwardmost one being the canopied cockpit with its lethal nose, on either side of which were the engine nacelles with their three-bladed airscrews. From wing tip to wing tip, the ship measured fifty-two feet, which meant that once inside the cockpit, you were looking out past the flanking engines onto twenty-six feet of metal on either side of you. It was nice to have two engines in case one decided to quit or was helped to quit by the GAF; it was also nice to have that 23-mm Madsen cannon in the nose surrounded by four 50-caliber machine guns, which was, to be modest, exceptionally heavy armament. The engine booms tapered like torpedos back to the twin fin-and-rudder tail assembly, with the main undercarriage wheels jutting from the twin booms, just back of the wings. Those wings were six feet off the ground when the plane was sitting on the flight line. The over-all impression was one of enormous size and power. *Tyler's Luck*, the legend read—Amen.

If there was anything that characterized the flight-line wait before take-off, it was our absolute silence. There was no radio chatter between the pilots, no need even for the formality of tower clearance. At precisely 0845, the leader of White Flight thundered down the runway and took off, followed by his wingman seconds later, and then by the element leader and his wingman. I was the element leader of Red Flight. With Ace Gibson on my wing, I taxied onto the wire mesh landing mat, following the two planes ahead, and did a final run-up check, propeller switches in AUTOMATIC, governors in full-forward take off position, magnetos at 2300 rpm, toes holding hard on the hydraulic brakes. I pulled the left governor back until I got a reduction of 200 rpm, and then returned it to the full-forward take-off position, making sure I got 2300 rpm again. Then I checked out the electrical system—volt-meter approximately twenty-eight volts, ammeter charging below fifty amps. I was ready. As White Flight circled the field overhead, waiting to be joined by the rest of the squadron, I thought This is number nineteen, thirty-one missions

235

to go, and then Archie Colombo, leading Red Flight, poured on the juice.

At 0848, I was airborne.

The people of Foggia did not like P-38 pilots. This made it difficult to form any alliances with girls, and so we were extremely lucky to get Francesca. The reason they did not like the P-38 pilots was that the Air Force had repeatedly bombed the railway marshaling yards when the town was still held by the enemy, and the villagers had repeatedly repaired the damage done in the raids until finally the Air Force dropped leaflets telling them to stop fixing the yards or the town itself would be bombed. The Italians went right ahead with their reconstruction work after the next raid, so the Air Force naturally sent in its P-38s to bomb and strafe Foggia. Whereas *we* were in no way connected with those long-ago pilots who had done the dirty deed, the moment a girl from Foggia found out you flew a P-38 you were dead. It didn't pay to lie, either, because they knew more about the Air Force than the Air Force did itself, and they could tell (by which field you were stationed at in the Foggia complex) whether you flew a bomber or a fighter. Moreover, the 94th Fighter Squadron was one of the few Air Force units permitted to wear an additional piece of jewelry above the silver pilot's wings: our identifying squadron insignia, a top hat in a ring. Fifty-cent pieces were very difficult to come by on the base, because enterprising machinists were turning them into this insignia jewelry, which was then traded to pilots for anything from two or three fresh eggs to a half-dozen cigars. But if you wore the insignia over your wings, it immediately identified you as one of those hated P-38 pilots who had shot up the town, and instantly brought pride in one's squadron into direct conflict with one's natural desire to get laid.

Francesca either hadn't heard about those fearsome P-38 pilots of yore or simply did not give a damn. We had met her on the road one day while we were trying to hitch a ride into town, all the jeeps having disappeared by the time Ace and I got out of debriefing. Our flight leader and his wingman had been shot down in a raid over Odertal, and Ace and I, presumably having witnessed every enemy pass, had been detained to answer Major Dimple's interminable questions. Were they in flames, Did they hit the deck, Did you see silk? and so on. Francesca was not exactly what one would have called a beauty, but she was a girl, and she was *there*. She came down the road on a bicycle, rare for these parts, since the Germans had taken with them almost anything that had wheels, wearing open sandals, one of those flowered housedresses with buttons down the front, and a threadbare black cardigan sweater fastened only at the throat and flapping loose around her shoulders like a short cape. She was a chunky girl with curly black hair and brown eyes, a lot of hair under the armpits, some on the legs, but then again, even the higher-type broads in Rome hadn't learned to shave like American women. Ace hailed her and asked her in English if she would give us a ride to town, and she smiled in a shy, frightened manner and shook her head and shrugged her shoulders, indicating she did not speak English, which we later learned was an absolute falsehood. She spoke English as well as any other Italian in Foggia, in fact better; she had been shacking up for some three months with a bomber pilot who caught very heavy shit over Budapest and had never been heard from since. She also told us later that she was afraid of us that first day on the road because she thought we might rape her, and had pretended not to speak English so that she could listen to and understand everything we were saying and therefore be forewarned if we decided to jump her. If we had any designs at the moment, however, they were on her bicycle and not her hot little body. We kept waving our hands around and trying to explain to her that we wanted a ride into town, and finally Ace demonstrated a method whereby the three of us could share the bike, he sitting on the seat and pedaling, she sitting sidesaddle on the crossbar, and me straddling the rack over the rear wheel, legs sticking out almost parallel to the ground, a system that worked for a distance of perhaps six feet before we all fell into the ditch at the side of the road, Francesca displaying a great deal of inviting white thigh as her dress went up over her tumbling legs. I think it was then that we decided she might not be so bad to fuck.

She lived, as it turned out, in a stone farmhouse about seven kilometers from the field, which made it all very convenient. Her mother was dead, and her father was a smelly old wop who had a cataract over one eye, and who would have sold his only pair of pants for a good meal and a steady supply of *vino*. There were only two rooms in the house, a bedroom and a sort of combined kitchen-living-dining room. But there was also a barn and the arrangement we later worked out was that Gino, the old man, would sleep in the barn whenever Ace and I came over to see his daughter.

On the night of the Kraljevo raid, Ace and I stopped to lift a few at the Officers Club, and ran into the pilot who had flown the lead bomber. He told us that everytime he went onto Automatic, turning the plane over to his bombardier to fly through the bombsight, he experienced all the qualms of a man running through a thunderstorm without an umbrella, certain he would be struck by lightning at any moment. It was always with an enormous sense of relief that he took back the controls after the bombs were away, as if returning his fate into his own hands once again. It turned out that his airplane was the one Ace and I had picked up off the target and escorted home, or at least close enough to home for him to contact Big Fence for a vector without getting jumped by bandits. In gratitude, he kept buying us drink after drink, and we didn't get to leave the club until ten o'clock that night. By the time we got over to the farmhouse, Gino was already asleep in the big lumpy double bed in the bedroom at the rear of the house. We had thoughtfully brought over two packs of cigarettes, and therefore felt no qualms about shaking him out of the sack and sending him off to the barn. The obsequious old bastard gratefully slipped out of bed in his underwear and thanked us for the pleasure of being banished from the house, while tucking one package of Camels (the other we gave to Francesca) into the waistband of his droopy long johns and praising the United States Army Air Force for its noble and courageous pilots, *grazie, grazie, mille grazie* for bomba the town, for fucka the daughter, but especially for bringa the cigarettes.

Only stupid women ask questions, only beautiful women ask favors. Francesca was neither. She knew why we were there, and she knew what she could expect in payment for her small sacrifices. We were reasonably decent fellows, though involved in the occupation of escorting bombers, and we never beat her or abused her, even when we were drunk. We were drunk whenever we went to her after a mission (which was sometimes five days a week and sometimes twice a week, and sometimes not at all for a week or ten days or two weeks or however long it took for the weather to break), and we always brought additional whiskey to the farmhouse because we wanted Francesca to have a drink with us before we went into the bedroom. I don't think Francesca enjoyed whiskey, but she always had at least one with us before we went to bed.

There was no electricity in the old farmhouse; if there ever had been any, the repeated bombing raids had effectively knocked it out, and nobody involved in the war was worrying about repairing electrical lines to Gino's cruddy little spread. Ace and I undressed in the light of the single kerosene lamp burning on the round table in the center of the large room, then went into the bedroom wearing only our khaki undershorts and climbed into bed to wait for her. In the beginning, when we had first started with Francesca, one of us would go into the bedroom with her while the other waited outside. But a fireplace provided the only heat in the farmhouse, and wood for fuel was going at premium prices, and it got pretty damn cold even on a summer's night, sitting in that big empty stone room without a fire. So one night Ace came into the bedroom, shivering, and said, "I hate to disturb you," and I said, "Then please don't," and he said, "Move over, Francesca," and climbed into bed on the other side of her, and it had been that way ever since.

She blew out the kerosene lamp on the round table now, and came padding across the stone floor of the house and into the bedroom. The door on the wooden *guardaroba* creaked open. In the darkness, she put on a cotton nightgown, and felt her way across the room to the bed, and crawled in between Ace and me.

She let us do whatever we wanted to do.

I don't know whether she enjoyed it or not.

She never said a word in bed, not a single word.

In the morning, we went back to the field at seven a.m., in time for briefing, knowing that if the weather was good we would fly to Hungary or Yugoslavia or Germany or Poland or Austria to bomb.

My hands and feet were always cold in the airplane, and I always came back with a headache.

October ❧

That Sunday afternoon, Allen Garrett called me a Bolshevik.

Nancy was in the kitchen doing the dishes with Allen's wife. He and I were in the parlor, drinking and talking and smoking cigars, a habit I had picked up from him out at the mill. He got up out of his chair suddenly and stretched himself to his full six feet two and a half inches, raised his arm and pointed his forefinger at me, his eyes blazing, and shouted, "Bert, you're a goddamn Red!" Even though everyone was calling everyone else a Red or a Bolshevik along about then, I was surprised anyway by Allen's accusation. And hurt. And angry.

The hysteria had started back in April, I guess, when Mayor Ole Hanson of Seattle (who had previously been making trips all over the country to alert it to the menace of a world proletarian revolution as openly promised by the Russians themselves at the formation of their Comintern) found a bomb in his mail. On the very next day, in Atlanta, Georgia, a colored girl had her hands blown off. She happened to be working for Senator Thomas R. Hardwick, who was chairman of the Immigration Committee, and who was strongly advocating stricter immigration quotas in order to keep the Bolsheviks out of America. It had been her misfortune to open a package addressed to her boss, presumably with his permission, the servant situation in Georgia being what it was. And on the last day of April, sixteen bombs bearing the same false Gimbel Brothers return address were discovered on a shelf in a New York City post office. It was not considered coincidental that they were addressed to such capitalists as J. P. Morgan and John D. Rockefeller, or to such high government officials as Attorney General A. Mitchell Palmer and Supreme Court Justice Oliver Wendell Holmes.

The situation only got worse in the weeks and months that followed. We were a people who had mobilized more than four million men to make the world safe for democracy, and suffered close to 365,000 casualties in history's bloodiest war. We were not ready to have our sacrifices rendered meaningless, we were not ready to lose our country to wild-eyed anarchists and dedicated revolutionaries. We knew how to deal with imminent danger, and we dealt with it effectively and mercilessly, the way we had dealt with Kaiser Bill's misguided troops on the battlefield. On May Day in New York City, the offices of a Socialist newspaper named the *New York Call* were ransacked and seven members of the staff were beaten up so badly they had to be sent to the hospital. A parade of Socialists in Cleveland was stopped by a mob of soldiers who insisted they get rid of the red flag they were carrying, leading to the throwing of a punch, and then a fistfight, and then open combat, and finally riots all over the city in which one man was killed and dozens more injured.

It was my opinion that people were getting a little crazy only because the country was about to go completely dry. I was not a hard-drinking man, but I had learned a little bit about alcohol on my recent trip abroad (Nancy always giggled when I referred to my war experience that way), and I knew that there was nothing wrong with a nip or two, especially when the weather was as miserable as it was this October. The Wartime Prohibition Law had gone into effect on the first of July, just in time for Independence Day, and the Volstead Act had been passed by Congress this month, putting teeth into the already ratified Eighteenth Amendment by making it a crime to distill, brew, or sell any beverage containing more than one-half of one per cent alcohol by volume. In the meantime, Allen and I were *still* drinking Bronxes in the parlor of my own home that afternoon, while waiting for the Eighteenth Amendment to go into effect in January. But it was not surprising to me that a nation deprived of its right to consume alcohol, however moderately, was a nation that would go looking under its bed for bearded bomb-throwers.

It seemed to me, I had been saying, that we could not blame everything that was happening in this country on the Communists. The Boston police had had every right to strike last month, they were only earning eleven hundred dollars a year . . .

241

"That's more than what you and I make, isn't it?" Allen said.

"We're new on the job," I said, "and we don't have to buy our own uniforms and guns. There's nothing wrong with a man striking for a decent living wage."

"There's nothing wrong with a strike that isn't instigated by the Bolsheviks," Allen said.

"Are you telling me the Boston cops are Bolsheviks?"

"I'm telling you there's no right to strike against the public safety by anybody, anywhere, anytime! That's what the governor of Massachusetts said, and that's what I'm saying."

"Then how about the steel workers? Do *they* have a right to strike?"

"Bert, don't you know that whole crowd there is infested with Reds? Who's the man who did the most to organize the steel workers, can you tell me that? Well, *I'll* tell *you,* Bert. It was William Z. Foster, a left-wing syndicalist. The whole damn strike there is a conspiracy. If I owned a steel mill, I'd do just what they're doing over in Gary. I'd bring in strikebreakers by the thousands and protect them with the National Guard, that's what I'd do. You wait and see how quick this strike'll be settled now that they're wise to those Reds."

"Well," I said, "you can't bring in strikebreakers every time there's a strike. John L. Lewis has called one for November first, now are you going to . . . ?"

"The UMW voted for public control of the mining industry," Allen said. "What's public control if not Communism?"

"They want more money," I said. "How would *you* like to work underground twelve, fourteen hours a day, breathing all that stuff into your lungs?"

"The hell with them," Allen said. "Palmer's got the right idea. He told them if they go ahead with this strike, they're violating the Lever Act. Do you know what the Lever Act is?"

"What's the Lever Act got to do . . ."

"It gives the President the power . . ."

". . . with here and now?"

". . . to step in whenever anything inter—"

"It was a wartime measure!"

". . . feres with the production of . . ."

"The war's *over,* Allen!"

"Coal is fuel!" Allen said. "And the President can tell those Red bastards to cut the crap and start producing it! That's the power the Lever Act gives him!"

"Gives the Attorney General, you mean. Wilson's a sick old man, he doesn't know *what's* going on in this country any more. If you want my opinion, I think Palmer's a lot more dangerous than either the Boston police *or* the steel workers *or* . . ."

That was when Allen jumped out of his chair and said, "Bert, you're a goddamn Red!"

"No, Allen, I'm not," I answered, surprised, and hurt, and angry.

"What's going on out there?" Allen's wife called from the kitchen.

"It's nothing," Allen said.

"It sure *sounds* like something," she answered.

"It *is* something," I whispered to Allen. "It's very *definitely* something when a friend of mine can call me a Bolshevik simply because . . ."

"I didn't say a Bolshevik!"

"You said a Red!"

"I said you *sounded* like a Red."

"No, you said I *was* a Red."

"Is that *you*, Bert?" Nancy called from the kitchen.

"The girls are getting upset," Allen said.

"No more upset than I am," I said.

"I see you've managed to smell up the entire parlor," Nancy said, coming into the room. Rosie Garrett followed immediately behind her, a tall slender girl with long black hair and dark eyes, wearing lip rouge ("The devil's own paint," Nancy called it, though she herself had begun putting powder on her face) and a tan suit, skirt tight above the ankles, tan spats to protect her from Chicago's winds. Congress had passed the Nineteenth Amendment in June, making it illegal to deny the right to vote on account of sex, and the thought of Rosie Garrett casting a ballot next year, when the law would go into effect, was somewhat frightening. Both she and Allen were older than either of us, each in their early twenties and terribly sophisticated. (They had spent Allen's week-long vacation in New York City this past summer, and had seen *Up in Mabel's Room*, which Rosie claimed had not shocked her the slightest tiny bit.) Rosie smoked cigarettes. Together, she and Allen

243

made a very striking couple, and I was always conscious of my own, well, not exactly handsome looks when I was with them; my nose especially, though Nancy insisted it was a quite regal nose. Nancy, of course, looked fresh and lovely *anywhere*, in *anybody's* company. She had put on a little weight since we got married, but those few extra pounds only brought her up to where she'd been before her illness. Slightly flushed as she came into the parlor, she flapped her hands at the cloud of cigar smoke. Behind her, slender dark Rosie put a cigarette between her rouged lips and struck a match.

"What was all the shouting about?" she asked.

"Allen thinks I'm a Red," I answered.

"Allen thinks Douglas *Fairbanks* is a Red," Rosie said, and Nancy burst into laughter. Rosie blew out a puff of smoke and then went to sit on the arm of her husband's chair, putting her hand on his shoulder. He was still frowning, though God knew why. *He* was the one who'd called *me* a Red.

"A *goddamn* Red, in fact," I said.

"Please, there are ladies present," Rosie said in mock affront, and wiggled her black eyebrows at Nancy, who again laughed.

"We were talking about the strike," Allen said.

"Grrrrrrr," Rosie said. "He reminds me of a grizzly when he's this way. Look at him. Grrrrrrrr," she said again, and tousled his short blond hair, and said, "Doesn't he look just like a bear, Bert?"

(He lay silent and motionless with one hand still clasped over the base of his skull, just below the protective line of his helmet. There was no blood on him, no scorched and smoking fabric to indicate he'd been hit.)

"Bert?"

(And then I saw the steel sliver that had pierced the top of his helmet, sticking out of the metal and the skull beneath it like a rusty railroad spike. "Timothy?" I said again, but I knew that he was dead.)

"Bert's out gathering wood violets," Nancy said.

"No, Bert is sulking," Rosie said.

I did not answer. I was wondering all at once about having made the world safe for democracy. As Allen sat opposite me and glowered in suspicion, I found myself

244

thinking something seditious, thinking something trai-
torous, thinking (God forgive me) that perhaps Timothy
Bear had been duped into giving his life for a slogan that
was meaningless, that maybe there was no such thing as
freedom, not in America, not anywhere in the world, that
perhaps the boundaries of freedom would always be as
rigidly defined as the boundaries of the Twenty-ninth
Street Beach had been this past July, where trespassing had
led to stoning and to death. I found myself overwhelmed
by a wave of patriotic feeing such as I had never experienced before (not even when the German guns were
sounding all around me), and I suddenly realized that
America was only now, only right this minute beginning to
test the strength of a political idea that was more revolutionary than anything that had ever come out of Russia,
testing it in a hundred subtle and unsubtle ways, not the
least of which was the unexpected appearance of a lone
Negro on a forbidden beach. And I wondered, exultantly,
hopefully, fearfully, what would happen when America
decided to find out *exactly* what freedom meant, *exactly*
to what limits freedom extended.

"All right, I know you're not a goddamn Red," Allen
mumbled at last.

"Grrrrrrrr," Rosie said.

November ⚜ ⚜ ⚜

It was two days after Thanksgiving, two years and a bit
more after President Kennedy had been shot and killed.
We stood in an early morning drizzle along the stone wall
that was the eastern boundary of Bryant Park in this city
where I'd been born. There were fifty of us, more or less,
waiting for the bus that would take us to the nation's
capital, where we could make our protest known against
the war in Vietnam.

Similar groups were waiting at thirty other pickup points
throughout the city, and two special trains hopefully

packed with demonstrators were scheduled to leave from Pennsylvania Station later that morning. The march on Washington had been conceived and co-ordinated by the National Committee for a Sane Nuclear Policy, and the group's expectation was that a crowd in excess of 50,000 concerned Americans from all over the country would surround the White House demanding peace in Southeast Asia. Sixty-five hundred demonstrators were supposed to be leaving from New York City, and SANE had calculated that 141 buses would be needed to take them south. By Friday evening, they had received definite commitments for 84 buses, and were hoping to charter an additional 31 coaches from Greyhound, and another 50 from a Connecticut company, more than enough to carry even a larger crowd than anticipated. But now, on Saturday morning, as a gray and sunless dawn broke over the New York Public Library, there was trouble already and we were being told by the marshal of the Bryant Park contingent that a rally had been scheduled for nine that morning for those of us who might never make it to Washington.

The problem, it seemed, had originated with the bus drivers' unions. Jackie Gleason had elevated the bus driver to the plane of a national folk hero with his weekly portrayal of the boisterous Ralph Kramden, and thus intellectually inspired, thus cognizant of their role in history and eager to protect and preserve the republic against subversives, anarchists, beatniks and the like, the bus drivers of America had refused to man the buses chartered for the trip, and only forty-eight of the committed vehicles had arrived at the scheduled pickup points. It appeared to the SANE officials that this was surely an illegal restraint of interstate travel, but in the meantime we demonstrators stood chilled and despondent in a city silenced by the long weekend holiday, the leafless trees around us sodden and stark against a monochromatic sky.

Dana had once written a skit about some North American Indians called the Ute, their unique characteristic being that everyone in the tribe was under the age of twenty-five. (*Ute*, don't you get it? she said, *Ute!* and I advised her that her sense of humor was far too excellent to be wasted on a cheap pun. Later that same day, when I told her we needed a new light bulb for the fixture over the sink, she convulsed me by replying, "Sure. What watt, Wat?") Anyway, it dismayed me to discover that not too many Utes were now in evidence in Bryant Park. The drizzle may have had something to do with that, or perhaps the fact that so many of the sponsoring organizations had such long names; the Ute of America, Dana had pointed out in her witless skit, preferred ideas to be short and to the point, preferably capable of being expressed in a single word, or better yet, a symbol. It was now close to seven a.m., I guessed, and the crowd had grown to perhaps sixty or seventy people, but I saw only a dozen kids our age, half of whom were obvious beatniks with long hair, dungaree jackets, and boots. The absence of more Utes in the assemblage may have accounted for our very orderly controlled manner; we looked less like demonstrators than we did a queue of polite Englishmen waiting outside a chemist's shop. The steady drizzle did nothing to elevate our spirits, nor did the nagging knowledge that perhaps our early morning appearance here was all in vain, there would be no goddamn transportation to Washington. Even the arrival of a bright red Transit Charter Service bus elicited nothing more than a faint sigh of relief from the crowd. Had there been more Utes present, the sigh might have become a cheer. In this crowd of octogenarians, however, it sounded more like a groan from a terminal cancer patient. Well, octogenarians wasn't quite fair. There was, to be truthful, only a sprinkling of very old people moving quietly toward the waiting bus. The remainder belonged to that other great Indian tribe (also made famous in Dana's skit) the Cholesterol, easily recognized by balding pates and spreading seats, strings of wampum about their necks, golden tongues (never forked) spouting pledges, promises, admonitions, and advice to their less fortunate brothers, the Ute. Maybe that wasn't fair, either. What the hell, we were *all* standing there in a penetrating November drizzle, all with our separate doubts, all hearing the marshal advising us that we would load from the front of the line (a senseless piece of information since I had never waited on any line that loaded from the *rear*) and then asking, "Where are those two girls?" to which a long-haired beatnik replied, *"Boy,* if you please!" and the marshal said, "You can't prove it by me. Am I that square?" and a member of the mighty

Cholesterol shouted, "No, you're not!" a good homogene-
ous mixture of marchers we were taking to Washington
that day.

There was not enough room on the single bus for all the
people moving in an orderly line toward the Sixth Avenue
curb. But a row of private cars with vacant seats in them
was pulling in behind the bus now, and people began
dropping out of the line in twos and threes, always in
order, to enter the cars and be driven off into the gray
wet dawn. Dana and I waited our turn. By seven-thirty we
were aboard the bus, and in another ten minutes the doors
closed and we pulled away from the curb and headed for
the Lincoln Tunnel.

I felt apprehensive, but I could not explain why.

It had rained in Washington, too, and the streets were
still wet when we assembled outside the White House at
eleven o'clock that morning. The sun was beginning to
break through. Looking across the Ellipse, I could see the
obelisk of the Washington Monument wreathed in clouds
that began tearing away in patches to reveal a fresh blue
sky beyond. It was going to be a beautiful day after all,
clear and sunny, the temperature already beginning to rise,
and with it the spirits of the protesters. The organizers of
the march were passing out signs on long wooden sticks,
each bearing a carefully selected slogan. My sign read,
vertically:

WAR
erodes
the
Great
Society

Dana carried a sign in the shape of an American flag,
the field of stars in the left-hand corner replaced by a
slogan, the bottom three white stripes lettered with a second slogan, so that the message read:

There were additional slogans as well, all of them muted in tone as befitted the dignified approach of the sponsoring groups, all of them professionaly printed by the hundreds, except for the dozen or so hand-lettered posters carried by some of the more militant forces who seemed to be shaping up into cadres of their own, signs that blared in blood-dripping red U.S. IS THE AGGRESSOR or AMERICA, GET OUT NOW! I noticed, too, as I lifted my sign and rested the wooden handle on my shoulder, that some of the hard-core cadres were carrying furled Vietcong flags, and my sense of apprehension grew, though I could not imagine trouble in this orderly crowd, the soft-spoken monitors explaining what we would do, the clouds above all but gone now, a robin's egg blue sky spreading benignly over the glistening wet white clean buildings of the capital.

The appearance of the first swastika was shocking.

We were marching along three sides of the White House, STEPS TO PEACE, STOP THE BOMBINGS, flanked by the wrought iron fence surrounding the lawn and the wooden police barricades set up to bisect the wide sidewalk, RESPECT 1954 GENEVA ACCORDS, the police watching with a faint air of familiar boredom, apparently without any sense of impending trouble, "NO MORE WAR, WAR NEVER AGAIN"—POPE PAUL, no one chanting or singing, even the militants looking oddly suppressed save for the anticipatory fire in their eyes and

249

the color of the now unfurled Vietcong flags, when suddenly the storm troopers appeared in Army fatigues and combat boots, swastika armbands on their shirtsleeves, George Lincoln Rockwell's American Nazi elite, one of whom held in his right hand a fire-engine red can with the label GAS on it, and in his left hand a sign reading FREE GASOLINE AND MATCHES FOR PEACE CREEPS.

The reference, of course, was to the two immolations within as many weeks this November, the first having taken place outside the river entrance to the Pentagon, not three miles from where we now marched, when a thirty-one-year-old Quaker named Norman Morrison drenched his clothes with gasoline and, holding his eighteen-month-old daughter in his arms, set fire to himself in protest against the Vietnam War. An army major managed to grab the child away from him in time, but Morrison could not be saved, and he was declared dead on arrival at the Fort Meyer Army Dispensary. A week later, a twenty-two-year-old Roman Catholic named Roger LaPorte set himself ablaze outside the United Nations building in New York City, and died some thirty-three hours later, still in coma. The immensity of those gestures, ill-advised or otherwise, coupled with the memory of Jews being incinerated by Nazis in the all-too-recent past (*Judgment at Nuremburg* had taken two Academy Awards not five years ago!) transformed this *American* Nazi's at best insensitive offer into an act at once barbaric and intolerable. It was no surprise that someone rushed him, yanked the armband from his shirtsleeve, and began tearing his poster to shreds. (The surprise came later; his attacker turned out to be an ex-Marine who, like the Nazi, was *opposed* to the march.)

I expected trouble to erupt full-blown then and there.

I saw another Nazi rushing forward with a poster that read IN WAR, THERE IS NO SUBSTITUTE FOR VICTORY, wielding the sign like a baseball bat, Vietcong flags on poles being lowered like spears now, a minor war paradoxically about to begin on the fringes of a protest *against* war. There was a lunatic aspect to the scene, the row of orderly marchers with their beautifully rendered posters, a middle-aged phalanx that circled the White House in the company of a sparse number of Utes, while Vietcong flags confronted Nazi swastikas, schizophrenia in the sunshine, the Washington police seemingly as dazed as the photographers, but only for a moment. Swiftly, efficiently, they moved in to break up the scuffle. Flash bulbs popped too late. My head was turned away, there was no danger that a recognizable photograph of me would appear on the front page of the New York *Times*. (Was this in my mind even then, the persistent rumor that draft boards were deliberately calling up peace demonstrators in reprisal, was this what caused my apprehension?)

We marched across the Mall later to the Washington Monument and listened to speeches gently urging peace. Looking north across Constitution Avenue, we could see the White House, and to the southwest across the Tidal Basin, the glittering white temple of the Jefferson Memorial. I did not know what to think. President Johnson had only yesterday affirmed through his Press Secretary Bill D. Moyers that the anti-war demonstrations were "a part of the freedom guaranteed all Americans." But Moyers had gone on to say that the President was "obviously impressed also by the other kind of demonstrations taking place in South Vietnam where tens of thousands of Americans were serving their country and offering themselves in support of freedom." Johnson seemed certain that the great majority of Americans were in favor of his Vietnam policy (but not the many thousands who were gathered here at the monument; and he had delivered through Moyers what sounded ominously like a warning to those of us who were opposed to the policy there, asking us again to "weigh the consequences" of our actions. I did not feel we were accomplishing too terribly much as we listened to the speeches. I felt a sense of helplessness, a certain knowledge that however many of us rose in protest against what Norman Thomas later called "this monstrously stupid chess game in which the pawns bleed," no matter how many of us made our views known and our voices heard, the course had already been charted; there were empires at stake of which we had no inkling.

All the way back to Talmadge, I could not shake my gloomy despair nor my edgy apprehension.

The Talmadge *Advertiser-Dispatch* published only two editions a week, one on Monday and the other on Thursday. Since the march had taken place on a Saturday, the earliest mention of it could only have appeared on the following Monday.

It was my father who brought the item to my attention. He had told my mother that he wanted to speak to me, and when I went into the living room, he was sitting in one of the Hogarth chairs flanking the fireplace. I took the chair opposite him. A pitcher of martinis was on the end table near his right elbow. It was nearly empty, and he was holding an almost-drained glass in his hand. I hoped he was not drunk.

"How come we never have heart-to-heart talks?" he asked.

"I don't know. How come?" I answered.

"When I was a kid," he said, "I used to go see all the Andy Hardy movies—you ever hear of Andy Hardy?"

"Yes, I have."

"Old Judge Hardy would take Andy into the library for these heart-to-heart talks, and they would get things all squared away. I used to wish my father would take *me* into the library and have one of those talks with me, but he never did. We used to have a library upstairs in the house on East Scott, well, you've never seen that house, you wouldn't know. It was a nice room. I'm sorry we never used it. I mean, to talk."

I didn't say anything.

"This is a nice room, too," my father said, "though of course not a library. Your mother's got good taste. This is a nice room, don't you think?"

"Yes, it's a very nice room," I said. "I've always liked it."

"Shall we have a heart-to-heart talk?"

"About what?"

"I try to be a good father," he said suddenly.

Again, I said nothing.

"Did you see this?" he asked and handed me a copy of the *Advertiser-Dispatch* folded open to page four. I was surprised to see my high school graduation picture there, with a caption over it that read:

TALMADGE YOUTH MARCHES

The single paragraph under the picture merely stated that I was one of an estimated thirty-five thousand protesters who had gone to Washington the week before.

"Is this today's?" I said. Idiotically, all I could think was TALMADGE UTE MARCHES.

"You didn't tell me you were going to Washington."

"You didn't ask me."

"Do I have to ask?"

"I guess if you're interested, you have to ask."

"No, I *don't* have to ask. A father doesn't have to ask his own son what he's up to. You're supposed to *come* to me and tell me. *That's* the way it's supposed to be."

"Pop," I said, "maybe we ought to talk some other time."

"No, let's talk now."

"Dinner's almost ready . . ."

"Dinner can wait!"

"How many of those have you had?"

"I can drink you under the table anytime you'd like to try it, Wat, so don't give me any of *that!*"

"Okay," I said.

"Okay," he answered.

We sat opposite each other silently. I put the newspaper down on the oriental rug. My father poured what was left of the martinis into his glass.

"What's your plan?" he asked.

"My plan for what?"

"You drop out of school, you go on a goddamn march, you get your picture in the paper for everybody to see . . ."

"I'm not ashamed of what I did."

"No, *I'm* the one who's ashamed."

"Then I'm sorry. I guess we all have different things to be ashamed of. If I embarrassed you, I'm sorry."

"You may be sorrier when your draft board sees that newspaper. You think they're kidding up there? You think this war is a joke?"

"No, I most certainly don't think it's a joke."

"You've been 1-A ever since you dropped out of Yale," he said. "What'll you do when they draft you. Refuse to go? Let them send you to prison?"

"No, I haven't got the guts for that."

"Then what? Run for Canada?"

"I don't think I could leave America."

"You love it so much you can't leave it, huh? But you can go on a march . . ."

"Pop," I said, "if you love something enough, you should

253

be able to say it's wrong." I paused. Still without looking at him, I said, "The way I think you're wrong, Pop."

"About what?"

"About . . . a lot of things. About this. Your ideas about this."

"And what else?" he said sharply.

"Nothing. Nothing else."

"Join the Navy," he said. "Nobody wants to get killed, that's understandable. I joined the Air Force because I didn't want to end up in the Infantry. The Vietcong have no fleet and no air power, you'd be safe in the Navy. Give them your two years or whatever you owe them, and then come home and live your life."

"No," I said. "It may be too late, but I've already decided to appeal my classification."

"What do you mean, too late?"

"I've been lucky so far. They're drafting guys left and right."

"What kind of an appeal?"

"I want it changed to 1-A-O."

"What's that?"

"Noncombatant."

"That's very smart," my father said, "you've got a lot of smart ideas. You'll put yourself on a battlefield without a gun, very smart."

"It's a matter of principle," I said.

"It's a matter of bullshit," he said. "You anxious to get killed?"

"No, but . . ."

"The idea is to stay alive, Wat."

"That's only *part* of the idea."

"Stay alive," he repeated. "However you can. Do whatever you have to do to stay alive." Our eyes met. "Do you understand me?" I shook my head. "What don't you understand?"

"I don't understand staying alive by hurting someone else. If . . . if that's what *you* have to do to stay alive, Pop, then you go ahead and do it. But don't ask me to . . . to hurt anyone. I can't do that."

"What are we talking about?" he asked, suddenly frowning.

"Pop . . ." I started, and then only shook my head.

"Say what you have to say, Wat."

"No, I don't have anything to say."

254

My father drew a heavy breath. "If anything happened to you . . ." he said, and hesitated. "Do you want to kill your mother?"

"Do *you?*" I said.

That was the closest we came to bringing it out into the open. That was the closest I came to saying, You son of a bitch, who are you fooling around with, some cheap cunt from the office, some college girl you picked up on your lunch hour, some Park Avenue whore, how *dare* you tell me how to live my life when you haven't yet learned to live your own? That was as close as we came.

My father turned away from me. Looking into his glass, he said, "Son, I . . ." and shook his head. I had the sudden feeling that he was going to cry. Without looking up at me, he quickly said, "I don't want you to get hurt." His lip was trembling. He kept staring into his glass. "Wat, I only . . ."

It occurred to me that I could help him. It occurred to me that he was trying to say he loved me. But I watched him from across the room, watched him struggling with whatever it was inside that made it impossible for him to say the words to his own son, and when at last he began sobbing, I swiftly left the room.

I did not stop hating myself for a long time afterward.

December ❦ ❦

She came limping away with her number four engine gone, Ace and I hovering above her, the pilot already feathering her number two; we were going to have a straggler not a minute and a half off target. Major Kander, our flight leader, said, "Springcap Seven-Nine, cover her," and I pressed the transmitter button in the center of the control wheel, and said into the oxygen mask microphone strapped over my chin and mouth, "Springcap Seven-Nine, Wilco," and peeled off with Ace on my wing not four feet to the right.

There was a big hole in the bomber's belly, and I saw

now as we dropped down over her that her rear turret was gone as well, how the hell were we going to to get her back to Foggia? The heavies were supposed to cruise at one-sixty after target, but if she was doing a hundred and thirty, she was lucky, already beginning to lose altitude and dropping more speed as the blades on her number two feathered and the propeller stopped. She had made a sharp right turn away from the bombing line and was now flying on a southerly course to the rally point, but there was no question of her keeping up with the other B-17s, we would have her on our hands all the way back to Italy. In the far distance, I saw some of the bombers already forming up, and suddenly Ace's voice shouted, "Break left!" and without stopping to think or to question, I immediately turned the wheel to the left, put in the left rudder, went into a roll, sucked back on the stick, goosed the airplane into a screaming climb with Ace clinging to my wing, and only then looked down to see what he'd been yelling about—four FW-190s dropping out of the clouds for a pass at the bomber's right side, apparently unaware as yet that Tail-End Charlie was gone and that the bomber had a blind spot. They came in on her in trail, all their firepower—four 20-mm cannons and two 13-mm machine guns for each plane—spraying the bomber in sequence from her nose to her tail as they made their first pass. It was too late to break up their formation, they came screaming up level on the poor stuttering bastard, approaching her over half the clock, twelve to six, staggered four abreast and filling the sky with thunder, black-spinnered each and every one of them, big black white-trimmed crosses on their gray flanks, smaller black swastikas on their tails, cannons blasting from the wing roots and the wings themselves, machine guns spitting from the cowlings of each plane as they came in level, one after the other, and then swung low under her for a try at the ball turret in the belly.

We were waiting above them as they broke clear of the bomber on her left-hand side and began to climb. The ball turret had swung around, and the gunner was following them as they rose, joined in firepower now by the gunner in the upper turret, and the waistgunner on the left, all of them shooting steadily as the enemy planes screeched for the cover of the cirrus clouds above, through which Ace and I dropped down on them, hoping the B-17's gunners would let up when we joined the fray and not get two of their own little friends. We did not surprise the Germans; they had known we were there when they began their attack. But their own surprise was complete; as we dropped down on them, a second pack of FW-190s appeared on the bomber's tail and a third formation dove in on the right again, all of them apparently having hidden in the cloud cover until the first pass was completed. Their timing was absolutely perfect. The attackers aft came in one behind the other in a single line, their flight leader learning immediately that the tail position had been knocked out by flak over the target, and safely diving and firing and ripping the tail assembly to tatters and then swooping under the belly as the three other planes in the flight followed close astern. I knew the bomber was done for. As the tail attackers dropped out of sight to reform for another pass, the third pack came in, using the same tactics the lead flight had employed, four planes attacking in trail at two, three, four, and five o'clock, perpendicular to the bomber's long right flank, in slightly escalated altitudes from the tail to the nose. They raked the big ship and then pulled up over her this time, and I saw the upper turret explode with what must have been a direct cannon hit, and Ace shouted, "Three o'clock high!" and it was then that I thought we'd *all* had it, the bomber, Ace, me, every fucking United States Army Air Force plane in the sky over Poland that day because just then a pack of six Messerschmitts dropped out of the clouds on my right wing.

The bomber was losing altitude fast. Smoke was pouring from the waistgunner's position aft of the radio compartment. The first flight of FW-190s had reformed and were diving on her nose now in an attempt to deliver the knockout blow, coming in one after the other in a straight single line, shooting at the cockpit and then peeling off just out of range of the nose guns. Ace was swearing into his radio. We had not seen the Luftwaffe on our last six missions, their habit being to hoard ships and gasoline for strikes they could be certain were coming, and now the sky was swarming with them. They were not concerned with us, we were only incidental. They were after the B-17. To each of those German pilots, the big brown bomber must have seemed the symbol of everything that was destroying the German dream, relentlessly pounding

257

oil refinery and synthetic plant, aircraft factory and railway line. We had lost three B-17s to flak over the target, and now the German Air Force wanted to make it four, and they furiously attacked that poor descending bastard in successive determined waves as Ace and I tried desperately to break up their formations, buzzing in and out and around their superior force, going for the lead ship each time, diving in at the nose, pressing the machine-gun button on the rear of the wheel the instant an enemy spinner appeared in the illuminated ring sight, trying to rake the cowling and the cockpit, and then pulling back on the stick and climbing for another dive as another flight zoomed in on the bomber.

It was hopeless.

My hands and feet were freezing, I found it difficult to breathe. My eyes, my head kept jerking around to every minute of the sky-clock ("Keep your head moving!" Lieutenant Di Angelo had shouted in Basic Flying at Gunter Field) and the headache was upon me full-blown, beating in my temples and at the base of my skull. Together, Ace and I managed to knock down two Focke-Wulfs, but the bomber was losing altitude steadily, dropping closer and closer to the ground, and there was almost nothing we could do to save her. The German fighters followed her down as we kept trying to drive them off, persistently closing in on her, and finally scoring direct hits on the navigator's compartment and the cockpit. The big lumbering crippled airplane went into a slow flaming spin toward the ground, and the German pilots broke off contact at last, streaking for home, one of them having the audacity to waggle his wings at us when he left. We got out fast before the flak started again, and picked up the rest of the flight some fifty miles beyond the rally point. We did not see any other enemy fighters on the way home, but we ran into heavy flak over Hungary, losing two more bombers to a rocket battery, and picking up another straggler with her number one engine gone. At Trieste, which we could see clearly below us from 20,000 feet, I dropped down on her left wing and lifted my hand in the three-ring sign, letting the pilot know I was leaving him there, and he threw the sign back, and I veered away with Ace on my left, and called into my microphone, "Big Fence, this is Springcap Seven-Nine. Request a fix, over."

"Big Fence reading Springcap Seven-Nine. Give me a long count, over."

"Springcap calling Big Fence. Commencing long count. One, two, three, four, five, six, seven, eight, nine, ten. Ten, nine, eight, seven, six, five, four, three, two, one. Over."

"Springcap Seven-Nine, your position forty-five thirty-nine north, fourteen four east, approximately five miles east of Trieste. Take heading one-six-six, you are approximately two hundred and sixty miles from base."

We made it home in fifty minutes. As soon as I landed, I slid off the wing, opened my pants, and fired seven hours' worth of piss at the runway while Sergeant Balson looked the other way and tried to pretend I wasn't sending up a steaming stinking cloud to envelop his precious airplane.

We could not stop thinking about the bomber we had lost.

The pilot had been a guy named George Heffernan, a soft-spoken law student from Minnesota. We had often ribbed him about his gentle manner, telling him he would never win a court battle because he was not an aggressive type, this in spite of the fact that he had flown the lead bomber in a massive flight of five hundred bombers against the crude oil refinery at Floridsdorf on the fifth of November, and again on the eighteenth. Now, in December, a week before Christmas, flying for the first time after a long spell of bad weather, he had been shot down over Poland, and we had watched the spinning flaming airplane he and his crew had named *Mother's Milk* explode on contact with the ground while the Messerschmitts and Focke-Wulfs hovered.

We had also been informed by Archie Colombo in our tent (we still referred to it as a tent, even though the mason had finally finished our tufa-block house and we were living in unprecedented luxury that included a tank and heater built for us by one of the T-3s and fueled with 100-octane aviation gasoline) that a recent strike against Odertal had brought up two ME-262s, the dreaded twin-engine German jet. It was his opinion, an opinion shared by many of us in the Air Force, that if the Germans could produce enough of those airplanes, we would lose our air superiority and stand a good chance of losing the war as well. I had never seen the jet, but other pilots had related tales of it rising suddenly and frighteningly to attack at speeds better than five hundred miles an hour. Firing four cannons from its fuselage nose, the ME-262 could out-climb, outmaneuver, and outshoot any piston-driven airplane we possessed. Ace and I were not happy about Archie's wide-eyed report, and we were even less happy about having seen Georgie Heffernan go down in flames over Poland. And since we were miserable, and tired, and perhaps a little scared, we drank a lot that night.

There was no shortage of scotch just then because the squadron had learned of a cache of Haig & Haig in Cairo, and had chipped in a small fortune to buy a full case in anticipation of our Christmas celebration. Tommy Rodwin had been elected to fly the secret mission. In Cairo, they had tried to tuck the contraband into the gondola around him, but the cramped cockpit would not accommodate all twelve bottles. So Tommy had been forced to cache three of them in the left engine nacelle, and they got so damn hot on the return flight that they shattered. He had landed in Foggia in a heavy fog, the nacelle stinking of booze, and had almost been lynched by the rest of us because of the breakage. But there was still plenty of scotch around, and Ace tucked a full fifth into the waistband of his trousers before we grabbed a jeep and headed for Francesca's place.

I don't know how we got there alive; I don't even remember who was doing the driving. It must have been a little past midnight when we drove into the courtyard and almost knocked over the fence penning in Gino's single pig—a relative, we suspected. We reeled over to the darkened farmhouse and Ace threw open the door and yelled, "Frankie, where the fuck are you?" and then said, "Will, you see anybody?" and I said, "No, it's dark in here," and he said, "Of course, it's dark in here, there's no light in here," and I yelled, "Frankie!" and Francesca came out of the bedroom pulling a woolen robe around her.

"It's late," she said.

"It's fucking early," Ace said.

"You flew," Francesca said. It was not a question.

"Yes, we fucking flew," Ace answered. We were still standing in the dark, the door closed behind us, the only illumination coming from the moon that glanced through the window at the far end of the room. "Put on some lights," he said. "Isn't there any electricity in this dump?"

"You know there is no electricity," Francesca replied.

"I don't know anything," Ace answered. The kerosene lamp on the table sputtered and then flared. Yellow light spilled onto the stone floor in a wide flickering circle. "What's *that?*" Ace asked. He was pointing to a flimsy structure at the far end of the room, shaped somewhat like a skeletal isosceles pyramid with four shelves. It was difficult to see anything too clearly in that dim corner, but the bottom shelf seemed to contain tiny figures representing the Holy Family, and the Three Kings, and a few shepherds and sheep and angels and what appeared to be a lopsided camel, all of them standing on a pile of straw Francesca had doubtlessly brought over from the barn. The other three shelves, spaced at intervals inside the open pyramid, each smaller than the next in ascending order toward the apex, were empty.

"*Il presepio,*" she explained.

"Tell her to talk English," Ace said. "Talk English!" he shouted at her, before I could say a word.

"It is a custom," she said, and shrugged. "For Christmas."

"What're the empty shelves for?"

"Gifts."

"Don't expect any from us," Ace said.

"I was not expecting any from you."

"Damn straight," Ace said. "Where's the glasses? I thought you were bringing glasses."

"Coming," Francesca said, and went barefoot to the wooden cabinet near the stove. "Was it bad?" she asked.

"It was marvelous," Ace said. "Fucking marvelous."

"We lost Georgie Heffernan," I said.

"We lost some others, too."

"Yes, but we *personally* lost poor Georgie."

"So what? She doesn't even know who poor Georgie is."

"Was," I said.

"Was. So what? Fuck him. Come on, Frankie, bring those glasses over here."

"He's upset," she said to me.

"Who's upset?" Ace said. "Here I am in lovely Italy a

261

week before Christmas about to fuck a pig I wouldn't look at back home, why should I be upset?"

"He didn't mean that," I said. "Come on, Ace, come on."

"I *meant* it," Ace said.

"He meant it," Francesca said softly, and put three glasses on the table.

"Give her a drink," Ace said.

"I don't want anything," she said. "I was sleeping when you came."

"Give her a drink, Will. We sent a man all the way to Cairo for this scotch, you damn well *better* drink it. You better drink a whole lot of it, Frankie dear."

"Have a drink, Frankie," I said.

"All right, but just a little."

"A *lot*," Ace said. Pouring, he mumbled, "Bet old *Skipper* ain't fucking a pig like you, you can bet on that."

"Tell him to stop," Francesca said. "He doesn't have to come here if he doesn't want to. No one forces him to come here."

"Oh, shut up," I said. "Drink your fuckin' whiskey, and shut up."

"You too," Francesca said, and angrily lifted her glass and threw off the three fingers of booze without stopping to take a breath. "More," she said, and held the glass out.

"Thinks it grows on trees," Ace said, but he poured the water tumbler half full again, and again Francesca drained it without batting an eyelash.

"Where's the governor?" Ace asked. "Out with his prize pig?"

"Asleep," Francesca said.

"He falls asleep quicker than most of us, you know," Ace said.

"How come?" I asked.

"Only got one eye to close."

"Ask me, he's only got one *ball*," I said.

"Just between you and me, Mac, you better have *four* of them," Ace said, and burst out laughing, and then said, "You know that one, Will?"

"Yeah, I know that one."

"This guy walks into a bar, and he says . . ."

"He *knows* the story," Francesca said.

262

"So what?" I said. "If Ace feels like telling a little story, what's wrong with him telling his little story? Did *you* fly to Poland today?"

"No," Francesca said.

"So shut the fuck up, and let him tell his story. Go on, Ace, tell your story."

"I forget the story."

"It was about Georgie Heffernan," I said.

"No, Georgie's dead, the dumb bastard. Have another drink, Francesca."

"I hate you both," Francesca said, but she held out her glass.

"So hate us, who cares?" Ace said. "I'm going to bed."

"So am I," I said.

"Buona notte," Francesca said, making it sound like a curse, and not moving from the table.

Ace and I went into the bedroom. Gino was snoring away in his underwear. Ace pulled back the blankets and said, *"Out,* shithead!" and the old man sat up and stared into the darkness with his one good eye, and then realized is was us, the liberating Americans, and immediately got out of bed, and shuffled and scraped his way out of the room. He said something briefly to Francesca outside, and then we heard the front door open and close, and we knew he was on his way to the barn. As we undressed, I could hear Francesca muttering to herself in Italian, the repeated click of the bottle's lip against the rim of her glass, the sound of the whiskey being poured. Ace and I climbed into bed.

"Come *on,* pig!" he roared, but Francesca did not reply.

In a little while, we were both sound asleep.

Perhaps it happened because we were both so drunk. It happened many times afterward, however, when neither of us was drunk, so I can't use that as an excuse. Perhaps it happened because we had seen Georgie Heffernan go down in flames. But we had seen bombers knocked down before, and our reactions were always the same, and they had never precipitated anything like this. Perhaps it happened because of Archie Colombo's story about the jet, and the possibility that we might meet one on the raids to come and be defenseless against it.

Or maybe, I don't know, maybe it had something to do

with the fact that we had already flown thirty-two missions, with rest leaves to Rome after the twelfth, Capri after the twenty-fifth, and eighteen missions to go before we would be sent back home. Maybe after thirty-two missions with your hands and your feet freezing cold and your head pounding, you got too tired or too scared and just didn't give a damn any more. Maybe you could only pretend for so long that everything was quite normal, thank you, and that escorting bombers over enemy targets was exactly what you'd be doing if asked to decide on any given day ("You anxious to get killed?" my father had said at the dinner table in our East Scott Street house on a day in March of 1943, when my mother was still alive and I was in a hurry to fly airplanes).

I heard someone weeping, and at first I thought Francesca had crawled into bed and was crying because of the way we'd talked to her earlier. I guess that was why I reached out, I'm sure that was the reason, thinking that Francesca was the person crying, and putting my arm over her shoulder next to mine, and then hearing Ace say, "Skipper, I'm afraid," and knowing all at once it was not Francesca, knowing that Francesca was not lying between us, she had not come to bed. "I'm afraid," Ace said, "I'm afraid, I'm afraid," and I kept my arm over his trembling shoulder, and he moved his face in against my chest, his tears falling on my skin, and said, "I'm afraid, oh Jesus I'm afraid, Skipper," and I said, "Come on, Ace, it's okay, come on now." He must have recognized then that I was not his older brother but only a friend named William Francis Tyler who had flown a harrowing mission with him that morning and afternoon, he must have realized then that we were not brothers. But he did not move away from me, he seemed to come closer instead, and I suddenly found both my arms around him, cradling him as though he were a baby, while he wept against my chest.

I'm certain it was Ace who started what happened next, but it doesn't matter. It may very well have been me. I'm certain, though that his hand as he lay cradled in my arms accidentally brushed against me, and I'm equally certain that I was unaware of it at first. And then it happened again, and this time I felt the whisper of his fingers and this time I *knew* he had touched me, and I felt myself lengthening in response, felt quick creeping tendrils of excitement in my groin and along my cock, and was suddenly

264

embarrassed. I think I wanted to move away from him, I think I wanted to call for Francesca, wanted her to bear the onslaught of whatever was beginning there in that pitch black room, but I could not turn away from Ace—he was my friend, he was crying bitterly, he was terrified. His hand tightened around my cock, he clung to my cock as if it were his own, as if by clutching the stiffening member between my legs he was reclaiming whatever maleness had been robbed from him in the sky over Poland that day. I moved my hand onto his groin. I reached in the darkness for him. To my surprise, I discovered that he was already hard, and I began crying too, inexplicably, uncontrollably. Sobbing together, we fitfully jerked each other into oblivious orgasm, and the next morning accompanied a thousand Fortresses and Liberators against transportation chokepoints in Hungary.

III

___

January ✤ ✤

There was, I had not expected, it appeared so suddenly, gray, shark-gray, shark-nosed, turbojets streaking fire from beneath swept-back wings, I was not sure, I thought at first, "Nine o'clock high!" I shouted to Ace on my left wing, but it was gone. I snapped my head around. "Did you see it?"

It came again. I could not believe there'd been enough time to execute a turn, but it, there, Colombo flying wing to the element leader shouted, "Jet above you, Ace!" and in that frozen moment *Aces High* burst into flame. The jet was gone. Streaking high over the formation, it swept up and out of sight, and I heard Ace yell, "I'm hit!" and Colombo shouted, "Where the fuck'd it go?" and I found myself unable to speak, unable to utter the commands a flight leader should have known to, Get out, I thought, "Ace!" I shouted, "What was that?" a pilot in one of the other planes asked.

We were fifty P-38s on a mission over Fiume, forty-eight actually because we had lost two to flak as we swarmed over the refinery, Ace in flames now, Get out, I thought again. He was on my left wing, slightly below me, and I could see the three big holes the shells had left at his wing joint, between the gondola and the engine nacelle, flames lashing up out of the shattered wing tanks, and

Ace's voice erupting into my headphones, "I'm on fire!" and I thought, Yes, I can see, and he screamed, "Selector valve! Fire in the cockpit!" and I thought Get out, Ace, ditch her, get out, get out, "Get out!" I yelled, "Fast!" I yelled, and saw him reaching forward and up for the emergency hatch release control and then suddenly pulling his hand back to slap at his flight suit, "I'm on fire!" he screamed, and I saw flames enveloping the cockpit as he rose from the armor-plated seat, still struggling with the release handle, desperately trying to get it open, "Hatch is stuck, Will," he said very quietly, eyes wide above the oxygen mask, hands fluttering wildly, and in that instant the tanks blew. My own airplane rocked with the blast, I pulled my head to the right in reflex, left shoulder coming up protectively, and then immediately looked down to see that the right wing and nacelle of *Aces High* had sheared off in the explosion and was dangling helplessly from the boom, suspended for only a moment before it broke away completely and began falling toward the ground. The gondola was gone, there was a jagged open hole where it once had been, blackened twisted metal like a gaping rotten mouth.

The demolished hulk of the airplane started a plunging deadfall.

There was another explosion when it hit the ground.

February ✿

I woke up trembling.

In the dream, my brother-in-law Oscar had come to me in full tribal regalia, headdress bristling with feathers, strings of beads and bones dangling from his neck and spread across his chest, lifting his hand, extending one long brown finger, and solemnly intoning, "Why did you steal our lands from us?" I backed away from him, close to the open mouth of the drum barker, and shouted over its tumbling roar, "Why did you steal my sister?" but he kept moving closer to me, closer and closer until I thought I would fall into the drum and have my clothes torn from

268

me, thought I would be tumbled and tossed until I came out at the opposite end stripped to my skin, naked and white. I sat up. I was wearing a flannel nightshirt, and the bed was cozy with the warmth of Nancy's body, but I could not stop shaking. The image of Oscar lingered, and then faded slowly. I blinked my eyes against the approaching dawn. It was almost time to get up. It was almost time to get dressed for work.

I did not know what was happening to me. I guess maybe I had hoped to set Chicago on its ear, become a paper tycoon within a week, branch out into New York and London, Paris and the world. I guess I'd nurtured, while listening to the pounding of the drum barker, wild dreams of owning countless mills, monopolies, *cartels,* the bark dropping down through the open still ribs and being whisked away together with remnants of the forest, twisted leaves and clinging dirt, my dreams soaring upward—Bertram A. Tyler, Chairman of the Board, I would smoke big cigars and hold meetings and they would whisper my name in the same awed breath as J. P. Morgan and Andrew Carnegie. But I had been with Ramsey-Warner for almost ten months now, and whereas I was now earning twenty-seven dollars a week, I was still rolling logs over to the woodpecker, still caught between the pounding and the drilling and the grinding, a long long way from becoming the powerful magnate I imagined in my fantasies. In fact, I considered myself just a step outside the poorhouse door, what with eggs costing eighty-three cents a dozen, and bacon selling for fifty cents a pound, and butter priced at seventy-four cents a pound, and shoes (which you could get before the war for three or four dollars a pair) now selling for upwards of ten dollars. And even though prices were government-fixed for coal, milk, and bread, twenty-seven dollars a week didn't go very far when there were two mouths to feed and two people to keep clothed against the bitter Chicago winter. (February so far had been a prize month, with temperatures recorded at six below zero, and the wind—as Nancy put it—"whistling to blow the marrow from your bones.")

I got out of bed.

The floor was cold. I pulled on a pair of pants over my nightshirt, and then put on my slippers and went into the kitchen and banked the fire in the stove and shoveled in some coal from the scuttle, and then put up a pot of water to boil. The toilet was in the hallway outside, shared by us and the Grzymek family downstairs. Mr. Grzymek was a Pole who worked for the McCormick Reaper Works, across the railroad tracks and within walking distance of where we lived.

The seat was cold.

Everything in the building was cold at this hour of the morning. I squatted there with my nightshirt pulled up and my trousers hanging down over my knees, and I thought Bertram A. Tyler, Chairman of the Board, living in a two-unit structure (small, but terribly comfortable) with a toilet in the hallway (modern plumbing, though, all very nice), overlooking the Sanitary and Ship Canal on the edge of the city's colored section, and boasting of a view that featured the House of Correction, the International Harvester Company plant, the railroad tracks of the P.P.C. & St. Louis, and Mr. Grzymek's reaper works. Bertram A. Tyler wiped himself, pulled the flush chain, and went back into the apartment to wash and shave.

I longed for a luxury home on the lake, longed for membership in the Union League Club where, standing outside on the sidewalk, I had seen women in furs and men in tuxedos floating out like visions in the make-believe world I'd created beside the drum barker—what worries did *they* have about the price of food or clothing? I had tried to explain all this to Nancy, I had tried to tell her that the world was moving very quickly and we were standing still in it, and she had said, (this was before we'd gone to see a doctor) Do you think there's something wrong with us, Bert, that we can't have a baby?

Nancy, I had said, don't you sometimes get the feeling it's all rushing right by us? They're putting a dial on the telephone, Nance, you won't have to jiggle the hook any more and ask for an operator, you'll get your number just by twisting a dial set right there in the base—Nancy, do you see what I mean? I went down to pick up my Victory medal at the armory last week, and I held it in my hand and looked at it, and it made me feel like a dinosaur. It's as if the war happened a hundred years ago, Nancy, it's as if everything has already moved way out and *beyond* the war, we're already living in a new era, only we haven't yet caught up with it. Am I making any sense to you, Nance?

Well, she said.

Look, I said, it's that everything seems to make me dizzy nowadays, I don't mean physically dizzy. I mean not knowing which way to turn because as soon as I decide I'm in favor of something or against something else, it all changes in the next minute, and I'm not sure any more.

Bert, she said, you *did* get a raise, they at least know you're on the payroll, they *must* have their eye on you.

Nancy, I'm not making myself clear to you, I said. I'm trying to tell you I don't understand what's happening in this country, and unless I can draw a sure bead on it, I'll be standing alongside that damn drum barker, excuse me, for the rest of my damn life, excuse me. Do *you* know what's going on? Does *anyone?* I get the feeling sometimes that everybody's rushing someplace, only they don't know where. And the worst part is that *I'm* standing still, *we're* standing still. I used to think I'd own that mill inside of a year. Now I think I'll be lucky if I get to operate a chipper inside of five years.

Well, Bert, she said, you've got to be patient.

I carried the kettle of hot water to the sink, turned on the light bulb over the mirror hanging there, and poured some water into the basin. Then I set the kettle down on the drainboard of the washtub, and stropped my razor, and worked up a lather in my shaving cup, all the while wondering how Oscar had got in my dream, I'd never stolen a piece of property from him in my life. The kitchen was beginning to warm up. There were only three rooms in the flat, the kitchen, the parlor, and the bedroom. The kitchen was in the center of the house, and the big black coal stove threw off a lot of heat, but rarely enough to warm up the bedroom which was on the northeast corner of the building and got some really terrific winds. Nancy had wanted me to buy a kerosene heater for the bedroom, but I'd heard of too many fires starting in those things, and I'd refused to do it. What annoyed me most, though, was that I couldn't afford to get her one of the new electric heaters.

Well, I thought, at least we don't have a baby to worry about too, and suddenly opened a big gash on my cheek. I looked up at God (hovering somewhere around the ceiling) and silently assured him I was only joking. I had never been a particularly religious person, but I was beginning to think more and more lately that I was being repaid by a vengeful deity for the sinful ways of my youth. Nor had I really believed what Dr. Brunner had told us; wasn't it possible that I'd inhaled some of that rotten stale mustard gas lying in holes all over France, stinking of death, and that it had somehow messed up my insides?

Frantically, I wiped at my cheek with one of the good towels Nancy's mother had given us when we got married. I'll silently bleed to death here, I thought. When Nancy wakes up she'll come into the kitchen and look down at me and say, Oh, Bert, you *shouldn't* have! Nothing can be *that* terrible! I smiled at my own slashed face in the mirror. I was mortally wounded, getting blood all over my nightshirt and Nancy's expensive towel, a near-pauper in a dead-end job in a city I despised, and all I could do was grin idiotically at myself, though I could not for the life of me see anything funny in our situation.

We had gone to visit Dr. Brunner one night at the beginning of January, Nancy clinging to my arm, her head ducked against the fierce wind as I led her up Twenty-sixth Street. He was a tidy little man wearing a long white coat, a stethoscope hanging from his neck, an air of sympathetic efficiency about him. But in spite of the fact that people were mentioning sex much more freely wherever you went these days, thanks to Dr. Freud, whose ideas about sublimation had quickly traveled from Vienna to New York to Chicago, I still found it extremely embarrassing to reveal to Dr. Brunner the things Nancy and I could not even comfortably discuss alone together. I kept turning the brim of my hat over and over in my hands, without looking at either him or Nancy, fumbling for words, certain that Nancy was blushing, and beginning to think we'd made a terrible mistake by coming here, we'd only been married nine months, why hadn't we given it a little more time before running to a doctor? Dr. Brunner kept nodding all the while I talked, and once he said, "I know this is difficult for you," and I said, "Yes," and went right on talking, afraid that if I once lost steam I'd quit altogether. When I finished, the doctor said, "Good, I understand. Let me assure you immediately that there are many healthy young couples who find themselves in your identical situation. We may have nothing to worry about here. But let's examine you both first, and make whatever tests are necessary, and then we'll be able to tell better, eh?"

The examinations were a nightmare, I'd never been so embarrassed in my life. Dr. Brunner matter-of-factly told us afterward that he had found nothing wrong with my testicular size, and that his routine (!) internal examination of Nancy had revealed no pelvic defect, but of course he would be able to tell us more after he had taken an ejaculated specimen (which he wanted before I left the office) and also a post-coital specimen (Nancy would have to come back the day after tomorrow) and had studied my sperm count and Nancy's ovulatory temperatures (I could not believe I was hearing these things spoken by a man, doctor or not, in the presence of a lady! By turns, I wanted to melt into the carpet, cover Nancy's good ear, or strangle Dr. Brunner). Nancy and I were both silent in the trolley car on the way home. Her face was still flushed, she kept her muffed hands in her lap, she did not even glance at me. I was certain I had exposed her to the most humiliating experience of her life, and I silently vowed never to take her to Dr. Brunner's office again. We went to bed without discussing any part of the horrifying incident, nor did we mention it at breakfast the next day, or at supper when I got home from work that night.

In bed, in the arctic zone of our northeast corner room, Nancy turned her head toward me and unexpectedly whispered something in my ear.

"What?" I said, "I didn't hear you, Nance."

"I'm the one supposed to be deaf," she whispered.

"I'm sorry, I just . . ."

"Bert," she whispered, "we have to make love tonight."

"What?"

"I'm going to see Dr. Brunner tomorrow morning," she whispered.

"Oh," I said. We lay stiffly beside each other in the darkness. I could hear her expectant breathing, the sound of the water tap dripping in the kitchen, a train chugging along the tracks a mile away to the south. "Nancy," I said, "are you sure you want to go back to him? Maybe we ought to . . ."

"Bert," she whispered, "a person's not worthy of the honeycomb if he shuns the hive because the bees have stings."

I nodded in the darkness.

"Don't you *want* to do it to me?" she asked.

273

"Yes, sure . . . what'd you say?"

"I feel like one of those women you told me about a long time ago," she whispered. "The ones who jazz," she whispered, and suddenly, surprisingly, began giggling, and threw herself into my arms, and kissed me with her mouth open.

At the end of January, we climbed the steps to Dr. Brunner's office again, dreading what he might tell us. He shook hands with me, nodded to Nancy, and then led us into his consulting room, where we both took chairs opposite his desk. Dr. Brunner glanced at a sheaf of papers, moved a tongue depressor to the side of the desk where he neatly arranged it parallel to the edge of the blotter, cleared his throat, and told us that there was nothing wrong with either of us, the laboratory tests had shown the number and motility of my sperm to be normal (how casually he discussed *my* sperm in the presence of *my* wife!) and he had been able to determine from the daily record of Nancy's oral temperature that she was indeed ovulating. In other words, we were both healthy and normal and not what could be even remotely considered an infertile couple. Very often, though, perfectly healthy normal couples like us could go for five years (Nancy winced) or even ten years (she turned to give me a swift hopeless glance) without having a baby, but then suddenly the woman would get pregnant, and would go on to have a dozen children after that, it was all a matter of patience. Nancy cleared her throat and asked the doctor whether the influenza might have had something to do with her not being able to conceive, and he said, "Nothing at all, Mrs. Tyler, I've just told you, there's nothing wrong with either of you." But she persisted, asking next about the encephalitis, and receiving the same response, and then telling him that she had come out of her illness a bit deaf, wasn't it possible that something else—finally causing Dr. Brunner to shout (I remember thinking he would not have lost his temper that way if we'd been rich) "My *dear* child, I assure you you're a healthy young horse, and that you *can* have children and probably *will* have children if only you'll be patient." Thank you, Nancy had said politely, and we left his office in silence.

As we walked down the narrow steps to the street outside, I said, "Well, Nance, we'll just have to keep trying, that's all. He says there's nothing wrong with us."

Nancy only nodded.

I remember thinking that if a woman could get pregnant just by nodding her head in a certain way, Nancy would have conceived right that minute on Twenty-sixth Street.

A paper mill is not an attractive place.

Aesthetically, Ramsey-Warner Papers, Incorporated, was perhaps as beautiful, say, as the prison at Joliet, with stacks puffing great billows of smoke onto the air, giant digesters rising like steel barn silos from the landscape, concrete buildings cramped side by side, each a different height and shape, some as tall and as narrow as machine-gun towers, others squat and lying close to the land, railroad sidings twisting past the mill or curving into it, freight cars clacking and clattering, huge rolls of stacked wrapped paper silently waiting, jackladders lifting logs onto stockpiles, chains clanging, wood looming in tangled pyramids, trucks and men in motion, everything painted a flat institutional gray, as bleak as February itself, as depressing as my own state of mind. I needed something to happen, but nothing ever did. And so I shouted my complaints over the tumbling bellow of the drum barker, and Allen Garrett shouted back, and in that way we made the days pass.

"I'm not siding with the radicals, Allen, but you can't expect me to side with Palmer, either!"

"He's a good man!"

"Oh sure! 'My motto for the Reds is S.O.S.—ship or shoot.' Is that a way for the Attorney General of the United *States* to be talking, like some ignorant uneducated greenhorn? 'Ship or shoot,' what kind of language is that for a man in high office?"

"You always quote only half!" Allen shouted.

"That is not half!"

"He also said, 'I believe we should place them on a ship of stone, with sails of lead . . .' "

"All right, all right."

" '. . . and that their first stopping place should be Hell.' That's good language, Bert. It's almost poetic."

"Poetic or not, it's crazy! Reacting this way to some kind of imaginary takeover of America . . ."

275

"It's *not* imaginary, damn it!"

". . . is just plain crazy. And I don't care if you start calling me a Red or a Communist or . . ."

"Did I call you anything?"

". . . whatever, I just refuse to get as crazy as everybody *else* in this country is getting. Do you know how many Communists there are in America?"

"Yes."

"Why, if there are fifty thousand . . ."

"There're more like five *hundred* thousand!"

"Oh *sure*, there are! Who's counting them, would you like to tell me? And why aren't we worrying about the Klan, that's going around tarring colored people and hanging them, now *that's* a terrible thing, Allen, that's worse than what we were told the Germans were doing during the war. But instead—now here's what I mean, Allen, here's exactly what I mean . . ."

"I think you'd *like* some coon to get your job, that's what I think."

"No, you just listen to me. There're two Dixieland bands right here in Chicago who wear the same costumes that the Klan does, the same white sheets and hoods, you know, with the eye holes in them, and one of the bands calls itself The Phantom Four, and the other one's The Night Riders. They're both very good bands, I hear, but what happens to the whole idea of right and wrong, Allen, if you can wear the same costumes as killers and make *music* in them? Where's the reality, Allen, do you see what I mean? What's real?"

"These logs are real, the drum barker's real, the mill is real. America is real," he said.

March ✾ ✾ ✾

I was in Saigon.

The army had flown me (via a commercial carrier called Saturn Airways) to Cam Ranh Bay three days ago, with orders to report to the 2nd Battalion of the 27th Infantry in Cu Chi, about eighteen miles northwest of

Saigon, and not too distant from the Cambodian border. From Cam Ranh, a Chinook had lifted me to the Tan Son Nhut Air Base, where I was billeted at a processing center called Camp Alpha, awaiting transportation.

There was a permanent party of about forty-five men on the post, the rest of us being soldiers in transit to base camps all over the country, or headed out on R and R tours. Peter Lundy was a guy from Stamford, against whom I'd played football when I was on the Talmadge team. He was in Army Finance now, and part of the permanent party at Tan Son Nhut. I met him in the mess hall my first night there. We talked a little about the old rah-rah days, and then he filled me in on the chow situation, and the girl situation, and told me how fortunate I was to have run into him because only permanent party were allowed off the post and into Saigon, but he thought he could get me past the security guards at the gate if I wanted to go in with him tomorrow afternoon.

He also told me that I had arrived in Vietnam at a particularly bad time weather-wise, since the country was blessed with a monsoon climate, which meant that there were only two seasons, the wet and the dry. The worst time of the year was between February and April, when the weather was hot and humid, as I may have noticed. He then went on to tell me some other pleasant little things about this prize nation we were saving for democracy, like the fact that the rats in Vietnam were as large as alley cats, and that there were twenty known species of poisonous snakes here, including cobras, kraits, and vipers, and that there were sharks in the coastal waters and leeches in the jungle underbrush, and mosquitoes carrying malaria and dengue fever, not to mention spiders, bedbugs, scorpions, and cockroaches, an altogether delightful place. Not for nothing had Saigon been named Pearl of the Orient. I thanked Pete for the information and made a date to meet him at four o'clock the next day. The night air, as he had promised, was oppressively muggy. In the distance over Saigon, I could see flares drifting brightly against the sky, like a summertime fireworks display over Playland. There was not much else to see. I went back to the barracks to write a letter to Dana, expecting to be bitten on the ass by a spider at any moment. I was asleep before lights-out.

The next day, we passed through the guards at the gate

277

without any difficulty. Pete was known to them, and all that was required was a discreet nod from him; it was nice to have important friends in high places, even if the importance was only that of a slick-sleeve sergeant. I was wearing a boat-necked sports shirt and pale blue slacks, loafers and socks. Pete, who had been a pretty flashy dresser even back in the old days, had on a bright purple silk shirt that had been made for him when he was on Rest and Recreation in Hong Kong, together with a pair of beautifully tailored tan slacks and a pair of sandals he had bought for 1200 piasters on Le Loi Street. In the fifteenth century, Le Loi had waged ten years of guerrilla warfare against the occupying Chinese, finally driving them out of the nation and becoming a king, only to die of beri-beri in Hanoi six years later. It was an interesting comment on this new war five centuries later, that the street named after a famous Vietnamese hero was one of the two streets in Saigon notorious for the sale of black market goods.

We had our choice of transportation from Camp Alpha—taxi, minibus, or cyclo. My mother had once shown me pictures of herself and my father on their Atlantic City honeymoon, and they were both being pushed along the boardwalk in a big wheelchair with a canopy over it. A cyclo looked something like that, except that the man pushing it was not on foot. There were, in fact, several varieties of cyclo, and all of them were on display and being hawked by their drivers outside the base. The cheapest cyclo (five to ten pee for the ride into Saigon, depending on how strenuously you felt like arguing) was a wheelchair with a bicycle attached to it; you sat in the chair and the driver pedaled the vehicle from behind. A cyclo with an attached motorbike was twice as expensive to hire, and a Lambretta with a van behind it had a variable fare that depended on how many passengers were being carried, its capacity being eight. Pete and I chose two motorized cyclos at an agreed price of fifteen pee each. The exchange rate in 1966 was a hundred and seventeen piasters to the dollar, so when you considered that the ride into Saigon must have been four or five miles, for a fare of less than fifteen cents, we weren't doing too badly. My driver, sitting behind me and wearing Army fatigues which he had undoubtedly purchased on either Le Loi or Nguyen Hue Streets spoke English reminiscent of the chop-chop variety invented by Chinese cooks in Gold Rush movies.

"You here long time?" he asked.

"Just got here yesterday," I said.

"Oh, you like Saigon," he said. "Much nice thing in Saigon. Number One town. Same like Paris."

"Mmm," I said.

"Where you from?" he asked.

"Connecticut," I said.

"You like Saigon," he said. "Better than Kennycunt."

Series I.—CLAIM FOR EXEMPTION

INSTRUCTIONS—The registrant must sign his name to either statement A or statement B in this series but not to both of them. The registrant should strike out the statement in this series which he does not sign.

(A) I am, by reason of my religious training and belief, conscientiously opposed to participation in war in any form. I, therefore, claim exemption from combatant training and service in the Armed Forces.

· ·
(Signature of registrant)

(B) I am, by reason of my religious training and belief, conscientiously opposed to participation in war in any form and I am further conscientiously opposed to participation in noncombatant training and service in the Armed Forces. I, therefore, claim exemption from both combatant and noncombatant training and service in the Armed Forces.

· ·
(Signature of registrant)

As we came into the city, as the city opened before us the way a melody line will open into a wider exploration of theme, implemented by a full orchestration where there had earlier been only a piano statement; as Pete in his bright purple silk shirt purchased in Hong Kong and I in my boat-necked shirt purchased in New Canaan came into this city that was the Paris of the East, I experienced the oddest sensation of believing suddenly and with the sharpest sense of conviction, that the entire war was a put-on, that there really *was* no war in Southeast Asia, that the daily communiqués from the battlefield (together with the ghoulishly required body-count of enemy dead) were comparable to the battle-action reports in *1984*, Eastasia is winning, Eurasia is losing, War is Peace, Saigon is Schenectady.

There were, of course, clues in these traffic-cluttered streets that this was the capital of a nation at war, the Army jeeps, the two-and-a-half-ton trucks, the Skyraiders streaking contrails over head in a sky as blue as that of Talmadge in the spring. But the Army no longer required its officers or men to wear uniforms except while on active duty, and it was impossible to tell whether the hundreds of Occidentals riding cyclos or taxis or stepping out of buses or standing on street corners or ogling girls or idly looking in shop windows were civilians or servicemen since they were all dressed, like Pete and myself, in clothes that would have been acceptable at any second-rate American resort. The city did not look truly oriental. It had instead the half-assed appearance of a movie shot on the back lot in the thirties or forties, a *Shanghai Gesture* that didn't quite make it for believability. Even the Vietnamese women, strikingly beautiful in their traditional *ao-dais* with paneled overdresses and satin trousers, seemed to have been supplied by Central Casting to satisfy the American stereotype of what an oriental woman *should* look like, long black hair and slanting brown eyes, narrow waists, delicate smiles, a France Nuyen or a Nancy Kwan to play the romantic interest in a movie about a white man in love with a Negro girl (carefully disguised as a white man in love with an Oriental) the motion-picture clichés springing to life everywhere around us, these slender inscrutable lovely girls chirping to each other in singsong ululation on every street corner or shouting in pidgin English across the bedlam of tooting horns. Saigon was *Dragon Seed* and *Macao* and maybe even *The General Died at Dawn,* and I was Gary Cooper, grinning somewhat sheepishly when a Vietnamese male approached my cyclo to satisfy yet another stereotype, that of the working pimp in a sinful city. He had undoubtedly learned his trade in the years when the French still controlled this garden spot, there was the promise of Parisian sin in his eyes and on his mouth as we waited for the light to change, *Quelques choses que vous desirez, monsieur?* the master pimp peddling pussy and pornography. But he recited it instead the way they'd written it in the hack script about the Mysterious East, gold tooth flashing in his mouth, lopsided grin (what no pigtail?), "You like Num-

280

ber One fuck, GI, I fix?" I shook my head as the light changed, and he shouted after me, "You lousy Number Ten, GI," and Pete yelled over from his cyclo, "That's the gook version of the bestseller list." To Pete, every Vietnamese in the country was a gook. The Vietcong were gooks, the ARVNs were gooks, the NVA were gooks, the Buddhists were gooks, the cyclo drivers, the bar girls, the policemen, the Prime Minister, each and all were only gooks. We moved slowly through tree-lined streets echoing Aix-en-Provence, designed by the French colonialists for a projected population of half a million people, and now trying hopelessly to cope with more than two million people, 150,000 automobiles and trucks, and another 500,000 bicycles and motorbikes. The sense of unreality persisted, was there truly a war being fought a hundred miles, fifty miles, twenty miles away? The horns honked, the lights changed, the cyclo drivers called to each other in Vietnamese over the roofs of Fords and Volkswagens, Toyotas and Triumphs, Citroëns and Chevrolets. I could not believe I was really here, but more than that I could not believe that here was real.

Series II.—RELIGIOUS TRAINING AND BELIEF
INSTRUCTIONS—Every item in this series must be completed. If more space is needed use extra sheets of paper.
1. Do you believe in a Supreme Being? ☐ Yes ☐ No
2. Describe the nature of your belief which is the basis of your claim made in Series I above, and state whether or not your belief in a Supreme Being involves duties which to you are superior to those arising from any human relation.

· ·
· ·

You could buy pot on any street corner in Saigon; the stuff grew wild in the countryside and even the school kids were selling it for five dollars a bag. This wasn't the same nickel bag you got back home, though; here it contained about two ounces of the stuff, enough for maybe ten or twelve cigarettes. In a bar on Tu Do Street, Pete and I bought a bag from a girl who kept insisting she'd be fired if her boss knew she was peddling grass on the side. We told her we wouldn't tell him if she didn't, and then bought her another glass of Saigon tea for a hundred and fifty pee, which seemed to mollify her for a little while at least. There was a jukebox going in the bar, stacked with records that were a month or two behind what was being played in the States, all rock, country-western, and blues, old hits like The Dave Clark Five's "Over and Over" and Herman's Hermits' "A Must to Avoid." The bar was crowded with young guys in civilian clothes, most or all of them servicemen, I guessed—Negroes, whites, a few Koreans. (*Pete* told me they were Koreans; I thought they were Vietnamese.) A Negro standing alongside of us was very proud of the United States Army jungle boots he had bought in the black market on Le Loi Street, and kept showing them off the way a newly engaged girl shows off her diamond. They had cost him ten thousand pee, about eighty-five American dollars, but he was expecting to be transferred out to the boonies any day now, and he had heard of guys waiting six to eight weeks to get boots issued while meanwhile they were walking around in the paddies all day and getting seven kinds of jungle rot. It had been a hell of a lot easier to buy them on Le Loi Street, the Negro said, and then asked Pete and me if we thought he'd made a mistake. The girl draped on his shoulder said, "You no makee mistake, Lloyd, them Number One boots."

"You think so, Annie?" Lloyd said.

"You jus' lookee them fine boots," Annie said. "Hey, mistah, you tell Lloyd here them Number One boots."

"Those are sure Number One boots," I said.

The girl who'd sold us the grass came over just then and said, "Hey, Cheap Charlie, alla girls *soooo* thirsty, you wanna talk some?"

"He wants to *fuck* some," Lloyd said, and Annie burst into tinkling laughter and buried her face in her hands.

"No talkee fuck," the grass-girl said. "Alla girls *sooo* thirsty here, my goo'ness, le's drink some nice tea, okay?"

"It's getting awful," Pete said. "You used to be able to go into any Saigon bar and work your points with these girls for the price of, oh, three, four glasses of tea—but then the tea only cost about eighty pee. What you were doing, you know, was trying to get yourself a steady shack, buying for the same girl every time you came in, hoping you could get to take her home one night. There's an eleven o'clock curfew here, Wat, so most of these joints close around ten-thirty, quarter to eleven, and if you're lucky and you get to take one of them home, why you can maybe get something good going, you know? You can rent

282

places for these girls for about thirty bucks a month, and then all you got to do is, you know, bring the usual crap, some C-rations every now and then, cigarettes, fans, goodies from the PX, and that way you got yourself a great thing going, a relationship, you know? I mean, you can always get laid in Saigon, there's a hundred short-timers working this street, they'll give you a quick one on a mattress out back for three or four hundred pee, but what a man needs is a *relationship*, Wat, that's what he needs."

"Hey, what you say, Cheap Charlie?" the grass-girl said.

"Fuck off, sister," Pete answered. "We're busy talking, can't you see?"

3. Explain how, when, and from whom or from what source you received the training and acquired the belief which is the basis of your claim made in Series I above.

. . . .
. . . .
. . . .
. . . .

4. Give the name and present address of the individual upon whom you rely most for religious guidance.

. . . .
. . . .

The Buddhists came into the streets as flares filled the nighttime sky over the city. They had rallied outside Saigon's brightly lighted Buddhist Institute, the Vien Hoa Dao, and now they marched in flowing white robes, followed by shouting citizens carrying hand-lettered banners and the saffron, red-striped flags of South Vietnam. There had been unrest in the streets ever since President Johnson's February meeting with Premier Ky in Honolulu, at which time it had seemed to the Vietnamese that our wily Senate cloakroom negotiator had tucked their man into his vest pocket. But three days ago, on March 10, Ky had dismissed a Buddhist-supported general from his ten-man military Directory, and now the priests were out in force to demand the overthrow of his government. Riot policemen in Army fatigues and helmets flanked the route of march, expecting trouble, expecting perhaps the same kind of big trouble they had known on June 11, 1963. On that day, at the intersection of Le Van Duyet and Phan Ding Phung Streets, at nine o'clock in the morning, the Venerable Thich Quang Duc, a member of the Buddhist clergy, had set fire to himself, thereby giving undeniably visual form to the flaring anger of the priests, who claimed that the Catholic President Ngo Dinh Diem was discriminating against the country's sizable number of Buddhists, variously estimated as between fifty and seventy per cent of the population. Being an American raised in the Judaeo-Christian tradition (as it was euphemistically called, forgetting for the moment the centuries of strife behind that handy twentieth-century label) I had no idea what a Buddhist believed. There had once been a Buddha, true; very good, Wat Tyler. There had also once been a Confucius, and his teachings formed the basis of yet another Vietnamese religion. But it was there that beliefs such as Cao Dai, and Hoa Hao, and Taoism entered the picture and caused a Westerner like myself to become hopelessly mired in a culture as deep and as resistant as the muddy rice paddies through which we pursued our war, a culture that surely included the throngs of Buddhists and their followers who demonstrated in the streets now against the very government we were supporting.

A Mercedes-Benz convertible, ten thousand dollars on the hoof, was being rolled over, and someone ran up to it with a flaming torch, right arm back, wrist slightly bent, left arm out for balance like a tennis player coming in to return a powerful serve, swinging the firebrand in a wide arc and then releasing it and allowing it to sail through the open window of the overturned car. The convertible top caught, there was an expectant hush as the crowd awaited the inevitable, and then pulled back and ducked and ran as the explosion came and flames billowed up toward the sky. The riot policemen charged into the group of demonstrators, gas masks pulled down over their faces, wicker shields hooked over their arms and thrust forward to deflect the stones and tin cans being hurled at them. There was a hiss, a puff, a cloud of tear gas erupted in the middle of the street, and the crowd screamed, barefoot school children wearing shorts and white shirts, older youths in Army trousers and American sneakers, plastic bags appearing here and there among the crowd, pulled over heads in defense against the gas, had no one ever told these people about the Great American Plastic Bag Scare? There were television cameramen shooting footage for news programs to precede "The Tonight Show starring Johnny Carson," another explosion as a motorbike burst into flame. And then a slender Buddhist monk, pate shaved, raised his white-robed arms and strode on floating sandals into the crowd of dispersing followers while behind him a riot policeman approached with upraised club. "Behind you!" I shouted, and Pete grabbed my arm and said, "For Christ's sake, Wat, keep out of it! This is gook business!" The club fell, a bright red gash appeared across the top of the priest's head. He dropped to the sidewalk running blood, his white robe glowing eerily in the light of the flames from the motorbike nearby.

5. Under what circumstances, if any, do you believe in the use of force?

. . . .
. . . .
. . . .

I had told my father during our unsuccessful Judge Hardy chat in the living room of our house last November that I was going to appeal my classification and ask to enter the Army as a noncombatant, but that was before I knew what was actually involved. I had thought it was merely a matter of running over to my local draft board the next day, showing them my classification notice, and saying, "I know I'm classified 1-A, but I'd like to change that now if it's all right with you. I'd like to be put in 1-A-O, which as you know means I object to taking up arms against an enemy, but I don't object to military service in a noncombatant status. So will you please make the necessary changes?"

"You mean you want to appeal your classification?"

"Yes, I'd like it changed to 1-A-O."

"You're asking for an exemption."

"I'm asking for reclassification."

"You're appealing your present classification and asking for an exemption."

"Okay, yes."

"Fill out this form. Mail it back to us within ten days."

"All I'm asking . . ."

"There are no automatic deferments or exemptions. Fill out this form. The Selective Service will decide whether to accept or reject your appeal."

6. Describe the actions and behavior in your life which in your opinion most conspicuously demonstrate the consistency and depth of your religious convictions.

. . . .
. . . .
. . . .
. . . .

It occurred to me, as I looked over the form for the first time, that it would have made an excellent mid-term examination for a graduate student in theology. I visualized a bare-assed southern Baptist, dunked into a river at infancy and subsequently raised as a God-fearing citizen, trying to cope with the complexity of language in the form, and finally throwing up his hands in despair—fuck it, I'd druther go fight. My own situation was not too dissimilar. To begin with, I knew beforehand that a Supreme Court decision in March 1965 had broadened the legal interpretation of the first question in Series II. RELIGIOUS TRAINING AND BELIEF, so that belief in a supreme being did not necessarily have to mean belief in God, but could instead mean "belief in and devotion to goodness and virtue for their own sakes, and a religious faith in a purely ethical creed." I knew all about the Seeger case, and I knew about the decision, and I was therefore surprised to discover, as late as November 30 of that year, that the question "Do you believe in a Supreme Being?" was still on the form. I recognized, of course, that I could answer "No" to the question if I so chose, supposedly without prejudicing my appeal, but I was honestly unprepared for the emphasis on religion throughout the remainder of the form. I was not a religious person. Oh yes, I had been in and out of the First Congregational Church every Christmas Eve as part of the ritual of singing carols around the enormous firehouse tree, and then going over for midnight mass, and I had also been there for services on the day after President Kennedy got shot, but I could not be considered a "churchgoer" in any sense of the word, nor had there been any really strong religious influences in our home (though my mother did try to get me interested in

286

Ethical Culture and took me to a meeting in Stamford one Sunday morning). My objections to the war in Vietnam were purely moral, and it seemed to me unfair that I was now being asked to justify those beliefs by pretending they were religious—in other words, by lying.

For if I wanted to qualify for an exemption, I would have to answer questions like 7. Have you ever given public expression, written or oral, to the views herein expressed as the basis for your claim made in Series I above? If so, specify when and where, keeping in mind that the basis for any claim in Series I above had to be "religious training and belief." I suppose I could have stretched a point, turned a corner in my mind that would have allowed me to explain as "religion" my sincere aversion to murder. But it seemed to me that this would have necessitated a duplicity that severely compromised my convictions.

I could not bring myself to complete the form.

I could not admit that I was a witch.

NOTICE—Imprisonment for not more than five years or a fine of not more than $10,000, or both such fine and imprisonment, is provided by law as a penalty for knowingly making or being a party to the making of any false statement of certificate regarding or bearing upon a classification.

Besides, it was too late, the wheels were already grinding. That Wednesday, I received a notice from my local draft board, advising me to report for induction into the Army of the United States a week later. On December 8, 1965, I was sent to Fort Gordon, Georgia, for eight weeks of basic military training, after which I went to Fort Jackson, South Carolina for an additional eight weeks of Advanced Infantry Training. At the end of March 1966, I was flown to Saigon where I met an old football opponent from Stamford who told me all about the weather, the rodents, the serpents, the parasites, and the insects of Vietnam, and later showed me the whores, the pimps, the pushers, the profiteers, the protesters, and the policemen preserving law and order. The next morning, I climbed into the back of a deuce-and-a-half, and was escorted in convoy with fifteen other men to the base camp at Cu Chi.

Lloyd Parsons, the Negro who'd been showing off his jungle boots in the Saigon bar, was in one of the trucks with me.

April ❦ ❦

Once you passed the target area, even if the mission was later scrubbed, it counted as part of your tour of duty, and the squadron clerk recorded it as such. In the Fifteenth Air Force, a tour consisted of fifty missions, after which you were entitled to be sent back to the States in one noncombatant capacity or another, usually as an instructor. (A fighter tour in the Twelfth Air Force consisted of a hundred missions, but that was because they were making shorter-range strikes, going out to dive-bomb and strafe, coming back to load up, going out again, three or four times in a single day.) You didn't *have* to go home after your fiftieth mission. You could elect to stay and fly another tour, the way Archie Colombo did in February. He went to Rome for three weeks, and came back in March to join the squadron again. He was shot down flying the third mission of his second tour, which coincidentally was my fiftieth and final mission for the United States Army Air Force.

Colonel Spiller gave me the usual rah-rah pitch about signing over for a second tour, telling me that the war in Germany was almost over, hell, General Marshall had expected it to be over by last November, it was just taking a trifle longer, that was all. Patton's Third Army had already crossed the Rhine and only last night Allied bombers had dropped 12,400 explosives and 650,000 fire bombs on Berlin, it was worth seeing through to the end, wasn't it? Besides, there was the possibility that if I signed over for a second tour, I might be immediately discharged after we knocked off Germany, instead of being redeployed to the Pacific where I would have to fly my ass off against the Japs. I thanked Colonel Spiller for his consideration, knowing he had only my welfare in mind, but I told him that I was very tired just then and that I thought it might be nice to go home. The colonel looked me in the eye, the tic in his own eye beating erratically, and said, Sure, Tyler, I'll okay the necessary papers. On April 3,

288

1945, two days after Easter, I left Foggia in an ATC airplane and after interminable stops at Iceland and Gander, finally landed at Mitchel Field, two miles northeast of Hempstead, Long Island.

There was the scent of imminent victory in the New York streets that April, much stronger, more easily sniffed than it had been in Italy. It was as though, paradoxically, the civilians knew more about the progress of the war than the men who were overseas fighting it, and thus informed could safely predict its early end. Even my father, when I spoke to him on the telephone from a bar in midtown Manhattan (the phones at the field had men standing in line ten deep) seemed to possess secret intelligence that the war in Europe at least, would be over before the end of the month. I told him that I certainly hoped so, and then I asked about Linda and told him how anxious I was to see them both, but that I didn't know exactly when I'd be getting to Chicago because the Air Force seemed to be fairly confused (situation normal) about what to do with all these returnees. My father asked if I wanted him to come down to New York, and I said I didn't think that was necessary, and he told me again how happy he was that I was home and safe, and asked me if I needed any money, and then said he hoped to see me soon, and to please keep in touch with him. The call ran seventeen minutes overtime. I went back to the bar where the ice was melting in my scotch, and asked the bartender to freshen my drink, and then walked over to the jukebox and put in a quarter and punched out five records, and went to sit down again. An Air Force captain was sitting at the far end of the bar, a jigger of whiskey and a glass of beer on the polished top in front of him.

I did not recognize him at first.

I looked him full in the face, and he looked back at me, and then we both turned away. I lifted my scotch and sipped a little of it, and listened as my first jukebox selection fell into place, a song new to me, its melody haunting, its lyric evocative, ". . . on a train that is passing through, those eyes . . ." and I drank silently, listening, and then ordered another scotch and glanced again at the captain. He was wearing a jauntily tilted crushed hat and he had a blond mustache and blue eyes, silver pilot's wings over the left-hand pocket of his blouse. He turned toward me as though aware of my casual glance, his own look becoming one of scrutiny, and all at once he said, "Will?"

Our eyes met, his probing tentatively and uncertainly, mine searching for a clue. "Will Tyler?" he said, more confidently now, and I suddenly knew who he was, the face registered, the voice registered, "Michael?" I asked.

We were rising simultaneously off our stools, slowly, slowly, our faces cracking with wide grins, our arms coming up ("Michael?" I asked, "Michael Mallory?") and we rushed toward each other like some crazy Klondike prospector brothers meeting in the middle of a muddy Main Street after months in the wilderness ("Michael, you son of a bitch!") and threw our arms around each other and let out blood-curdling yells that must have shattered a dozen glasses behind the bar. We jigged all around that room, we threw our hats in the air, we put six quarters in the juke and turned the volume up full, and bought the bartender a drink when he complained, and laughed and slapped each other on the back, yelling over the sound of the music, roaring our amazement and our pleasure, "Let's call my sister!" I shouted, "Let's call Charlotte Wagner!" Michael shouted, our words tumbling over themselves, overlapping. You look great, When'd you get back, Where've they got you now, What were you flying, How do you like my paintbrush, I've seen more hair on a strip of bacon, Hey, remember that night, Remember old Ronny Booth passing out on us. Remember those jigs chasing us out of Douglas, remember? remember? remember?

The party was being given for a bombardier who had lost an eye over Ploesti. Michael had met him at Fort Dix (where the poor bastard was being discharged with a Purple Heart), and he had invited Michael to the big bash tonight, promising him plenty of girls, booze and music. Michael had assured him he would show, but then had lost his courage, and had wandered into the bar for a few fortifying drinks. We finally decided to brave it together, hero fighter pilots that we were, and we managed to find the Sutton Place address, a high-rise overlooking the East River, but then Michael chickened out again. I think he really was afraid of contact with, well, people who hadn't been dropping bombs or firing machine guns. People.

So we stood on the edge of the river, and watched the

shimmering reflection of a tug's lights on the water, and Michael softly said, "Reminds me of the lake, doesn't it you?" and I said, "Yes, it does," though I wasn't really sure, I think anything that night would have reminded us of Chicago. Michael began talking all at once about how strange it felt to be back in the United States, and then asked me if I'd taken one of those returnee tests at Mitchel, and when I told him I hadn't as yet, he went on to explain that the Air Force had developed a questionnaire to assist them with the enormous task of redeployment and that some of the responses given by bomber pilots and fighter pilots were pretty surprising, hadn't I heard about that questionnaire?

"Well," he said, "you might be interested in knowing that only twenty-eight per cent of the bomber pilots thought they should be shipped overseas again, whereas forty-six per cent of the fighter pilots figured they *would* be sent over and actually *wanted* to go."

"So what does that prove?" I said.

Michael shrugged. "Nothing, I guess." He looked out over the water again. "I don't remember all the figures, Will, but the guys who said they *didn't* want to go overseas again gave a lot of different reasons. Some of them felt they'd already done their share of overseas duty— almost twice as many bomber pilots said that as fighter pilots. Or they just couldn't take another tour either physically or mentally—the percentage was in favor of the fighter pilots on that one. Or . . ."

"You think they're going to ship *us* to the Pacific?"

"I don't know," Michael said, and shrugged again. "There was another question on one of the tests, Will. This one was given only to enlisted men, maybe the Air Force didn't want to hear what its flying officers had to say. Anyway, the question was 'Do you ever feel this war is not worth fighting?' "

"What were the answers?"

"The majority, forty-five per cent, said 'Never.' Twenty-three per cent said 'Once in a great while.' Twenty-four per cent said 'Sometimes.' And eight per cent said 'Very often.' " Michael paused. Turning to me, he said, "What would you have answered, Will?"

"I've never once thought this war wasn't worth fighting," I said. "Have you?"

Michael looked out over the water. Very softly, he said,

"I was scared to death. All the time. Every minute. I kept thinking it'd catch up to me. I kept thinking it *had* to catch up. I kept thinking my grandfather got out of the Spanish-American War alive, and my father got out of World War I alive, but I wouldn't get out of this one, I wouldn't make it, Will, the world's fucking idiocy would overtake me at last." He sighed deeply then, and turned to me again, and I looked at his face in the light of the street lamps, and knew why I had not known him in the bar, and wondered suddenly what had taken him so long to recognize me.

"Look," I said, "why don't we go upstairs, huh? Might be a good party after all, what the hell. Come on, Michael, what do you say?"

"Sure," Michael answered. He grinned suddenly, the old hell-raising grin I remembered, and linked his arm through mine and cheerfully said, "Off we go!" and together we turned from the river and walked directly into the building, past the doorman who called behind us, "Excuse me, gentlemen, whom did you wish to see?"

"Lieutenant Douglas Prine," Michael answered.

"Yes, sir," the doorman said, "that's apartment 14B."

In the elevator, a pimply-faced operator said, "You fellows just back from overseas?"

"Just back," Michael said. "How can you tell?"

The elevator operator shrugged. "You can tell guys who're just back. You see any action?"

"A little," Michael said.

"Fourteen," the elevator operator said.

She had hazel eyes and brown hair, and she came into the party at about one a.m., wearing a gray Persian lamb she had undoubtedly borrowed from her mother. Our host, Douglas Prine, a black patch over his right eye, helped her off with her coat, and then kissed her on the cheek and shook hands with her escort, a sallow-faced kid of seventeen or eighteen who stood awkwardly shuffling his feet and gazing into the living room, where all us grown-up soldiers and dolls were drinking and dancing and laughing. Michael Mallory was unconscious on the sofa, his head in the lap of a buxom brunette who huskily sang "Long Ago and Far Away" while idly running her fingers through his hair. The record player was indifferently spinning the cast album of *Carousel,* June bustin' out all

292

over the room as couples tried to dance to the hardly rhythmic beats of a Broadway orchestration. As I watched from a vantage point near the piano, the new girl said goodnight to her escort, who pecked her self-consciously on the cheek and then sidled out the front door. She stood hesitantly in the entrance to the living room as though trying to decide whether she should join the party, and then smiled and turned on her heel and started up the staircase leading to the second floor of the duplex. I bounded out of the living room.

"Hey!" I said.

The girl turned. She looked at me with vague bemusement, head tilted, brown hair falling loose over one eye à la Veronica Lake, the opposite eyebrow raised in imitation of God knew how many other movie queens. I had a sudden feeling of prescience, I thought I knew for one insane moment exactly what dumb thing she would offer in response, and I hoped against hope that she would not say it, but she lifted her eyebrow impossibly higher, and in a very young and hopelessly affected voice said exactly what I knew she would, "Hay is for horses."

"Oh shit," I answered, and snapped a smart salute at her, and then executed a military about-face, and marched into the living room. She came in directly behind me, but I didn't know she had followed me until I turned from the bar, where I was refilling my glass, and found her standing at my elbow.

"Would you like to apologize?" she said.

"For what?"

"For what you just said."

"What did I say?"

"You *know* what you said."

"Okay, I apologize."

"Thank you," she said. "Goodnight."

"Hey, hold it a minute."

"What do you want?"

"You live here?"

"I live here."

"Who are you?"

"Dolores Prine."

"Oh. Is the guy with the patch your brother?"

"Yes."

"How old are you?"

"Why?"

293

"I like to know how old people are."

"I'm almost eighteen."

"Which means you're only seventeen."

"If a person is almost eighteen, why yes, I guess that *does* mean she's only seventeen, how clever of you."

"Where're you running to?"

"I'm going to bed."

"Why?"

"I'm tired."

"Big night on the town with your pale little boyfriend?"

"Yes, big night on the town."

"Radio City Music Hall?"

"No, the Roxy."

"What's the Roxy?"

"It's a theater. You mean you don't know the *Roxy?*"

"I'm not a New Yorker."

"Where're you from?"

"Chicago."

"Foo."

"What do you mean *foo?* It's a good city."

"It's not as good as New York."

"Have you ever been there?"

"No. But no city in the world is as good as New York."

"How about Ocracoke, North Carolina?"

"Never heard of it."

"Would you like a drink?"

"A drink? I'm only seventeen."

"You're almost eighteen."

She was only seventeen and still attending the McKeon School. I felt somewhat like Lazarus the following Monday waiting outside the building as little girls in uniforms came skipping down the steps into a New York April gilded with sunshine. "Aren't you going to carry my books?" she asked, and I sensed that she was kidding me, but I took them anyway because I hadn't yet learned to decipher the meaning in her hazel eyes, my mother's own green with an overtint of the palest brown, flecked with pure cat's-eye yellow, remarkable eyes that claimed complete attention whenever she spoke.

It was, of course, her youth that attracted me, though I myself was not yet twenty, born on June the sixth, nineteen hundred and twenty-five, A date to remember, my mother had often said when she was still alive, though generally she said it when I was being particularly abominable, fun in *her* eyes too, broad midwestern sarcasm, You don't *know* how long we hoped and prayed, Will, you don't *know* how your father and I longed for our first child, and then to be blessed with *you,* oh surely we were chosen, flinty green sparked with humor, and then a hug and a slap on the behind, I loved that woman, I loved her still.

Dolores Prine's mother called her Dee, and her brother called her Lolly, and she asked me to call her one or the other because she hated the name Dolores, each diminutive sounding equally childish to my octogenarian ears, each reminiscent of a world I had left behind a long time ago, those walks home from Grace School in the afternoon, Michael Mallory cracking his dirty jokes and Charlotte Wagner bellowing her horse laugh in response, educated elbows and compliant breasts, ice cream sodas on Division Street, portable record players on the Oak Street Beach. The name Dolores conjured images of a tall Spanish lady, hair pulled back into a bun, mantilla falling in a lacy cascade from a high comb, eyes brimming with sorrow and pain, her walk erect and dignified, but each long stride so sensuous besides, a promise of surging passion under that long black skirt. But Lolly? Dee? Lolly was the child who skipped along beside me and prattled about the latest Woody Herman record, flicking her brown hair back and away from the eye it had been trained to cover, giggling unexpectedly, asking me if I ever killed a man, and then opening her hazel eyes wide (hand flicking at the falling brown curtain, fingernail revealed as bitten to the quick) when I said that I had been credited with four and a half enemy planes, "How can you shoot down only half a plane?" she asked. I explained to her that my wingman and I (it was amazing how I could mention his name without feeling pain any more), a fellow called Ace Gibson, from Reading, Pennsylvania, had shot down this one enemy airplane together, and therefore had to share credit for the kill, and she nodded in quick understanding and then said, "It must have taken guts," and that was all. Lolly had become Dee in the crack of an instant, the girl child had become at least the adolescent and in the adolescent there was some promise of the woman. I wanted to put my arm around her narrow shoulders, wanted to hold her close and touch her breasts beneath the gray school jacket, green-gold crest over the left pocket, green tie separating the twin mounds under the white cotton blouse, so young, so very young. And yet Francesca could not have been much older, and I had done things to her, we had done things to her, so why did I feel so guilty now, why did I feel that if I touched this slender coltish thing beside me, I would be arrested and imprisoned for life? If she was only seventeen, then I was only nineteen; if I was almost twenty, then surely she was almost eighteen. I did not touch her. I carried her books like a tongue-tied oaf, discovering sunlight along the fine down on her wrist where it jutted from the too-short sleeve of her jacket, and listened as she explained to me in all seriousness the tremendous sacrifices Clark Gable, James Stewart, and Tyrone Power had made for their country in wartime by giving up their profitable Hollywood careers and going off to fight. "It must have taken guts," she said, and bingo, we were back in the third grade again, with little Lolly swallowing the finger paint and getting her frock all messy besides.

If the Air Force had permitted me to go back to Chicago while awaiting redeployment orders, I probably would never have seen Dolores Prine again after that awkward Monday. But at Mitchel Field there was only confusion and procrastination; everyone seemed to know that the war in Europe was rushing to a close, yet no one seemed prepared for its end. The Air Force could hardly allow an experienced combat pilot to go home for even a few days, because nobody knew what was going to happen once Germany surrendered; the Japanese might launch a wholesale Kamikaze attack against San Francisco, in which case we'd all be rushed to the West Coast. Since the Air Force didn't know what the hell to do with me, all they asked was that I check in for formation each morning. If my orders had not yet arrived (and God only knew where those orders were supposed to be coming from), I was free to leave the field until formation the following day. It was a very sweet setup. Michael, enjoying the same country-club status at Fort Dix would take a bus in to meet me in the city, and together we wandered through those early April days, bright with sunshine, sparkling with just enough of winter's lingering bite. As far as I was concerned, the war was already over. I did not for a moment believe I would be shipped to the Pacific, and I found myself talking to Michael about plans for the future—should I go into my father's business, should I go to college, should I try writing—I had written some very good letters while I was overseas. Together, we explored our philosophies and our ideals, our hopes and our ambitions, usually in one or another of New York's bars. I only mentioned Ace Gibson once, and that was because Michael and I had been talking to a lieutenant-commander in a Third Avenue bar, and the guy started telling us about a Dear John letter he had received, and it called to mind that other bar in Los Angeles, where a drunken captain in Supply had told Ace and me about his wife running off with the local—dentist, had it been?

It was Michael who suggested that we stroll over to McKeon and surprise the little Prine girl. I wasn't so sure that was a good idea, but we'd been sitting in a bar for close to two hours, and it was so beautiful and bright outside that it seemed a shame to kill the rest of the day that way. So we paid for the drinks, and then walked east toward Madison Avenue, and at three-fifteen were standing before the wide front steps of the school waiting for her to emerge. Michael seemed immediately at ease with her, even though I could not yet shake the thought that I was robbing the cradle. He cracked a few exploratory dirty jokes which caused her to burst into delighted laughter (I remembered all at once the day he told the Confucius Say joke in Lindy's presence) and then asked her if she was old enough to drink beer, and when she said they wouldn't allow her inside a bar unless she could show identification, went into a grocery store on Lexington Avenue (I *guess* it was; I was still unimaginably confused by New York's simple layout of avenues and streets; and we walked over to Fifth Avenue and took a double-decker bus up to Fifty-ninth (outside the Plaza Hotel?) and walked into the park there and sat on the grass and drank the beer and spent the afternoon together.

It must have been five-thirty, a quarter to six, when we decided to take Dolores home before her mother called out the National Guard. We were coming out of the park when we passed an old man snuffling into his handkerchief (I don't think we really noticed him at the time, I think he only registered in retrospect) and several yards behind

297

him was a woman, a younger woman obviously in no way connected with the old man, and she was openly weeping. And the next person we passed had a stunned look on his face, and there was an odd ominous buzz on the air as we walked past the fountain outside the hotel, and Dolores suddenly turned to me and said, "Something terrible has happened. We've lost the war."

A sailor was standing alongside the plate glass window of the department store on Fifty-seventh and Fifth, blinking as if trying to hold back tears. I went over to him and said, "What's the ... ?" but before I could finish my question, he snapped to attention and threw a salute at me, and I patiently returned the salute, and then said, "What's the trouble, sailor?" and he said, "The President is dead, sir."

"What?" I said.

"Roosevelt," he said.

"Roosevelt?" I said, and felt enormously stupid all at once, as if we were engaged in a baggy-pants vaudeville routine. He had *told* me the President was dead, hadn't he? And the President was Roosevelt, wasn't he? Then why had I repeated his name as though saying it aloud would deny the fact—no, he could *not* be dead, he had been President for as long as I could remember, he could not now be dead, we would lose the war, oh Jesus, we would lose the war and the world would be enslaved.

Dolores suddenly threw herself into my arms and began weeping against my shoulder.

It was then that I began to think I was falling in love with her.

The war in Europe, which had seemed so close to ending, now seemed fiercely determined to prolong itself. A rattle was sounding on the expectant air, signaling the death of something quite familiar, something almost loved, this war that had been with us for so long a time and which now refused to expire the way a proper invalid should have, coughing itself out in the stillness of the night. Our new President, Harry S Truman, said, "Our demand has been, and it remains, unconditional surrender," but Allied Supreme Headquarters in Paris announced that despite persistent rumors to the contrary, there had been no substantial advances toward Berlin, and our closest units to the city were still more than fifty miles

298

away. It was a time of dying, that April, beginning with the death of Roosevelt, the largest death I had known since my mother's, and then dwindling into a series of anticlimactic smaller deaths as we awaited the ultimate collapse, the end of the European war—the deaths of cities, the deaths of rivers crossed, the deaths of bastions stormed and bunkers demolished, the death of an era. Into this time of dying, into this loud and raucous, constant and endless communiqué from the front, there was insinuated like a delicate flute refrain, the beginning of Dolores Prine and me, or rather (like the smaller deaths) a series of smaller explorations that were leading, we suspected, to a larger beginning for us both.

Troops of the Third Army were thirteen miles from the Czech border on the north and on the west, the Seventh Army pushed to within fifteen miles of Nuremburg, the Canadians advanced toward the Zuider Zee, the United States First swept northward through the Ruhr pocket and engaged in bloody street-to-street combat in Halle, the French took Kenl on the Rhine, and in a hamburger joint on Sixth Avenue, when I asked Dolores if she minded my eating onions, she answered, "Yes, I mind terribly," and suddenly kissed me for the first time. The French marched to within ten miles of the Swiss border, the United States Seventh crossed the Fils River and took Weilhelm, we were ten miles from Bremen, we had occupied Bologna after a nineteen-month campaign, the Soviet High Command announced that Russian troops "had marched a thousand miles from the gates of Moscow" to capture Erkner at the eastern limits of Berlin, and in a taxicab heading for Sutton Place, I put my hand under Dolores Prine's skirt, and she tightened her thighs on it at first, catching it and stopping my advance, and then opened slowly to my pressure, my fingers touching the mound bulging crisply beneath her cotton panties, "Will," she said, "please," but I did not remove my hand, the American armies were standing on the banks of the Mulde River, and the Russians were only forty-eight miles away.

Who was this girl?

I hardly knew.

Beautiful, yes, I thought she was perhaps the most beautiful girl I'd ever met, but I had thought that from the very start, when she'd walked into the apartment on the arm of her Lebanese rug salesman, and that had never changed. There was too, I suppose, the promise of passion in her hazel eyes, daring me, mocking me, a passion only partially unleashed—her twistings beneath me on the grass in Central Park, dusk falling, "We'll get mugged if we don't watch out, Will," and a schoolgirl giggle—it was only a matter of time, she knew it, I knew it, and I dreamt each night at Mitchel Field of entering her and hearing her shriek aloud in ecstasy. That was there, then, the promised passion of Dolores my flamenco dancer, that and a suspected capacity for pain, too, which seemed equally Spanish in origin, though her father was Irish ("With a fifth of scotch thrown in," he told me) and her mother was Dutch. But beyond the wild expectation of taking her to bed—she seemed to me the materialization of every pin-up picture I had hung on barracks walls from Mississippi to Italy and back again—was there really a beginning here, a gentle flute song floating on the wind of a dying April, was there really anything to *love* about this lovely girl? (She was, it occurred to me once, when I was feeling unusually Freudian, the total opposite of Francesca, the beauty of Foggia, and perhaps to me the symbol of everything clean, innocent, and alive, as opposed to everything soiled, corrupt, and dead—well, not the total opposite, I suppose, since the old man Gino had a cataracted eye and Dolores' brother wore at patch over an empty socket. I didn't too often think psychoanalytically, however, and I was probably dead wrong.)

She wrote poetry. She showed me one of her efforts several days before I finally took her naked on her quilted bed in the back bedroom of the Sutton Place apartment while her one-eyed brother was out dancing and her parents were visiting friends in Connecticut for the weekend and two Russian armies were pushing the Germans further back into Berlin. The poetry was terrible.

> *Now how can*
> *The eagle soar*
> *With but a single eye?*
> *I have witnessed*
> *Lesser feats*
> *But never on this earth.*

I told her what I thought of it—we were in a Chinese restaurant on the fringes of Harlem, she *did* know the city well, I had to give her that. She looked at me solemnly for a moment, and then asked, "What do you know about poetry?"

"Nothing," I said.

"Then how do you know it's terrible?"

"It doesn't move me."

"It moves *me*," she said.

"You wrote it," I said. "Listen, you asked for my opinion, and I gave it to you."

"I asked for your *praise*," she said.

"I thought you wanted my opinion."

"I don't need opinions," she said. "Every cheap critic in the world has an *opinion*, but only poets have *ideas*."

"Excuse me, I didn't know you were a poet," I said.

"I'm *not*."

"Then what are we arguing about?"

"If you love someone, you're supposed to say her poem is good."

"Your poem is terrible."

"Then you don't love me."

"Did I say that?"

"*Do* you love me?" she asked.

The first real contact was made on April 25, when a four-man patrol of the United States 273rd Regiment came upon a Russian outpost at Torgen on the Elbe, two miles west of the advancing American forces.

The bedspread had been quilted by Dolores' mother. "We shouldn't be here alone," she told me, "maybe we'd better go out to a movie or something."

"We've seen everything around," I said. "We've been to twelve movies in the past week, if I never see another movie as long as I live . . ."

"Then let's go for a walk."

"It's raining," I said.

"Will . . ."

"Yes?"

"Don't do this to me. Please."

"Do what?" I said.

"If you don't love me, then please don't."

"I never said I didn't love you."

"You never said you did, either."

"Come here."

"No. Please."

"Come here, Dolores."

"Don't call me that. Please."

"Lolly? Dee?"

"Please," she said. "Please."

"Come here, Dolores. I won't touch you. I promise."

"You will," she said, and came to the bed.

On April 28, Benito Mussolini was shot to death by partisans in the village of Dongo on Lake Como, together with his mistress Clara Petacci and sixteen Fascist leaders. On the last day of April's dyings, large and small, Il Duce's body and that of Signorina Petacci were hung upside down from a steel girder in what had once been a gasoline station. Signs were placed above their bound feet, black-lettered onto white, proclaiming their names to the assembled populace. They were cut down later and taken to the morgue, but only after Mussolini's head had been kicked to a bloody pulp by a crowd that once had cheered him in life. On that same day, in a bunker below the Reich Chancellery, Adolf Hitler and his mistress Eva Braun committed suicide. The announcement from Berlin read, "At the head of the brave defenders of the Reich capital, the Fuehrer, Adolf Hitler has fallen. Inspired by a determination to save his people and Europe from destruction by Bolshevism, he has sacrificed his life."

By that time, I was humping Dolores Prine day and night.

May ❧

It was shortly after the end of my lunch hour at the mill when a runny-nosed kid came over from Building 17 to tell me that Mr. Moreland in Personnel would like to see me at two o'clock. I told him I'd be there, and then asked if he knew what it was about, but he just shrugged his shoulders and wandered off across the yard with his hands in his pockets. Since it was then a quarter of two, and since the walk to 17 could conceivably taken fifteen minutes (if a person had a cork leg) I advised Allen

302

Garrett that I was going up to the executive building, and then put down my picaroon and left the conveyer belt.

Ramsey-Warner, like most paper mills, manufactured several grades of stock, and I had begun to understand during my year's apprenticeship there that different types of pulp were blended to make those various papers. I guess you could say I was an essential employee in the manufacture of both groundwood and sulphite pulps in that it was I (along with Allen) who spiked the logs off the conveyer belt if we saw any defects in them, it being absolutely necessary for wood to be glistening clean before it was transported to either the chippers or the grinders. Mr. Moreland's office was in the building behind 12-A, where the big grinders were housed. (*All* the buildings at the mill were numbered, and I was convinced that Joliet used the same identification system for its cell-blocks. I often wondered if the prison, unlike R-WP, Inc. had a building numbered 13.) On the way to Mr. Moreland's office, I peeked into 12-A to see what was going on, figuring that if I was ever going to own this place, I had better familiarize myself with every phase of the operation whenever I had the opportunity.

There were twenty grinders in the room, each pair of them flanking a 3000-horsepower motor. If you looked at a grinder from a certain angle, it resembled the front of a locomotive, cylindrical, with a covered drive shaft jutting out of it where the locomotive's headlight would have been, a metal plate somewhat like a cow-catcher just below it, and a narrow cylinder looking very much like a steam whistle, high up on the right. The first impression lost itself quickly enough in a labyrinth of pipes, dials, valves, and wheels, the clean logs moving on their conveyer belt to be fed into three metal pockets equipped with hydraulic plungers that forced the wood against the huge grindstone revolving inside the machine. The logs were ingested parallel to the face of the twelve-ton stone, the resultant friction against their sides separating the wood fibers and dropping a warm thick soupy pulp into the pit below. That was how the grinder worked. I had asked a hundred questions about it the first time I discovered Building 12-A, standing around and chatting with the guys who operated the machines and took the big empty pockets off the line for refilling whenever their contents had been ground away. One of those guys, a Swede named

303

Bertil Åkeson (our private joke was always the same: "Hello, Bert," and "Hello, Bert"), greeted me now as I poked my head inside the door. I went over to him, hoping he would be involved in some mysterious operation about which I could ask some casual questions without causing him to think I was after his job. But all we did for five minutes was discuss the wonderful weather we'd been having, and when he finally mentioned something about checking the stone pit temperature gauge, I couldn't stay around to watch or I'd have been late for my appointment in Building 17.

I had been in Mr. Moreland's office last April, when he'd hired me, and it seemed to have changed little in the intervening months. His desk, leather-topped walnut, dominated the room, sitting large and cluttered before the twin windows that overlooked the company's digesters in the yard outside. There were glass-enclosed bookcases on the wall to the left of the entrance door, and three portraits (two of the Ramsey Brothers, Amos and Louis, and a third of Martin Warner) unevenly flanked the fireplace and mantel on the right. The walls were wood-paneled, the carpet was brown, the room was inviting and cozy in contrast to the cheerless gray exteriors of all the buildings at the mill. Mr. Moreland beckoned to the single chair angled before his desk. I sat.

"Tyler," he said, "do you know how many strikes there were in America last year?"

"No, sir," I said.

"Two thousand, six hundred and sixty-five," Mr. Moreland said.

"Yes, sir."

"Four million men walked off their jobs, that's a rather impressive figure, wouldn't you say?"

"Yes, sir."

"Here at Ramsey-Warner, we did not have a single strike in 1919."

"No, sir."

"Nor do we intend to have one *this* year, either."

"Yes, sir."

"Tyler," he said, "Ramsey-Warner is letting you go."

I don't know what I had anticipated. I'd had no idea where his conversation was leading, no clue as to why he'd been throwing strike statistics at me. I guess I'd thought for a single soaring moment that he'd been telling me about Ramsey-Warner's good fortune only as a prelude to giving me a raise or a promotion, I guess that's what I secretly thought and hoped. I looked at him now in stunned silence, his brown suit blending with the warm comfort of the room, his face impassive, brown eyes watching me from behind gold-rimmed eyeglasses.

"This is Wednesday . . ."

"Sir, did you say . . . ?"

". . . but you may draw your wages to the end of the week. I think you'll agree that's more than is called for."

"Sir, I don't understand . . ."

"Yes, what is it you don't understand, Tyler?"

"I don't understand . . ."

"We no longer have need of your services, I thought I'd expressed myself quite clearly."

"But I thought . . ."

"Yes, what did you think, Tyler?"

"I thought I was doing my job, I thought . . ."

"Yes, yes," Mr. Moreland said.

"I've never missed a day, I've always . . ."

"Tyler," Mr. Moreland said, "we do not want a strike here in 1920, is that clear?"

"Yes, but . . ."

"Your sympathies are well known around this mill. If you want my advice . . ."

"My sympathies?"

"A man can't go around talking the way you do, and not . . ."

"*What* sympathies?"

". . . expect word to get back to Management. There's no place at Ramsey-Warner for radical ideas."

"Radical?"

"Yes, *radical*, now damn it, Tyler, you're trying my patience."

"Sir," I said, "I'm not a Communist, if that's what you're . . ."

"Did I *say* you were a Communist?"

"No, but . . ."

"I did not say you were a Communist, nor do I *know* whether you're a member of the Party or not. It has been estimated by the National Security League, however, that there are 600,000 resident Communists here in America,

305

and I can assure you, Tyler, that we don't want any of them here at this mill. Now if you want my advice, you'll draw your wages and be quietly grateful for our generosity, that's my advice to you."

"Sir," I said, "this is America. A person can . . ."

"Yes," Mr. Moreland answered, "and we're damn well going to keep it that way."

There was dazzling sunshine in the yard outside. It reflected from the flat gray of the buildings, so that the walls surrounding me seemed so many mirrors bouncing back light without image. Allen, I thought. Allen Garrett told them. Allen is the only person I've ever considered a real friend here, the only person with whom I've exchanged ideas, it must have been Allen who said I was a radical. Stunned, I walked across the sunlit yard and tried hopelessly to reconstruct every conversation we'd ever had. "They are little Lenins," I remember quoting sarcastically, "little Trotskys in our midst," this was at the beginning of the month, when we were talking about the New York State Assembly's vote to expel its five elected Socialist members. Yes, of course, oh God, and Allen had quoted in rebuttal a clipping from the *Times*, sent to him by his uncle in New York, "It was an American vote altogether, a patriotic and conservative vote. An immense majority of the American people will approve and sanction the Assembly's action," and I had told him that the *Times* was crazy, and so was his uncle, and so was he. And hadn't (no, it couldn't be true, it couldn't have been Allen who'd cost me my job) but hadn't we argued only last week about those two Italians up in Massachusetts, whatever their names were, who had supposedly committed murder and armed robbery, but who were also —coincidentally—radicals who'd taken part in several strikes and who'd organized some kind of protest against the Department of Justice? Hadn't I said, Oh God, what *hadn't* I said, what *hadn't* I felt free to discuss with my good friend Allen Garrett?

When I got back to the conveyer belt, he was rolling a log off toward the woodpecker. He squinted down at me from where he stood on the platform, sunlight stabbing his eyes, and said, "What'd Moreland want?"

"I've been canned," I said.

"Why?" Allen asked, looking genuinely shocked.

* * *

I did not think it would be difficult to find another job.

We were in the midst of what seemed like lasting prosperity, and even though some gloomy forecasters were predicting a full-scale depression before the end of the year (based, I supposed, upon the recent collapse of farm prices) I could not imagine unemployment walking hand-in-hand with inflation. So in that second week of a Chicago May that quickened my step and elevated my spirits, I put on my best suit each morning, with a clean white shirt and collar, tie held in place by a stickpin made from a pearl my mother had given me as a wedding present, and went off to seek work. I left the house early every day, trying to get to as many mills as possible, but I was usually home by two or three o'clock, and it was Nancy who suggested that the Grzymeks downstairs must have thought I was a gangster selling illegal whiskey or something, since I kept such elegant hours. I encouraged this idea all during my second week of job-hunting, tipping my hat to Mrs. Grzymek whenever I met her in the hallway, affecting the air of a very successful if somewhat shady businessman off to a strategy meeting, after which I would have lunch at the Commercial Club and then come home in time for an afternoon nap. But at the end of the second futile week of hunting, Mrs. Grzymek ran into Nancy at the butcher's, and asked, "Has your husband found work yet?" puncturing even that balloon. We had fifty-six dollars in the bank when I lost the job, and by the last week in May, we were down to thirty-two. I was getting just a trifle nervous. Moreover, Nancy was beginning to nag me about not having seen the Garretts in all this time. Sounding like a phonograph record of my own arguments, and probably ticking off the points on her fingers one by one (we were in bed when she treated me to this particular sermon, and I could not see her in the dark) she explained that (1) I was reacting quite hysterically to a climate of suspicion and fear, (2) I was behaving as abominably as Mr. Moreland had, and (3) I was condemning and hanging poor Allen without even giving him the opportunity to defend himself. I politely said, "Pardon?" and rolled over and went to sleep. I had more pressing things on my mind than Allen Garrett's supposedly injured feelings.

It was raining when I woke up the next morning. The bedroom was chilly and damp. I did not want to get out

307

of bed. I did not want to travel in the rain to Ogden Avenue, where I had a job interview with a Mr. McInerny of Dill-Holderness International. But I thought of those thirty-two dwindling dollars in the bank, and I thought of how tempted I had recently been by a recurring classified advertisement in the *Tribune* for a washroom attendant at the Blackstone Theater. So I pulled on a pair of trousers over my cotton nightshirt, and went into the hall to perform my morning *toilette,* even as Bertram A. Tyler might have done in Paris, France, before leaving for his highly profitable automobile agency on the Avenue Neuilly. Then I shaved and dressed myself in the clothes that had so successfully fooled Mrs. Grzymek, kissed Nancy on the cheek, and went out into the rain. I was drenched before I reached the streetcar depot.

Mr. McInerny was a tolerable old bore who apprised me of the fact that forest products ranked seventh in the United States industry in this year of our Lord 1920, and would no doubt rise even higher on the scale in years to come. There are unlimited opportunities in paper for a young man who's not afraid of hard work, he said. I assured him that I was not afraid of hard work, and then told him of my not inconsiderable experience in lumbering—the font, so to speak, of the paper industry (Ah yes, the font indeed, Mr. McInerny said, nodding)—and of my apprenticeship at Ramsey-Warner, all of which seemed to impress him favorably. But at last he got around to the part of the interview I was dreading, "Why did you leave your last place of employment, Mr. Tyler?"

"I was let go," I said.

"Why were you let go?" Mr. McInerny asked.

I had coped with this question on every interview I'd had during the past three weeks, debating whether I should lie in answer to it, knowing it would take nothing more than a telephone call to ascertain the truth of whatever I said, and finally developing a sort of compromise answer, a lie that wasn't quite a lie, a truth that wasn't quite that either.

"There was a personality conflict with another employee," I said.

Mr. McInerny looked at me very closely. "What *kind* of personality conflict?" he asked, surprising me. On my last several interviews, the clever answer I'd evolved had not been challenged. I sat now in silence, wondering what to say next. "What *kind* of personality conflict?" Mr. McInerny asked again in his gentle boring voice.

"A man I worked with was making false accusations about me," I said, and realized I would now have to define the accusations and do a dissertation besides on innocence defiled, realized in short that I'd already lost the job.

"What *kind* of accusations?" Mr. McInerny predictably asked.

"Well," I said, figuring honesty was the best policy, "they thought I was a radical."

"Who thought so?"

"Mr. Moreland who fired me."

"*Are* you a radical?"

"No, sir."

"How do I know you're not?"

Throwing caution entirely to the winds, I said, "How do I know *you're* not, Mr. McInerny?"

"*I'm* not looking for work," he answered.

We stared at each other in polite silence, Mr. McInerny smiling in his bored and gentle way, I knowing for certain that the smoke had gone all the way up the flue. Mr. McInerny shook hands with me, and promised to let me know his decision by the end of the week, but I knew I had not got the job. My suit, which had begun to dry out a little in his office, got soaked all over again the moment I stepped outside. With my luck, I was sure it would shrink to half its size before I got home. It had cost me thirty-five dollars and ninety-five cents less than a year ago.

It was still raining when I got off the streetcar. A tall slender girl wearing a white raincape was standing on the front stoop of my building, her dark head bent, studying the falling raindrops in the sidewalk puddles. She looked up as I approached, seemingly on the verge of glancing away again immediately, as though she had wrongly greeted too many strangers during her wait and was now ready to reject even the person she expected.

"Hello, Bert," she said.

"Hello, Rosie," I said, surprised. "What're you doing out here in the rain?"

"Nancy asked me to stop by, but she doesn't seem to be home."

"Well, come on up," I said. "No sense getting wet."

"I *would* welcome a hot cup of tea," Rosie said.

"Sure, come on up."

We climbed the steps to the second floor in silence. There was the aroma of mustiness in the hallway, the steady sound of rain drumming on the roof, the angrier splash of the waterspout in the areaway. From the flat downstairs, I could hear the eldest of the Grzymek children practicing scales on the parlor piano, a dreary accompaniment to the rain. There was no light on our landing, save for the natural illumination from the airshaft window at the top of the stairs. I moved closer to the window, searching through my keys for the one to the front door, and then turned and felt for the keyhole. Rosie stood silently beside me. When I opened the door, she went into the kitchen and walked directly to the stove.

"Damn rain," she said.

"I'll bank the fire and put up a kettle."

"I'd prefer a drink if you've got anything."

"I think so."

She did not take off her cape. She stood huddled near the stove while I shoveled coal into it, and then she reached into her bag for a package of Sweet Caps, shook one loose, lighted it, and blew out a long stream of smoke, almost as if it were a visible sigh.

"You should get a telephone," she said. "For situations like this."

"Can't afford one. Especially now."

"How's it going, Bert?"

"Nothing so far."

"You'll find something."

"Unless everybody already knows I'm a Communist."

"You shouldn't say that. Not even in jest."

"Who's jesting?" I said.

"Bert," Rosie said, and then stopped. I turned from the cabinet near the stove, where I was rummaging through the bottles, but she only shook her head and puffed again on the cigarette.

"Looks like all I've got is some Rock and Rye a fellow at the mill made."

"Fine," she said.

"It's sort of sweet."

"I only need it to take off the chill."

"Wait, here's some scotch."

The bottle was almost empty, the last of the wedding reception whiskey Nancy and I had brought from Eau Fraiche. I poured a little into the glasses and carried them to where Rosie was standing near the stove.

"To your finding work soon," she said, raising her glass.

"Amen," I said, and drank with her.

"Bert," she said, and again shook her head, and puffed on her cigarette, and then lifted the stove lid and dropped the butt onto the coals. She walked to the table, put her glass down, turned to me, folded her arms across the cape, and said, "Bert, Nancy won't be back until two o'clock."

"What do you mean?"

"We arranged this between us."

"Why?"

"Because I want to talk to you."

"Is this going to be about Allen?"

"Yes."

"Then why didn't Allen come himself?"

"Because he doesn't know anything about your fancied grievance."

"Oh, is it fancied?"

"Yes."

"Rosie," I said, "I've been out of work for close to three weeks. I've got thirty-two dollars in the bank, and the rent's about due, and that isn't fancied."

"Your grievance is."

"I lost my job."

"Allen had nothing to do with that."

"Didn't he? Then why hasn't he come around?"

"Because he's ... no, I won't tell you. It'll only convince you you're right."

"What is it?"

Rosie shook her head.

"Well," I said, "my feet are wet, so if you'll excuse me, I'd like to change my socks and put on some slippers."

"No!" she said sharply. "I told Nancy we'd have this settled by two, and damn it, we *will!*" She reached into her bag for another cigarette, struck two matches before she managed to get it going, and then glared at me angrily, as if I'd been responsible for her inability to light it.

"As for Nancy," I said, "I never thought she'd be a party ..."

"That's right, start imagining things against your own wife, too."

"No one asked her to start meddling in . . ."

"*I* did. Allen had nothing to do with your getting fired."

"Then why hasn't he been around to inquire about the state of my health? You *still* haven't answered *that* one, Rosie."

"He's been busy."

"Ahhhh. Poor fellow. I've been busy, too."

"He got a promotion. He's been trying to learn . . ."

"Marvelous!" I said. "What was it? A reward for turning in the anarchist?"

"That isn't fair, Bert!"

"No? What's fair? I'll be begging in the streets if I don't find a job soon. What's fair, Rosie, you tell *me!*"

"Oh, give me another drink," she said.

"The scotch's gone."

"Then give me some of that crappy Rock and Rye. You really get my goat, Bert, I've got to tell you."

I walked back to the cabinet, found the bottle of homemade stuff, and carried it to the table. Rosie handed me her glass. I rinsed it out at the sink and then went back to where I'd left the bottle. The only sound in the kitchen was the ticking of the big clock on the shelf over the drainboard. The rock crystals banged against the side of the bottle as I poured.

"Thank you," Rosie said. She raised her glass. "When shall I bring Allen?"

"Never," I said.

"Bert . . ."

"Your husband is a liar and a rat. I don't care if I never see him again as long as I live."

"You stink," she said, and drank. "Flffff," she said, pulling a face. "*This* stinks, too."

"Rosie," I said, "why don't you just go home?"

"I think I will," she answered. She carried the glass to the sink and poured the Rock and Rye down the drain. Then she rinsed out the glass again, and put it on the drainboard. She checked her rouge in the mirror over the sink, touching one corner of her mouth with an extended forefinger, then turned and walked swiftly to the door. At the door, she said, "This isn't the end, Bert," and walked out.

                    *   *   *

Since I was not starring in a motion picture about
virtue or courage rewarded, and since the age of miracles
was otherwise dead, I did not hear from Mr. McInerny by
the end of the week, nor did I get the job at Dill-
Holderness. Instead, I drew twenty-six dollars from the
bank to pay the landlord when he came around for the
rent, and then I wired my brother-in-law Oscar in Arizona, asking him for a loan of a hundred dollars to tide
me over until I could find a job. He sent the money by
return wire. The telegraph operator asked me, "Are you
Bertram A. Tyler?"

"That's right," I said.

"Sender requires that you answer a question."

"What do you mean?"

"Wants you to answer this question before I turn the
money over to you."

"Oh. Sure. What's the question?"

"Name his tribe."

"I beg your pardon?"

"Name the sender's tribe."

"Oh . . . uh . . . Apache. No, wait, it's . . . that's right,
Apache."

"That's right, Apache," the operator said.

June ✿ ✿ ✿

Darling Wat,

I sometimes get the feeling it's all an enormous put-
on.

Do you remember my once telling you that there were
really no such places as Cairo, London, Rome, etc.? When
you go up in an airplane, the stage crew on the ground
merely changes all the scenery, moving around the sets
and the props, and however long it takes to transform
New York into some other place is exactly how long they
figure the "flying" time will be. Actually, you're just circling Kennedy for seven hours, and when you come down,
voilà—Paris! An extension of the One World theory, my

love, and worthy of a doctorate. Is there really such a place as Cu Chi, and is Wat Tyler really there? Oh darling, if I could just go up in a jet and have them change the scenery below to Vietnam, so that when I landed you'd be there waiting for me. I miss you so much.

I don't know if you get news about what's happening in the rest of Vietnam, but I guess you know about the various immolations there this past week, starting with the Buddhist nun who burned herself to death outside the Dieu De Pagoda in the old capital of Hué, wherever that is. Dieu De being French for God of, Pagoda and Buddhist being of course Oriental, gasoline being five gallons of American-made, origin of match unknown. Have them change the scenery, Wat, *please* have them change the scenery to a peaceful island in a sunlit sea where we will lay (sic!) on the beach and count floating coconut shells. Nine suicides in a week, all in protest of Premier Ky's treatment of the Buddhists in Danang, and all our beloved leader could say on Memorial Day was, "This quite unnecessary loss of life only obscures the progress that is being made toward a constitutional government." Just before the big weekend, Wat, they were warning motorists about holiday accident tolls, and forecasting the number of deaths to be expected this year if we didn't drive carefully enough, while at the same time the New York *Times* runs weekly figures on the boys being killed in action over there. It is all so ludicrous and so senseless. Come back to me safely, Wat, I love you so terribly much.

I was home over the holiday weekend to visit my parents (reading days happily coinciding), and I called your mother in Talmadge to say hello. Your father, I guess you know, has been in Los Angeles talking to Ronald Reagan about doing a picture book on his career, it being at least a fifty-fifty chance he'll be elected governor of that progressive state come November, in which case your father will have stolen a march on the competition. But your mother didn't know quite what to do about renting the Rosen house on Fire Island again because if your father *does* get a go-ahead on the book, he'll naturally be spending a lot of time in Los Angeles with the old Gipper. Apparently a man named Matthew Bridges in Talmadge (your mother said you would know his daughter) wants to rent them his summer cottage at Lake Abundance, but your mother feels this won't be much of a change. I suggested that perhaps she might be able to talk your father out of the project *entirely* by reminding him that Reagan is an avowed Goldwater Republican who flatly refused to repudiate the John Birch Society. But she seemed to think the prospects of *that* were pretty slim indeed. Anyway, we had a very nice conversation. She told me you've been writing regularly, which is only what I expected of you.

Hey!

I saw a great piece of graffiti in the 86th Street stop of the Lexington Avenue subway:

> *We are the Black Knights,*
> *We travel by the night lights.*
> *The Moon and the stars are our guide,*
> *The night is the time that we ride.*
> *We are the Black Knights.*
> *Lawrence (the poet)*

And just below that, Wat, written in another hand in a different colored ink was: *Fuck you, Lawrence.*

Critics everywhere.

Write soon. I adore you.

Dana

June 5, 1966

My darling Wat,

Question of the week: What is a boonie?

Runner-up question of the week: What is a hootch?

Here I am about to take my last final, and all you can do is prattle on about your boonies and your hootches and your deuces-and-a-half—which reminds me, what's a deuce-and-a-half?

Has anyone ever told you that a person could fall asleep reading your mailing address? The Army should simplify it. I have an excellent idea on how they can do that. They can discharge you tomorrow. Then your mailing address would become Talmadge, Connecticut, and I'd wrap myself naked in Saran Wrap and send myself to your house. I may send myself naked to Cu Chi, anyway, as a surprise for your E-8. Which reminds me, what's an E-8?

Carol is afraid she's going to flunk Descriptive Astronomy. I don't know what gives her *that* idea, Wat, since she hasn't yet bought the text for the course, and has attended only four classes since February. Just paranoid, I guess, completely out of her boonies, if you take my meaning. One of these days, I'll give her a kick right in the hootch which is even better than frontal lobotomy for certain types of mental disorders. Have I told you that I love you insanely? Here I am—just a minute, let me count—(is runner-up one word or two?) 231 or 232 words into my letter, and I haven't yet told you? Just for that I love you, I love you, I love you, I love you, I love you, I love you, I love you, I love you.

Insanely.

Try *that* on your old deuce-and-a-half, baby.

You remember my telling you that for Intro to Fine Arts (a real crap course) I had to make these charts graphically illustrating the various periods of architecture, sculpture and painting? Like, you know, Hellenistic and Renaissance and 17th Century and all that jazz, with examples of each type, a very hairy project, Wat, considering how few credits the course is worth. Anyway, it was due Friday, and when I carried it over to the school, it was naturally pouring bullets, so I had to wrap it in the plastic cloth from our kitchen table. The architecture chart got a little messy, but I think I'll get a good grade, anyway. I'd *better* get a good grade, after all that work. I've been at it steadily since the beginning of April, almost two months, I guess. You have no idea how great it feels to be *finished* with the damn thing.

Carol turned in an English paper at the same time, so we both went out to celebrate. Her boyfriend is in the Navy, and we are known far and wide as The Celebrating Celebrated Celibates, which is not a bad name for a rock group, what do you think? (Never mind, I *know* what you think.) Anyway, we went over to the North End for a *great* Italian meal, and it was too beautiful outside to go to a movie afterwards, so we wandered over to the docks and bought a six-pack and sat smoking cigarettes and drinking beer and looking out over the harbor and at Logan Airport across the way, and just talking. She's a really decent kid, Wat, even though she leaves the apartment looking like a boonie, if you take my meaning. We went shopping afterwards, each of us deciding that we deserved a reward for turning in our respective projects on time, and for having done such a hootch job, besides.

1st Soldier: What do you call a hootch in a town eighteen miles northwest of Saigon?

2nd Soldier: A Cu Chi hootch.

Carol is a nut for rings. I think she got the idea from Ringo, she's an absolute Beatlemaniac, plays their albums day and night and drives me out of my flak jacket. (I *know* what that means, smartie.) She bought this beautiful old ring that fits on her pinky and has a tiny snippet of braided hair behind its glass face. The woman in the store told us it was a mourning ring, you know, with the hair being from a *corpse*—enough to make the blood run cold, Wat, mine anyway. Carol didn't seem to care at all, though. She's going to take out the hair that's in the ring now, and replace it with a lock from her boyfriend's head, which seems terribly morbid to me, and also somewhat like tempting the fates, though he's not in any particular danger stationed as he is on Treasure Island.

I have to study now.

I love you, Wat. Be careful, darling.

Dana

June 6, 1966

Wat, my darling,

I am absolutely limp.

I just got back to the apartment after the most awful exam I've ever taken in my entire life, bar none. I was up cramming half the night, figuring it would be either multiple choice or true-false because that's what he gave his other section. I got there with my head full of facts, certain that if anyone accidentally jostled me in the hallway I'd start spilling campaigns and elections, bills and laws, state legislatures, and government finance all over the floor, and I sat down, and he handed out the exam, and it was a *discussion*-type question! He wanted to know all about the House of Representatives, structure and organization, officers, party leaders, committees, procedure, etc. I'm sure I flunked it, and I'm sure it's because I lost my study hat.

Wat, I feel totally and hopelessly miserable.

I'm going to take a hot bath, and wash my hair and put

317

it up in rollers so I can enjoy being a girl. Then I'm going to eat a full pound box of chocolates and read *The Magus,* which was my present to myself for having turned in the Art project. Still no grade on that, by the way. I'm entitled to a rest, don't you think? Tell me I'm entitled to a rest, Wat.

Wat: You're entitled to a rest, Dana.

Thank you, darling.

I have a late nomination for the Tyler-Castelli Award for April, having picked up a back issue of *Vogue Magazine* in the dentist's office last week. Trumpets. The envelope, please. Nominated for the Tyler-Castelli Award for Cramming Two Commercials Into A Single Sentence While Managing Besides to Spell "Colors" With Vast Affection—*Vogue Magazine* for April 1, 1966, in its PEOPLE ARE TALKING ABOUT feature: "People are talking about ... The Bleached-out girls of *The Group,* the new movie of Mary McCarthy's novel so Cloroxed that it took out all the author's grit and hard colours, leaving the design so faded that there is little to watch except Shirley Knight who has crammed a portrait into the gesture of reaching for a Kleenex."

Please cast your vote early.

Oh my God, I almost forgot to tell you about the kitten! We're not supposed to keep pets, you know, our landlady would throw a fit if she found out. But do you remember that terribly rainy Friday when I delivered my tablecloth-wrapped masterpiece? Well, on the same day, Carol found this bedraggled, half-drowned kitten cringing and mewing under the front steps, and she hid it under her raincoat and brought it upstairs. It is a piebald cat, which doesn't mean having very little hair, Wat, as I'm sure you know with a hootch intelligence like yours. Nor does piebald apply only to horses, as I'm sure you also know with your boonie education and your big deuce-and-a-half, not to mention your M-16—which reminds me, what *is* an M-16? Piebald is having black and white patches, which the kitten has. Because of her distinctive coloration, we call her Rusty. I think she's cross-eyed, and I also think I'm allergic to her fur, but she's so adorable you could die from her. She peed all over Carol's bed last night. Carol did not find it too amusing.

Off to my tub! I'm going to soak for an hour and a

318

half, and then go read my fat book. Oooooh, what a marvelous time I have ahead of me! You've cheered me up already, my darling, and I adore you.

Dana

P.S. Why are the people in *Vogue* always talking about things nobody I know is ever talking about?

June 9, 1966

Darling Wat,

You figure my grades.

Fine Arts project, on which I worked my kishkas to the bone for close to two months: C minus.

Intro to Modern Government, for which I studied all the wrong things: B plus.

English Lit, casual studying, no sweat: A.

French Lit, full night's cramming, much Dex: C.

Haven't yet received a grade in Renaissance Lit, but I'm fearing the worst because I studied hardest for that one. Do you think I'm paranoid? (That's what they keep whispering all the time, Wat, following me in the street and watching every move I make. I know they're after me, and wouldn't be surprised if they'd reached all my instructors and faked up all those cockamamie grades.)

Bumper Sticker of the Week: USE EROGENOUS ZONE NUMBERS

I don't want you to think that bumper stickers are becoming a fad here in Boston, but a lady got hit by a Cadillac the other day at the top of Beacon Hill where Joy crosses Myrtle, and imprinted backwards on her behind they found the words:

MARY POPPINS IS A JUNKIE

Hilarious?

Ho-ho.

Rusty the cat just looked up at me appreciatively, so I guess *she* thought it was pretty good.

Wat, I don't know what to do. Because of the big snowstorm we had back in February, with classes being canceled and all that, the semester's been extended almost two weeks beyond what's usual. But in spite of the grace period (school ends this Saturday), Carol and I *still* haven't found an apartment for next semester, and she's beginning to kvetch now about "Do we have to move, it's so nice here, etc?" She's got a point, in that we do have a lovely apartment in a nice old building, and close to the school besides. But she's such a slob, really. I love her dearly and all that, but I'm getting tired of tripping over her panties and books and records on the bedroom floor, and I thought I'd convinced her at last that it would be nice if we could find an apartment with a larger bedroom so that we wouldn't constantly be getting in each other's way. At first she said she didn't think her father would spring for the possibly higher rent, but she finally got the message, and we've been actively looking since the beginning of May. But now she's starting to waver, especially since it appears we'll have to stay over to keep looking past the 11th. I'm not too happy about *that* prospect, Wat. I've already arranged a lift down with a girl from Brooklyn who has a beat-up old Buick station wagon with lots of room in the back, and I've begun packing my clothes and things, and I honestly don't feel like hanging around Boston for however long it takes to find a new place, especially when Carol no longer has her heart in it. What to do, what to do. I'm sure this is all terribly fascinating to you out there waiting for somebody to say at least I love you.

At least, I love you.

In fact, I adore you.

To be perfectly frank, I am hopelessly attracted to you.

Is there the slightest possibility that you'll get that R and R to Hawaii, because if there is, I'll beg, borrow or steal the fare and meet you there. As it now stands, I may have to spend July with my folks on the Cape (do you know any analyst in the entire world who doesn't spend his summer vacation on Cape Cod?), but I'll change plans, rearrange plans, hijack a jet, do *anything* if you can get away from that damn war for a while. Please let me know.

I love you very much.

Dana

Dearest Wat,

Do you remember a boy named Bernie Lang from Harvard? We met him at a party here in Boston one weekend, a very tall kid with a sort of gloomy expression? At J.L.'s apartment? Anyway, somebody told me he was dropping acid, and I didn't believe it, but I understand he had a very bad trip just last week, convinced he was a race horse and challenging all the traffic in Kenmore Square. I know it sounds comical, Wat, but it was really quite serious. He was taken to Boston Psychopathic for observation, and the rumor is that he's gone completely out of his mind. Whether it's temporary or not is still anyone's guess, but it's enough to scare hell out of you, isn't it? When Carol heard about it, she flushed all our pot down the toilet, which I thought was going a little too far since I'd paid for half of it, and since pot simply *ain't* LSD.

Rusty is screaming her head off, I'll bet she's caught something!

(No, she hasn't.)

She's grown very big in the past few weeks and is beginning to lose all of her maidenly charm. In fact, there's a lecherous old tom who's already begun serenading her from the backyard, probably setting the poor dear up for an early conquest, you cats is all alike, man. Carol wants to get rid of her. She says it's because the landlady has been prowling around suspiciously outside our door, certain we're harboring boys. But I think it's because Rusty still seems to prefer Carol's bed to the litter pan we've put under the sink. I must admit the place is beginning to smell. We take the cat out every now and then for exercise, hiding her under our raincoats to sneak her past Mrs. Cooley, but we look like three-breasted creatures when we slink down the stairs that way, and besides it's getting too warm to be wearing raincoats, and it hasn't rained once since the beginning of the month. But the last time Carol suggested that we dispossess the cat, I said, "Okay, let's tie a brick around her neck and dump her in the Charles," which shocked her out of her pants. I guess I like that old dumb cat.

Look at her.

She knows I'm writing about her.

I'm still not too thrilled about going up to the Cape next

321

month, especially since my mother informs me that there's no sewing machine in the house they've taken. I recently had to shorten all of my skirts (again!) and I began to get the sewing itch, and was planning on making myself some clothes this summer. There are so many great styles coming in, Wat, and I'll bet I could whip up some of those Marimekko things in a matter of hours. Of course, it's the material that makes those look so great, but maybe I can find some cool material when I'm in New York. Without a machine, though, it'd be murder. And who wants to hear glove anaesthesia discussed by a multitude of shrinks as the sun sinks into the Atlantic and their wives envy my boobs and tell me I was a mere child the last time, etc. etc. etc.? Not me. I want to come to Hawaii and be with you.

Incidentally, I have a nomination for the Tyler-Castelli Fire and Brimstone Award for June, and I'd like your opinion on it. I think it should go to Billy Graham who told 19,000 listeners in London, "I fear that sex has become our goddess—and has that one-eyed thing in our living room become our God?" *Is* sex your goddess, Wat? I thought *I* was. And what about that one-eyed thing in the living room, huh? I keep talking to Carol about it, but she insists it must be one of *my* friends, as all of hers have 20/20 vision. Let me know about the R and R, and also about Billy Graham, as I want to contact him immediately if he's a Recipient. Actually, though, I think he's an Evangelist.

Dana

P.S. Your description of the base camp perimeter was very illuminating. *You're under arrest!*

June 17, 1966

Dearest Wat,

I miss you so much I can't think straight. How many months do we have to go? I know you have the days marked off out there, but I keep forgetting whether we have to count a year from when you went into the service or a year from when you got to Vietnam. Please tell me. Please date your next letter very carefully, and state in it exactly how many months and days it will be until you can come home. Then I'll mark it on my calendar, too, and at least that part of the uncertainty will be gone.

Too many things have been happening here at home. And a thing that seems terribly important when it occurs is almost immediately overshadowed by something even more important. I don't think I told you that James Meredith was shot eleven days ago down in Mississippi. He was on U. S. Highway 51, a few miles outside of Hernando, when a white man wielding a 16-gauge shotgun stepped out of the bushes on the side of the road and began yelling his name, "James Meredith, James Meredith, I only want James Meredith," and then firing four loads of birdshot into the highway. I guess he was avenging Old Miss for being forced to admit Meredith as its first Negro student back in the Dark Ages of 1962, or maybe he wanted to prove to Meredith that it was *not* safe for a Negro to walk from Memphis to Jackson in an attempt to inspire voter-registration. Luckily, he didn't kill him. But that wasn't the end of it, Wat, which is what I meant about more important events overtaking those that seem terribly meaningful at the time.

The shooting drew Negro leaders to the South from all over the country, naturally, some of them seeking publicity, I guess, but all of them determined to finish Meredith's march for him. But they ran into difficulty again just yesterday in the town of Greenwood, where the police wouldn't let them pitch their tents on school property and where Stokely Carmichael of SNCC was arrested with several other Negroes. He's now been let out on bail, Wat, but when they freed him, he yelled to the assembled crowd, "We want black power! Every courthouse in Mississippi ought to be burned down to get rid of the dirt." As you know, Carmichael's sentiments tend to be Black Nationalist, so the important thing wasn't his racist vehemence, which was expected, but the way the Negroes in the crowd isolated only two words of his outburst and began chanting them like a slogan, "Black power, black power, black power."

I can remember a girl who had to quit B.U. because her father was being transferred out to California someplace, telling me she was never quite certain about what she should call herself, the derogatory expression nigger having derived from Nigra, which was a mispronunciation of Negro—so was it okay to call herself a Negro? Wasn't that only a refined way of saying nigger? She had never heard a Negro woman referring to herself as a Negress, for example, because that was *certainly* derogatory. (Didn't the Nazis use the word Jewess in much the same way?) And whereas she thought it might be okay to call herself a colored person, she felt her uncle was putting on airs when he referred to himself as a person of color. So where did this leave her? Well, I think Mr. Carmichael has started something down there in Mississippi, for better or worse. I think Negroes will *know* what to call themselves from now on, even though black may be only another misnomer. (Have *you* ever met a black Negro?) It scares me, Wat, all of it. Martin Luther King keeps urging peaceful protest, but I sense that even *his* patience is wearing thin, and I wonder how long he can sustain his grander vision and his larger dream? Bobby Kennedy gets up on top of a car outside racist Johannesburg and tells the gathered people, "Hate and bigotry will end in South Africa one day," and he's *really* saying to the world that it will end in America, too. I say *aluvai* to both of them. I'd like to invite them to dinner one night. I think they would like Rusty the cat.

Hey!

Lenny and Roxanne have finally decided to get married after only two short years of sleeping together! The decision was all very sudden (though I'm sure she's not pregnant) and the wedding is set for June 25th, which is a week from tomorrow. I've been asked to be one of the witnesses. They're getting married by a justice of the peace, so it won't be a big production, but there'll be a reception afterwards at the 79th Street apartment, and I'm very excited about the whole thing. In her letter to me, by the way, Roxanne reported a fine piece of graffiti she spotted in the ladies' room of Schrafft's 88th Street, and which I now pass on to you:

MAYOR LINDSAY IS A LESBIAN

Write to me soon. I love you.

Dana

P.S. Do you ever discuss any of these things with Lloyd Parsons? I gather from your letters that he's your closest friend in the hootch, but I was wondering if your relationship is that free. I imagine the Army's integration is real enough—I can't, for example, visualize any racial conflict on a patrol into enemy territory—but sometimes I wonder.

June 22, 1966

Darling,

I have to run out to look at an apartment that suddenly materialized on St. Mary's Street—kitchen, living room, and two bedrooms, all for $125.00! (Its last occupant was a maiden lady who drove it only on Sundays.) Carol is yelling for me to hurry up, and we're going over to C'est Si Bon afterwards for some onion soup and those great pâté sandwiches, and won't be back till late tonight so I won't have a chance to write to you. I'll just stick a stamp on this and mail it when I go down, AWRIGHT, SHADDUP ALREADY!

I love you,
Dana

June 24, 1966

Dearest Wat,

I think we may get the apartment, but it's not a certainty yet. Two other girls had been to look at it before us, and they left a deposit on it. But they're not sure they're going to take it because one of the girls had rheumatic fever last fall, and it affected her heart, and she's not sure her parents will dig her climbing all those steps every day. I hope they're as much concerned about the poor kid's health as I am, because Wat this is the most terrific apartment ever, with this little entrance alcove lined with bookshelves, and a tiny kitchen off to the left and a fairly decent-sized living room and, of course, the *two* bedrooms. They're both very small, but can you imagine the luxury of not having to listen to Carol arguing on the phone with her mother, or not having to yell at her to put out the light? Can you imagine how nice it'll be to reach for a ribbon on the dresser top and not stick my hand into a cold cream jar Carol has left open? Darling, keep your fingers crossed for me. If we don't get this apartment, I'm going to enter a life of prostitution.

Meanwhile, other troubles loom.

What do you do with a cat when you go home for the summer? Carol's parents own a Great Dane who would swallow poor Rusty in a second. *My* parents would appreciate a cat as much as a case of German measles, and we can't find anyone here to take the poor beast, even though she's turning out to be an excellent mouser. (At least she doesn't run away from them any more.) It occurs to me suddenly that perhaps you could use a mobile mouse trap for under your hootch out there. The rat population being what it is in Vietnam, Rusty could perform a much-needed service while perhaps simultaneously becoming the company mascot, on lesser inspirations have entire wars been won. Vot you say, big boy? Shall we wrap her as a gift? Sorry we don't have any of the ball-bearing kind, but who knows what sexy Rusty may lure to the camp? She certainly seems to be doing all right with our back alley tenor? Yes? No? I send? I don't?

I won't even discuss how shitty I think it was of your C.O. to refuse the R and R. You've been there for four months already, and it'll be six months by August (when I could have gotten away very easily) and I think the old bastard *might* have broken his heart and said yes.

I miss you. I want you. I love you.

Dana

June 28, 1966

Wat darling,

Please forgive this odd-looking stationery. Carol and I are in the midst of packing all our things, and I can't find my usual dainty, ladylike, jonquil-colored, quality writing paper. You guessed it (God, are you intelligent!) we got the apartment! Papa of the rheumatic fever victim called his child prepaid from Tampa, Florida, to say he would *not* have her climbing five flights to an apartment even if it was the Taj Mahal, which it couldn't possibly be in a place like Boston, and the answer was No, definitely No, N-O, double O, O. So the landlady refunded the deposit, which was really very nice of her since she didn't have to, and then called us to report what had happened and to say the place was ours if we still wanted it. *Still wanted it?!?!* Carol and I ran from here to St. Mary's (eight blocks) in a matter of six seconds, showered a month's advance rent on the poor bewildered old lady and made wild promises such as we'd be in bed by eight o'clock each night after we had eaten all our Pablum. Anyway, it's ours, and we're moving in tomorrow, and then locking the place up for July and August. Mommy and Daddy are already on the Cape, and I'll be going there directly from here, so that's that.

Roxanne's wedding was absolutely beautiful, just a simple ceremony, but I wept all the way through it anyway, and practically couldn't sign my name straight when it came time to witness the certificate. The reception afterwards in her parents' apartment was somewhat crowded, to say the least. Try to picture four or five hundred relatives and friends packed into a place that's identical to my parents', Wat, only two floors lower down. It was possible to get intimate with someone just by being introduced! (Now don't start worrying about that, I'm only kidding.) The food was marvelous, and there was plenty to drink, and I met a lot of kids Roxanne and I used to go to Dalton with, and we got very weepy all over again, and it was a thoroughly enjoyable female experience. The only sad part of it was that you weren't there to enjoy it with me. But that, Wat, is the only sad part about my entire life.

Come home soon.

You hear me?

I have now marked the exact end of your tour on next year's little calendar at the back of my appointment book: March 30, 1967. I expect to meet you wherever your plane lands, and we'll throw champagne glasses in the fire and pretend there never was a stupid war. March 30th is exactly 276 days from now, you think I'm not counting?

Hey, guess what? We got rid of Rusty. I suppose I shouldn't put it quite so crassly, but I must admit the cat was beginning to be a severe pain, and both Carol and I were getting quite anxious about what to do with her come the end of the week. She chewed up my best nylons (the cat, not Carol) on Friday, and I had to rush out to buy another pair before going down for the wedding, as if things weren't hectic enough with the apartment hanging in the balance and with Carol moaning about having flunked Descriptive Astronomy. (She really *was* surprised, can you believe it? By the way, I passed Renaissance Lit with a B, so I expect you to send me some kind of award from out there in the jungle, like maybe an orchid picked from a tree, or a smooth pebble from a stream, or perhaps even a piece of bamboo drilled with evenly spaced holes upon which I can play ancient tunes like "And I Love Her." I will leave it to your imagination.) Anyway, we had a girl from Simmons up for dinner Sunday night when I got back from New York, oh, listen, this was *some* production. Candlelight and wine, you know, and Rusty cute as anything with a blue ribbon around her neck, cocking her head to one side, the whole adorable quizzical cat routine, Carol and I dressed to kill and stumbling all over ourselves in our efforts to please. When we were mixing the salad in the kitchen, Carol suggested that we turn the Simmons girl on, but I thought this might be a bit much for someone from Muncie, Indiana. In fact, she even declined the scotch we offered, and I thought our entire NBC Special might be preempted, as they say in TV Land, but Rusty rescued the day by climbing gently into her lap after dinner, and purring against her bosom, and I'm happy to report it was love at first sight. Carol is even now delivering Rusty to the girl's room on Park Drive, over near the Fine Arts Museum, so thank God for that! If I ever write to say I'm about to take in another pet, please send me a hand grenade by return airmail.

Wat darling, let me go pack the rest of my junk or we'll *never* get out of here. I'm so afraid the new apartment will vanish into thin air before we move into it. I love you, love you, love you. Write soon.

Dana

P.S. Something just occurred to me. I mean, it really occurred to me when I made my silly joke about people getting intimate with a handshake, or whatever it was I said. You've never asked, Wat, and I never thought it necessary to say so. But I think you should know that I stopped taking the pill the day you left for the Army. I love you. Be careful or I'll die.

July 🌱 🌱

I suppose I felt that Dolores should have had at least *some* sort of patriotic understanding for the sacrifices made and still to be made, considering the fact that her brother had lost his eye flying a low-level bombing mission over Ploesti. But she surprised me by saying it would certainly be worth a few thousand dollars to get myself out of the Army, and if I knew how to arrange it, I should make the proper inquiries at once.

I knew how to arrange it and also where to arrange it. The word had been passing around Mitchel Field for months now, the hangar talk being that you could get a medical discharge, a safe assignment, a furlough extension, or a transfer merely by contacting the right people and crossing their palms with silver. I knew the talk was true, and I personally resented its authenticity. Mind you, I held no brief with the Army's recently disclosed points system for discharge. It seemed to me that the scheme was heavily weighted in favor of two types of soldiers, those who were married and had children, and/or those who had received certain combat awards or decorations. Someone like myself, who had flown fifty combat missions over enemy territory with his hands and feet freezing and his head pounding, could muster only thirty-six points against the eighty-five required for discharge—a point for each month I'd been in the service, and another for each month I'd served overseas. The system was unfair, and it placed me in imminent danger besides of being reassigned to the Pacific to fight against the Japanese while some Army instructor stationed in Iowa got his discharge because he'd happened to sire three kids. But that didn't mean I was ready to buy myself out of the Air Force.

My father had written in his most recent letter to me that the United States Government might be a little slow in redressing grievances, but that it always made good sooner or later, as witness the bill President Truman had just signed, whereby we would pay the Sioux Indians for ponies the Army had taken from them after the massacre at Little Big Horn in 1876. With a stroke of not unexpected sarcasm, my father had written, "I'm sure your Uncle Oscar, though he is but a mere Apache, will be terribly pleased." Well, it was easy to become cynical about anything that had to do with the Army, but I sure as hell hoped it wouldn't take them another seventy years to revise the points system. Anyway, the day after I received my father's letter, I was glad I *hadn't* been lured into buying a fake discharge. The way the Army had finally caught up with its pony thieves, the Air Force finally caught up with the two commissioned officers and six enlisted men who were involved in what was described as a "nefarious and scandalous racket." The ring was arrested on July 6 at Mitchel Field; when I told Dolores that night about the furor on the base, she only shrugged and said, "You waited too long, love."

The "love" was an affectation acquired from her brother, who had of course been stationed with the Eighth Air Force in England. The cynicism was her own, somewhat unsettling to discover in a girl who would not be eighteen until next month, especially when her opening line had been "Hay is for horses." I suspected, though, that I was leaning a bit too heavily on that first impression, trying to create for myself the image of a beautiful dope. Because aside from humping her, which was delicious, I wanted no real involvement with Dolores Prine, and the easiest way to avoid any meaningful relationship was to convince myself she was incapable of tying her own shoelaces, which simply was not true.

Her older brother, Douglas, had graduated from Science (which Dolores assured me was the best high school in New York City) at the age of sixteen, and was in his second scholarship year at Columbia when the Army drafted him. Wearing his black patch with all the flair of a latter-day pirate, curly hair darker than his sister's tumbling onto his forehead, he would fix me with his one good piercing eye blazing out of his head like fire from The Green Lantern's ring, and engage me in polemic —political, religious, financial, artistic, it didn't matter. He loved to argue, and more often than not he would draw Dolores into our heated debates as well, and together sometimes they would strike sparks long into the night while I secretly yearned to touch her, and she knew I did, and glanced shyly at me, slyly, as if to say, But you see, love, I can *think* as well. The arrest of the Mitchel Field ring sent Douglas off into a lecture on the moral dissolution of America, his thesis gaining vigor the following day when it was revealed in Chicago that the use of counterfeit red ration coupons had reached a new high, some 8,000,000 points having passed over the nation's meat counters in June alone. Two days later, when federal agents in New York arrested twenty-four people on charges of selling or possessing narcotics, Douglas showed me the *Daily News* headline like a poker player exposing a

330

royal flush, shouting at me as though *I* represented the system—"This is what I lost my eye for!" he screamed, and his mother came in from the kitchen and advised him please to calm down as his father was still asleep.

Mrs. Prine seemed more concerned with her son's infrequent outbursts than with her daughter's daily wanderings. School for Dolores had ended on June 15, but before then I had made arrangements with a corporal out at Mitchel to use his parents' apartment on West End Avenue as soon as they left for Nantucket on the Fourth of July. I had been promoted to first lieutenant after the Fiume raid, which meant that I was now earning about two hundred dollars a month, when I added in my longevity pay and my subsistence allowance. I couldn't very well pay the corporal an exorbitant amount for the use of the apartment, but he was willing to settle for ten dollars a week, plus whatever small favors I could extra-legally confer as an officer—passes, use of Army vehicles off the base, bar duty at the Club, where he hoped to meet higher-type broads. (This was all before the scandal broke; afterward, I was pretty damn careful about anything I signed for him.) In any event, Dolores and I spent a lot of time at the apartment, and her mother's indifference to her whereabouts puzzled me. I asked Michael what *he* thought about it one day—this was before the Air Force transferred him out to Luke Field, where he was to begin training fledgling pilots—and he told me with a great deal of scholarly nodding of head and adjustment of imaginary spectacles that sexual mores were changing in America, harrumph, but that parents were still unable to visualize their children in situations any more compromising than those they themselves had experienced at the same age. Add to this the fact that Mrs. Prine was a phenomenally ugly woman who had probably never had a pass made at her in her life, and you could understand why she could not for a moment imagine, harrrrumph, what her nubile daughter was doing every day of the week, harrrrumph. I thanked Michael for his shrewd observation.

Mrs. Prine, now that I thought of it, *was* a singularly unattractive woman. Small-bosomed, narrow-hipped, near-sighted but too vain to wear eyeglasses, she squinted and flapped around the big Sutton Place apartment dictating letters to a temporary secretary who came in once a week, directing club activities and charities, arranging balls and parties, scattering papers like fallen leaves behind her, and constantly glancing back over her shoulder as though expecting something she had overlooked to grab her by the nape of the neck. It was reasonable to believe that the farthest thing from her mind was her daughter's sexual initiation, and I was grateful for her indifference, but at the same time felt oddly guilty each time she squinted her greetings to me at the front door.

On his days off, Mr. Prine followed his wife around the apartment like the executive officer on a battleship, wiping a white gloved hand into the angled joining of bulkhead and deck, fluttering helplessly in her boiling wake, bald pate glistening, eyebrows raised in anticipation of the calamities she constantly predicted. Douglas towered over his father by a full foot and a half, and it was somewhat comical to see Mr. Prine coming sleepy-eyed out of the bedroom at two in the morning to ask his huge, one-eyed son, calmly and patiently, to please lower his voice. Mr. Prine was chief counsel for a firm that manufactured ladies' girdles, corsets, and the like ("He's very big in ladies' underwear," Dolores said to me one day in our West End Avenue bed, and then wiggled her eyebrows as I burst out laughing at the old old gag), and he was constantly being sent to negotiate contracts in Minnesota or Maine, coming home a week or ten days later to hear his wife forecasting some new impending disaster. He was invariably too busy to concern himself with what was happening to either of his children, a failing that pounded itself home with frightening suddenness at the end of the month, when the vague calamity his wife had been expecting descended with fury upon his household.

I should have suspected that something was wrong with Douglas from the start, but I assumed only that he was too bright for me, that he was aware of meanings too subtle for me to grasp. He had purchased a wire recorder shortly after his discharge, and was now engaged in filling spool after spool with recorded notes for a documentary radio program he hoped to submit one day to the major networks. Whenever I went to see Dolores, I would find her brother closeted in his room, surrounded by open newspapers and magazines, the radio blaring the news as he selected and snipped the articles or items he needed for his project. There was no mistaking the seriousness with which he approached his task, nor his conviction that he was embarked on something that would prove enormously valuable to the world in its post-war reconstruction. Sometimes, as he played back his assorted gleanings, his voice took on the mannered cadences of a Walter Winchell or a Gabriel Heatter, but he always seemed to realize when he was hamming it up, and excused himself by saying he had not yet overcome the theatrical lure of the microphone. For the most part, he read his items into the machine in his normal speaking voice, dispassionately, and I was honestly impressed by the logical order in which he had arranged his news fragments, and forced to respect the purposeful clarity of even those parts of his indictment with which I disagreed. An indictment it was, no question about that. Only occasionally did he veer from his thesis, as though he had absent-mindedly strolled off a path that wound through a formal garden to find himself entangled in a patch of weeds. But he always found his way back again, always managed to extricate himself, the flat recorded voice returning to recite the facts he was laboriously compiling.

That was in the very beginning.

He became convinced early in June that the Japanese would never surrender and that he would be called back into the service to do more bombing. He did not know how they expected him to look through a bomb sight again, he had only one eye, didn't they realize that? Were they now redrafting blind men and cripples to fight their war? The Japanese would never surrender, despite the pounding we were daily administering in the Pacific, and even if they *did* surrender, it was all for nothing.

"Look at this," he would say, "*look* at this world we're attempting to save, what's the point?" He would pick up a clipping from his desk then and begin reading it in the portentous voice of a *March of Time* announcer, "July 8, 1945—an American guard at the POW camp in Salina, Utah, today machine-gunned the tents of sleeping German prisoners, killing eight and wounding twenty, how are we any better than they? Look at this one, July 13, 1945" (the *March of Time* voice again) "the House Un-American Activities Committee today assigned an agent to investigate Representative Rankin's claim that Hollywood is the greatest hotbed of subversive activities in the United States, and that big names are involved in one of the most dangerous plots ever instigated for the overthrow of this government. It's the goddamn Palmer Raids all over again, have you ever heard of A. Mitchell Palmer?" (What newspaper is that from? I asked.) *"Look* at this stuff, Will, this is all fact, look at it. July 14, 1945— General Eisenhower announced today in Frankfort-on-the-Main that United States troops may now converse on streets and in public places with adult Germans, do you get the significance of that, Will? They were only allowed to talk to *kids* before this, but Eisenhower says the new move is a result of rapid progress in de-Nazification. I say if we're talking to the Germans today, we'll be sleeping with them tomorrow, the same way you're sleeping with my sister. Oh, don't look so surprised, I'm not blind, I've still got *one* good eye, buddy. Anyway, who cares? What you're doing is only an infinitesimal part of the whole molecular structure."

In bed one afternoon toward the end of July, Dolores said, "Now there're these two buttons, okay? And if you push the one on the right a hundred million Chinese peasants will die immediately. You can save them all, though, by pushing the one on the left, but then *I'll* die. Have you got it?"

"I've got it," I said.

"Well?"

"Well, what?"

"Which one would you push?"

"This one," I said, and gently touched the nipple on her right breast.

Dolores looked down at herself and grinned. "You mean you'd sacrifice a hundred million Chinese just for me?"

"Two hundred million."

"Yes, but only peasants."

"Landlords, too."

"Mandarins?"

"Even emperors!"

"You must really love me then."

"Who said so?"

"I said so. What would you do if I told you I never wanted to see you again?"

"I'd come to your house and break down the door."

"But I wouldn't let you in."

"If I'd already broken down the door . . ."

"Yes, but I'd call the police."

334

"And get me sent to jail?"

"Why should I care? If you don't love me . . ."

"I love to touch you," I said. "Mmmm, where are those sweet buttons?"

"Will, please."

"I'm sorry."

"You make me feel very cheap sometimes."

"I said I'm sorry."

"You're . . . you're the first person I've ever done this with, you know, I'm not some . . . some damn old prostitute you picked up on Eighth Avenue."

"I know you're not."

"I'm only seventeen."

"I know."

"You might try remembering that."

"I will."

"The same age as Juliet."

"Juliet Schwartz?"

"Sure, Juliet Schwartz."

"*Now* what are you going to do? Start crying?"

"Over you? Fat chance," she said, and burst into tears.

"Juliet was only fourteen," I said, and handed her a corner of the sheet. "Here. And besides, you'll be eighteen next month."

"That makes me some kind of hag, I guess."

"No, it makes you a beautiful young lady."

"Yeah, crap," she said, and wiped her eyes on the sheet, and then reached for my khaki handkerchief on the night table, and noisily blew her nose. "I'm not a fool, you know," she said. "My father's a lawyer, you know."

"I know he is."

"I can get very mean if I want to."

"Dolores, I can't imagine a mean bone in your . . ."

"I *hate* that name."

"But I love it."

"But you don't love *me!*"

"Do you want me to say I do?"

"Yes."

"I love you," I said.

"What?"

"I love you."

"No, you don't," she said. "You're only telling me that now because you're afraid."

"Of what?"

"Of what I said. About statutory rape."

"When did you say *that?*"

"I didn't, but I had it all ready. I was going to say, 'There're only two things I have to say to you, Lieutenant Tyler,' and then you'd say, 'Yes, and what are those two things?' and I'd say, 'Statutory rape.' But it didn't come out that way because you got me so angry. Do you really love me, Will?"

"I adore you."

"Yes, I adore you, too. Can you get a pass this weekend?"

"I doubt it."

"Can you get tickets for *The Glass Menagerie?*"

"Why? What's . . ."

"For Friday night?"

"Well, I don't know."

"Daddy left for Los Angeles yesterday to negotiate another one of his panty deals, and Mother's leaving for Easthampton Thursday. I thought we could spend the whole weekend together . . ."

"Why didn't you tell me this sooner?"

"Because if you wouldn't admit you loved me, I was going to jump in the river."

"I'll get the pass, and I'll get the tickets."

It was easier to get off the base for the weekend than it was to get tickets to the play. But I managed both, and arranged with Dolores to meet her at the apartment at seven o'clock that Friday night. The bell rang at six-thirty. When I opened the door, I was surprised to find her standing there wearing a plaid skirt, loafers, and a white blouse, hardly appropriate attire for dinner and the theater afterward. She came into the apartment trembling and apologetic, telling me we couldn't possibly go out, explaining that she would have called me if the apartment's telephone hadn't been disconnected for the summer, but she *knew* I was waiting for her, and so she'd caught a taxi, and it was *still* downstairs, and she'd run out of the house without her bag, could we please go back to Sutton Place at once?

In the taxicab, she explained that she had heard sounds coming from her brother's room the night before, and had thought at first he was up late recording. But when she'd gone in to him, she'd found him sitting in the center of the

336

bed staring at the opposite wall, mumbling what had sounded like gibberish at first, Tupelo Lass, Thundermug, Utah Man, Hell's Wench, not understanding until her brother said the words King's Ransom, which she recognized as the name of his airplane, and realizing all at once that he was reciting a partial roll call of the B-24s that had flown low over the Ploesti oil fields on the day he'd lost his eye. When he saw her in the room, he told her that his eye socket was bleeding and begged her to get him something to stop the blood, and she had sat on the edge of his bed, and taken his hand, and convinced him that he was home and safe, talking gently and quietly to him until he drifted off to sleep again. Today, he had seemed completely calm, had in fact gone for a walk in the park this afternoon, leaving his important project for the first time in months. But he had returned just as she was getting ready to dress, and when she greeted him at the door, he said to her, "Shave your head," and went directly to his room where he turned on the radio full blast, in time for the six o'clock news. She was terribly worried now, feeling certain she should not have left him alone.

The apartment was still when we got there.

Dolores turned on the hall light. "Douglas?" she called.

There was no answer.

"Douglas?" she called again.

He was sitting in the living room near the piano, a blurred huddled shape in the velvet-covered easy chair, the carpet at his feet strewn with newspapers and magazines, the recorder resting on the piano top beside him. "Is that you?" he said. "I've been waiting for you," he said. "Listen to this," he said, and suddenly snapped on the recorder, and turned to us with his unwavering Cyclops gaze as the spool began to unwind.

Good evening, Mr. and Mrs. America, and all the ships at sea, the recorded voice said, the WPB has estimated today that the war cost us only $7,400,000,000 a month in the year nineteen hundred and forty-four, but the question we now ask and will continue to ask is what does that have to do with the price of fish, when glass eyes are going for a dollar a dozen? Perhaps you'd like to answer *that* one for us, Mr. Truman, while raising the American flag in Berlin, the same flag that was flying over Washing-

337

ton when we declared war, and telling everybody there that if we can put this tremendous machine of ours, which has made victory possible, to work for peace, we can look forward to the greatest age in the history of mankind, in which case why have they stolen my eye and refuse to return it though I've mailed countless petitions, give me back my eye you sons of bitches, they're buying soap in panic all over America, do they hope to wash away our sins, do they hope to wash away the blood, they've been warned there's no shortage, is it true that the Nazis made Jews out of soap, why are we hoarding, do you know that General Minami says, and I quote in Japanese, I always quote, I have the facts right here at my fingertips, don't try to con *me*, pal, I know you're putting it to my sister, Japan, I quote, Japan will be ready to talk peace only when the whole of East Asia is freed from Anglo-American colonial exploitation and when Japan and other nations in the world are assured of a peaceful life based on justice and equality, so where's my just and equal eye, did you look under the sofa, Lolly, do you remember once when I touched you in the tub and you began to cry, does *he* touch you, that prick, the Japanese have refused our ultimatum, I told you they would, listen to this, So far as the Imperial Government of Japan is concerned it will take no notice, of *what* I ask Premier Suziuki, no notice of *what*, of yellow men being bombed, of eyeless bombardiers sighting, dropping sticks and stones will break my bones and Lolly has no tits, who's this William Z. Foster who was named chairman of the national board and Party, if there's going to be one, why weren't we invited, I'll bring my cup and pencils, you can shove dimes up my ass and watch me dance the polka, the FBI has tracked down half a million draft dodgers, who would have dreamt, love, that so many Americans had no heart for this beautiful war, did you know that Henry Ford said today just before his eighty-second birthday that the nation and the world, I quote, are on the eve of a prosperity and standard of living that was never before considered possible, but ask old Hank what he was doing back in the summer of 1920 in Dearborn, Michigan, ask him how come, love, ask him should Jews buy his automobiles today, love, why not if they'll soon be buying the ones the Nazis make, I'm so damn tired, folks, we're running a little late, folks, the Japanese'll never surrender, they know I

338

haven't got a chance with just one eye, oh Jesus Lolly my eye is bleeding again, Oh Jesus Lolly save me, love, help me, love, save me (and then suddenly his real voice erupted over the litany coming from the recorder, his real voice burst into the room high and strident, Help, he screamed), Lolly save me help me save me (Help, oh Jesus, help!), and I remembered what Michael Mallory had confided to me so earnestly outside this building on the bank of the river, that he'd kept waiting for the war to catch up to him, kept waiting for the world's idiocy to overtake him at last (Help, Douglas Prine kept screaming over the sound of the recorder).

He was taken to Bellevue Hospital the next day and committed on July 31 to Four Winds in Katonah.

August ❦

I kissed Rosie.

I kissed her while inside the band played "Avalon" and Allen Garrett sat passed out at the table with his head cushioned on his folded arms, "I found my love in Avalon, beside the bay," both of us huddled in the shadowed alleyway in the angle where the speakeasy's kitchen and dining room joined, steam puffing from a vent onto the stifling August night, the aroma of roasting beef, "I left my love in Avalon, and sailed away," her mouth opening, the taste of alcohol, and my hand sliding into and under the low corsage of her white dress, "You shouldn't," she said, and pressed herself to me.

I kissed her because when I'd been dancing with her earlier in the evening, she had pushed tight against me and I had felt myself growing hard and had wanted to hold her closer still, and was embarrassed even though everyone on the floor was dancing that way, I did not know what to do, I did not know what to think. I kissed her because I knew with certainty there was nothing beneath the white tulle but an underslip and knickers of the flimsiest stuff, kissed her because she had said to me the moment Allen passed out, "Let's get some air, Bert." I kissed her because she was dark and slender and wore rouge on her wide mouth and laughed very loud when anyone told a dirty joke and smoked cigarettes and drank far too much gin. I kissed Rosie because she was the complete and total opposite of Nancy my wife, whom I loved.

I kissed her, too, because grudges die hard, and I was still harboring a grudge against Allen Garrett.

I had found a job at last in June, but that had been entirely by accident, and every time I got to thinking about the close call I'd had, I started hating Allen all over again. I had asked Oscar for two additional loans of a hundred dollars each, which he had readily sent, together with the assurance that he would continue helping me for as long as I needed it. But the new loans put me three hundred dollars in the hole to my brother-in-law, and I didn't like such a huge debt hanging over my head like a half-chopped tree. I had just about given up hope when I went out to the Circle Mill to apply for work as a loader. The job paid five dollars less a week than I'd been earning at Ramsey-Warner, but that turned out to be academic, anyway, because it had been filled by the time I got out to Joliet. I didn't know what to do. I hated going home to face Nancy, I actually hated the thought of going home. I walked across the Circle yard breathing in all the familiar scents of a paper mill, hearing all the familiar sounds, and thinking maybe I should take Nancy and head back to Wisconsin, I could always get a job in the woods there, always make a decent enough living to support her that way. I guess I'd been walking with my head bent, hands in my pockets, and I only chanced to look up as I started out the main gate, and saw three fellows in suits like my own, standing on line outside a covered staircase that ran up the side of one of the buildings, its galvanized metal roof reflecting sunlight. I walked over to the line and asked the fellow on the end of it what was going on, and he told me they were hiring salesmen, and I said, Oh, and was ready to leave again, when I thought Well, why *not* a salesman, you've already considered cleaning out toilet bowls, haven't you? and I got on the end of the line.

The man who interviewed me was named Gerald Hawkes, and he asked me six questions in rapid succession and then stared at me in silence.

340

Q: Have you ever sold paper products before?

A: No.

Q: Have you ever sold anything before?

A: No.

Q: Have you ever worked for a paper company before?

A: Yes.

Q: Which one?

A: Ramsey-Warner.

Q: Why did you leave?

A: I wasn't earning enough money.

Q: How much would you like to earn?

A: Fifty dollars a week.

Gerald Hawkes blinked at me. He stroked his mustache. He fingered his stickpin. He got up and walked around his desk and came over to my chair and circled the chair and studied me, my suit, my shoes, my shirt, my tie, and then went back to his desk and sat again in the big leather swivel chair behind it, and fingered his stickpin and stroked his mustache.

"We'll pay you ten dollars a week," he said. "Plus commissions. You won't be earning much in commissions at the start, but then neither will we be earning much in sales. When you've learned the territory, you should start making a lot more than the fifty you're asking."

"Will I have to travel?"

"Why, what've you got against traveling?"

"Nothing."

"Then why'd you ask about it?"

"Because you didn't mention anything about traveling expenses."

"You won't need traveling expenses, you'll be selling to retail stores in the Chicago area. Can you drive?"

"Yes, sir," I said, which was true. But I had been living in Chicago for more than a year now, and had not driven a car since I'd left Wisconsin, and was really a little apprehensive about driving in Chicago traffic. I did not tell him any of these things, though. I was learning fast that one way to get a job was to sprinkle a few lies here and there among the petunias.

"Can you start work tomorrow morning?"

"Yes, sir, I can."

"Good. Report to Mr. Goss in Room 314 at eight o'clock."

"Thank you," I said.

"Welcome," Gerald Hawkes answered, and stroked his mustache.

I began working at the Circle Mill on a Wednesday morning. That Saturday night, Allen and Rosie came up to the South Lawndale flat bearing gifts—a turkey Rosie had roasted, and a bottle of gin her brother had made. (He had actually made two *cases* of the stuff, which qualified him as the biggest bootlegger I personally knew.) The visit was not unexpected. Nancy had prepared me for it, or, to be more precise, had bludgeoned me into accepting it. There was a lot of embarrassed foot-shuffling and eye-shifting when the Garretts arrived, but at last Allen and I shook hands like two schoolyard kids who had had a knockdown-dragout fistfight and were now reluctantly making up. We all toasted my new job (including Nancy, whom I had never before seen drinking hard liquor), and then we toasted Allen's promotion, which I was still convinced he'd got by lying about me. Nancy and Rosie went out to the kitchen to warm the turkey and set the table. Allen and I sat opposite each other silently in the parlor.

He offered me a cigar, which I declined.

He cleared his throat.

He shifted his weight in the big easy chair.

Then he said, "Bert, no matter what you think, I never said anything to anybody about you being a radical."

"Okay," I said.

"Do you believe me?" he asked.

"I believe you," I said. But I didn't.

The job was a good one. Circle ran a huge operation, with two mills on the West Coast, another in New York State, and of course the one in Joliet. Since the company manufactured a wide variety of paper products—newsprint, industrial papers, bond and writing and ledger and manifold papers, bags and boxes, book and offset papers, butcher's wrap, you name it—my selling job took me to a great many different kinds of retail outlets, and I was certainly never bored. Circle's main paper product that year, though (as was the case with all of the Joliet mills, was wallpaper, and I guess I earned most of my commissions selling to the housewares sections of the big department stores, or to the smaller paint and wallpaper retailers scattered all over Chicago. By the end of my third week at Circle, I began to think that Allen had done me a big favor. My earlier ideas on how to become a corporation executive now seemed terribly naïve. The way to get into the board room was not by spiking and rolling logs off the conveyer belt. *This* was the way. I found myself outlining a plan for my rise through the Circle Mill ranks, allowing three to five years for each phase of the escalation, from salesman to District Manager, in which position I would begin supervising salesmen, and fighting with plant managers for deliveries, and influencing mill schedules, and meeting regularly with management, and then moving up to Sales Manager where my salary would take a sudden jump and company stock would be offered to me, and then on to Vice President-Sales where I would undoubtedly come into conflict with the Vice President-Manufacturing because the next job upward on the ladder was Executive Vice President, third highest position at Circle, with only the Chairman of the Board and the President of the company above. This was 1920. If everything went as I expected it to go, I could become President of Circle by as early as 1932, but certainly no later than 1940. None of it seemed beyond my grasp. I was, perhaps, just an uneducated lumberjack from the Wisconsin woods, but (as I had once told Mr. Moreland) this was America, and I knew that here a man could become whatever he chose to become.

The Garretts entered my life only peripherally in those early days at Circle. We saw them socially perhaps once a week, sometimes less, and I knew that our friendship was dying a normal death, and that it might have been dead already had his betrayal not, paradoxically, spurred a renewed interest in it. What I had earlier regarded as his inquiring mind, I came to realize was only a sponge invariably absorbing the wrong opinions of others. I can remember one night in the parlor of the Garrett flat when I mentioned that Circle had given me a brand-new Ford to drive, and Allen suddenly began endorsing all the horse manure being printed in the *Dearborn Independent*, rising to his full height and telling us that the claims about an international Jewish leadership were absolutely true, that the Jews *were* hellbent on confounding and confusing and finally overcoming the Gentile world by creating wars, revolutions, and civil disorders, that the Jews *were* getting all the profits from the sale of illegal whiskey, the Jewish

343

landlords *were* charging exorbitant rents, the Jewish manufacturers *were* making all the shorter skirts responsible for our decadence (while Rosie's skirt inched higher and higher every week), the Jewish producers *were* making movies about orgies and putting on filthy Broadway plays, the Jews were doing this, the Jews were doing that, the Jews in short were responsible for everything that was wrong in the nation and the world because, just as the *Independent* had reported, everything was "under the mastery of the Jews." I didn't argue with him. Nancy and I left early instead. I knew the friendship was dying, and yet I clung to it, telling myself at first that Allen really wasn't too bad a fellow, telling myself that Rosie was good company for my wife, but wondering even then, I suppose, if I wasn't just waiting for exactly what was happening now.

Now, two months and a little bit later, in an alleyway outside a speakeasy, I knew the sweet revenge of kissing Allen's wife, hot and trembling in the sweltering summer night as a gang of kids went by in one of Mr. Ford's tin lizzies, and inside the vocalist sang, "And so I think I'll travel on, to Avalon." She put her tongue into my mouth, she pulled her face away from mine and laughed, she arched herself against me, and said, "Where'd he park the car? Let's get in the car, Bert."

"Rosie," I said, "we'd best go back."

"No," she answered, and took my hand.

In the rear of the Jeffery Sedan, the windows open, passing automobile lights intermittently illuminating the interior roof, Rosie lay back against the cushioned seat and lifted her dress above her waist and said, "Do you like my stockings rolled?" and I touched her legs, touched the silk the color of her flesh (a year ago, two years ago, a century ago, girls wore stockings that were either white or black), "All the girls are doing it," Rosie said. (Doing what? Turkey trot? The world had changed, everything had been changed by the war.) Her mouth in the darkness was bright with paint, there was a vapid smile upon it, would she later claim that she'd been drunk? The smell of homemade gin climbed into the steamy interior of that silent automobile, our alcohol-scented breaths rushing to merge a moment before we locked lips again, my hands under her dress, clutching at her. She reached up with her thumbs to hook the elastic of her teddies, and then pulled

344

them down over her belly and her thighs. I could dimly
see the pale whiteness of her skin and against it a narrow
black triangle, "Kiss me," she said, my hands on her flesh
so warm beneath the white tulle, her legs opening now,
her slender fingers pressing the back of my neck, I
thought again of a silent forest (there was, as always, that
moment when she seemed to resist) and of a boy whose
dreams in the violet dusk were proscribed by an insulated
world, and I entered her, and she said, "What, Bert,
what?" and I think I whispered, "I don't know," (and then
she trembled, and I could hear her groan again, almost as
if she were in pain) and I sought her mouth, sought that
bright scarlet slash and drew from it whatever secrets
Rosie knew, drew from it prognostications, scathing
visions of what was yet to come, tasting of gin, long silken
legs enveloping me, distant music swelling through the
open car windows, "Here's the Japanese sandman, trade
him silver for gold," (and there was a long heavy shudder
and then a hundred echoing crackings, and then there was
silence).

I drove them home in the Chicago midnight.

There was the smell of gin in the automobile, that and a
stronger scent, but Allen Garrett was unconscious on the
back seat and incapable of detecting Rosie's lingering
feral aroma, incapable of knowing what I had done to his
wife not a half-hour before. She sat beside me now with
her legs recklessly crossed, coat open, skirt high on her
thighs, the rolled stockings lewdly suggestive (a Chicago
streetwalker had been quoted in last week's newspaper as
saying, "You can't tell the ladies from the trollops any
more"). I did not think Rosie Garrett was a trollop, but
I'm not sure I thought she was a lady, either. I knew only
that I had taken her with an explosive violence I had
never before experienced, and felt now the same confusing
aftermath of shame and guilt I had known in France,
when I'd failed to stop what was happening to that little
girl. I told myself as Rosie sat beside me with her head
thrown back against the seat, humming "Avalon" as
though I needed reminders of what we had together
accomplished in the space of five minutes, told myself that
this was the first time and the last time, and knew even
then that I was lying to myself. But I tried nonetheless to
understand what was happening, because it all seemed to
345

be part of the bewildering labyrinth that had been constructed around me without my knowledge or consent. I felt as though I had, in the past few months, become a very minor if not totally insignificant figure in a changing landscape over which I had no personal control, as though the events of my own life were only secondary to the much larger events taking place. But more than that, it seemed to me that the nucleus of my intimate universe had somehow become dislocated, the nucleus was no longer *me,* Bertram A. Tyler. I was, instead, only an expendable moon that could be burned to cinders in the upper atmosphere without being missed or mourned, in danger of being replaced in an instant by some other revolving satellite created in outer space from the boiling matter of our time. I was certainly blameless for what had happened (Rosie's hand on my thigh now, fingers widespread; strangers at eleven, lovers at midnight) if I could point to the speed of the modern-day world as the source of my confusion, the dial on the telephone, the closed automobile, the shorter skirts, the more liberal drinking habits (in themselves a confusing paradox), the whole surging momentum of a nation rushing back to a "normalcy" quite unlike anything it had known before. I blamed all these things, and hoped to become blameless in the process, but the guilt persisted.

So I blamed Nancy as well, blamed her for not being here tonight but being instead in Eau Fraiche with her sister Clara, blamed her besides for being not as *female* as she might have been, even though the doctor had said there was nothing wrong with either of us (I knew there was nothing wrong with *me,* but I could not believe there was nothing wrong with *her*), told myself that somehow her inability to conceive a child made her less womanly, while knowing of course this was not true, and suspecting that perhaps there were passions in her I preferred not to explore lest she become in my mind the equivalent of a whore, neither a mother (which she could not become, it seemed) nor a respected wife. The reception having failed, the guilt and the shame persisting, I allowed the excitement to take complete control, allowed Rosie's humming to envelop me, allowed her hand to work its way toward my fly, allowed her fingers to unbutton me and to enclose me while we drove slowly toward South Lawndale and Allen snored in the back seat.

And then we had a conversation that seemed to me representative of the precarious balance we were all trying to maintain between the simplicity we had known before the war and the sophistication rapidly engulfing us. With her hand curled around me, with her husband drunk and unconscious on the back seat of the automobile, Rosie Garrett casually asked, "How's Nancy's sister?"

"Still in bed," I said, "but coming along."

"What's wrong with her?"

"Oh, just a bad cold is all. But she's been running a fever."

"She's got how many children?"

"Two."

"It's terrible when the woman of the house comes down with something," Rosie said.

"Especially when she's married to someone like Ed."

"What's the matter with Ed?"

"Can't stand anybody being sick. Gets absolutely furious, treats Clara like a dog just when she needs him most."

"When's Nancy coming back?"

"Wednesday, I think. Or Thursday. It depends on how Clara's doing."

"Will you come see me Monday night?"

"What?"

"Monday night. Allen's staying late in Joliet."

"I . . . don't know, Rosie. Maybe we'd just better forget what happened."

"No," she said. "You'll come see me."

September ✿ ✿ ✿

There were five rows of protective barbed wire around the base camp at Cu Chi, and the sandbagged bunkers were spaced at seventy-five-yard intervals inside the perimeter, with one man in each bunker during the daylight hours, and three at night. During the daytime, the line troops manned the perimeter. But between six p.m. and six a.m., two men from the rear echelon joined a single combat-experienced soldier in the bunker, and it was then that things got a little tense. Rear-echelon troops were inclined to shoot at anything that moved, and orders had come down from above that no one was to fire a weapon without permission from the sergeant or officer of the guard in the CP bunker, it being reasoned that the folks out there could be a returning friendly patrol as easily as some Vietcong infantrymen setting up a mortar. So whereas there were plenty of weapons in each bunker—M-60s and M-50s, grenade launchers, M-79s, Claymore mines, and of course our own pieces, the M-16s—we weren't allowed to use them before we checked upstairs. It was a very comical war, all right.

The base camp at Cu Chi looked like a postage stamp from the air. Visualize those five rows of tangled barbed wire as the perforated edges of the stamp; and inside that the evenly spaced bunkers as the stamp's border; and moving toward the center, the line-troop hootches with their wooden frames and screened upper halves and tented roofs as a second khaki-colored inner border; and then the body of the stamp itself, a geometric abstract with battalion headquarters to the southeast, and the mile-long air strip running perpendicularly off-center, and to the southwest the rear echelon hootches, a base within a base with its own mess hall and motor pool, its own orderly room and EM's Club, its own showers and latrines and chapel—for those Remfs who had anything to pray about.

My own hootch was just inside the perimeter to the northwest, and it had a metal roof, which meant that it was very popular after dark, when all us guys would climb up onto it to watch the Night Show—the pyrotechnic display of the Hueys firing tracer rounds, or of the mortars (ours and the V.C.'s) chewing up the countryside. Fresh back from the boonies, there was comfort in watching the action from a safe distance; it beat *Batman* all to hell. Some of the rear-echelon hootches at Cu Chi were as sumptuously equipped as the Waldorf-Astoria, with electric fans, refrigerators, hot plates, lawn chairs, foot lockers (made by the gooks out of discarded tin cans, and sold at the PX) and even television sets. We were out in the boonies more than we were back at the base, however, and our hardback was only sparsely furnished. The only advantage this gave us over the Remfs was that our empty Spartan cells seemed infinitely larger than their crowded

Playboy pads, even though they all measured about the same—thirty feet long by fifteen feet wide. There were eight guys in my hootch, including Lloyd Parsons and myself.

Muhammed Ali, a man I enormously admired because he had announced to the world at large, "I don't have no quarrel with them Vietcongs," and then had been informed by the Illinois Boxing Commission that his spring title bout with Ernie Terrell was thereby canceled, later learning as well that he was persona non grata in such patriotic centers as Louisville, Pittsburgh, and Bangor, Maine, those guardian cities of America undoubtedly believing that a man who laid it on the line before millions of people each and every time he stepped into a ring was merely a downright yellow-bellied lily-livered coward for protesting his 1-A draft classification; Muhammed Ali, whom the press insisted on calling Cassius Clay despite his repeatedly stated preference for the Muslim name he had adopted; Muhammed Ali might have been surprised and pleased by the comfort in which we lived, exalted besides by the racial breakdown in our hootch, there being five white men and three Negroes present and accounted for, though I doubt he would have appreciated the democracy we experienced out in the boonies, where each of us, black or white, had a fair and equal opportunity of getting killed by them Vietcongs with whom, like Muhammed, many of us had no quarrel.

There were about twenty Chinooks and forty or fifty Hueys at Cu Chi and sometimes they choppered us to places that seemed a thousand miles away. The Air Force personnel at camp was limited to a dozen or so meteorologists, and so the fliers were Army pilots who would drop us in the middle of a clearing surrounded by jungle or rice paddy, and then go back to lay a short timer or two on a moldy mattress in a makeshift shack. Usually, though, we fanned out from the base in a radius no longer than twenty-five miles, going out on day-long patrols or ambushes, reconnaissance-in-force missions, and village sweeps that lasted for weeks and sometimes months, and then coming back to base for a day, or two, or four, and going out again. It was a very comical war, with no real front and with no place in Vietnam being positively secure against enemy action at any given time. Of the 190 guys in my company, I guess sixty per cent were smoking grass.

In the hootch, the only one of us who wasn't on pot was Lloyd Parsons, and maybe he had good and sufficient cause to avoid the stuff.

Lloyd was from 117th Street near Lenox Avenue, which he described as "New York's fashionable Upper West Side, man." He had begun smoking marijuana back in 1958, when it was still called Mary Jane, and before it was considered hip to bust a joint before dinner. He was twelve years old at the time, and a junior member in a bopping street gang called The Crusaders, which mounted regular armed forays into Spanish Harlem, a block and a half from its own turf. By 1959, The Crusaders ceased to function as an effective fighting unit, not because the Puerto Ricans had greatly depleted their forces, but merely because—of the gang's fifteen charter members, and twelve members later recruited, and six junior members-in-training—only four of The Crusaders had not graduated from blowing tea to shooting heroin. (The Puerto Rican gangs were beginning to suffer from the effects of a similar escalation along about then, and so peace of a sort was achieved between the warring factions without benefit of intensive social work; nobody had time to go around breaking heads when he was trying to figure out where to get his next fix.) The gang broke up shortly thereafter, but not before Lloyd—at the age of fourteen—had become a confirmed junkie. He was busted for possession in the spring of 1962, while he was still a high school sophomore barely attending classes, and elected to be sent to Lexington for a commitment of at least four and a half months. He could not wait to get out of the hospital, and when he finally returned to his street in November, he immediately sought out his friendly neighborhood pusher and was back on the shit again within seventy-two hours. He stayed lucky until the beginning of 1964, when he was again picked up by the zealous detectives of the 28th Squad, and again sent to Kentucky. This time, because Lloyd had apparently learned something about himself in the intervening years, the cure was effective. He came back North in January of 1965, eighteen years old and determined never to go near narcotics again. His determination was strengthened by a little thing the United States had going over here in Southeast Asia. It seemed, Lloyd learned, that he could join the Army and enjoy an equality he had never known on the streets of Manhattan, while simultaneously being whisked away from daily contact with bad company eager to encourage and supply any new habit he might care to develop. He enlisted in February 1965, and made E-4 inside of a year. When I met him in Vietnam, he seemed very much his own man, confident that he would survive this war the way he had survived the war against the Puerto Ricans, certain there was a real future for him in the United States Army, where a man's value was determined by the rating on his sleeve and not by the color of his skin. If anyone ever offered him a joint, Lloyd only shook his head politely, and said, "Thank you, no, I don't smoke." He was the coolest cat I'd ever met in my life. I think he considered me a friend.

In August, Dom Viscusi, a guy in our hootch, stepped on one of the V.C's punji sticks while we were on a vill sweep, the excrement-dipped, sharply-pointed bamboo piercing the sole of his boot and causing an infection that got him sent first to the 12th Evac Hospital on the base, and then to Japan for R and R, lucky bastard.

Rudy Webb was Dom's replacement.

He arrived in September with about six or seven other guys who must have thought (the way I did when I first got there) that Cu Chi was *really* the boonies. I suppose it was, in relation to Saigon. But to us who had been there for a while, it was home, it was safe, and the boonies were out farther, the boonies were wherever they took us to fight. Rudy was an E-2, a short squat fellow with a weight lifter's powerful build, crew-cut blond hair, and blue eyes slightly darker than my own. He came into the hootch somewhat shyly, the way most replacements did, and introduced himself to the other guys who were sitting around writing letters or listening to Armed Forces Radio on their transistors. He'd been flown over only last Tuesday, so we asked him the usual questions about the States and about the Saigon scene, and he answered us like fuzz being interviewed on a television news program, never once saying anything as simple as "We caught the crook" when it was possible to say. "We apprehended the perpetrator," peppering his speech with words he surely understood, but making them sound like a second language. I guess he was trying very hard to create a good first impression among guys who had been living together for quite some time. But not knowing our separate backgrounds, and not wanting to take any chances, he came on like what I suspect he thought a college professor sounded like, and the results were a little ludicrous. Nontheless, he seemed to be a nice enough guy, and I think all of us considered him a welcome addition to the hootch. Dom Viscusi had, in fact, been a terrible pain in the ass.

I did not get a chance to really talk to Rudy until evening chow, I was sitting alone at one of the mess hall tables when he came over and quietly asked, "Excuse me, is this seat occupied?"

"No," I said.

"You mind if I join you?"

"Not at all."

"Thank you," he said, and climbed over the bench. He was wearing his newly issued cotton jungle shirt and field pants, and he moved with the ponderous neatness of most very strong men, moving his muscles about like heavy furniture in a small room, adjusting his buttocks to the bench and his arms to the table. He ate as though he had come from a large family where it was imperative to finish everything in sight before somebody grabbed it off your plate. He did not look up at me again until he had devoured all the food on his tray, and then he raised his head and his eyes and abruptly said, "I'm not sure I caught your name this afternoon. I'm Rudy Webb."

"Wat Tyler," I said.

"Pleased to meet you, Wat," he said, grinning boyishly and engagingly, and then suddenly looked at me with a puzzled expression, and asked, "How was that again? Wat?"

"That's right. Well, Walter, really."

"Oh, *Walter*."

"But everyone calls me Wat."

"Yeah?" he said, and shrugged. "Well," he said, "regardless," and extended his hand across the table, slyly watching me to see if I'd caught his proper usage, no dolt mouthing nonexistent words was he, "it's a real pleasure," and took my hand in a firm grip, a good grip, not the kind some jocks give you when they were trying to assert something by crushing your fingers to a pulp. "Where are you from, Wat?" he said, like a genial master of ceremonies on a television game show, trying to put a nervous guest at ease.

"Connecticut."

"That's very nice up there in Connecticut," he said. "Whereabouts exactly?"

"Talmadge."

"I don't believe I know it. That anywhere near New Haven?"

"About halfway between New Haven and New York."

"I'm from Newark," he said. "New Jersey."

"Uh-huh."

"But I got people in New Haven. Relatives."

"I went to school there," I said.

"Yeah? What school?"

"Yale."

"Oh, yeah? The college there?"

"That's right."

"What happened? You flunk out?"

"No."

"What then?"

"I quit."

"How come?"

"Just like that," I said, and shrugged.

"Didn't you like it?"

"I liked it fine."

"Then why'd you quit?"

"It was a personal matter."

"You knock up a girl or something?"

"No," I said, and suddenly burst out laughing.

"If you did, who cares? This is Vietnam, we're lucky we get out of here without having our asses cracked," he said and, pleased by my spontaneous laughter, began laughing with me.

The red silk pajamas came as a surprise that night to everyone in the hootch. But it was Jimmy Wyatt, a black kid from Philadelphia, who started giggling when he saw them. Depending on what season it was, we slept either in our underwear or all our clothes, not because civilian pajamas were outlawed (they weren't), and not because we were worried about additional laundry charges (most of us sent our laundry out to be done, the way American sailors on Chinese gunboats did in the early 1900s, preferring the native work to the slob jobs done by the PX or QM concessions), and not because we thought it might be necessary to pull on our pants in a hurry (we were all fairly confident that Charlie would never get through the

353

perimeter), but merely because you didn't wear pajamas in the goddamn Army. I had never seen a soldier wearing pajamas, not at Fort Gordon where I'd taken my Basic, and not at Fort Jackson where I'd had my AIT, and certainly not here in Vietnam. But Rudy Webb reached into his duffle that first night, and pulled out a pair of blazing red silk pajamas we later learned he had bought in San Francisco's Chinatown, a big yellow dragon embroidered on the back, and without a sign of embarrassment or a word of introduction, put them on and then picked up his toilet kit and started heading out of the hootch toward the latrine. Jimmy Wyatt, who was tall and skinny and who had played center for his high school's basketball team, was stretched out on his cot reading a comic. It got very cold at night in September, even when it wasn't raining, and so Jimmy was fully dressed except for his boots, and he had wrapped his legs in a blanket besides, and he seemed very cozy and happy and thoroughly engrossed in his reading. His short-timer's calendar hung on the wall behind him, the gatefold from last month's *Playboy*, over which he had drawn a grid of tiny squares covering the girl's body and representing the number of days to the end of his tour. Each time we got back from the boonies, Jimmy filled in more of the squares with his pencil. He had forty-two days to go, and the only open squares were on the girl's huge breasts and belly. He turned a page in the comic as Rudy walked past, and I suppose the dazzling display of red silk caught his eye because he looked up and suddenly began giggling. Rudy stopped dead in his tracks, as though he had been anticipating some comment on his sleeping attire, and was now more than ready to deal with it. There was a smile on his face as he turned to Jimmy. I was writing a letter to Dana at the other end of the hootch, and when I looked up the first thing I saw was Rudy's smile, and I remember thinking what an odd smile it was, and then he said, "What's the matter, pal?"

"Man, those are some classy pajamas," Jimmy said, giggling in his very high, almost girlish way.

"You like them, huh?" Rudy said, still smiling.

"Oh, yeah, man, I really dig them," Jimmy said.

"Then what's so funny?" Rudy asked, and the smile dropped from his face.

Still giggling, Jimmy said, "Nothing."

"Then what the hell are you laughing like an idiot for?" Rudy said.

"*Who's* laughing like an idiot?" Jimmy asked, and since he was no longer giggling, there was a certain comic validity to the question. In fact, I expected the whole thing to fizzle right then and there, expected it to pass into company lore, Remember the night ole Rudy Webb put on them red p.j.'s and skinny Jimmy Wyatt start laughing like a fool, and then they both rolling on the floor in tears, oh, man, we sure had some high old times in Vietnam, d'in we? Lloyd Parsons, who was sitting on his cot just opposite me, glanced up, and with a note of authority befitting the highest-ranking man in the hootch, said, "Hey, you guys, knock off the shit," and that *certainly* should have been the end of it.

But without glancing at Lloyd, his eyes on Jimmy who was still stretched out on his bunk tensed now for a move, anticipating trouble, Rudy said, "Maybe he'd like to tell me what's so fucking funny about my pajamas."

"Hey, man, bug off," Jimmy said, "you and your pajamas both. You was going out to brush your teeth, so why don't you go brush them, huh?" He picked up his comic, searching for his lost place, and Rudy took one quick step toward him and slapped it out of his hands. It fell to the floor with a tiny flutter that crashed through the hootch like a mortar explosion. Jimmy lay still and silent for a moment. His hands were empty, but he deliberately held them frozen where they'd been when he was holding the comic. Slowly, deliberately, like a challenged gunslick, he raised his eyes to Rudy's face, and then opened the blanket, swung his long legs over the side of the cot and stood up.

Rudy was waiting.

With the toilet kit still clutched in his left hand, he threw his right fist full into Jimmy's face, sending him falling back onto the cot, and almost collapsing it. Dropping the kit and rushing up tight to the side of the cot, fists clenched, he waited for Jimmy to get to his feet again, but Jimmy was too smart to stand up into another punch. He swung out on the opposite side of the cot instead, giving himself the full clearance of the hootch aisle, and then backed cautiously toward the door to move outside, where he would have plenty of room to maneuver and where his longer reach might easily give him the edge in a jabbing fight. Rudy bounded out of the hootch, yelling something about the pajamas having cost him thirty-five dollars, and Lloyd and I both ran out after him, anxious to put an end to this thing; we had never had a fight in our hootch before, and we did not want one now. The two men were warily circling each other when we reached them. Lloyd stepped close to them and said, almost in a whisper, "Come on, you guys, save that for Charlie."

"This *is* Charlie," Jimmy answered.

They were referring, of course, to the Vietcong, the V.C., Victor Charlie in the Army's phonetic alphabet, shortened by the fighting men of America, ta-ra, to plain old Charlie, the enemy out there in the boondocks. Or at least I was certain that *Lloyd* was referring to the men in the black pajamas, but I wasn't too sure that Jimmy's man in the red pajamas wasn't another Charlie, a different Charlie, the Charlie who was the enemy back home in the really distant boonies of America, Charlie nonetheless, *Mister* Charlie the white man. For a startling moment, I wondered if the double meaning had been intended. We had never had any racial bullshit in our hootch, but news from home traveled very fast these days, and the race riots this month in Ohio, Illinois, Michigan, Georgia, Mississippi, and Christ knew where else had caused at least *some* consternation among the black troops. So maybe this was it, maybe Jimmy Wyatt had suddenly stopped worrying about the big Yellow-Red color war we were fighting out there in the boonies and was insisting instead on making *his* war very real and personal—stating it plainly in black and white, so to speak.

"We'll settle this ourselves," he said, and Rudy hit him.

There was no contest.

Rudy was a powerful man, and it was obvious from the start that he had also done some boxing back home in Newark, New Jersey. His first punch opened Jimmy's lip. Jimmy flailed his arms the way he must have as a twelve-year-old on the streets of South Philly, landing only a few wild haymakers that hardly fazed Rudy, who kept moving in with his head ducked to deliver blow after solid blow to Jimmy's body and head. Jimmy's face was covered with blood, there was blood in his hair, blood on his shirtsleeves and on his trousers. Rudy was going for his eyes now, battering punches at first one eye and then the other, and I thought, Jesus Christ, he's going to blind him.

"Okay, that's enough," I said.

"I can take him," Jimmy said, spitting blood, and Rudy hit him in the left eye again, opening a cut at least two inches long.

"That's *enough!*" I yelled, and threw myself on Rudy.

I knew he was strong, but I didn't realize *how* strong until his first punch connected. He hit me just below the heart, and I thought for a wild moment that his fist was going to bore a tunnel clear through to my back, tearing whatever flimsy tissues offered resistance, breaking ribs, ripping arteries, penetrating with the force of a shell fragment. I reached for my chest like a man in the midst of a cardiac seizure, clutching right hand crossing over, mouth open, gasping for breath, my left arm dangling at my side. Rudy hit me again, in the face this time, and as I staggered back and away from him, he whirled on Jimmy and clobbered him on the side of the head with a roundhouse punch that knocked him to the ground. I threw myself at Rudy again, certain now that he was going to kill us both and bury our bodies just inside the wire, throwing a punch that he easily knocked aside, and then feeling his fist collide with my throat just to the left of the Adam's apple, another inch and I'd have been choking in the dirt. He hit me on the ear, and then threw a straight jab at my nose, and I felt blood gushing from my nostrils, and I thought how glad I was that Dana wasn't here to see this, and then I heard Lloyd say, "Okay, Webb, that's it."

"You want some, too?" Rudy shouted, and whirled on him.

"Yeah, I want some, too," Lloyd answered and reached into the top of his boot and pulled out a hunting knife, because Lloyd did not kid around, Lloyd had lived with danger all his life, and was too used to coming back from it alive.

Rudy stared at the knife.

"Okay," he said.

"I can take him," Jimmy said again, and tried to get up, and fell back to the ground on his face.

October ❦ ❦

An old lady holding an open yellow parasol sat on a bench silhouetted against the cloudless sky and speckled water. I watched her from across the Drive, and saw her delicately rise, the sunlight filling the yellow silk for a final instant before she snapped the parasol shut, and hung it on her arm, and slowly walked away. Chicago, burnished with October's gentle light, had been silenced by Sunday. Looking out over the lake while the waiting cab driver impatiently revved his engine, I could imagine a time centuries ago when La Salle stood on this same shore with an Indian named Chikagou, chief of all the Illinois country, and talked of furs and kettles, hatchets and knives. Had there been gulls against the sky then as there were now, crying into the stillness? Had La Salle here in "Portage de Checagou," as he had spelled it in a letter, even remotely suspected the immensity or wealth of the land that lay to the west? For whatever you said about this city, however you compared her to New York, which was bigger and busier and had more restaurants and barber shops and easily as many gangsters, you could not take from her the certain knowledge that she was neither huddled nor crouched upon a tiny island, but towering instead on the brink of a continent. I felt the openness of prairies here. I felt space behind me and ahead of me and around me, the limitless space of a sky free of flak. I was happy to be home.

The driver honked his horn.

"Coming," I said.

Nothing had changed.

The Tyler crest was still there, leaded into the frosted glass panel on the front door, green spruces against a blue sky. I rang the bell below the small brass Tyler escutcheon set in the richly carved oak jamb, and Linda opened the door and flung herself into my arms. My father came through the sliding doors from the living room, and smiled

358

broadly and held out both his hands to me, and I thought, He looks the same, a trifle older perhaps, but essentially the same, nothing has changed. We went into the living room, and my father slid the doors shut behind us, and then poured scotch for himself and me, and a glass of sherry for my sister who was, after all, eighteen years old now, and going steady with a boy my age who expected to enter college as soon as he was discharged from the Navy.

"He wants to be an accountant," Linda said.

"That's very nice," I said.

"You'll like him."

"I'm sure I will."

"His name is Stanley."

"That's nice."

"I call him Stan."

The glasses were passed around. My father stood in the middle of the room with the portrait of my mother hanging behind him over the fireplace mantel, not a good likeness, I had hated that picture even when she was alive. He raised his glass and said, "To Will," and my sister echoed simply, "To Will," and I said, "To all of us."

My sister wanted to know whether New York was really as exciting as everybody said it was, and my father asked if I'd been to this or that restaurant which he went to whenever he was there on business, most of them too expensive for me. Linda went out to the kitchen to see how the new maid was managing with the roast, and my father and I talked some more about New York, and then he got around to asking me what my plans for the future were.

"I don't know," I said.

"Do you expect to go to college?"

"Yes, I guess so," I said.

"What do you want to study?"

"I don't know."

"Of course, there's no rush."

"No."

"I suppose you'd like to take it easy for a while."

"Yes."

"Do you have any school in mind?"

"No."

"I imagine you'd be given preference at a school in Illinois."

"Yes, I would imagine so."

"Of course, there's no rush."

"Mmm."

My father poured a little more scotch into each of our glasses.

"I'm glad you're home, Will," he said.

Critical revision, he had called it.

I was eight years old and sitting at the dining room table in another house, Linda on my right with her elbow in my ribs as usual, my mother listening attentively, oddly silent. He was telling us about the paper industry, and of how he would not have risen to his present position (Sales Manager, I think it was) had he remained inflexibly committed to an original false notion. When the opportunity for critical revision had presented itself (remember those words, son, critical revision) he had eagerly seized it and, as a result, his entire life had changed. (All of this was terribly fascinating to an eight-year-old boy who was anxious to get upstairs to his comic books.) Critical revision, he said again, and I remembered hoping he would not go into another of his long-winded sermons, but he sure enough did, explaining that all too often people pursued a wrong idea with the same zeal and energy that could be devoted to the *right one*, developing a life style that was based upon a fallacy or a series of fallacies. Or worse yet, people and even nations—failing to recognize that once-worthy goals, causes, or ideas could become obsolete, being creatures of habit, and lacking this capacity for critical revision—remained steadfastly devoted to a way of life that was no longer a valid response to the times.

It was funny the way words meaningless to me then, despite my father's eagerness to explain (my mother listening so attentively, as though he were telling her something private, not to be heard by the children, a glance exchanged at the table, their eyes meeting, had he said something to her that I did not understand, why had he been so insistent on defining the way of life a man chose, the way of life to which he irrevocably committed himself —well, never mind). The words had meaning for me now because, home and safe, surrounded by all the things I had known through eighteen years of boyhood, I suddenly felt a lack of direction or will, and wondered whether it wasn't time to engage in some of that critical revision my father had tried to promote those many years ago.

I told myself that what I missed most was flying. I had not been inside an airplane since I left Foggia early in April, and I wished now that I could climb the access ladder onto the wing of a Lightning again, open the top hatch and settle into the pilot's seat, lock my safety belt and run through all the familiar pre-flight checks, battery switch ON, cross-feed switch OFF, tank selector valves to OUTER WING ON, half a hundred more burned into my memory through repetition. I longed to taxi out to the end of a runway, and then hold hard on the brakes and open the throttles, manifold pressure and rpm mounting, the airplane trembling around me, and suddenly let her go, release the brakes and allow her to roll away, speed building, fifty miles an hour, eighty, airborne at a hundred, memory taking over completely as I thought again about flying. I wanted to be in the sky again. I missed flying terribly, I told myself, and had no right to deny myself its pleasure any longer. So I went out to the Elmhurst Airport one day, and rented a twin-engine Beech for fifteen dollars an hour, and took her up and put her through some simple maneuvers, and then landed her, and went back home to the house on East Scott, still filled with an odd sense of deprivation.

I took out Charlotte Wagner that Friday night, and discovered that she wanted to talk exclusively about the old days at Grace School, recalling incidents I had either forgotten or never been a part of, remembering classroom jokes and school outings, student and teacher characters, all the games she had cheered, and even the cheers themselves, turning to me in the parked automobile, eyes glowing, to chant, "With a G! and an R! and an A! and a C! and an E! With a Grrrrace School . . ." and then pulling away when I tried to kiss her, and telling me I had never answered the postcards she'd sent me from Cape Cod in the goddamn summer of 1944! I called Sarah Cody the next day, and went to pick her up in high expectation because she had always been a fun-loving kid with a fine Irish sense of humor and adventure, and a smile that broke like a sunrise, with a good figure besides and a reputation for being pretty easy, or so Michael Mallory had reported. She was even prettier than I remembered, sleek black hair and a pert fresh mouth and sparkling blue

eyes, the conjured image of every Irish lass who'd ever
been kissed in a haystack, but she told me almost immediately that she had been scheduled to go out with a senior
from Northwestern who had come down with a bad cold,
and so I was extremely lucky that she was free, it being a
Saturday night and all, and then expressed keen disap-
pointment when I told her that what I had in mind was a
movie when her original plans had been for dancing at
The Empire Room. Sarah Cody, it seemed, was being
dated almost every night of the week by university boys
who found her ravishing, witty, sexy, responsive, inventive, brilliant, and nothing if not perfect. The movie was
lousy. I did not try to kiss her goodnight because I didn't
wish to mar the flawless line of her lipstick. In desperation, I called Margaret Penner that Wednesday and said,
"Hello there, Margie, this is Will Tyler, I don't know if
you . . ." and she hung up, small surprise. In an agitated
state of extreme critical revision, I decided that perhaps I
missed Dolores Prine, I guessed.

We had said goodbye one October night, huddled together in a hotel bed, Dolores warm and trusting and
weeping in my arms as I let lies fall like autumn rain
around us, gently pattering on the sodden leaves of what
she thought was an undying love. Dolores, I said to her,
I've never met anyone like you in my life, I hate to leave
you now, but I've got to go back to Chicago, I've got to
go home to find my roots again, can you understand that
(and she said, Yes, love, weeping) and I said, I've been
through a war, Dolores, and there are a lot of things I
don't yet know about myself or about what's waiting for
me in civilian life, and so I've got to go back, and I can't
take you with me, not yet, can you understand that (and
she said, Yes, love, weeping) and I said, Maybe after I've
been there a while, maybe after I've had a chance to find
this person who is Will Tyler, to look at myself in the
mirror (Yes, love) and come to terms with myself, know
what it is I really want, why then maybe, Dolores, I can
send for you and we can be together again, but not now,
Dolores, can you understand that, not now (Yes, love,
weeping) and made love to her again before dawn because
if I was going to be a rat, if I was going to lie to this
eighteen-year-old kid (Yes, love, yes) and cause her to
believe that I would one day send for her, cause her to
believe that this was not truly the end, not truly goodbye,

then I might as well go whole hog, might as well be the consummate bastard, take all I could get from her before I left her flat, yes love yes love yes, and we said good-bye.

She had written eight letters to me, none of which I'd answered. I went upstairs to my room now, and read them over again. In the last letter, she had enclosed the snapshots we'd taken the day before I left New York. Clipped to the twelve prints was a slip of white paper with the single word "Remember?" scrawled onto it. I looked at the black-and-white photographs now, trying to reconstruct in my mind the exact moment when the camera's shutter had clicked to freeze Dolores into one or another characteristic pose, realizing all at once that the girl whose pictures lay spread out beside me on the bed was not just *one* girl, not *only* Dolores Prine, but really a rather extraordinary and startling *collection* of girls: Dolores munching on a jellied apple, her hazel eyes opened wide in surprise as the camera clicked on a ravenous bite; Dolores striking a mock sexy pose against a lamppost on Lexington Avenue, coat open, one hand on her hip, the very image of a Parisian streetwalker, eyes slitted, mouth curled in sensuous invitation; Dolores gazing down at the river outside her building, sunlight caught in the shimmering web of her hair, her eyes all but closed, her face in silhouette as clear as alabaster, as soft as snow; Dolores leap-frogging a fire hydrant, legs akimbo, hair floating, eyes and mouth wide open, shrieking in girlish delight as the shutter clicked; Dolores angry and frowning because I had been saying, "No, your head a bit more to the right, that's it, no, a little more, yes, perfect, no," until she shouted, "Go to hell, Will!" just as I snapped the picture. I studied this crowd that was Dolores, trebled it, multiplied it by a thousand, converted it into a mob of Doloreses, and then reversed the procedure, condensing, solidifying this universe of girls into one alone, Dolores Prine, who seemed to me now the most marvelous girl I had ever known. In those frozen snapshots on the bed, I detected a pulsating life, and I wanted to hold it close and fierce, and never let it go again. I went into my father's library, missing her desperately, telling myself that what I wanted to do was go down to New York for a few days, maybe a week, spend some time with her, nothing was happening in Chicago anyway. *Dear Dolores*, I wrote, and crossed it out, *Do-*

lores darling, I wrote, and crossed it out, and wrote *Dear Dolores* again, and then wrote, *I've been here in Chicago for several weeks now, doing all the thinking I told you I'd have to do before coming to any knowledge of myself and,* oh, shit, I thought, and crumpled the letter and threw it into my father's wastebasket. I got up from the desk and began pacing the room, walking past the floor-to-ceiling bookcases, my eye traveling over books that must have been bestsellers when my father was about my age, stuff like *Miss Lulu Bett* by Zona Gale and *The Valley of Silent Men* by James Oliver Curwood, and *Mooncalf* by Floyd Dell and a very hot little numer called *Jurgen* by James Branch Cabell, which I took from the shelf and thumbed through, finding a long underlined passage in it. I became curious about some of the other books then, and began leafing through them at random to see if my father had marked any more pages. Most of them looked unread. There was, however, a corner niche of World War I books which were dog-eared and heavily annotated. I carried some of those over to the desk and scanned the notes he had boldly scribbled into the margins, indignant outbursts like *Nonsense!* or *This did not happen!* sympathetic praise like *Yes, God, yes!* or *I remember the stink, too!* Intrigued, I found myself reading a paragraph in the middle of one book, and then turned back to the first chapter, and then moved from my father's desk to the big leather chair near the Franklin stove, and suddenly lost all interest in writing my letters. That afternoon, I discovered that I did not miss Dolores and I did not miss flying.

What I missed was war.

I missed the uniform, and I missed the routine, and I missed being awakened in the pre-dawn hours and going to the latrine with a dozen other guys and shaving and putting on my flying gear and going to the briefing hut and being told that today we would provide penetration, cover, and withdrawal for another bombing raid. I missed the excitement, I missed the killing, I missed the war.

That night, I went out to get drunk.

I found a bar on the South Side that reminded me a lot of The Eucalpytus on Wilshire Boulevard, which Ace and I used to frequent a lot when we were hotshot pilots in Transitional Training and making the long haul down from Santa Maria every chance we got because there was so much sweet pussy in those Los Angeles hills. It was late, the jukebox was going, a few hookers were hanging on the bar, there was a pleasant hum, a familiar clink of glasses. I felt warm and cozy. I knew I would get drunk and that pleased me because I did not feel like thinking about my future, or wondering whether I'd go to college or go to New York or go into my father's business or try writing or contact Pan-American to see if they needed a very good combat-experienced pilot to fly one of their airplanes. I didn't want to think about anything. I merely wanted to get drunk and then go home to sleep.

I don't know what was on the jukebox, I really can't remember. I'd had two or three drinks already when the guy sitting next to me at the bar turned and said, "This is a nice number," and I said, "I'm sorry, what . . . ?" and he said, "This song," and I listened for a moment, and then said, "Oh yeah, it is."

"I'm a musician," he said.

"Oh?"

"Yes, I play tenor sax and clarinet. I work with a little combo over on Woodlawn. Do you know a place called Frankie's?"

"No," I said.

"That's where I work. Tonight's my night off, though. It's the chord pattern that makes a song good or not, you know. This one's got a particularly good chart."

"There're so many new ones," I said, "I can hardly keep up with them."

"Especially when you've been away for a while," he said.

"That's right, how can you tell?"

"I don't know what it is, but a guy who hasn't been wearing civvies for a long time looks really weird in them. Take me, for example. I look as if I just got out of prison last week, and this is the *suit* they gave me, do you know what I mean?"

"I know *just* what you mean," I said and began laughing.

"I was with the Fifth Army in Italy," he said. "I just got back to Chicago in August."

"I was with the Fifteenth Air Force," I said. "Also in Italy."

"Oh? Where?"

"Foggia."

"Where's that?"

"Near Bari. Down on the heel."

"I didn't get over to that side of the boot. We landed in Salerno."

"No, Foggia was on the Adriatic side."

"Yeah. Well, I'm glad all *that* shit's behind me. What are you drinking there?"

"Scotch and water."

"Bartender, let's have another scotch and water, and a bourbon on the rocks here. My name's Bob Granetta, I play under the name of Bobby Grant, you can call me both or either." He extended his hand.

"Will Tyler," I said.

"Pleased to meet you, Will."

He was taller than I, leaner, with a thatch of curly black hair, dark brown eyes, a grin that climbed crookedly onto his face as he shook my hand briefly and then picked up his drink again. Leaning on the bar, he said, "How do you like being home, Will?"

I shrugged.

"Yeah, me too. I kind of got a kick out of Italy, you know. Hell, I ran into half my goombahs over there, it was like Christmas on Taylor Street. Were you born in Chicago?"

"Uh-huh."

"Me too. Ah, thanks," he said to the bartender, and then raised his glass. "Will," he said, "here's to rehabilitation or whatever the hell they call it, huh?"

"Here's to it," I said.

"*Salute,*" he said in Italian, and drank. "When I think of some of that piss we were drinking overseas," he said, "I get just *sick* thinking about it. Where do you live, Will?"

"Over on East Scott Street."

"Oh boy, I've met my first millionaire," Bobby said, and began laughing.

"No, not quite."

"I'm only kidding. I used to walk that whole Astor Street neighborhood when I was a kid, though, wishing I could live in one of those great old houses. Are you living with your folks?"

"With my father and sister. My mother's dead."

"Oh, I'm sorry to hear that."

"Well, it was a long time ago," I said, and suddenly realized that it was.

"I couldn't stand living with my folks any more," Bobby

366

said. "I was in the Army for three years, you know, I couldn't come back and all of a sudden have my mother telling me to pick up my socks. Pick up your own socks, I felt like telling her. So I have a place of my own now over on South Kimbark, do you know that area?"

"Yes, I do."

"It's a nice place, this guy I know helped me to fix it up real nice. Also, it's close to where I'm playing, which is very convenient. I don't finish till three, four in the morning, later on weekends because we usually hang around to jam, you know. It's great to be able to walk only two or three blocks and flop right into bed. How's that scotch doing?"

"I'll get the next round," I said, and signaled to the bartender. "I feel like getting drunk tonight."

"You and me both. We're lucky we ran into each other. I hate drinking alone, don't you?"

"Worst thing in the world."

"Hate doing anything alone, matter of fact."

"I had to fly that mother-fuckin' airplane alone," I said.

"What kind of plane did you fly, Will?"

"The P-38. The Lightning," I said. "Bartender, another round here, please."

"That's a pretty plane," Bobby said. "That's the one with the tail like this, isn't it?"

"Yeah, with the twin booms."

"Yeah, that's a great airplane."

"A *great* airplane," I said. "How come you didn't get into an Army band?"

"Not good enough, I guess," Bobby said, and shrugged. "You've got to realize the Army had its pick of some of the best musicians in the country. They were drafting guys from Benny Goodman's band, Glenn Miller's, even Al Di Luca's—which happened to be the band I was playing with before they grabbed me. I'm sure you've heard of *him*," he said, and laughed.

"Everybody's heard of Al Di Luca," I said.

"Certainly. So with all those musicians going in, there just weren't enough Army bands to go around. Really, Will, you can't win a war by sending people out to play 'American Patrol.'"

"Here we go," I said. "Drink up, Bobby."

367

"Here's to Al Di Luca," Bobby said, "wherever he may be."

"And here's to . . ." I started, and shook my head.

"Yeah?"

"No," I said, and drank.

"Have you got a quarter?" Bobby asked.

"Let me see." I took out my change and spread it on my palm. Bobby picked up a quarter, and then went over to the jukebox. By the time he returned, I'd finished my drink and ordered another one. A hooker came over to chat with us about the weather, and Bobby matter-of-factly asked how much it cost for the night and she told him it would be twenty-five dollars but that she didn't French. If he wanted somebody who Frenched, he was barking up the wrong tree. He told her to go peddle her ass someplace else, and then ordered another drink and angrily said, "High-class whore, working a bar on Stony Island Avenue. What's so special about *her* mouth, would you mind telling me?"

"They've been spoiled," I said. "Too many servicemen around."

"I'd rather go home and jerk off than risk getting a dose from something like that," Bobby said.

"You and me both," I said.

"Besides, there're too many *nice* girls in Chicago."

"Right."

"Have you got a girl, Will?"

"Not here."

"Where?"

"New York."

"That's a long way off."

"Not even a girl, really."

"What then, a boy?" Bobby said, and laughed.

"Not a *girlfriend*, I mean. Just somebody I was fucking steady."

"What's her name?"

"Well," I said, and shrugged.

"Listen, I'm not going to dash down to New York and *call* her," Bobby said, and put his hand on my shoulder.

"Dolores," I said.

"I knew a girl named Dolores in Georgia. Dolores Greenberg. I suspect she was the only Jew in the state. She was fabulous in bed."

"So was mine."

"Do you think maybe *all* Dolores are marvelous in bed?"

"Maybe so."

"Or maybe it's just you and I who're marvelous, and we made them look good."

"Maybe, who knows?"

"Are you finished with your scotch? We'd better order another round."

"Must be a hole in this glass," I said.

"Listen," Bobby said, and put his hand on my shoulder again, "why are we wasting a fortune for liquor here when I've got a bar full of the stuff at home? Why don't we go up there, listen to some records, and drink all we want to, without having to call the bartender every two minutes. What do you say?"

"Well," I said, "we're here now, we might as well stay."

"I've got some really good records," Bobby said. "I don't know if you dig jazz or not, but I've got stuff that goes all the way back to Jimmy Blythe and King Oliver. What do you say?"

"Well, it's kind of late," I said. "I thought maybe I'd have a few more drinks and then head home."

"Why? Is your Daddy waiting up for you?" Bobby said, and laughed.

"It isn't that," I said, "but we're here now, what's the sense moving?"

"Come on up to my place," Bobby said.

We were facing each other now, we had turned our stools to face each other, our knees touched, our eyes met.

"Come on," he said.

He put his hand on mine.

"Come on."

I woke up to brilliant sunshine.

I was naked.

There were tiny spatters of blood on the sheet.

I could hear the shower running someplace in the apartment. I got out of bed and picked up my undershorts rumpled on the floor, and pulled them on and put on my pants and shirt and jacket and stuffed my tie into the pocket and hurriedly put on my socks and did not bother to lace my shoes.

369

In the street outside, I ran.

I kept looking back over my shoulder.

From a telephone booth on Cottage Grove, I placed a call to Dolores in New York, hoping I would catch her before she left for school. She answered on the fourth ring.

"Hello?" she said.

"Dolores? This is Will."

"Will! Where . . . ?"

"Dolores," I said, "Dolores, I . . . I need you. Will you marry me, Dolores?"

"Yes," she said.

November ❧

It had been snowing heavily since four o'clock. A huge Election Day bonfire had been set in the middle of Sixty-third Street, and from Jackson Park, where I waited for Rosie, I could see the flames leaping up against the falling snow. There was a sharp wind blowing in off the lake. Sparks raced into the sky like incandescent flakes, and the marchers around the fire struggled to hold onto their makeshift signs as they bravely chanted their election slogan into the wind, "We Want Harding, We Want Harding!" Farther up the street, a second fire flared in the late afternoon darkness, and another chant joined the first, so that they merged bipartisanly in the blinding snow. "Harding, Cox, Roosevelt, Coolidge," one becoming the other, indistinguishable.

I had come directly from the mill, telling Nancy beforehand that I might be home late tonight as I wanted to stop by the polls to see how heavy the voting was. I would not be old enough to vote until January, but she knew I was keenly interested in this presidential election, and readily accepted my alibi. From Joliet, I had called Rosie and asked her to meet me in Jackson Park at five o'clock, and she had said, "In this storm, Bert?" and I had answered, "Yes, Rosie, in this storm." I stood hatless on the edge of the park now, my hair blowing, the snow thick underfoot and swirling in the air, clinging to my coat. My gloved hands were in my pockets. I was cold, and I was wet, and I had no stomach for this tryst, but it was something that had to be done, and I aimed to get it done today.

When we were relieved by the 5th Division in October 1918, and I received Nancy's letter in Montfaucon, I got drunk with a worldly French corporal who told me he would never understand the American attitude toward marriage and sex, making it sound as if one were quite naturally exclusive of the other. He told me that no Frenchman in his right mind would dream of a life that did not include a *garçonièrre* and a pretty little lady with whom to share it on a rainy afternoon (he was, significantly, from Paris and perhaps his description of the French ideal did not apply to places like Les Eyzies or Vence). But he told me that before the war he had known at least half a dozen married American businessmen who had become utterly demoralized after falling in love in Paris. Since falling in love, and being in love, and making love were to the corporal the very essence of life, he could not fathom what seemed to him a juvenile, unrealistic, totally unsatisfying, and uniquely American approach to sex. He had demonstrated his premise by picking up two out of the three tavern whores and taking them both off to bed, he being a married man with four children, the youngest of whom was almost my age.

I was not in love with Rosie Garrett, of that I was certain, and yet I had been to bed with her at least a dozen times since that night in August, and had felt that same guilt described by the French corporal, felt a less understandable guilt for meeting with her now, as though we were lovers when in my heart we had never been anything like, when in my mind whatever had happened between us was already finished. I reached under my coat and fumbled in my vest pocket for my watch, clicked it open, studied it, snapped it shut angrily, and looked off at the orange-yellow flames searing the afternoon darkness. I had been driving since eight this morning, driving first through a Chicago gray with the threat of a storm as I went from store to store, and then driving out to the mill to check on several shipments that seemed to have gone astray, and then driving all the way back from Joliet in what had become a fierce snowstorm. I was irritated now,

371

and tired, and feeling foolishly guilty for an affair that had hardly ever been.

She came up behind me and gently looped her arm through mine, and smiled, her face wet with snow, her black fur hat crowned with white, I could remember her smile in the automobile that very first time, and in the stifling heat the strains of "Avalon," too long ago, too tenuous a bargain to hold me to now.

"I'm sorry I'm late," she said, "the trolleys are all . . ."

"That's all right," I said.

"You must be frozen, Bert. Shall we go somewhere for coffee?"

"No, I don't think we should take that chance."

She turned to me and looked into my eyes, and nodded, and said, "All right, Bert. Can we at least sit down?"

I dusted one of the benches free of snow, and we sat side by side, Rosie with her hands in her black muff, I with mine in my pockets. We might have been strangers, and I suppose we really were.

"You sounded so desperate on the telephone," she said. "I couldn't imagine . . ."

"Well, I've got to talk to you," I said.

"Nancy knows, is that it?"

"No. No, she doesn't."

"Allen doesn't suspect a thing, if that's what you're . . ."

"No, that's not it, either."

"You look very handsome," she said, "with all that snow in your hair."

"Thank you, Rosie . . ."

"Yes, Bert?" she said, and brushed a snowflake from her cheek and then turned to me again. She knew what was coming, of course, they always know, women, there are sensors they possess that reach out and delicately probe, touching the core of the matter long before it is broached. Her face took on a pinched protective look, poor Rosie, poor dear Rosie married to a jerk and seeking God knew what from me. I wanted to say Rosie, please understand that I don't want to hurt you, please understand that there's a time to choose, dear Rosie, and this is that time for me. I can't continue, Rosie, unable to look my wife in the eye, fearful that each time she says "Pardon?" she is questioning a fresh lie, I can't do this to

372

her, because I love her dearly. Forgive me, please, for taking what I took from you, and for turning it aside now, for seeming to spurn it now, I don't want to hurt you, I truly don't. But Rosie, please understand that there's a way of life I cannot follow and yet remain the man I once hoped to become, *still* hope to become. Rosie, I wanted to say, please know that I can't commit to this, I can't give to it the energy or devotion it demands, it would destroy me, it would take whatever's good or real or honest in me and crush it forever. Rosie, I wanted to say, please understand. Rosie, I wanted to say, but she already knew, she looked at me with a small sad smile on her painted mouth, her black fur hat tilted precariously on her head, covered with a crooked crown of snow, she looked at me and waited for me to kill her.

There is only one way to say goodbye.

"Rosie," I said, "I want to end it."

I dreamt that night that I addressed a thousand deaf Indians in full battle regalia.

I dreamt that I mounted a platform, carrying a bass drum and a harmonica, and held up my hands for silence, and then hit the drum three times in succession and blew a sustained chord on the harmonica and held my hands up once again. When I began speaking, I spoke clearly and distinctly because all the Indians were deaf and had to read my lips—all of them were lip readers, so to speak. And since I had talked to them many times before, and since each time they had been fooled by my bass drum and harmonica into thinking I was only a song-and-dance man, I wanted to make absolutely certain that *this* time they understood me.

I dreamt that they watched me silently as I began to speak, their arms folded across their beaded chests, faces impassive, feathers rustling slightly in the wind. The sky behind them was blue, the platform rose from the center of a vast plain that stretched beyond me and the gathered Indians. My fine feathered friends, I said, I know that I am not one of your highly exalted paper tycoons whose every uttered syllable clears your normally clogged eustachian canals, I know in fact that my own beginnings were humble indeed, for where did I start if not with pulp, where I had to talk loud and talk fast to be heard over the pounding of the drum barker, where if not there? But listen to me, I dreamt I said.

Please, I dreamt I said.

Oh, I know that you have seen me standing here before you on many a previous occasion and perhaps you thought I was trying to sell you fraudulent medicine in glittering bottles, though I tell you now in all honesty my offers were sincerely made, and whatever small ills and tiny ailments I hoped to cure seemed terribly important to me. And should you now, my gathered tribal brothers, should you now fail to recognize the elixir because of what you once erroneously thought to be snake oil, well—the loss will be mine, of course; I am exposed alone to the angry wind here. But the loss will be even more seriously yours.

There was suddenly in my dream an enormous bonfire shooting sparks to the Chicago night, and more Indians dancing about it holding signs that read HARDING-COOLIDGE and chanting "We Want Harding, We Want Harding," while white men stood beyond the circle of light proscribed by the flames and jeered and taunted, "Harding is a nigger, Harding is a nigger!" I held up my hands for silence while everywhere around us the white men passed their leaflets surreptitiously into the crowd, black type flaming against the orange and red of the fire:

To the Men and Women of America

AN OPEN LETTER

When one citizen knows beyond the peradventure of doubt what concerns all other citizens but is not generally known, duty compels publication.

The father of Warren Gamaliel Harding is George Tryon Harding, second, now resident of Marion, Ohio, said to be seventy-six years of age, who practices medicine as a one-time student of the art in the office of Doctor McCuen, then resident in Blooming Grove, Morrow County, Ohio, and who has never been accepted by the people of Crawford, Morrow and Marion Counties as a white man.

"I ask you now," a white man shouted, "is this the one you want in the White House, is this the one you would choose to lead this great nation to its proper destiny, is this the one you will vote for tonight against James M. Cox and Franklin Delano Roosevelt, the men who deserve to become the President and Vice President respectively of this our bountiful land, and not a person whose colored ancestry can be traced back through four separate lines! Do we want, I ask you, this blackguard in the White House?"

I dreamt I fell to my knees and said, But you do not understand, surely you do not understand. I am no longer involved with Rosie Garrett, I saw her only a baker's dozen times, it was the heat, I beg you to understand it was only the dire heat that drove us near to crazy with temptation and desire, it was only the heat that caused our fornication, copulation, then and but a dozen times more in the parlor of her flat, but that was all, I swear to you!

The Indian chants rose from around the fire, sparks fled upward into the night, "We Want Harding, We Want Harding," and now there was a cross-chant from the white men, "Cox, Cox, Tyler is a Coxman! Cox, Cox, Tyler is a Coxman!"

Wait, I dreamt I begged them, wait, please listen to me, I am a veteran of the Great War, ask these noble savages if I did not personally know Geronimo and Cochise, ask them if I did not fight bravely and watch my comrades fall, ask them if I am not now incensed by these false charges against Mr. Harding and determined to vote for him despite this vicious slander, although I am only twenty years old, having been born on the first day of January in the year 1900, and will not be eligible to vote until two months from now—but I would if I could, I swear to you! Please understand, I know you will understand, I do not speak with a forked tongue, I am no longer forking Rosie, I swear that to you, Nancy, please don't cry, I am no longer seeing her, it is over, it is done.

"It is over, it is done," the Indians chanted.

The white men faded into the distance, scattering their leaflets behind them, tossing them into the fire, flames of blue and green changing the colors on the redskins' faces. The Indians stared at me. Behind them, the sky turned a promising mauve. There was music now, somewhat celestial, harps and violins, a gentle wind sweeping from some secret plain.

We are on the threshold, I said, of greatness, the threshold of greatness. We can go either way, you or I, we can take this treasure that we hold here in our hands, my friends, we can take it and squander it, toss it into the fire there where it will burn like those leaflets bearing malicious slander, libel—is there a lawyer among you, my tribal brothers? Is it libel or slander? Which one is printed and which one spoken? No matter. I tell you now that we can take this gift magnanimously bestowed upon us by a generous Lord, yours or mine—what do *you* call Him, my friends? Is it The Great Spirit? That's a good name for a righteous God. I have nothing against your God, I tell you we are all one and the same and we all have the duty to make sure we do not squander this heritage of ours, do not scatter it to the winds or toss it on the flames. Side by side we have hunted the buffalo and defended our homes against the invaders from over the mountains, planted our corn and—no, my friends, wait, don't leave, make no mistake, I do not come to you in Indian guise now, I do not come to you in feathers and buckskin, face painted, it's just me, just Bertram A. Tyler, your old song-and-dance man, don't be afraid, don't leave yet, please wait, please listen.

I think you know what I'm about to tell you. I have the feeling that we've shared this dream together, shared it often enough before, lived it together for a long long time, and that we are too wise now to— Damn you, I'm losing my patience!

Shall I talk to you like the ignorant savages you are, shall I promise dire happenings, heap curses upon your feathered heads, the witch doctor warning of what may come if you do not purchase from me this colorless, tasteless, odorless liquid I've naïvely labeled—well now, where's the label, must have come unglued. There *is* no name for it then, my friends, you'll just have to trust me, I suppose. You'll have to drain bottle after bottle of this stuff, pour gallons of it into your systems to rid your bodies of the sores and chancres, purge the liver and the bile, make yourselves pure again, for Christ knows, The Great Spirit knows, we are sullied and scorned, we are on the edge of an abyss so deep it might just as well be bottomless. Take it, my tribal brothers, pull the cork and drink deep draughts, it will not hurt you, it can only help. For if you ignore my warnings, here then are the things that will happen to us, to you and to all of us, if you do not hear, if you choose to remain deaf to the music coming from somewhere out there—is there a musician among you? Can anyone tell me what that lovely instrument is?

Though you are brave, you will tremble before ghosts.

Though you are free, you will remain as slaves to the past.

Though you are provident, you will shun visions of the future.

Though you are considerate, you will slaughter your leaders.

Though you are wise, you will engage in thoughtless battle.

Though you would populate the earth with sons, you will send generations yet unborn to perish in their youth.

Though you would stand a hundred thousand years, you will witness the end of your nation instead, and neither it nor you will ever again rise from the ashes.

There was the sound in my dream of feathers blowing on the wind. And then one of the Indians stepped forward, came close to the foot of the platform in the light of the fire and, looking surprisingly like my brother-in-law Oscar, stared up into my face and said only, "Why did you steal our lands?"

December ✤ ✤ ✤

There was, the surprise was complete, we realized instantly, I stopped, I, the noise, sudden automatic rifle and machine-gun fire coming from ahead and from one side of the jungle trail. Bravo had followed Alpha into an L-shaped ambush, the first fire-team fully contained within the right angle and caught in a deadly crossfire, my team only partially enclosed with Rudy Webb and I just entering the long side of the trap. Everything screamed urgency— Hit it! Move!—but I did not leap instantly into the bushes on the left because I'd been caught in this kind of ambush before and had learned that the side of the trail from which no enemy fire came, the supposedly *safe* side, was often lined with angled punji stakes waiting to impale the man who hurled himself reflexively into the undergrowth. I hit the dirt where I was standing instead, and then crawled swiftly off the trail on my belly, elbows working, eyes scanning the ground ahead, and whirled to find Rudy beside me already returning fire.

I was Private Walter Tyler of Captain Finch's D Company, 2nd Battalion of the 27th Infantry, 2nd Brigade of the 25th Infantry Division. We had started Operation Ala Moana on the first of December, two weeks ago today, and were pushing now through the dense jungles in Nau Nghia Province, some thirty miles northwest of Saigon, where only yesterday we had found an enemy cache of 10 AT mines, 46 tons of rice, a ton of sugar, and 570 gallons of pickled fish.

(The jungle off the trail has not been booby-trapped. Wat Tyler hugs the ground, his M-16 on automatic, and fires long bursts into the trees across the trail. He hears someone calling for a medic. This one is going to be very bad, he knows that. He cannot imagine anyone in Alpha having survived the ambush, and he suspects that Bravo's lead rifleman and the grenadier five meters behind him have also been hit and possibly killed. He recognizes the voice of the man yelling. It is Lloyd Parsons. But he cannot tell whether Lloyd himself has been hit, or is only calling for a medic to help the men ahead of him in the order of march.)

A mechanized unit had yesterday discovered seven bunkers and two tunnels in the area just to the rear of us, and had captured twelve 81-mm rounds as well as 11,200 small-arms rounds, more than a ton of rice, and a Russian-made radio. A recon patrol filing out into the jungle had reported back with the information that a V.C. base camp with two dozen buildings was located a mile to the southwest. Our march this morning was intended as an encircling maneuver, similar to the procedure we used in a vill sweep, where we surrounded a suspect hamlet during the night and then attacked at first light, hoping to catch Charlie before he left his woman and his rice bowl to go off into the jungle again. The difference here was that this was 0905 in the morning, and we were still a half-mile away from the enemy position, and Charlie had obviously known we were coming, Charlie had closed the trail and lined it with rifles and machine guns, and was determined now to annihilate each and every one of us. I heard Lloyd yelling for aid again, but nobody seemed to be going to him, and so I assumed our medic had been hit in the initial burst. Somewhere off on the left of the trail, I heard Jerry Randazzo, our RTO, radioing back for help, and then there was renewed intensive fire, and Jerry's voice stopped. The jungle was still.

(Wat Tyler is wearing a fiberglas flak jacket over his cotton jungle shirt and field pants, leather-soled, canvas-topped jungle boots with holes for water drainage, black nylon socks, a helmet liner, and a steel pot with a camouflage cover on it. Hanging from his belt suspender straps are a first-aid kit containing gauze, salt tablets, and foot powder; an ammo pouch containing magazines for his automatic rifle; a Claymore pouch containing six M-26 fragmentation grenades and two smoke grenades; a bay-onet, a protective mask, and two canteens of water. He is dressed for war, but he is frightened. He thinks he will be killed this morning.)

"Wat . . ." The voice was Lloyd's . . . a whisper in the jungle stillness. "I'm hit," he said, and the V.C. opened up again. There was no question of marksmanship here, the jungle was too dense, they fired only at the sound of his voice, spraying the undergrowth with automatic bursts, pausing only long enough to reload and doing that in an overlapping pattern so that the fire was constant. They had the machine gun going in there, too, adding its heavier clatter to that of the rifles, ripping through the leaves on this side of the trail some fifteen meters ahead. I did not think Lloyd had a chance, he was too deep inside the trap.

(Wat Tyler does not want to consider the possibility that the entire squad has been annihilated, and yet he does not hear any answering fire from this side of the trail, and he knows that an ambush such as this calls for heavy return fire, blind return fire, spray the bushes, spray the trees, rip the jungle apart, keep firing, keep hurling grenades, keep everything going until help arrives or until it becomes possible to withdraw. But no one else is firing.)

"Cover me!" I heard Lloyd shout up ahead, and sud-denly a grenade exploded on the V.C. side of the trail, and Rudy and I began firing again as Lloyd pushed free of the hanging vines, stepping out of the tangled brush in a long loping stride, one arm bloody and dangling, the other pulled back to toss a second grenade. The V.C. machine gun opened up, cutting him down before he'd moved six inches out of the jungle, the grenade dropping in the center of the trail not a foot from where he fell. The explosion tore a hole in the ground and ripped off one of his legs. There was a tick of time, a hiatus the length of a heartbeat between the explosion and the renewed Vietcong fire. Lloyd was lying motionless in the center of the trail. The bullets kept striking his body, nudging it slightly with each soft steady plopping hit, as though trying in concert to roll him off the trail and back into the jungle. The ground around him was covered with blood.

(Wat Tyler is frightened. The one thing he does not want to do is get killed in this stupid fucking war. In the eye of the camera, he sees himself as a terrified child crouched on the edge of a jungle trail, trembling on the narrow brink of death in the company of an idiot from Newark, New Jersey. He suspects that even now the Vietcong are moving their machine gun further up the trail so that they can fire directly across it into the thicket where he and Rudy are waiting. He does not want to die this morning.)

"Let's get the nigger before they do," Rudy whispered to me.

"What?" I said.

"Your buddy. Let's get him off the trail before these mother-fuckers butcher him."

"He's dead," I said.

"You want them to slice him up like a piece of meat?"

"He's dead," I said, "it's too fucking late."

"It could be you out there," Rudy said.

"It isn't," I said.

"You coming or not?"

"I'm not."

There were two things you did not do in Vietnam. I had learned both of those things from Lloyd Parsons, who had been my closest friend and who now lay dead on the trail fifteen meters ahead, with one of his legs blown off besides. The first thing you did not do was leave a dead or wounded buddy, it did not make any difference, dead or alive the Vietcong or the NVA would hack him to pieces

380

and throw him in an open pit. The other thing you did not do was get yourself into a situation that looked suicidal. Suicide was for heroes, and there were hardly any heroes in Vietnam, there were only guys wasting time till they were short, only guys trying to stay alive. I was not a hero, and everybody else in the squad was dead, and going out there to get Lloyd's body would be suicide. I was too scared to think.

"You coming, Tyler?" Rudy said.

His helmet was very close to mine, he nodded his head for emphasis as he whispered to me, and metal clicked against metal, and for an instant I thought of a Talmadge playing field and a football huddle, thought I would call a Roger-Hook-Go, after which we would run out there with rifles blazing and pull Lloyd off the trail before they cut him limb from limb, though one limb was already gone, wasn't it, and Lloyd was dead. I wanted to stay alive. I did not want to die this morning.

"Let's go, Tyler," Rudy whispered.

On the other side of the trail, I heard movement in the underbrush, the snapping of twigs, the rustling of leaves. There was a small mechanical click.

"No," I said.

(Wat Tyler remembers that he would not have died for Larry Peters in Mississippi in the summer of 1964, either, and suddenly wonders if there is anything in this world that he *would* die for, and realizes just as suddenly that there are a hundred things, a million things he would *live* for, but none that he would care to die for, thank you. To Rudy Webb perhaps, it was important to pull the body of a black man off a jungle trail after he had been shot to tatters and had his leg blown off, but Wat Tyler does not see how he can help Lloyd now except by staying alive. He knows for certain that if he steps out of these bushes he will be killed in an instant. There is too much to do, he thinks, to much to live for. Go fuck yourself, Rudy Webb, he thinks, you and *all* the Rudy Webbs of America.)

"Up, Tyler," Rudy said. "Up or I'll put a bullet in your head."

I looked at him in amazement. He had turned the muzzle of his rifle toward my chin, and his finger was curled around the trigger. He was wearing a two-week beard stubble caked with jungle grime, and the armpits of his shirt were stained with sweat, and there was a thin line

381

of spit running from one corner of his mouth, a dull glitter in his eyes. From across the trail, there came another small mechanical click.

"Jerry must have reached Battalion," I said reasonably and calmly.

"Jerry reached *shit*," Rudy said. "They cut him down before he said two words into that fuckin' radio."

Lloyd had told me, a long time ago, "If you want to stay alive out here, you better start getting angry, Wat. You just listen to your old Uncle Lloyd. He knows all about being angry, 'cause he's been angry all his goddamn life." Rudy was angry now, angry at me, and angry at the Vietcong setting up their machine gun across the trail, and angry at Lloyd, too, I think, because it was Lloyd's dead and riddled body that was making it necessary for Rudy to live up to a ridiculous code, Lloyd's black and bleeding and smoking corpse that reminded Rudy he was only a man who could be likewise killed and possibly hacked to pieces afterward if good old buddies did not perform for him the service he was ready to perform for Lloyd—even if it meant putting a bullet in my head. There was something completely insane about this. He knew we would not last a minute if we stepped out of the bushes. He knew that we would be killed as dead as Lloyd, and that *all* of our bodies would be hacked apart, if that's what Charlie had in mind this morning, and he also knew that the Cavalry *might* just possibly arrive in time, the Cavalry always arrived in time, didn't it? There was a whole fucking battalion someplace in this jungle, eight hundred men who had heard all the shooting and who had maybe got Jerry's radio message, eight hundred men ready to come to our rescue, so what the hell was his rush? I could not understand. I knew only that I did not want to get killed, and that I stood a very good chance of being killed in the next ten seconds, either by my side or their side, it would not make a hell of a lot of difference. A bullet in the head was a bullet in the head.

The machine gun opened up.

(Wat Tyler is hit. He sees Rudy's face above him, the mouth opening in shocked surprise, the bridge of the nose dissolving into a slow motion shot of a red flower opening, and then Rudy is falling toward him, and the hanging jungle canopy begins to wheel overhead, Hold the ball, Wat tells himself in idiotic litany against the fear, Hold the ball, and clutches his rifle to him like a woman. Rudy's helmet smashes into his face, his neck snaps back, he thinks for a moment he has broken something in his spine, and then the ground hits him, and he is splayed flat against the earth by a hundred and ninety pounds of muscle and bone.)

I clung to my rifle against my chest, I could smell the tumbled jungle floor, that's right you little shits, I thought, kill your star quarterback, and smiled, and lay still and helpless, and thought suddenly of something Mr. Jarrel had said in American History I, about Giles Corey being pressed to death in Salem, Massachusetts, because he would not admit he was a witch, rock after rock being piled upon his chest, and all he ever said was, "More weight," and had died for his refusal to betray his own conscience. I could not move, they had broken something inside me. I felt wet and sticky below the waist. I lay and waited. An odd buzz hovered over the jungle. I could hear strange voices. I could not understand what they were saying. I thought of Dana. I listened to the voices in bewilderment and fear because I knew now that something terrible had happened to me, that they were all talking about what had happened to me, that maybe my neck was twisted at a funny angle, maybe there was a line of blood trickling from under my helmet. The buzz was incredible. Dana, I thought. Dana, I hurt. Dana, I love you. From the tail end of my eye, through a tiny wedge between my head and Rudy's shoulder that was pinning it to the ground, I saw a pair of feet in sandals moving swiftly over the jungle floor, saw the bottoms of black pajamas stark against the brilliant sunshine.

(Wat Tyler sees the enemy soldier from a foreshortened angle, the camera shooting up the length of the black silk pajamas to the pinched and narrow face. There is no joy on that face. The camera holds on the tired eyes for only a moment. Wat stares into them, trying to understand something. He is not afraid, he only feels betrayed. And he hurts. He hurts very badly. Look, he thinks, why can't we just, and the enemy soldier fires a short burst into Rudy's back, and then swings the rifle past Rudy's shoulder, and puts the muzzle against Wat Tyler's cheek, and pulls the trigger.)